Green Eyes

Blair Burns

Published by Blair Burns, 2024.

Also by Blair Burns

Murder on the Emerald Coast
Green Eyes

Watch for more at https://www.blairburnsauthor.com.

Dedication

I dedicate my book to Phillip Morris Calhoun

Born August 4, 1944 and passed away August 5, 2023

The joy of Phil's life was his years of performing music with fellow musicians, friends, family, and strangers. How proud he was of his years performing as Phil Calhoun & Trashy White Band at the Green Knight Lounge in Destin. Phil became a Super Star/ Legend in this area because of his entertainment abilities and his incredible vocal sounds. His greatest love of singing was for the Lord Jesus Christ at Faith Assembly Christian Church and his pastor, Toy Arnett, and the congregation there loved him so greatly.

This book is like reading the diary of a dear friend, who is struggling to keep her and her children's lives on a positive course, despite real life heartbreaks and hardships she encounters.

You will celebrate her hard-won blessings, fear the hard decisions she will have to make.

The author incorporates insights into the lives of coastal realtors and touring musicians. She shares from history facts of local restaurants, and people who make her story seem like you are part of it.

Linda Lytle Duvall

Birmingham, Alabama

***Green Eyes* by Blair Burns** has the ring of truth, though it's veiled as fiction. The author doesn't shy away from mentioning actual places in Destin, Fort Walton Beach and Nashville. In this bitter-sweet love story, Green-eyed, single mom and independent professional woman Harper Hamilton is drawn into a love affair with tattooed county music star Cade Fox. Their relationship appears ideal until it takes a heartbreaking turn. Can their love survive? You have to read the story to find out. The country stars referred to as working with Cade are famous names **you will** easily recognize. As for me, I enjoyed sharing Harper and Cade's story and I think you will too. Five stars.

Sandy Semerad, Author Seagrove Beach, Florida

Take a trip to the Emerald Coast & the past through the pages of this delightful book! Transporting you beyond the sandy shores, it unravels the essence of a bygone era when this coastal beach community remained a hidden treasure, known intimately by the locals; a community "where everybody knows your name". With a blend of romance and the Nashville music scene, "Green Eyes" offers a compelling tale and a nostalgic glimpse into the simpler times when Destin was but a quaint fishing village and where neighbors were more like family. Immerse yourself in this heartwarming story filled with romance, local lore and the charm of yesteryear before the area was "discovered", it is a truly enjoyable read that will leave you longing for more and for the days gone by! DONNA FOX, NICEVILLE, FLORIDA

Blair Burns has asserted her right to be identified as the author of this work in accordance with copyright.

First Published 2024.

Blair Burns lives on the Emerald Coast of Florida. She has been a realtor for the past thirty years and is now semi-retired. She has time to write, garden, paint, travel, and volunteer with her Standard Poodle, Saban, as a read-therapy team in the local elementary school and library.

She writes about the beaches and towns where she has lived and raised her family. Her work includes murder mysteries and love stories. Keep in touch with Blair on her website and blog at https://blairburnsauthor.com on Facebook and Instagram. You can email her: blair@blairburnsauthor.com and she will respond personally.

Other titles by this author

Murder on the Emerald Coast.

Acknowledgements

I would like to acknowledge the people of Destin, Florida, who gave me the opportunity to use them in my book and assist me with timelines and characterization for Green Eyes. I would like to thank Norma Calhoun, wife of Phil Calhoun, for giving me permission to dedicate this book to Phil and The Trashy White Band.

I am thankful to have found Barbara Unković to assist me with the final editing. Not only does she give great instructions, but she also praises you when you write a wonderful description.

I would like to thank singer-songwriter Bryan Bludworth for the use of his songs,

I'll always be Crazy Because You Love Me, and *Here Tonight.*

You can follow Bryan on his website <u>https://bryanbludworth</u> On YouTube and all music streaming platforms.

Kathleen Sweeney and her designers with Book Brush did a fantastic cover for my book.

Florida 1991

Chapter 1

Sunday afternoon my colleague, Suzanne, from the bank called.

"It's Melody's birthday and we need to take her to party," she said.

"On a school night? We have auditors at the bank in the morning. I don't know how I can make it," I replied.

"It'll be fun. I'll pick you up in an hour."

"Where are we going? How should I dress?" I asked.

"Wear your jeans and bring a jacket. We're going to the Boat House in Destin on the harbor."

"Seriously! They don't have liquor, just beer and oysters."

"There's an amazing guitar player from Nashville playing tonight. He comes in October, so he can fish in the rodeo. You can drink a Coors Light beer."

"Okay, pick me up. I'll be on time."

I needed jeans that fitted tightly. Then I looked in my closet and dragged out my old cowboy boots and a long-sleeved patterned shirt. If we were going to hear a country music star, I knew I should dress the part.

We walked in and found a table. The windows were open, and a pleasant breeze was blowing off the harbor. The Boat House resembled a shack on the water. The shack hung over the water on crooked pilings. I wondered if it was safe, but it had been there for years. Boaters motored up to get gas, buy beer, and stayed to eat oysters. I loved the smell of the harbor front. Fishermen next to the Boat House were cleaning their catch. The sun was going down, and the weekend boaters were heading back to their docks.

I looked around at all the money hanging around the bar. We were probably the best-dressed women in the place. Girls with tattoos and way too short, tattered jean shorts were dancing together in a sexy way. The guys had scraggly beards and large beer bellies. Deckhands from the marina wandered in after a day of fishing. I spotted a couple of good-looking guys at the bar. They must have been from out of town. The music was blaring from the speakers. It was becoming crowded, and we were lucky to find a table not too far from the band. The Boat House had a reputation for being loud and wild. It appealed to many kinds of people, from fish heads to millionaires. Not my usual place. I preferred the disco and never went out on Sundays. That was the day I spent with my kids.

The server came to take our order for oysters and beer. Suzanne told the her to ignore me when I complained they only served beer and rot-gut wine.

We were bankers at the First Beach Bank in Fort Walton Beach. We hung out together and enjoyed each other's company. Suzanne had divorced a jerk, and she had one son, the age of my Lizzie. She was the shortest one in our group, and got teased about it all the time, so we protected her in crowds.

Melody was dark-headed with striking brown eyes and curly, shoulder-length hair. She was of Italian descent and loved to cook. Good cooking had made her curvy.

Kate was the statuesque younger one among us. She had long blonde hair. We nicknamed her *the baby* because she was a mere twenty years old. She was a die-hard country music fan and the reason we went out together on this occasion.

We couldn't afford to go out often and I was grateful that they gave me a raise when I became the president's secretary. My parents were great. They bought school clothes and paid for the kids' extracurricular activities. It was difficult financially with two children and no child support.

The server brought our beer and oysters. The oysters from Apalachicola were cold and delicious. I dug in, put one on a cracker and dosed it with hot sauce. Yum, they were good. In thirty minutes, the band would start. The house band was a country band called The Trashy White Band. I wasn't a fan of country music, but they were popular in Destin. The younger girls loved them and went to the Boat House often.

"Who's the guest musician?" I asked.

"Cade, something or other, from Nashville," Kate replied. "I saw him playing on the Grand Ole Opry awards and he is hot. He has the sexiest tattoos on his arms and neck."

Mercy, why did I waste my Sunday afternoon to come see a tattooed music star? We finished our beers and ordered another round of drinks. Beer was not my favorite, even though I ordered another Coors Light. It was tolerable. I hoped this would be our last round of drinks. We could go home after this guy had played.

Out he strutted, guitar thrown over his shoulder, long hair swinging. There was applause from the crowd and Phil Calhoun, the lead musician from The Trashy White Band, introduced him.

"This is Cade Fox from Nashville, Tennessee. You've all heard his new single, *Green Eyes*. It's number one on all the charts."

I'd never heard this single or any of his other music. The band and Cade played. I was impressed by how he picked that electric guitar. I stared at his tattoos. There were two on his arms and one on his neck. Oh my, his arms were steel, thin and long. I wasn't sure what was tattooed on them, but it looked good. He wasn't tall, about five feet ten. He wore a T-shirt, tight jeans, and I mean, tight jeans, boots and a silver and leather bracelet on his right wrist. You couldn't help noticing the bracelet on his arm, because he was stroking that guitar as if it were a woman. Not my preference in a guy, but indeed sexy. He played *Green Eyes* first. It was a slow song with lots of melancholy.

My friends were transfixed by him and sung along with the band. They adored country music and knew all the words. Melody and Kate stood up and started swaying to his song. Oh, my heavens, they were embarrassing. I hoped no one there knew us. The entire audience stood up, clapped, and stomped their appreciation. I got up and joined them. I must admit, he was a talented guitar player. When the band played other songs the crowd settled down. People were hanging out the open-air windows and standing by the bar. I hoped the place didn't get more crowded.

Oh no! I needed to pee. The bathrooms were outside the bar and I would have to walk in front of the band to get to them. Could I hold on? I tried to wait until the band took a break. I hoped they would hurry and finish their set.

When Cade sang another song, *Here Tonight,* he was looking right at me.

> *Tried to do a life with you*
> *But it always got cold*
> *If the truth had been exposed,*
> *May have left a while ago*

You can't build your dreams
With pain from the past,
And you can't count on things
You know will never last
So baby take my hand
Let go of your pain
There's a safe place here
You can remain
You Gotta keep going till you find where you belong
Crawling through heartache until you find your way home,
Cause there is someone out there that can make you feel alright
Maybe that someone's here tonight
It's the scars that make you perfect. I can see the honesty in your eyes
Looking back into mine, I hope you can see where my heart lies
So baby take my hand
Let go of your pain
There's a safe place here
You can remain

The band played a few more songs. I didn't recognize any of them. Cade joined in with The Trashy White Band and they played their famous song, *She ran off with a Fish Head*. I wasn't crazy about that song. As I glanced around, the whole place was singing it with them. Again, I hoped no one was there who knew me.

The band took a break, and I rushed to get to the bathroom. I walked past the bandstand and tried to be as inconspicuous as possible. Oh yikes! Cade reached out and grabbed my arm. I was paralyzed. Then he looked at me.

"You have the most gorgeous green eyes I've ever seen," he said.

"Thank you," I mumbled and escaped to the bathroom. I wasn't sure what happened during that split second. How did he see my eyes? I had my head down as I passed him. The other women in the bathroom stalls were talking about his tattoos, his arms, his tight jeans and were swooning over him. I hoped my gang was ready to go home. As I left the bathroom and headed toward the deck, there he was. An enormous group of people were hanging around him and asking for his autograph. I stopped to watch.

"Okay guys, I came down here to Destin to get away from the spotlight. I came to fish at the Destin Rodeo. I don't want to spend my time signing autographs. I need a real drink, not a beer," I heard him say as he pulled a silver flask out of his back pocket and took a swig. The groupies understood and backed away.

How could I get off the deck and back? I'd have to push my way back to my friends. Or should I risk passing the groupies? Was it possible to return the way I came? Pushing past the groupies was the easiest way.

"Hey, green eyes," Cade said as I tried to slink past. Oh, my! He was talking to me. Everyone looked at me and he tried to grab my arm again. I stopped—petrified.

"I just want to say hello," he said.

"I have to go back to my friends." Thank heavens at that moment they called him back on stage and I slunk to my seat.

"What in the hell happened up there?" Kate asked.

"He called me green eyes and grabbed my arm. We have to go. Now!" They stared at me as if I was nuts.

Cade sang another song and looked right at me as he sang *Welcome to My World.*

I was frozen. I didn't let dangerous men into my world.

"We have to leave," I told the girls again.

"You're nuts. He's interested in you," Kate said.

"I'm getting a taxi. I'll see you tomorrow at the bank." After picking up my purse, I headed for the front door. That way, I didn't have to pass the band. When I asked the bartender to call me a taxi I was worried about how much it would cost. For emergencies, I kept a secret hundred dollar bill in my wallet. This was an emergency.

Destin was fifteen miles from Fort Walton Beach. The fishing village was mostly beach cottages and restaurants. The drive across the Eglin Reservation was always relaxing. I could look at the beach on the south side and the bay on the north. The dunes were replenishing themselves after Hurricane Charley in 1986. The pine trees were coming back too.

My cab driver dropped me off at my little 800-square-foot house behind the bank. The ride was only $40. I still had emergency money left. I gathered my composure and walked into the house. My dad had helped me purchase it after my divorce. Built in 1950, of brick, it had a detached garage and a wonderful, fenced backyard. Thank heaven the previous owner had renovated it. I had no more money when I moved in.

The kids had eaten their pizza and left a mess in the kitchen. I didn't care. I'd clean it up in the morning. It was eight p.m.

"Get ready for bed, brush your teeth and you can skip a bath tonight," I said. Lizzie was twelve, tall, for her age, with long blonde hair and a beautiful face. Sean was six, a rambunctious boy with lots of energy. His complexion, hair, and eyes favored mine.

Lizzie did a great job of babysitting her brother and I was thankful. "Love you," I told them before I took two aspirin to prevent getting a headache after drinking beer. I couldn't relax. The evening had been exciting—I had to admit.

Chapter 2

It thrilled me to be in Destin and enter the Destin Fishing Rodeo. The owners of The Boat House had invited me to be their guest. They paid my entry fee for the rodeo and all I had to do was play with their house band. They called themselves The Trashy White Band. The leader of the band was gigantic; he made me look like a runt. He must have been six feet five inches tall, had a handle-bar mustache, and he wore cowboy boots and a black cowboy hat. I'd met his friend Burt in Nashville when he was recording, *You Can Eat Crackers In My Bed Anytime.* Burt told me how much fun The Boat House was and that I would love it. So, I agreed to come.

So, there I was on stage, playing their songs and my new number one single, *Green Eyes.* The crowd was big on a Sunday night. Fans stood on the deck and hung out the windows. As I played, I noticed a redhead in the second row. She was with her girlfriends, although she wasn't acting as excited as them. I was star struck. She had the most gorgeous green eyes I'd ever seen. With her red hair and green eyes, she would make a perfect cover for an album.

As we finished our set, she got up and crossed the bandstand. I couldn't help myself. I grabbed her hand and commented on her green eyes. Oh shit! She wasn't happy that I'd grabbed her hand and she pulled it away. I watched where she was going—the bathroom. There were lots of women on the deck lined up there. During the break, I went outside to have a drink. Hopefully, I could talk to her. I leaned against the railing and enjoyed the cool breeze off Destin Harbor. Beer was not my favorite drink, and I reached into my back pocket and brought out my flask. I took a swig of Jack Daniels. That tasted better. I climbed up on the stage. "Do y'all know the words to *Welcome to my World?* I want to play it for that cute redhead with the green eyes," I said to Burt.

Burt laughed at me. "I saw you grab her hand. She didn't look too thrilled. Yes, we can play that song. Do you want to play it now?"

"I sure do." The Trashy White Band started the beat. I stroked my electric guitar and started singing it to her. Her friends in the audience poked and teased her. When the song was over, she got up and left. Well, hell! Why did she leave? I'd grab one of her girlfriends at the next break and ask.

We played a couple more sets until it was almost time to close. Her friends were still there, so I jumped down from the stage and walked up to the tall, blonde one. "Hello, I'm Cade Fox. Where did your girlfriend go?"

"Hi, I'm Kate. Harper needed to get home to her children. It's a school night. We work with Harper at the First Beach Bank," the blonde replied.

"Okay. I want to send her some flowers—to the bank. Will you give me her full name and the address of the bank? I'm here for a few days. I'll be playing at the Boat House for a few more evenings. If you want to come back, I'll buy y'all a drink." I watched Kate grin at her friends.

"She'll definitely be surprised. Her name is Harper Hamilton and send them to The First Beach Bank at 2121 Eglin Parkway, Fort Walton Beach," Kate said.

"I'll get Bob, my manager, to send them tomorrow while I'm fishing. I'm going to invite her to the rodeo dinner."

I don't know why, but for some reason her friends found this amusing and they giggled among themselves as they left.

Chapter 3

The next morning, the bank auditors were there to audit my dear friend Doodle Harris. It bothered me because Doodle and I were good friends. I met *The Doodle,* the first weekend I came to Fort Walton Beach with Michael Hamilton. He was promoting a dance at the Quonset Hut in Mary Esther. Michael was great friends with him, and they were both lifeguards at Fort Walton Beach. Michael's friends were there, and the dance was so much fun until Norton pinched my butt.

"Who the hell did that?" I screeched.

Norton smirked. "I did! If you come over here much, you better get used to it." Michael, my date, just laughed. Fort Walton Beach was different from my small town of Milton.

While I was getting files for the auditors, the florist arrived with a bouquet of white roses.

"Who is Harper?" the florist asked Kate and Kate pointed at me. The florist set them on my desk. I couldn't imagine who was sending me roses. I opened the card. It read, *Green Eyes, will you come to the captain's dinner for the fishing rodeo with me? I need to bring a date. Can you call Bob, my manager? I'm fishing today. Tell him where to send a car for you.*

"Did you tell that musician my name and where I work?" I asked Kate.

"Yes. He came over to our table after you left and asked where you went. I told him you had to get home to your children. He wanted your name and where you worked. So, I gave it to him. Don't kill me."

Should I go? I'm sure it'll be fun. Lots of clients at the bank fish big charter boats for a living. At least I'll know people. I went into the break room for privacy, so I could call the phone number on the card from the florist.

"Bob Little speaking," said his manager.

"Hi Bob, my name's Harper Hamilton, and Cade told me to call you."

"Yes, he hoped you'd call. Did you get the flowers?"

"Yes, they were a delightful surprise. I accept his invitation. I live at 210 Greenbrier Drive in Fort Walton Beach. Cade's note says you are sending someone for me?"

"We are. Be ready at six. The dinner starts at seven."

I walked over to Kate's desk at the switchboard. "Guess who needs to babysit my children tonight and feed them? I left them on Sunday night to go with you all to the Boat House. I can't leave them by themselves again."

"Sure," said Kate. "I don't want you to miss this date. The only pay you have to give me is the details tomorrow." She laughed.

The workday ended. I told Lizzie and Sean where I was going. Lizzie thought it was cool and Sean couldn't have cared less. He wanted to know who was feeding him supper.

I put on my best jeans, cowboy boots and jean jacket. I had read in the paper that the dinner was at The Wharfe on the harbor in Destin. Charter boat captains don't dress up and neither do their wives. I knew I'd be fine in jeans and boots.

At six p.m. I glanced out the window. Oh my, there was a big white limo outside my door.

"Hello, I'm Bob. Cade's cleaning up after a big day of fishing. We'll meet him at The Wharfe." Bob was older than Cade. I guessed around fifty. He was balding, and he wore a fancy suit. It looked like the ones worn by country music stars in *People* magazine. It was definitely not what men in Destin wore. He helped me into the limo and offered me a glass of champagne. I took it, thinking it would relax me. It did. The stereo was playing the latest country songs.

"Do you like Cade's music?" Bob asked.

"I'd never listened to his music before the other night at The Boat House. I'm a disco girl. But yes, his songs are excellent."

Bob looked at me strangely and we didn't talk anymore.

We were the only limousine to arrive at The Wharfe. Everybody else was parking their beat-up Fords and Chevrolet trucks. Several of the boat captains and their wives turned and looked at me. How awkward. *Oh, my heavens, there's Buck and Muriel Destin. They're my favorite bank clients.*

"Hi," Muriel said. "What're you doing in the limo?"

"Hi Muriel, just meeting someone." I grinned and winked at her. As usual, Muriel was dressed in a silk dress with a colorful scarf around her neck. She was wearing her black mink coat, even though it wasn't that cold. We walked up the stairs and into the bar. Cade was at the bar, dressed in tight blue jeans, a cowboy shirt, and had a hat on his head. He turned and saw us coming. He excused himself from the guys at the bar. When he reached for my hand, I got an electric shock.

"Hello, Green Eyes. You're a sight for sore eyes. I'm so glad you came."

"Thank you for the limo ride. It was different. And the roses are beautiful."

As Cade greeted me, I glanced around the bar. Hung on the walls were huge, mounted fish that boat captains must have caught. There were plaques under each fish that gave the size, weight, and type of fish. Past the bar, there were views of the harbor. The lights on the condos across the water twinkled and made the harbor look like a fairyland.

"Let's go find our seat." He guided me to the front of the restaurant where the chairman of the rodeo, Royal Melvin, was sitting. Buck and Muriel were also up there. I hoped we could sit near them. Our seats were by Royal and his wife. Buck and Muriel were across the table. Cade introduced me to Mr. Melvin. He saw that the Destin's were my friends, so I introduced him. Muriel gave me a sly grin. She was having a good look at Cade. I could just hear her saying the next time they came to the bank. *Why were you with the guy with the tattoos?*

Most of the boat captains were dressed in jeans, long-sleeved fishing shirts, and deck shoes. Some of the wives had on simple linen dresses and low heels. Other women wore jeans and plaid shirts. Muriel was the most striking among them. Somehow, she got her husband, Buck, to wear a sport coat with his white shirt and jeans. Across the table were Kelly and Mary Ann Windes, more clients from the bank. Kelly was so handsome, and Mary Ann Windes was cute as can be in a floral dress.

Royal started the dinner by welcoming the captains, wives, dates, and special friends to the banquet. "This is the 1990 Rodeo," he said. "There are seventeen boats registered, and we expect big fish to be pulled into the dock this year. We welcome our famous angler from Nashville, Cade Fox."

Cade nodded. "Thank you, sir. It's a pleasure to be here."

The servers brought out fried crab claws and hushpuppies. Sweet tea was on the table. The smell of all that delicious food had my mouth watering, although there wasn't much time to talk to Cade because the food was being served. I was nervous and he was sexy for sure.

We enjoyed a medley of fried snapper, grouper, and triggerfish. The fish had been caught in the Gulf of Mexico earlier in the day. The rodeo celebrated those who caught blue marlin, Warsaw grouper, amberjack, king mackerel, snapper and more.

When the dinner was over, Cade shook hands with several captains. Then he leaned toward me. "Green Eyes, we need to leave this crowd. Where should we go?"

"There's a bar close by. It's called Harbor Docks. Can the limo take us there?"

"The boat I'm fishing from is behind that location. That'll be perfect. Can you go and get the limo for us?" he asked Bob.

Bob left us at Harbor Docks where we sat at a table by the window. Harbor Docks was one of my favorite places. I loved the long wooden bar with the brass top and footrest. The bar stools had local names on their backs. You had to ask the bartender before you sat in one just in case the namesake was coming. It was a favorite afternoon hang out for anglers and businessmen and it was a place I could take my children to eat on a Sunday afternoon. Sean loved to go downstairs to throw a fishing line into the water. He only caught small pin fish, but he was entertained.

It was October and the weather was fantastic. The temperature was a balmy seventy-eight degrees. Cade asked what I wanted to drink, and I asked for a glass of white wine. Cade got a bourbon at the bar and brought me my wine. Harbor Docks was empty on a Monday night; we had the place to ourselves. We discussed normal things. How did he find Destin? How many children did I have? He told me he'd never been married, and his music career was just beginning and Nashville was enjoying the style of country music he played.

"I'm not a country singer like Willie Nelson or Waylon Jennings. I like their songs, but I play a little more electric guitar and move like Elvis. It's kind of country rock," he said.

"I don't listen to country music. I must admit, I'm a disco music fan."

"Well, I can teach you to like it."

"It's getting late," I said. "I need to go home soon. It's a school night for my children. We have to be up early."

"Can we go on the back deck before we leave?" he asked.

The new moon shone over the water. It was so calm and all I could hear was the tinkling of the lines on a sailboat behind Harbor Docks. Before I realized it, he drew me to him and kissed me. Electric sparks happened again. That was the second time being touched by him had given me a shock.

Cade released his grip on me. "Green Eyes, would you like to go fishing with me on Wednesday?"

"I've always wanted to go deep-sea fishing. I'd love to. What time should I be here? I can drive myself. Please don't send the limo. And can you call me Harper please?"

"Sure, I'll call you Harper, but I like Green Eyes. Can you be here by 8 a.m.? It isn't tournament fishing on Wednesday for me and I can have you back by two. Your children must get home from school soon after that time."

Moments later, Cade went to find the limo driver and we left for Fort Walton Beach. He held my hand on the way home and gave me a huge kiss when we arrived at my door. I had to admit, he was dreamy.

"Goodnight. I can't invite you in as my neighbors are nosey. I'll be there Wednesday morning."

Kate rubbed her eyes, woke up slowly and got off the couch. "How was your date?"

"Much better than I expected. Our clients, Muriel and Buck Destin, sat next to me and across the table were Kelly and Mary Ann Windes. The rodeo dinner was excellent. Then we went to Harbor Docks for a drink."

"Anything else? Don't hold back."

"He kissed me out on the back deck of Harbor Docks. Yes, it was exciting. I'm going deep-sea fishing with him on Wednesday ... thanks for babysitting."

"Okay, if that's all you are going to tell me, I'll leave. I'll see you at the bank tomorrow."

Chapter 4

On Wednesday morning, I couldn't wait to go fishing. I dressed in a sweat suit with sneakers and took a waterproof jacket. It could get windy on the Gulf of Mexico. As soon as the kids were off to school on the bus, I drove my little yellow Chevrolet Chevette to Harbor Docks. I strolled along the dock to the boat. I was so excited I could hardly control myself. Cade jumped off the boat and helped me into it.

"Hello. Say hello to Al for me." The captain of the boat, Gary Jarvis, welcomed me on board.

Cade looked at me with curiosity. "You look fantastic. This is going to be fun. But who's Al?"

I laughed. "Al's my boss, the president of our bank. He knows Gary and told him I was going fishing with you. This's a small town. We all know each other."

"Al has told me all about you. I promise we'll take good care of you. Let me tell you a little about my boat. It's a thirty-eight-foot Infinity built in 1988. It has two diesel engines and is rigged for sport fishing," Gary said.

Cade and I settled ourselves in the back of the boat. Gary backed it out of the dock and idled toward the Destin Pass. We passed the fuel dock and a couple of restaurants and cabins for tourist anglers. The boat turned south at the pass which led to the Gulf of Mexico. Our pass and the Gulf of Mexico are one of the most gorgeous places in Florida. The water was emerald-green mixed with cerulean blue. The sand dunes were so white they glistened. I needed to wear sunglasses to protect myself from the glare.

The fishing boats had gone out earlier for the tournament, so we had the pass to ourselves. I enjoyed the salty smell of the Gulf. As the boat passed the jetties, a pod of dolphins followed us into the Gulf of Mexico.

"Isn't that a wonderful sight? I never tire of watching the dolphins," I said to Cade.

"Yes, they're fantastic creatures. Today is going to be fun." He was standing next to me and moved even closer. "I love this," he said. "It's so much fun to share it with you." He bent his head and kissed my forehead.

"We need to motor out fifteen miles for offshore fishing. I have my own markers where I like to drop anchor," Gary told us. When we arrived at the spot, he dropped the large anchor and helped Cade get his pole in the water. Then he turned to me.

"Do you want to fish?"

"Do you think I can? I'd love to catch a snapper for dinner."

"Sure, I'll help you catch a fish. You're probably a natural," Gary replied.

"Okay, rig me up. I'm excited."

The boat was pleasantly rocking with the rhythm of the waves when suddenly Cade's line zinged. He reeled in a fish. "I think it's a snapper," he said. "Is it big enough to keep?"

"Yes, that's a keeper. They have to be at least ten inches long. That one looks to be twelve inches," Gary replied.

Then next thing, my rod was zinging. "I've got a fish too." Gary came over to help me land it. Cade was laughing at me.

"Hey, cowboy, don't laugh at me. I've never caught a fish before."

We fished until lunchtime when Gary brought out sandwiches and beer. The fresh air and exercise reeling in fish had made me hungry.

"This is a wonderful way to spend a morning. A great day of fishing and good company," Cade said.

After eating our ham and tomato sandwiches, Gary took the boat back through the pass. It was busier then, with boats returning to weigh in the fish they had caught for the rodeo.

"I'm going to win that rodeo one day on my own charter boat," Cade said.

Gary and I smiled at him.

Gary docked the boat and when his deckhand hung the snapper we'd caught on a board for a photo, along came Mary Ann Windes. She was the local dock photographer. I had told her last night that we would be fishing with Gary Jarvis and docking behind Harbor Docks. She said she would come take our photos with the fish we'd caught.

"Do you want your photo taken with the fish? It'd be a great story for the paper," she asked Cade with excitement.

"Sure, take my photo, please. Harper and Gary come over here and be in the photo with me."

How exciting! My photo with Cade would be in the paper.

Cade bade Gary and Mary Ann goodbye and walked me to my car. "We can have a local restaurant cook the snapper. Do you want to eat dinner with me?"

"I can't go out again tonight. Would you like to bring them to my house? I'll bake them and make you cheese grits and coleslaw. You can bring Bob if you like."

"That's an even better idea. What time should we come?" he asked.

"Six is best for me."

"Fabulous. I'll bring beer and a bottle of white wine for you." He leaned in my car window and gave me a kiss. His kisses gave me tingles. "I'll see you tonight." He walked back to the boat.

Chapter 5

On my way home, I stopped by the grocery store and picked up what I needed for cheese grits and homemade coleslaw. I wanted this dinner to be superb. Thank heavens I had cleaned the house the other night. My house was tiny and built in the fifties. I bought it after Lenny and I broke off our engagement. I loved it being near the bank and my children's schools. My dad bought me central air conditioning and because it had no dryer, he fixed me a clothesline in the backyard. I didn't argue with him. I was so thankful for the AC.

Lenny, my ex-fiancé, sold his beach condo and gave me his rattan furniture. It fitted perfectly because it was smaller than normal furniture. There was room for a double bed in my room and a small dresser. The kids slept on twin beds in their rooms. It was amusing to watch in the mornings when we were getting ready for school and work because we only had one bathroom. All three of us were in front of the sink and the mirror.

The kids came home from school and tumbled in the front door. "Please get your homework done now. We have company coming for dinner."

"Who?" Lizzie asked.

"Cade Fox and his manager, Bob. We caught lots of snapper this morning and I'm cooking them tonight."

"Wow, Mom, we'll try to be on our best behavior."

"Thanks, honey. Get your homework done and make sure you brother has his bath."

Lord help me! Cade and Bob arrived in the limo. I forgot they didn't have a car. I greeted them at the door. "Come into my humble abode. I have dinner cooking."

Lizzie and Sean appeared and I introduced them.

"You're as beautiful as your mom. Let me look at you. Do you have green eyes too?" Cade said to Lizzie.

She blushed. "No, mine are brown like my dad's. Sean has green eyes like mom." They scampered back to their rooms.

Bob handed me the wine and beer to put in the refrigerator. I told them this house was the first one I'd ever owned and apologized for how small it was.

"You should see where I grew up in Middle Tennessee. Your house is a mansion compared to where I was born," Cade said.

I opened the wine and gave each of them a beer. They sat in my little living room while I got the dinner ready. When the kids came into the kitchen, I fixed them plates of food, then let them go to the sunroom to eat. There was only room for four at my small dining table.

"Come into the kitchen, guys. Dinner's ready." Cade and Bob sat and I served them from the stove. I laughed when they sat in my small rattan dining chairs. Bob was tall and barely fitted in the chair. Cade, at five feet ten, fitted a little better.

"Yum, this is delicious," Bob said. "You're an excellent cook."

Cade was stuffing his mouth with the cheese grits. "It sure is," he mumbled.

"Thank you. I try."

We were quiet while we ate. The baked snapper was fabulous, and everyone loved my cheese grits and coleslaw. When we had finished eating, Lizzie came in and helped me clear the table.

"I'm sorry, I didn't have time to make desert."

"No problem. I don't have room for another bite," Cade replied and Bob nodded.

"Excuse me while I take the children to bed, please."

I kissed each of them and tucked them into bed. "Cade's a hunk, Mom," Lizzie said.

"Where did you learn that word?"

"From MTV."

When I returned, the guys were drinking another beer and chatting. "I've had a great time this past week," Cade said. "I hate that we have to go home tomorrow."

"I'm glad I got to meet you and go fishing. I promise to keep up with your career."

"Could you come to Nashville one weekend when I'm playing in the Flamingo Room?"

"That would be exciting." We walked toward the door; Bob went ahead and got in the limo while Cade lagged behind. Then he pulled me close and gave me a heavenly kiss. Fireworks went off for me again.

"Goodbye. Meeting you was terrific. I hope you will come to Nashville one weekend."

"I'll do my best. We come from different worlds. Do you think a romance is possible between us?"

"It's worth a try." He left, got in the limo and I watched them drive away. A tear dripped down my cheek. A couple of neighbors were outside and watched the limo leave.

Chapter 6

"Harper's a charming woman. Her children are well behaved, and I admired her home and it didn't embarrass her to tell us it was small. Do you think where I come from would stop her from dating me?" I said to Bob as we were driving back to the hotel.

"Of course not. I can tell she likes you," Bob replied.

"Let me tell you my story," I said. "I don't think I've told you before. I grew up in the small town of Dunlap, Tennessee. Dad was a coal miner and he was forty-eight when he died in a mining accident. Mom taught second grade in the small schoolhouse at Sequatchie County Elementary School. She raised three boys by herself after Daddy died. She was paid some money because of his accidental death, but it was never enough. Thank heavens Grannie took us in to live with her. She cooked for us and kept our clothes clean. Both were adamant we had to get our high school diplomas."

"That's terrible about your father. Your mother sounds like a strong woman. Kind of like Harper."

"Mom is the strongest woman. She put up with Dad's drinking and raised us boys by herself. I started picking a guitar with Daddy when I was twelve. Tucker played banjo and Sawyer wrote music and played drums. Dad was an excellent guitar player and encouraged us to use our talents. Our high school band was called Three Foxes. I'm the eldest and I left home first. After graduation, I headed for Nashville. I was itching to be a country musician.

"My first job was sweeping and cleaning up at the Grand Old Opry. I thought if I could hang around the greatest country singers, one of them might take a liking to me. It was the summer of 1989. I played back-up guitar at the Opry for a few stars when they needed a fill in. Then I overheard Waylon Jennings talking to his manager, Bud. Where the hell is Billie Ray?"

"He called in sick with the flu this morning," said Bud.

"Who the hell's going to replace him for the show tomorrow?"

"I don't have anyone."

"I remember walking up to them both and saying, Mr. Jennings, I play a mean guitar. Would you let me sit in with you at practice today?"

"Well, why the hell not? Let's hear what you got, boy. What's your name?"

"Cade Fox, sir. I've played for a few bands when they're short a guitar player."

"Be at practice at two p.m."

"The rest is history. They let me play. They liked me. I got to fill in for anyone who needed an electric guitar player.

"One night I was in the kitchen cooking a beef stew. It was one we could eat for a week. Tucker was picking and singing and I asked him the name of the song."

"*Green Eyes.* Sawyer wrote it and sent it to me to surprise you. Do you like it?" he replied.

"I love it. Can you tune it for my electric guitar?"

"Sure. We can practice it after we eat. Your stew smells good. Almost as good as Grannie's."

"We ate, then we played the song. I felt it had potential. Get Sawyer down here this weekend with his drums, I told him. We'll set up in one of the back rooms at the Opry.

"That weekend we rehearsed at the Opry. Chet Atkins listened to us playing and poked his head in the door. Y'all sound pretty good, boys. I cut my teeth at Skull's Rainbow Room in Printer's Alley. You need to do a gig there. I can give you Skull Schuman's phone number. Tell him I sent you," said Chet.

"Can you believe our luck?

"I called Skull the next day. He said there was an opening in two weeks. We took it. The crowd wasn't large, but everybody liked our music. Skull asked us to play every Wednesday for a month. Then he moved us to Friday, Saturday, and Sunday nights. The crowd grew and Skull clapped us on the back after our Saturday performance. He loved the crowd, liked us and our song.

"One weekend, Chet Atkins came to listen to us."

"Boys, you are good. Especially that song, *Green Eyes*. Owen Bradley, my record producer, should allow you to record it. I'll set it up with him at The Barn."

"You are aware of the rest. I'm thankful Owen recommended you to be our manager. Thanks to you and Owen, our single has been in the number five slot on Hot County Singles for five weeks in a row. It was exciting that our song was just behind Waylon Jennings and Willie Nelson's song *Mamma's Don't Let Your Babies Grow Up to Be Cowboys*."

"You boys are doing very well, considering you've only been in Nashville a short time," Bob said.

"Do you think it would impress Harper? Or would my past scare her off?" I asked.

"If your story scares her off, you don't want her. Call her when we get home and ask her to listen to your story."

"Thanks, Bob. You're a good friend."

Chapter 7

Why was I spoiling my day thinking of Cade? He'd gone back to Nashville to better his music career and a broken heart was something I didn't need. Country music stars must have normal families. I wondered if Cade wanted one. I knew he would have to travel on the road to become famous and he had told me he and his brothers wanted to be successful.

That weekend I decided to take the children to visit my parents. That would take my mind off Cade. I dialed their number. "Hi Mom, the kids and I want to come visit you for the weekend. Do you and Dad have any plans?"

"No, dear, that would be wonderful. We'll heat the pool so the kids can swim. What do you want me to fix for dinner?"

"We love your macaroni and cheese. Can Dad grill some pork chops?"

"That sounds terrific. What time are you coming?"

"We'll leave here Saturday morning around ten. Love you, Mom."

On Saturday morning, we loaded the Chevette and drove to Milton. From Fort Walton Beach, we went west on highway 98 until we came to Navarre, then we turned north on Highway 87. It was an hour's drive through pine trees and across the Blackwater River. I reminisced about learning to water ski on that river with my dad. Every summer weekend, we put the boat in and went water skiing. Our ski team competed in Pensacola and Fort Walton Beach. I was their girl. The boys threw me on to their shoulders for pyramids. I won trophies for slalom skiing. My slalom routine was like the one at Cypress Gardens. I was a daredevil, but afraid of ski jumping. The summer after my junior year in high school, we took a family trip to Cypress Gardens and they offered me a summer scholarship. They wanted me. But Dad took a look around. 'That is too much freedom for a teenager,' he said. My Dad was strict. There was no summer at Cypress Gardens for me.

Dad had built their brick three-bedroom ranch home on a country road. He wanted at least an acre so they could have a swimming pool and a garden. The kids bailed out as soon as we arrived. Lizzie ran straight to Mom and Sassy, the miniature poodle. My mom was born in London and met my dad during the war. She had more energy than any woman I knew. Everyone loved her for her smile, kindness, and laughter. Her hair was turning white, which fitted her grandmother role. Sean and I followed Dad to his garden. My dad was a superb role model for Sean. He spent lots of time teaching him to throw a baseball, swim, and about the vegetables he grew. He took him on the back of his motorcycle to pick up cans from the side of the road and then donated the money from their sale to the church. Sean and I loved the vegetables he grew. Dad was a natural gardener. He planted marigolds between the rows, and he never sprayed chemicals on the plants. We picked enough yellow squash and green beans to eat for an early supper. Dad cooked the pork chops to perfection, and his fresh vegetables were a treat. Sean asked for seconds of macaroni and cheese.

"Mom, can we put on our swimsuits now?" Sean asked. "Papa wants me to dive in."

"Okay. Lizzie and I will put on ours too." My children loved the pool. Mom had had them swimming since they were babies. My parents swam with the kids and I relaxed on the lounger and worked on my tan. My mind drifted back to Cade. Mom dried off with a towel and sat on the lounger next to me.

"Why so thoughtful?" she asked.

"Oh, I met someone who may not be a good fit for me. He's a county music singer from Nashville. He has a song out that's popular."

"Really, he sounds different from others you've dated. Tell me about him."

I told her how we met. That he took me to the rodeo dinner and charter-boat fishing. I mentioned that I was afraid to get too involved. I told her I was attracted to him, tattoos and all.

She laughed. "Give him a chance. It wouldn't be like he'd be in your life every day. You could fly to Nashville and see how he lives. Dad and I will look after your children if you decide to go." My parents were the best in the world.

Chapter 8

Bob and I were back in Nashville and my brothers were ready to go to work. It was nice to have The Barn to practice and record. Sawyer, our younger brother, had been writing while Tucker and I had left to live in Nashville. Sawyer was still finishing high school and came to Nashville on weekends. At six feet two, he was much taller than me and Tucker. He had dark hair and brown eyes like Mom. Because he was the youngest, Mom was more protective of him and didn't want him exposed to Nashville too early.

I told Sawyer about Harper, and how his song *Green Eyes* fitted her and I asked him to write another song about her. He loved hearing how Harper had snubbed me at The Boat House and how I'd enjoyed the dinner at the rodeo, fishing and her cooking for me and Bob.

"You got it bad, brother. I'll work on one for her," he said.

Bob got us another gig at Skull's Rainbow Room in Printers Alley. We were playing back-up when Chet Atkins needed us at the Grand Old Opry.

In the 1970s, a distinctive rock music style was emerging in Nashville. Charlie Daniels became the leader of southern rock music. His style was closer to country music than the blues. My brothers and I aspired to be more like Charlie Daniels. The three of us were tired of the Grand Old Opry style of music. Charlie Daniels was sponsoring a volunteer jam and he invited us to play. It was being held at Middle Tennessee State University in Murfreesboro. Sawyer had finished his new song and we planned to play it that weekend at the volunteer jam.

I called him. "Brother, you better plan to come over here this weekend. Charlie Daniels has invited us to play at his volunteer jam. Shine up your drums and get here Friday night."

"Wow, how exciting is that? I can't wait to tell Mom when she gets home from school. I'll bring you some biscuits and honey from Grannie and be there this weekend."

Bob came over Saturday afternoon to pick us up in his van. "I've booked a hotel. Nothing expensive, but we should be comfortable. Bring your instruments and let's get on the road. It's forty-five miles to

Murfreesboro from here. We need to check into the hotel and get something to eat," Bob said.

Sawyer put in the tape of *When I Saw You*. And we sang the words several times to be sure we could do it. "This is a great song. You're getting better at songwriting all the time." Sawyer beamed and everyone agreed with me.

We arrived at the stadium where the musicians were milling around and testing their equipment. Charlie Daniels strode over to meet us. What a giant of a man he was, all six feet two inches. He wore an off-white Stetson, along with white boots and a buckskin fringed jacket. His eyes sparkled with excitement and he had a strong handshake. "Hi Foxes, I'm so glad you joined the jamboree. We'll have a full house tonight; they've sold all the tickets."

"Charlie, you're the best. I sincerely appreciate this opportunity for the guys. Wait until you hear their new song," Bob said.

"Fantastic, y'all are the tenth band to play tonight. Make sure you pay attention when one group leaves and the next one starts," he replied.

"We will. This is too exciting to miss. Thank you again for the opportunity," I said and shook Charlie's hand.

Our band had on white shirts, blue jeans, boots, and string ties. The idea was to appear casual. The other bands started playing at seven and played two songs each. Our time to play was around ten p.m. The lights were shining on a stadium full of country music fans. They sang along with the bands, stomped their feet, and clapped.

"This's the biggest group we've ever played for. Don't get nervous, just pretend we're practicing," I said as we tuned our instruments before we walked onto the stage. I had butterflies, and I imagined my brothers did also. It was a cool October night in Tennessee, near sixty degrees. But it was not so cold that the fans wouldn't enjoy themselves. They had packed the stadium tightly and the lights were bright. *Green Eyes* was the first song we played. The entire stadium sang along. Then I made an announcement. "My brother Sawyer has written a new song we want to play for you. It's called *When I Saw You*. We hope you like it." The crowd loved it, although they couldn't sing along because they didn't know the words. Instead, they swayed in time to the rhythm. After we left the stage, the fans swamped us and asked for autographs. "Can you believe it?" My brothers' smiles were huge. "I think they like *When I Saw You* as much as *Green Eyes,*" I said to Sawyer.

"I'm going back to the hotel and call Harper," I said. The Jack Daniels bottle was sitting on the counter. I poured myself a shot to help me relax then dialed her number, even though it was midnight. When she answered the phone I could tell I woke her. "It's me, Cade. I have good news. I'm sorry it's late."

"It's okay, I'm awake now. Tell me."

"We just played at Charlie Daniels' Jamboree in Murfreesboro. Sawyer's new song about you, *When I Saw You,* was a hit. Everyone loved it and wanted our autographs after we left the stage."

"I didn't realize he had written another song. It's about me?"

"Yes, I wanted to see how the fans reacted to the song before I told you. I'll send you the cd tomorrow."

"That's wonderful. I'm happy for y'all. It sounds like your career is going well. What's next for you?"

"We're going home for Thanksgiving. Grannie's back has been hurting her and Mom wants us home through the holiday. I'd love for you to meet Grannie and Mom. Would you like to come?"

"I'd love to meet your family. My kids are out of school, and I think my mom would be glad to have them for me."

"Let me send you a ticket. Do you want to fly from Pensacola? Check with your mom and tell me what time and dates work for you. I can't wait to set eyes on you."

"I will. Can't wait to see you either. When I find out about the flight schedule, I'll call you. Good night."

I was so excited. I hoped I could sleep. Another shot of Jack Daniels would settle me. I finally drifted off, dreaming of Harper—her red hair and green eyes.

Chapter 9

The next morning, I couldn't wait to call my mom and ask her if she would mind me going to Chattanooga for Thanksgiving. "Mom, I'm so excited. I'm beside myself."

"Yes, dear, what is it?"

"Cade wants me to fly to Chattanooga, meet his Grannie and Mom for Thanksgiving. His Grannie isn't doing well, and he's afraid I might never meet her. Would you mind if I went? I realize I always spend Thanksgiving with you and Dad. Would you have the kids? I can fly out of Pensacola."

"Mercy girl, slow down. I'm sure it'll be okay with your dad if you go to Chattanooga. We'd be happy to have the kids. Find out what flight you need to take. We can take you and pick you up. Do you want to visit Cade? This is exciting for you."

"Oh Mom, you're the best. I'm going to tell him I can go. Thank you, I love you."

I called him at nine a.m. my time. His phone went to voicemail. He must've been so excited last night that he slept late. I left him a message to say that I could come for Thanksgiving.

I woke the kids so we could go to church. Then we went hunting for shells in Walton County. Plenty of shells roll up on the beach in the fall around Topsail State Park. As we climbed the dunes to the beach, we spotted three deer watching us. The beach was calm after the storm the previous night and there were shells everywhere. Sean and Lizzie had their buckets and we did the shell crawl for at least a mile or two. We loved to collect them and make Christmas presents. It was a fun family project. We made shell mirrors, boxes with shells on top, and Christmas ornaments to give to friends and family.

At three o'clock we arrived home. The red message light was blinking on my recorder and I couldn't wait to listen and see if it was Cade. Sure enough, he'd left a message saying he'd slept late and was sorry he missed my phone call. He'd booked a ticket for me the day before Thanksgiving with Eastern Airlines. I would from Pensacola to Chattanooga. He was sending my ticket in the mail. He sounded so excited that I was coming and he couldn't wait to tell his mom and Grannie. His band were going to play at Tootsie's that night. He said he'd call again soon.

I had worn out the kids with our shell hunting. It was early when I fixed hamburgers for dinner. Tomorrow was work and school. It would be early to bed. I dreamed of Cade and how much fun we'd have at Thanksgiving.

Chapter 10

Tucker was sleeping on the couch with a pillow on top of his head and he was snoring. He looked like he used to when he was ten. His blonde hair had fallen over his face, his blue eyes were closed. He was a damn good-looking guy. Women always gave him a lot of attention when he was dressed to play his banjo at a concert. But like me, he hadn't had a girlfriend in ages.

"Get up Tucker; we need to pack and head for home."

Tucker rolled over and brushed his hair out of his eyes. "Is it time to leave already? I feel like I didn't get enough sleep. What time did we go to bed?"

"It was around midnight. We promised Mom we'd be home for dinner tonight. And I need to pick up Harper in Chattanooga tomorrow morning."

We got on the road about noon. The beautiful drive from Nashville to Dunlap would take us a little over two hours. Tucker went back to sleep as I drove. I was glad. It gave me time to daydream about Harper. I couldn't wait to smell her hair and gaze into those green eyes. I hoped she was as excited as I was about this visit. And Mom was excited I had a girlfriend. But poor Grannie. Not unexpectedly, at eighty-eight, her health was declining. Her memory wasn't as sharp as it used to be either. Her back hurt and she took naps often. Grannie was our rock, and I didn't want anything to happen to her.

I thought about our band's good luck. We had two songs on the country music charts. Bob was an excellent manager and I was thankful he handled all our gigs and performances. It sure took a lot off my shoulders.

I hoped I could buy a new truck soon too. My 1970 Ford had two hundred thousand miles on it. I was dreaming of the shiny new black one I'd seen at the Nashville dealership.

I drove out of the city down Highway 24. It was a peaceful drive up and down the mountains and we passed Stonewood Bluff and the Ascend Amphitheater. I remember Tucker and I played there the year I graduated from high school. Tucker was still sleeping and snoring. I reached over and gave him a poke in the ribs. He grumbled but stopped snoring. By the time we turned south on Highway 127, it was time to wake Tucker. It would only take another thirty minutes to get home.

"Wake up Tucker! We're almost home." I jabbed him in the ribs again. Snorting and grumbling, he straightened himself up in the seat.

"Okay, I'm awake. Where are we?" he asked.

"Ten minutes from home."

As we drove up to Grannie's house, it flooded me with memories. I wondered what they'd cooked for dinner. The house looked weather-beaten and needed a paint job. The steps looked somewhat rotten too. Sawyer should have fixed those issues. I knew Tucker and I had better stay a couple of extra days and help repair them. I don't want Grannie to fall. It was time for a railing. When I beeped the horn as we pulled into the yard Mom came flying out of the house. She gave us both a big hug. I was so proud of Mom. At fifty-six, she was still a gorgeous woman with wavy very black hair and blue eyes. She was small-boned. She didn't wear make-up, but if she did, she could have been a model. Trim and tall, she kept herself in shape with the work around the farm.

"I'm so happy you're both home. Come in. Grannie's waiting in her rocker. I have fried chicken for dinner."

Chapter 11

I was too excited for words. I spent the night with my mom and dad in Milton. Lizzie and Sean were glad to be with them for Thanksgiving. Dad drove me to Pensacola at nine. My plane left Pensacola at eleven. Our little airport was small. Nothing like Atlanta would be when I had to change planes.

"I hope you have a great time," my dad said. "Watch your heart this time. See how he lives and gets along with his mother and grandmother. You can tell a lot about a man by how he treats them. A long-distance romance can last awhile because sometimes absence makes the heart grow fonder. Although that didn't happen with me and my girlfriend when I left Michigan for England during the war. I forgot about her as soon as I met your mother. Your Uncle George made me go to a dance at the enlisted men's club. He was already married to your Aunt Maria. I was tired of flying from London to France and back. He wouldn't accept a no. He said Maria was bringing her sister, Hilda. I shaved and took a shower, put on my white dress uniform. When I got there, they had a seat for me beside Hilda. She was an English girl. She laughed easily and was a superb dancer. You know the rest. We were married three months later. That was wartime. This is a different time. Just be careful."

"I will, Dad. Thanks for bringing me to the airport. I love you. I'll let you know when I arrive."

The flight only took an hour from Pensacola to Atlanta. I found my seat and stowed my small suitcase in the overhead bin. I was thankful I knew how to find my way in the Atlanta Airport where the tram took me to the gate for Eastern Airlines. After about an hour's wait, I flew to Chattanooga. I wore my navy-blue suit with a white blouse and low navy-blue heels. I wanted to impress the Fox family.

As I walked off the plane, Cade was standing there waiting for me. He looked as excited as I felt. He rushed toward me, took my bag, and grabbed my hand.

"You made it! How was the flight?" he asked.

"Smooth," I replied. "I'm happy to be here and can't wait to meet your family."

Outside the airport his truck was parked by the curb. Chattanooga is a small airport too. Luckily, he didn't get a ticket for parking at the curb in front of the airport. He opened the door, gave me a big kiss, and helped me in. My suitcase went into the truck bed.

"We'll be at Mom's in forty-five minutes. Are you tired? Need something to drink?" he asked.

"No, I'm just fine. I have never been to Tennessee. I can't wait to see everything you have to show me."

We held hands all the way and he brought me up to date on what he had been doing. How the two songs were number one and number six on the country music radio channels and that Sawyer was writing more. They needed at least ten songs for an album. I could tell his career was on the way up.

We drove up the hill to his mother's place which was in a rural area. A metal gate had to be opened. They didn't have camellias and azaleas like there were at my parents' house. There was one big maple tree that shaded the house. The driveway was dirt, not paved. The white house was cute as a bug with black shutters and a large, covered front porch. It could have used a fresh coat of paint. His brothers were out front, nailing boards on to the steps. Their black and white hound dog was lying in the dirt. He jumped up as he saw Cade's truck pull into the yard.

Cade laughed. "Outstanding, you two are rebuilding the steps. Thank you so much. This is Harper. Come meet her," he said. When they turned and looked me over I wondered what they were thinking. The tallest one came forward first. Cade was rubbing the dog's ears.

"I'm Tucker. I live with Cade in Nashville." He put out his hand. I pulled him close and hugged him. He looked a little bashful.

"You must be Sawyer, the songwriter," I said. "Let me give you a hug too. Sawyer walked toward me with enthusiasm and hugged me.

"Look at her green eyes. I can see why the song fits her. And she's a redhead too," he said to Cade. "How's your temper?" he asked me.

"I have one," I told him. "But unless someone makes me furious, I try to control it." I laughed with the three brothers.

"Okay boys, let's take Harper inside to meet Mom and Grannie." He walked me up the new steps on to the porch and opened the screen door. "Mom, Grannie, Harper's here. Dog, stay outside."

Cade's mom was beautiful. She was dressed in blue jeans and a checked shirt. Oh my, had I overdressed? Grannie was sitting in her rocking chair. She looked like my Grannie Michigan, with white hair and faded blue eyes. Her flowery dress was cotton, and she had a white apron over it. She was doing needlepoint. She put the needlepoint on the table and rose to meet me. Cade's mom got up too.

"Welcome, Harper, I'm Dorothy. We're so happy to meet you. This is Grannie. She lost her real name years ago when the boys came along."

I was thankful she didn't embarrass me and comment on my suit.

"Come sit on the sofa next to me. Cade, get Harper some tea, please."

We chatted about my flight. She asked about my children and what I did at the bank. Grannie smiled and had only one comment. "Do you want to change your suit? It's lovely, but you don't have to dress up in Dunlap."

"Thank you, I will." Grannie took me to a tiny bedroom. It had one twin bed with a crocheted blanket and lace curtains. There was a small wooden chair to put my suitcase on and a sewing machine sat in the corner. I spied a bathroom across the hall.

"We're glad to meet you," said Grannie. "Cade hasn't brought a girl to our house since he was in high school. All we have are boys around here. He's told us so much about meeting you in Destin, going fishing, and you cooking snapper for him. He's a nice young man. All of Dorothy's boys are dutiful sons. They fixed the stairs so I wouldn't fall. In the morning, they're building a railing for me to hold on to. You make yourself at home. I'm going to check on our dinner."

They all made me feel welcome. I removed my suit, hung it up in the antique wardrobe. The room obviously didn't have a built-in closet. I pulled out a shirt, jeans, and tennis shoes. I wondered what Grannie and Dorothy were making for dinner. Whatever they were cooking smelled delicious. The boys were in the living room watching television. Cade got up when I came into the front room.

"I'll take you to the barn to see the horses. We have enough time before dinner." Dog followed us. When Cade opened the door, inside the stables were two horses. The first one was a beautiful black one. "This is Satan," said Cade. "When he was a young colt, he got into trouble all the time, so we named him Satan. He's four years old now and sweet as molasses. Next door to him is Suzie. She is an eight-year-old mare. You can grab her tail and swing between her legs, and she won't move a muscle. Dog loves to run behind her and sleeps in her stall."

"Why do you call him Dog? Doesn't he have a real name?"

"He just walked on to our property one day. 'Whose dog is that?' Sawyer said. None of us knew who he belonged to. He hung around. Grannie fed him and we just kept calling him Dog."

"He's sweet, for sure. I love horses. When I was in high school we had two. I love to ride." Suzie let me stroke her ears and rub her soft muzzle. Satan was bobbing his head to get me to rub him too.

"We can ride in the morning before Thanksgiving dinner," Cade said before he walked me out of the barn and showed me his mother's garden. It was by the fence and full of beans, squash, corn, and tomatoes. Our families were probably more alike than I thought. As I turned away after picking a perfect tomato, Cade pulled me to him and kissed me. We melted together for a moment until I saw Sawyer running toward us with Dog. "It's dinnertime," he yelled and we broke apart.

"Thanks, we're coming now," Cade said. I blushed as we walked toward the house. "It's okay. They know I like you."

Dorothy and Grannie had cooked smothered pork chops, cornbread, and collard greens. They sure knew how to cook. After dinner, I helped Dorothy clean up the kitchen. She smiled at me for offering and we got it done in a flash. The boys were outside on the porch with Grannie and I could hear music.

"What are they doing?" I asked Dorothy.

"They love to jam on the porch. They play old country songs and hymns for Grannie. Let's go join them," she said. We sat in the rockers. "The one they are playing is *Old Rugged Cross,* Grannie's favorite." Cade was playing a regular guitar, not his electric one. Tucker was playing his banjo and Sawyer was using the tambourine. All three were singing and they sounded terrific. Grannie was smiling, rocking, and doing her needlepoint. "Let's play *Green Eyes* for Harper," said Cade. I blushed as he leaned toward me when he sang.

His mom was grinning at me. The next one they played was *When I Saw You*. I'd only heard the CD and not had Cade sing and play it for me. I was embarrassed. Once they finished the song they put down their instruments and Cade walked over to me and took my hands. "Sawyer wrote that song about you for me when I got back from Destin. I'm so glad you're with us this weekend so I could play it for you."

A tear dropped onto my cheek. I hadn't felt that way about a man in a while. Shortly after, everyone went to bed. Cade reminded me we were going horseback riding in the morning.

Chapter 12

I woke around six because I wanted to brush the horses so I could take Harper riding. I thought we'd be able to ride for a couple of hours. In the barn, Satan was pawing at his door. I brought him out and tied him up so I could groom him and put on his saddle. I had to saddle him first, or he'd act up. Suzie didn't mind waiting. She was used to Satan being first at everything. First, to leave the barn in the mornings. First, to be fed and watered; we spoiled him rotten. Next I groomed Suzie before I put on her bridle and saddle. After taking hold of both their bridles, I walked between them to the house. As I was about to hitch them to the railing, Harper walked out of the house in jeans, plaid shirt, and boots. She looked ready to ride.

"Good morning," she said. "I wondered where you went. Your mom gave me a cup of coffee and a biscuit. Have you eaten anything?" she asked.

"I wanted to get the horses ready," I said as I tied them to the railing. It was time for coffee and a biscuit for me. "I hope you slept well."

"I did. Your mom's house feels so comfortable. We can't ride for too long because I want to help prepare Thanksgiving dinner," she said.

"No, you're a guest. The kitchen is small and we have a routine. How about you and the boys do the dishes afterwards?" Mom said when she overheard Harper.

"Are you sure? I don't mind helping. You and Grannie are such fabulous southern cooks, I'm jealous. I wish I could fix vegetables like you."

"Thank you. Go enjoy your ride. Sawyer and Tucker are going to finish the railing on the steps for Grannie."

"Come on, Suzie is waiting for you to ride her. I'll ride that devil, Satan. He always wants to be in front. If you're too far behind me, yell," I said.

We mounted the horses and headed down the dirt road. I jumped off and unlatched the gate. *Oh dear, here comes Dog.* I locked the gate behind me. "Dog, go back to the house. You can't come this time," I told him. His eyes lost their sparkle and he tucked his tail between his legs and went back to the house.

I tried staying next to Suzie and Harper. But Satan was chomping on his bit and pulling to go faster. I kicked him. "Stop it, Satan. We need to go slower today."

"No, you don't," Harper said. Next thing I knew, she and Suzie were flying down the road. Her red hair was streaming behind her; she was an experienced rider. Satan and I flew after them. We galloped for about ten minutes until I pulled Satan up under a gigantic oak tree by the small lake. Harper saw me and reined in Suzie. The horses were breathing hard. They needed a break and we dismounted. "Let's walk them down to the lake for a drink of water," I said and walked toward Harper to help her dismount. But she had already gotten off Suzie and was leading her toward the lake. I needed to remember she was an excellent rider. We were both breathing rapidly too. After the horses had drunk enough, I tethered them to the branch of a nearby tree. Then I took Harper's hand and led her to the grass. I stroked her hair off her face gently and leaned over and kissed her as we lay on the grass. My heart was pounding. I didn't want to be too forward, but I was dying to touch her under her shirt, yet it was too soon. My body was stirring and I wanted to make love to her. I pulled back and sat up. If I hadn't, I might not have stopped. Harper sat up too. Her face was flushed.

"I didn't mean to give you the wrong idea. It's all I can do not to make love to you," I said.

"I know. I feel the same way. Is it too soon to feel this way?" she asked.

I shook my head. "I don't think so. I feel like I've known you all my life."

When Harper reached out and drew me on top of her I reached under her blouse and undid her bra. Her nipples were firm and I could tell she wanted me to touch them. I lifted her blouse over her head. I kissed her neck, her breasts, and down to where her jeans began. She moaned. Then she unbuttoned my shirt, one button at a time. I had the urge to rip it off. The feel of her skin on mine was everything I had dreamed about. I unbuttoned her jeans and pulled down the zipper. She didn't stop me. I stroked her stomach and moved my hand lower. She kissed me more fiercely. Then I unzipped my jeans. I wanted her so badly. I took it slowly. *Hold yourself back.* Harper grabbed my shoulders and moaned again.

Our joint orgasm was earth shattering. I kissed her and murmured in her ear. "Oh, Harper, you are everything I ever dreamed of loving." We rolled on to our backs in the grass to regain our composure.

"That was wonderful. I've been dreaming of you too," she whispered.

I walked down to the lake with my scarf. After wetting it, I wiped my face, then rinsed it and brought it to Harper. I wiped her face. She smiled at me. "Do you want to rinse off?" I asked.

"Yes, let's wade out just a little way," she said before we both took off the rest of our clothes. Lord, she was beautiful without clothes. I took her hand and helped her down the bank. We stood in the water and looked into each other's eyes. We didn't speak. A short time later, we walked hand in hand back to where we'd left our clothes.

"Are you okay?" I asked her.

"Yes, more than okay," she replied. "We better dry off a bit before we try to put our jeans back on." As we struggled to pull them on to our damp bodies, we were both laughing. We mounted our horses and headed back to the barn. I took care of the horses and Harper went into the house.

By the time I came in, Harper had changed into clean clothes and was peeling potatoes for Grannie. As I went to my room to take a shower and put on clean clothes, I thought about how special the morning had been.

Mom rang the bell on the porch and summoned everyone to the table. Sawyer and Tucker had put away their tools and were ready to eat. Mom, Grannie, and Harper brought the turkey and vegetable dishes to the table. We stood and held hands. Mom gave the blessing. "Thank you, Lord, for bringing Harper to meet our family," she said at the end.

What a meal Mom and Grannie had prepared. We stuffed ourselves until we could eat no more. Then Mom and Grannie went out to the porch to rock while the rest of us cleared the table and started the dishes. "Can I call my parents and wish them a happy Thanksgiving?" Harper asked.

"Of course," I replied. "Use the phone in Mom's bedroom so you can have some privacy."

I walked on to the porch to join the rest of the family. Everyone was almost asleep. "This one is a keeper," Mom said to me.

"I know, Mom."

We were all too full to eat dessert. We would wait until later.

After we had rested our full stomachs, Grannie called us back into the house to have pumpkin pie with whipped cream. After that, the boys and I returned to the porch to play music for an hour. By then everyone was yawning and ready for bed.

Chapter 13

When I woke up in the sweet bedroom I stretched my arms toward the ceiling. Cade's family was so nice, and they made me feel welcome. My thoughts turned to Cade. Making love with him yesterday was exciting and intense. *Slow down your feelings, girl.* How could I like someone so much? I wondered what we'd do next. I knew I'd better get dressed. Everyone got up early in that house.

In the kitchen, Dorothy was making pancakes. Everyone was up before me. "I hope I didn't sleep too late. Your bedroom is just so comfortable," I said to no one in particular.

Dorothy laughed and Cade stood up to greet me. "Come sit down and have some pancakes. What do you want to do today?" he asked. "Most of the attractions are in Chattanooga. We could visit Lookout Mountain, ride the Incline Railway, and see the Caverns. I think you'd enjoy the sights."

"Oh, that sounds like fun. I've never been to those places."

We left after breakfast and as we got into Cade's truck, Dog was begging to go. "Please, grab his collar so we can get through the gate?" Cade yelled at Sawyer.

"Sure, brother. You two have fun. We'll be here fixing the railing for Grannie." He gave Cade a knowing look.

"I feel bad about not helping them, but I think they understand I want to spend time with you." He leaned over and gave me a sensual kiss. My heart fluttered. *I'm doomed.* As we drove to Chattanooga, I sat next to Cade on the bench seat of his truck. Why did trucks quit having bench seats? It was so nice to sit next to him. He had WSM Radio playing and I was learning to appreciate country music. "This is the station that we want to play our songs. They've been around since 1925 and are the most listened to," he said. "The first time I heard *Green Eyes* played on WSM, I was thrilled. It's great to have Sawyer in the family. He's a talented songwriter. We should have enough songs for an album soon."

"That'll be wonderful. Hope it happens soon," I told him.

We drove to Lookout Mountain where the view from the park was over seven states. When Cade helped me out of the truck, it mesmerized me.

Then I wondered how the settlers traversed these mountains to settle in Tennessee. Cade put his arms around me as we enjoyed the view. It felt so peaceful to be with him.

"Let's go to Ruby Falls next. We can ride the Incline Railway. Hope it won't scare you too much. Then we can go to the Caverns," he added.

We arrived at Ruby Falls, where there were lots of tourists. I laughed to myself. I was also a tourist. Cade got our tickets to go into the Caverns and we descended in an elevator 260 feet below the surface. What a wonder of nature. Miles of caverns and the waterfall were breathtaking. Cade took my arm to make sure I didn't slip.

"I don't know how my dad worked in the coal mines for all those years. I can't imagine being underground all day," Cade said.

"Me either. I like sunlight too much."

As we went up the elevator, we looked for the Incline Railway. It was within walking distance and as we approached to buy tickets, something strange occurred to me. "Do we sit backwards in the seats?" I asked him.

"Yes, are you afraid? It's very safe."

The guide told us they had established the railway in 1895. It was not that scary, just funny to be riding backwards.

"Are you a Yankee?" Cade asked me as we exited the railway car.

"No, I was born in Virginia and raised in the South. My dad and all my cousins are Yankees. My brother and I were lucky. Mom had us in Portsmouth, Virginia, at the navy hospital

"Why do you ask?"

"I want to take you to Point Park. It's a ten-acre Confederate memorial park overlooking Chattanooga. It has several historic tablets, Confederate artillery, and a scenic outlook. We can eat our picnic lunch there," he said.

We walked together to the park. By then I was hungry and wanted to sit down and rest. Cade found a picnic bench, and we were both glad to eat and rest. I noticed he'd brought his flask. He took a swig and asked if I wanted one. I never drank during the day and he didn't do that at his mother's house. Because my ex had been an alcoholic, I was a little worried. I said nothing, but I intended to be watchful of Cade's drinking.

After lunch, we walked around and read the historic tablets. The Civil War was a terrible time in our country. Cade, asking me if I was a Yankee, showed the scars were still there between the North and South. The South suffered when many young soldiers were killed. Women had to be strong back then to survive. Cade's mother and Grannie were survivors of that time. I couldn't imagine losing a husband and raising three boys. I asked Cade to tell me about losing his dad.

"It was an awful time in our lives," he said. "Dad was forty-eight when the accident happened in the mine. I was twelve, Tucker was ten, and Sawyer was only eight. I remember very little about the first year after he died. Mom cried a lot. We tried to stay out of her way and play outside. We were renting a house close to the coal mine, and I guess Mom couldn't pay the rent because Grannie stepped in. Grannie was dad's mother. After we moved in with her, our family life was much better. Grannie had social security and a miner's widow pension. Mom got the miner's pension too, which helped with her teacher's salary. When I was sixteen, I got a job at the hardware store in town." He took a second swig from his flask.

"I sure was lucky during my young life. I don't know how your mom did it. It's hard enough for me to raise my two without a father or child support," I said.

"You do a great job. Your children are precious and well mannered. I like them and hope to get to know them better," he said. "Ready to go back to the house?"

"Yes, it's been wonderful to see this part of Tennessee."

We drove back to Dunlap and Cade drove through downtown to show me his high school and the hardware store where he'd worked. It was a quaint town filled with old brick buildings that looked as if they might fall down. We passed a courtyard with the courthouse and jail in the middle. I was glad I lived near the beach. The mountains were different for a change, but nothing beat our beach.

When we arrived back at the house, the boys were finishing the railing. "I think I'll lie down for a nap," I said to Cade. I knew that way he would help them finish the job.

When I woke up, everyone was on the porch. Grannie was thrilled with the new railing and praised all of them.

"Well, sunshine, did you have a nice nap?" Dorothy asked.

"It must have been all the fresh air and sights that made me sleepy," I replied and smiled at her. Cade pulled up a chair for me. Tucker was picking on his banjo and helping Sawyer with a song he was writing. *What a wonderful family.*

"Tucker and I are taking everyone out for barbecue tonight," Cade said. "Mom and Grannie have been cooking so much we want to treat them. Grannie's favorite is the Sticky Fingers Smokehouse. It's about twenty miles from here. We'll leave soon. Mom, we better take your SUV so we can all fit," he added.

We arrived at Sticky's, which looked like an old-fashioned restaurant with ancient red brick and a cracked sidewalk. Cade asked for a table for six in the back.

"How large are the portions?" I asked Cade.

"Huge. We usually order two slabs of ribs and pulled chicken for Mom and Grannie. Then we get all the sides of cornbread, deviled eggs, baked beans, and fries. We'll get an appetizer of pretzel bites. You'll love them. They soak the pretzels in beer and dip them in cheese before frying them. I know you'll love it all," he said.

The pretzels were delicious. Then out came the platters of food. Oh, my goodness! It was a good thing I was taking part in this feast and sharing the food. "I've never had barbecue this good," I said. "This is a real treat. Thank you."

"Did you like the sauce? I'll get you a bottle to take home. I think you'll like the sweet sauce," Cade said.

Cade and Tucker threw their credit cards on the table to pay. Cade told the server to put a bottle of the sauce on his tab.

No one talked on the way home. We were all too stuffed. It was dark by the time we arrived. Dog was licking his lips as he smelled what was in the paper bag that came home. We sat on the porch and Cade gave him a rib to chew. There were lightning bugs on the lawn. How peaceful and fun to watch are they? Everyone went into the house except me and Cade. He brought his rocker closer to mine and stroked my hand. "Your visit has been a blessing to me and my family. Mom loves having another woman around and I hate that I have to take you back to the airport tomorrow."

"I hate to leave, but I don't want to take advantage of my parents. The kids and I will go to church with them on Sunday, then I'll drive back to Fort Walton Beach. We better go to bed, my flight leaves Chattanooga at eleven."

Cade stood up, took my hands and pulled me from the rocker. He gathered me in his arms and kissed me with desire. My pulse was racing, but I wasn't about to do anything that would make his mother disrespect me. I pulled away and said goodnight.

Chapter 14

When I woke at dawn, I dreaded the day ahead. I had to take Harper to the airport. I lay there thinking about what a great time we'd had. Making love to her was amazing. I would love to do it again. She said a long-distance romance would be difficult. She was right. Once she was gone, I would have to concentrate on my music. I had a quick shower before everyone else got up.

I had walked out of the bathroom with only a towel around me when I ran into Harper. We were both startled. I saw her stare at the tattoos down my arms and neck. She had never asked me about them and I wondered why. "Good morning, Green Eyes. Did I startle you?"

"Yes." She blushed and stepped back. "You better get dressed. I can't imagine what your Grannie would say."

"I'll go to my room. You can use the bathroom now." She smiled at me and closed the door. I sure wished we were alone. I would have loved to ravish her.

Grannie and Mom were in the kitchen making breakfast for everyone. When Harper joined us at the table, Grannie brought her a plate of biscuits and gravy.

"Thank you, Grannie," she said. "I've had a wonderful time with you. I don't know when I've eaten this good."

"Doesn't your mom cook like me?" Grannie asked.

"No, my mom has many talents, but cooking isn't one of them. Food was rationed during WWII in England, where she grew up. The English aren't known for their cooking. When I want some good southern cooking, I go to my girlfriend's house. Her mother makes the best field peas. I've really enjoyed yours and Dorothy's good food."

We finished breakfast and I asked Harper to get her suitcase. As we got ready to leave, everyone hugged her and told her to come back soon. I saw a tear slip down her face. I put her suitcase in the truck and opened the door for her. We waved at my family and left the farm. As we drove down the road, neither of us spoke. I held Harper's hand and she rubbed my palm.

"Why did you get those tattoos?" she asked as she looked right at me.

I laughed. "I wondered when you were going to ask. It was high school graduation night and several of us drove to Nashville to celebrate. We were passing a tattoo parlor and went inside We'd been drinking and celebrating our freedom from high school. I thought the (fox)would look great on my neck. My friend was getting a heart tattooed on his arm with his girlfriend's name in the center. I thought that was stupid. What if he broke up with her?"

"Why the fox with a tail?"

"My last name is Fox, so I thought it would look cool on a musician. Something for everyone to remember me by. What do you think?"

"Well, at first, it shocked me when I saw it on your neck while you were playing at the Boat House. But as I heard you play and sing, it grew on me. The other women loved it. I've never dated anyone with a tattoo before. I admit they're sexy on you and I love the arrows on your arms."

We were on a deserted part of the road on the way to the airport in Chattanooga when I saw a driveway in the woods, so I pulled off the road. I had to kiss Harper. I shut off the engine and gathered her into my arms. She sighed and returned my kiss. I tried to stop, but my passion was overruling my head. I slipped my hand down her pants and inside her lace underwear. I was as hard as a rock in my tight jeans. Luckily Harper unzipped them. "I need you," I whispered in her ear just before I reclined on the seat and pulled her on top of me. Her body urged me on. "I love you," I whispered as once again we reached the height of passion.

"I love you too," Harper cried.

I drove on to the airport and arrived thirty minutes before Harper's plane was scheduled to depart. She jumped out of the truck and I handed her the suitcase. She hugged me and turned to run to the check-in at the gate. They were calling her flight. As she left, I stood beside my truck to wave as I watched her airplane head for Florida.

I drove back to the farm dreaming of her body and those gorgeous green eyes.

Chapter 15

I was breathing hard as I ran to hand the gate attendant my boarding pass. She stared at my blotchy face and disheveled hair.

"It looks like you had a good time," she said and laughed. I could only nod at her as I looked for my seat. We sure cut it slim. I could've missed my plane. After putting my suitcase in the overhead bin, I collapsed into my seat. The pilot began revving the engines and moments later, we cruised down the runway. I fastened my seat belt and tried to relax. Stopping in the woods and having sex was thrilling. I was afraid I was in love. A little voice in my head was saying, *Dummy, you are going to get your heart hurt.* I might have been, but I hoped Cade would be worth it. I reclined my seat and fell asleep.

The plane landed with a thump and I woke up. We had stopped right in front of the gate and they connected the stairs to the plane so we could deplane immediately. I grabbed my bag and left. I was back in reality.

As I entered the airport, I spied Lizzie, Sean, Mom, and Dad waiting for me. They ran up and hugged me and I hugged them back.

"Did you have a good time?" Lizzie asked. "Tell us all about it."

"Wait until we get in the car."

Dad took my suitcase and we found his car in the parking lot. When I sat between the children in the back seat the questions started. I told them about riding the horses on Thanksgiving morning. Then I told them about all the good food I ate and the places I visited. Sean perked up when I talked about the boys singing and playing music on the front porch. Mom was smiling at me.

"It sounds like you had a wonderful time," she said.

"I did. Thank you for having Lizzy and Sean. I'm sure they had fun too."

"We went to watch The Little Mermaid. I bought them both new shoes. We had turkey, dressing and green peas for Thanksgiving. Do you want to stop at the Quick Burger before we get home? I don't feel like cooking."

"That sounds good and I'm sure the children will enjoy it."

As we pulled into Quick Burger in Milton, memories of Steve Bass, whose parents owned the restaurant, came into my mind. Steve was my tenth-grade boyfriend and always available when I didn't have a boyfriend. It had been twenty-five years since we graduated. I wondered if by then he was running the restaurant. As we walked in to get a booth, nothing had changed. There were the same red vinyl booths and stools at the bar. I smelled hamburgers and French fries cooking. My stomach growled and I longed for one of the quick burgers. We ordered lots of quick burgers, French fries, and cokes. Mom and I were chatting when a large person loomed over us. It was Steve.

"Hi, Harper, I recognized your mother's English accent. What a surprise to see you here. You're looking fantastic and you haven't aged a bit."

"Steve! I have some wrinkles now, you know. It's great to see you. I often recall the fun times we had."

He laughed. "My favorite memory of you is you helping me toilet paper Mr. Amos's house on Halloween. I had just got my Corvette, and you and I were cruising. I thought it would be fun to throw toilet paper into the tree in front of Mr. Amos's house. But Mr. Amos heard my mufflers as we were leaving and the next day at school, he put me in detention. He didn't know you were with me. Lucky for you. Coach Madison was mad at me and didn't let me practice for our bowl game. Fortunately, he let me play and we won. That made us Class A State football champions in our senior year."

Mom and Dad gave us both a horrified look.

"We had some great times," I said.

"You should have married me," he said.

"Probably so. But then I wouldn't have Lizzie and Sean. Say hello to Mr. Steve, you two." They looked up at Steve shyly and said hello.

As we were about to leave, Dad asked for our check. "Steve took care of it," our server replied. I left a good tip.

Dad drove us home to watch television and relax. We watched Mom and Dad's favorite show, Lawrence Welk.

"Are we going to bed now?" Lizzie asked. "Can I sleep with you?"

"Of course, honey. Did you miss me?"

"Yes, Mommy. You won't leave us and go live with Cade, will you?"

"No, honey, I would never leave you." We climbed into bed and she snuggled up to me. She fell asleep while I caressed her hair. I had a hard time sleeping, thinking of all the things I'd done in the previous few days. I prayed I wasn't making a mistake with him before I finally fell asleep.

Chapter 16

"Mom, we have to return to Nashville. We'll be leaving in the morning. Thank you for having Harper for Thanksgiving. I know she had a great time and I hope we can continue our long-distance relationship. As always, the food and company were the best."

"We love you, Cade. Harper is adorable. Keep the lines of communication open with her.

"I told you she's a keeper," Mom replied.

I hugged Mom and Grannie and went to bed.

Tucker and I left early in the morning. I tried to check my voicemail, but the phone service is terrible in the country. After we had driven for an hour, I pulled off the road to see if the service was any better. "I'm going out to check my phone and see if Bob has called. You can drive the rest of the way to Nashville," I said to Tucker. There were two missed calls from Bob and a voicemail message. "Call me urgently," it said.

When I returned Bob's call, he told me that Amy Kurland wanted us to play at The Blue Bird Café the following night. The singer had canceled, and she thought we would be an excellent replacement. She had heard us play at the jam in Murfreesboro and liked our songs. We needed to be at the café by seven. I relayed the message to Tucker. It was great news because there was a lot of publicity when you played at The Blue Bird Café. We could play our two songs and a lot of other artists' songs.

We arrived at The Blue Bird Café in Green Hills an hour early. There was a big blue awning over the plate-glass window at the front door. We stepped inside where they focused spotlights on the singers in the middle of the room. The large bar was in the back, flanked by lots of barstools. They had arranged four top tables and chairs around the room. The hostess greeted us and said she'd get Amy and her stage manager. They were doing a set-up where we could play a duet to the patrons in the restaurant. It was so exciting. Many country music stars have played at The Blue Bird Café and become famous. Lynn Shults from Capital Records discovered Garth Brooks there the previous year. It might have been the break we needed.

Tucker set my guitar and his banjo on the stand, then we sat at the bar and ordered cheeseburgers and fries. The cute girl behind the bar flirted with us.

"Hey, I'm Cindy, and I'll be your bartender tonight. Will you want anything brought over while you play?" I was in love, but if I hadn't been, Cindy with her bright smile, long black hair, and perky breasts would have got my attention.

I looked at Tucker and winked. "Thanks, Cindy. We could use a pitcher of water and two glasses. We'll come back to the bar and get a Jack Daniels during our intermission." I gave Tucker a nudge and a grin after she turned her back to order our food. He laughed at me. After we had eaten, I headed to the bathroom to take a swig from my flask. I was nervous and excited at the same time.

As soon as we sat in our chairs, the crowd went quiet while I strummed my guitar. I spotted Bob in the crowd with a man I didn't recognize. He looked out of place in his tweed jacket, corduroy pants, and Fedora hat. I nodded Bob, and we played *Green Eyes* first. The crowd was listening. I'm sure many of them didn't know who we were. At the end of the song, they clapped. I could tell they liked it. There were plenty of smiles and head nodding.

"Thank you, folks. I'd like to introduce my brother, Tucker Fox. Tucker stood up and they gave him a round of applause. I'm Cade Fox and we are from Dunlap, Tennessee, but we're living in Nashville now. Our next song is also a song our brother Sawyer wrote. It's called *When I saw You.*"

I wished Harper were there to listen to us sing her song. We got another round of applause. After that we livened up our performance with other artists' songs. After playing for forty-five minutes, we took a break. I wanted a shot of Jack Daniels. Cindy saw me and set it on the bar. "Nice songs," she said. "Your brother wrote them? He's talented."

"Yes, he's our younger brother, Sawyer. He's still in high school. Mom is keeping him at home until he graduates."

"Wow, how cool is that?" She walked away with her little butt bouncing.

I slugged back my shot of Jack Daniels and turned around. Bob, our manager, was walking up to us with the guy who had been sitting with him.

"Great job, Cade and Tucker. The audience like you a lot. I want to introduce you to Bill Welch from the Tennessean." Bill reached forward to shake our hands.

"Glad to meet you both. I like your style. I'd like to interview you. How about meeting me for lunch? I'm a reporter for the Entertainment Weekly for the Tennessean."

"Sure, that'd be great. When would you like to meet?" I replied.

"Let's meet at the Belle Meade Cafeteria at noon this Wednesday. I want to get the article in the paper for the weekend. It's great to meet you both. Right now, I've got to get home to the missus and kids."

"That was fast," I said to Bob.

"Yes, Bill doesn't mess around. You and Tucker dress nicely for lunch because he'll take your photo. Speaking of running, I need to get home too. You guys sounded great."

Tucker and I took our seats in the center of the room and I spoke into the mike, "We're going to play a few songs that Sawyer didn't write. You'll recognize them, *What's Going on in Your World, Nobody's Home, Let It Be You,* and several others."

When we finished the set, Amy Kurland, the owner of the Blue Bird Café, came over to thank us for filling in and handed me an envelope. "Don't worry about your tab at the bar. Hope you guys will come back again," she said. It surprised me how young she was. She looked to be only in her mid-thirties. She was very short, had her dishwater blonde hair in a long braid that hung down her back, and she was wearing wire-rimmed glasses like John Lennon.

When People spoke to us while we packed up our instruments it felt good to be admired and complimented. Tucker and I left and headed for my truck, which was parked down the street. After putting the instruments behind the seat, I took my flask out of my back pocket. Tucker looked at me as I chased down some whiskey.

"Do you feel you have to drink to play and sing?" he asked me.

"No, why do you ask?"

"Lately, it seems you are swigging from your flask more and more. Mama wouldn't like it."

"Right. When we perform, I'm a little nervous. I'll do better. We have a lunch date on Wednesday with the reporter from the Tennessean. That'll give us some great exposure." I high-fived Tucker and drove to our apartment.

Chapter 17

"Can you come into my office?" Al said. I loved working for Al. He was only forty years old, and a graduate of the University of Alabama. He was handsome and dressed in quality suits. Plus, I didn't have to answer to the women vice-presidents who were extremely bitchy.

"Sure, boss, what's up?"

"We've had an exceptional year at the bank. I want to give a party to celebrate our success and invite all our best clients. All the directors of the bank, the attorneys we use, builders, developers and all the real estate agents who use our mortgage department and bank with us. Oh, and I almost forgot about the car dealers. Mr. Lee would fire me if I forgot David, Gator, and John. I want you to get the list together for me."

"Sounds like fun. Do you want it before or after Christmas?"

"I'll leave that up to you, but I think after Christmas and before New Year's Eve. It can be on a weekday night. Say we start at five and go to eight."

I was excited and started planning it right away. Being the president's right hand allowed me the privilege of planning the party. I called the Holiday Inn in Destin and the Ramada Inn in Fort Walton Beach to see which one had an event room for one hundred and who would give us the best price. After making the calls, the Ramada Inn had the best venue and price. We intended to serve beer, wine, and a special cocktail and finger food. I would ask Margo Redd to be the bartender who mixed the cocktail.

The best date was Thursday, December 28th. I called Susan at the Friendly Florist. She banked with us and made fabulous flower arrangements. I needed music. I wished I could get Cade to come, but his music wasn't suitable for a bank party. Sherry & Bob Rockwell from Playground Music would find us a nice trio to play soft music. I went through the list of directors for the bank and Al's top clients.

When lunchtime came, my girlfriends were in the breakroom. It was time to stop and tell them the news.

"Guess what? Al said we can throw a big party after Christmas for our important VIPs. Make a list of any special customers you think I should invite and give it to me before Friday. I'll be sending out the invitations soon. Do you want to be my hostesses? It'll be Thursday night, December 28."

"Oh, that sounds like fun," said Melody.

"Include me, please," Kate chimed in.

"What about you, Suzanne?"

"I'm planning to go visit my family in Atlanta for Christmas. I want to make sure I'm back before I commit."

"Let me know soon. And I want y'all to wear a festive Christmas dress. Something red, green, or black, plus stockings and heels."

"Sounds good," they replied in unison. We finished our lunch and I returned to my task. Next I needed to order invitations. I went to see Al in his office to ask if I could leave early and go downtown to the Coach-n-Four to do that. I filled him in on where it would be, the date, and the hostesses I had picked to help me.

"Good choices, yes check out anytime and get those invitations in the mail. I know you'll do a great job planning this party."

As I drove along main street to the Coach-n-Four, I was excited about overseeing the party. The business connections would be fantastic. I decided I'd go to Smith's and look for a dress. Once I'd finished ordering the invitations, I walked across the street to Smith's. I had to look confident and poised so the shop women wouldn't look down on me. I'd always been uncomfortable shopping in that store because the wealthiest women got all their clothes there.

A woman with glasses and a pinched nose looked at me. She had on a black tailored dress, black stockings, and black high heels. I imagined she was about sixty-five. She was skinny and had an abundance of silver bracelets on her arm that jangled every time she gestured with it.

"Welcome to Smith's. Are you looking for something special today?" she asked.

"Yes, ma'am, I want a dress for our bank Christmas party. It needs to be red, green, or black."

"Well, that limits you," she said as she looked down her nose at me. "Follow me upstairs, please. That's where we have the nicer dresses. What size are you, a six?"

"You are correct, I'm a six." She showed me to a dressing room and brought in four dresses. When she left, I peeked at the price tags. Mercy! Two hundred and fifty dollars was too steep for me. I poked my head out of the fitting room curtains and spotted her. "Ma'am, could you come here, please? Do you have a less expensive item? Say around one hundred dollars?"

"I'll go look. Do you want to pass the other four back to me?" she replied with a smirk.

I handed them back and she returned with two, a black one and a red one. I tried on both. The red one was pretty and sexy. The black one was more sedate. Which one to choose? I got my cell phone out of my purse and called Suzanne. As I was calling her, the woman looked in the dressing room. "Have you decided?"

"No, I'm calling my girlfriend to ask her opinion. We're having a Christmas party for our clients at the bank, and I'm overseeing it. I imagine once I send out the invitations, you'll have a wealthier group of women looking for dresses." I pulled the drapes shut. *Bitch, I bet you make less money than I do.* Suzanne answered and I described the dresses.

"Go for it. Buy the red one."

I followed the bitchy woman to the cashier's desk. When she asked if I needed shoes to go with the dress, I ignored her and paid with my credit card. I knew shoes would be less expensive some place else. I was glad to get out of that store and drive home to the kids. As soon as I told her about it, Lizzie was dying to see the dress and I took it out of the garment bag.

"Wow! Mom, that's gorgeous. You'll knock them dead in that."

My phone rang as I was hanging my dress in the closet. I hoped it was Cade. I hadn't talked to him since last week. My heart was beating loudly as I said hello.

"Hello, Green Eyes. I've been missing you."

"I was afraid you'd forgotten me."

"Are you kidding me? All I do is dream about you. I've been busy. Tucker and I got to play at The Blue Bird Café. Have you heard of it?"

"Yes, I know it's a great place to get discovered. Did someone discover you?" I said and laughed.

"Well, a reporter for the weekend stories in the Tennessean wants to interview us. He's writing a story for the paper. I'll send you a copy when it comes out. Who knows what that will lead to? What have you been doing?"

"I'm in charge of planning the bank's Christmas party. It's keeping me busy, and I just bought a new red dress to wear. The party's on December 28. I wish you could be here."

"I'd love to see you in your red dress. Let me see if Bob has us booked that week. I'll be at Mom's for Christmas, so I could fly out of Chattanooga. We hope to be going on the road in January. Bob is lining that up for us now. I won't have any time off for a while if we get to tour with Garth Brooks."

"I hope you can come. I didn't know you were going on the road so soon. Are you excited?"

"Bob just told us. Going on the road will further our career and get us more fans. Sawyer only needs to write two or three more songs to make it ten for an album. He can't go with us until he graduates in May. Mom is firm on that."

"Okay. Listen, I need to go and feed my starving babies. They're both standing here making noises at me."

"I understand. Tell them hello from me. I'll talk to you again soon."

Chapter 18

Tucker and I met Bill Welch at the Belle Meade Cafeteria. We both dressed in tan slacks and plaid button-down collar shirts and made sure we had shined our boots. Bill stood up as we entered the restaurant and waved us over to a booth in the corner.

"Hello guys, thanks for meeting me." It looked as though he was dressed in the same clothes he wore the other night.

"Sure Bill, we're honored you want to do a story about us. What do you want to know?"

"Tell me about your upbringing and how you got to Nashville. But let's order first and we can talk while we eat."

I filled him in on our past and told him we were waiting for Sawyer to join us.

"You three have an interesting story. Everyone comes to Nashville for fame and glory. Do you see this in your future?"

"We hope so. We're working hard, playing wherever and whenever we can. We're both hoping your newspaper article will get us more attention," Tucker replied.

"I'm sure it will. Let's go outside so I can get a photo of you both." Bill paid the tab, and we followed him outside and he took our photos in front of the restaurant.

"Thank you, guys. Look for my article this weekend." A quick wave and he was gone. Nothing slow about Bill.

I looked at Tucker. "That was slam, bam, thank you, ma'am. I hope this article will help our career. By the way, Bob says he might have found more work for us."

As we were driving in my old Ford pickup, we passed the Ford dealership. "Let's pull in and look at the new trucks. This one is on its last legs with 200,000 miles on the speedo." We drove over to the truck lot and started looking around. A salesperson in a pink leisure suit and burgundy shiny shoes walked up. He was about twenty and still had acne on his face. I couldn't get over his obnoxious leisure suit. Perhaps that was the style for car salesmen. I wouldn't be caught dead in his clothes.

"Hi, y'all looking for a new truck?"

I thought about being a smart ass, and almost said, *No, we want a convertible,* but kept it to myself. "We're just looking and getting an idea of what we want when we hit it big."

"You must be an aspiring country music star, but you're dressed kind of snappy for that profession," he said and laughed.

"The reporter for the Tennessean just interviewed us," I replied. "Look for his article in the paper this weekend. How much is this black 4x4 Lariat?"

"It's $14,677 and we have special financing on it right now. You want to fill out a loan application?"

"No, but we'll be back soon. I know it." When we headed to my truck he followed.

"Wait, take my card. I'll get the paper this weekend and keep your article in my drawer until you show up again. Good luck."

Tucker looked at me. "That's a pile of money, brother," he said.

"We're going to have that truck soon."

We drove to The Barn to meet Bob.

"Hello Foxes, great to see you both. Did you meet Bill?"

"We did, we ate, we talked fast, and we said goodbye."

"I should have warned you; we call him fast-talking Bill. He'll write a good story about you. Anyway, I'm sure you're wondering why I wanted to meet you here."

"Yes, we are kinda wondering," I said.

"Well, I want you to meet Garth Brooks. Follow me."

Garth was in the recording studio and when he saw Bob, he finished his song and came out.

"Garth, this is Cade and Tucker Fox who I told you about."

We shook hands with Garth. "Let's sit down and talk a bit," he said. We sat. "I'm playing at the Hew Haw on January 19, here in Nashville. I'm looking for a band to open for me. If y'all do a good job, I'll need you to go on the road with me in 1991." He looked at us and waited for a response.

"We'd love to play for you that night. Our drummer, Sawyer, can't join us until May though. If you agree, I can find someone to work in his place."

"Round up a drummer and let me hear you three play together soon. There's a little time left."

"I know a drummer you'll like. We can use one of the back rooms at the Opry this week," Bob said.

"Let me know when you'll be at the Opry," Garth said. "Bye guys, I have to get back to the recording studio."

"Wow, Bob, this is great news. Who's the drummer?"

"Can you meet this Friday at the Opry? I'll call Richard Boone and tell him to come, so be prepared to play some of Garth's music. Familiarize yourselves with *The Dance*, *The Thunder Rolls*, and *Friends in Low Places*."

"Got it. We know those songs, but we'll practice them before Friday. Thanks Bob," I said with a grin. "That black Ford is looking better and better. Let's go home and practice," I said to Tucker.

I called Harper to tell her our news. "Hello Green Eyes. I've been missing you."

"I was afraid you'd forgotten me," she said and sounded like a record stuck in a groove.

"Are you kidding me? All I do is dream about you. I've been busy. Tucker and I got to play at The Blue Bird Café. Have you heard of it?"

"You told me that last time we spoke. Remember?" she said and laughed.

I laughed too. "What have you been doing?"

"Still working on the Christmas party. It's keeping me busy. There's a lot to do. Do you know if you can come yet?"

"You know I want to see you in your red dress. We're still hoping to tour with Garth Brooks and Bob is still working on it. We have to audition for Garth in a couple of days. As soon as Bob finds us a drummer."

"I really hope you can come. When will you know?"

"Soon, I hope. As soon as I do, you'll be the first to know."

"Okay. I hope you find out soon. I better go. It's been wonderful talking to you. I love hearing your voice. Bye."

Chapter 19

I had a wonderful time with Cade's family. He called the last night he was with them. I got to talk to his mom and Grannie. They were all resting on the front porch. He didn't know if he could take a few days off. I would be busy with the party anyway, so I tried not to think about it too much.

The day of the party finally arrived. Most of the invitees rsvp'd to say they were coming. The Ramada Inn was ready to entertain us at five. The band was set up and Margo was preparing her famous cocktail. Kate and Melody had arrived in their gorgeous dresses. Kate's was emerald-green to complement her blonde hair, and Melody had chosen a slim-fitting black dress that showed off her legs. I had slipped into my red dress and touched up my make-up. We were all set to get the party started.

I stopped by Margo's bar to see how she was getting on. "Hi, Margo, you look fabulous. Thank you for coming to make your notorious cocktail," I said. Margo was my favorite bartender in Fort Walton Beach. She knew everyone, had a beautiful smile and long, long red hair that reached down to her behind. I was lucky she was available for our party. "What's in your cocktail tonight?"

"I've made up gallons of vodka, cranberry juice, triple sec, and lime juice. I'll top it off with a lemon twist and serve it in those glasses on the table over there. It's a very sexy drink for a Christmas party. Do you want one now?"

"Yes ... I think it might calm my nerves." After she poured me one, I took a sip. "Yum, that's delicious. I better go slow on these. I bet I could get drunk quickly without realizing it."

"Yes, be careful how many you have. Your body mass is small, if you know what I mean, so I'd suggest you only drink this one and one more later."

When I arrived in the bathroom, my girlfriends were already there, touching up their make-up. I twirled in my red dress and waited for their approval. "Wow! That dress is a knock-out," Kate said.

"You're going to get looks from lots of our clients, especially the men," Melody added.

"Thanks, girls. It's fun to dress up occasionally. I really appreciate you being here to help me. We better get out there and start greeting people."

Al and his wife, Dorothy, came in the door. Al had on one of his navy-blue suits, a Christmas tie and shiny black shoes. Dorothy looked glamorous. I could tell she had bought the dress from Smith's. I hope the rude lady didn't wait on her. It was an emerald-green, silk, mid-length dress that showed her cleavage.

"Do you want to greet the clients or have me do it?" I asked Al.

"Why don't you greet them? Dorothy and I will just circulate. You look great in that dress, doesn't she, Dorothy?"

"You sure do. Where did you find it?"

"Smith's," I said and blushed.

"Well, it looks fabulous on you," she added. "I got mine there too."

"It looks fantastic on you. You two go enjoy the party. I'll be at the door if you want me for anything."

Our first guests were Gary Lee and his wife, Helen, who were in their seventies. He was the chairman and founder of the bank. Behind him came his eldest son, Bobby, with his wife Nancy. Bobby was on the board of the bank and a local attorney. Nancy was as beautiful as she was sweet. Bobby was lucky to have her as his wife. Next came David and Linda Lee with Gator and Connie Lee. They ran the Pontiac, Oldsmobile, GMC, and the Jeep dealership. They were all attractive and the women were wearing expensive dresses. John and Susan Lee were next. He was the youngest brother and had the Dodge dealership. John was the most handsome boy in the family, tall, slim, and dressed in a more expensive suit. His wife complimented his good looks. Jim Lee, their brother, and our local dentist arrived. He had the best smile of all the brothers. Maybe he would play the piano for us. I was proud to work for such a successful and astonishing family.

"Welcome, it's so nice y'all are together. Al and Dorothy are mingling, and my job is to greet everyone. Margo is at the bar with her specialty drink. The ladies might enjoy her Cosmo. We also have whatever you prefer. Enjoy yourselves," I said as I encompassed them with my smile.

More people arrived, including Muriel and Buck Destin. I hadn't seen Muriel since the Destin Fishing Rodeo. She had on her gorgeous mink coat and Buck was wearing a suit. He usually wore his overalls to the bank. Muriel always dressed impeccably.

"Come in, come in, you two." As I gave Muriel a big hug she whispered in my ear.

"Anything come of that good-looking guy you were with at the rodeo?"

"Yes, we need some time alone so I can fill you in. I might get one of the other girls to do the greeting and join you soon," I whispered. They moved on through the door and Pat Champion, one of our realtor clients, along with Delys Dearmon, who owned a title company, walked up. These two were definitely opposites. Pat had on a well-tailored evening suit and high heels with a purse to match. Delys liked to make a statement and she wore a sexy black dress and stilettos.

"Hi, Harper," they said in unison. "This should be a fun party," Delys added.

"Go check out Margo at the bar. She's made a special cocktail." They walked toward the bar and in walked Don Dewrell with Cash Moore. Those two were a story in themselves. Don always wore his cowboy boots, white shirt, string tie and a suede jacket. Cash never dressed up. He had wrinkled linen pants and shirt. I don't think he ever took any clothes to the cleaners. He hugged me, and Don looked down the front of my dress. They were both single and many of the women in Fort Walton Beach chased them.

"Great dress," Don said to me. Two of my best friends worked for him, so he knew me well and knew he could get away with his behavior.

"How ya doing?" Cash asked me. He had known me since I was nineteen and too young to go into his bar, The Faux Paux on Okaloosa Island. He used to let my ex, Michael, sneak me in occasionally before I was twenty-one. My ex sold liquor to Cash's many stores, and they had been friends for years. Cash had always respected me, which I appreciated.

"I'm great, Cash. Thanks for asking and thank you both for coming."

Several developers arrived separately, Jerry Dorminy, Bob Black, Jay Odom, and Doodle Harris. I watched Jerry head for Delys Dearmon; he'd been trying to date her for a while. They all interacted in real estate business together. Our small town had produced several successful developers and builders. Doodle winked at me, and Jay shook my hand.

A few couples were dancing to the band, and I wished I was dancing with Cade. He was probably playing somewhere in Nashville. By then, I needed a break and asked Melody to take over the front door. Then I went over to Muriel and Buck. Muriel had a Cosmo, and it looked as if Buck was drinking a beer. "Can I join you two?" I asked.

"Of course, darling. Sit down." Buck got up to get food. He probably didn't want to hear us gossip. I told Muriel all about Cade and that I was afraid I might be falling for him.

"You never know who the love of your life will be. I've told you how Buck and I met and what opposites we were. Look how long we've been happily married. Give the guy a chance and you'll decide if he's right or wrong for you in six months," she said.

"Thanks, Muriel, you are such a good friend. And thanks for coming. I'll let Buck come back to you. I need to chat with a few others."

I was at the bar getting my second Cosmo when Pat Champion spoke to me. "Hey, Harper, bring your drink over here. I want to ask you something." As I sat down with Pat, I wondered what she wanted to ask me.

"You know, you have the right skills to be a good real estate agent. I'd love to train you. Come work for me as an assistant. I'll pay for you to take the test and your fees to get started."

I was surprised and curious. "Thank you. I've never given being a realtor any thought."

"It a great career. I'll call you after the New Year. Let's have lunch. In the meantime, think about how much more money you could make if you become a realtor. I understand you are a single mom. With hard work and tenacity, I know you could do it."

"Thank you. I look forward to our lunch ... oh, my goodness! My boyfriend just walked in the door. He's supposed to be in Nashville. I better go greet him."

My heart was fluttering. Cade looked great. He had on a sport coat, tawny pants, and newer-looking cowboy boots. Melody greeted him and then looked around for me. I couldn't contain my excitement and hugged him tightly.

"Hey, Green Eyes, surprise!" he said.

"What a surprise you are. Do you want a drink? Let's go over to the bar and see Margo."

He took my hand and as we walked people stared at us. I wondered if they were aware of who he was.

Margo beamed. "I'll be damned, it's Cade Fox. Welcome. What can I fix you?" she said.

"Jack Daniels on the rocks, thank you." We turned away from the bar and Muriel walked up to us. She winked at me and smiled at Cade.

"Mr. Fox, I see you found something to return to Destin for."

"Yes, ma'am. It's good to see you again. Her green eyes captured me that night in The Boat House."

"I'm glad to hear it. You two have fun. I better take Buck home. He's got to fish in the morning."

We sat down. "How did you find me? How did you get here? Can you stay? I'm so glad to see you," I blurted out.

"Slow down, honey. I've got plenty of time to tell you. I don't want to interrupt your bank party."

"It's almost over. Let me go talk to my boss and ask if I can leave." As I rushed over to Al, I stumbled. I was glad I didn't have a drink in my hand. "Al, Al, my boyfriend just showed up from Nashville. The party's almost over, can I leave now?"

"Slow down. Is that your boyfriend with the tattoos?"

"Yes. He got them to make a statement about his music career."

"Al, her boyfriend is Cade Fox. I've seen him on the Grand Ole Opry show. He was playing with Chet Atkins. Let's go over and meet him," Dorothy said.

"Okay, if you say so," Al said to his wife. They walked with me to meet Cade and I introduced them. Cade shook Al's hand.

"Harper has told me so much about you. Thanks for giving her the day off a while back to go fishing with me."

"Speaking of days off, I think Harper deserves tomorrow off for hosting this terrific party. You two leave now and enjoy tomorrow."

I was dazed and waved goodbye to Kate and Melody before we left. "Where do you want to go?" I asked once we were outside.

"I've rented a room at the Hawaii Kai. Do you want to go there? Are the kids home with a babysitter? I saw Kate at the party."

"The kids are with my parents. They knew I had this party tonight. My parents like to have them when they are out of school. I can follow you to the hotel. I don't want to leave my car here."

Cade pulled me to him and kissed me passionately. I felt as if I was on cloud nine. I could stay the night with him.

"Okay, Green Eyes, follow me."

Chapter 20

As we drove in separate cars to the Hawaii Kai, I was so glad I flew to Fort Walton Beach. Harper's red dress was enough to drive a man crazy. I couldn't wait to make love to her and tell her how much I'd missed her.

I jumped out of my rental car and waited for her to drive into the parking lot in her little yellow Chevette. It was so easy to spot. I opened the door and pulled her into my arms for another long kiss. She put her arms around my neck and held me close.

In the elevator, I pushed the button to the eighth floor. I couldn't keep my hands off her.

"Spend a few days with me in my slice of heaven. Come out and listen to the waves," I said as I pulled back the sliding glass door from my room on to the balcony. I had never booked a hotel room this luxurious. It had beautiful drapes you pulled back to look at the Gulf. The carpet was brand new and matched the expensive bedding and light fixtures. There was a minibar with a refrigerator and a sink. I glanced in the bathroom and couldn't wait to get Harper in the shower that had variable sprays and a large shower head.

"Do you realize it's December and cold outside?" she said.

"Honey, I just want to look at you out here in that red dress. I'll put my arms around you to keep you warm." In the cold air, she was shaking. Floridians must have thin blood. "Come on, we can go inside where you'll be warmer."

"That's much better. This dress is not suitable for balconies on the beach."

"It's gorgeous on you, but I want to see what's underneath."

Harper laughed at me and turned around for me to unzip her dress. As it fell to the floor, I gasped at the sight of her red underwear. "I hope you weren't expecting someone else tonight. Perhaps I shouldn't have surprised you."

"Don't be silly. You're the only man in my life. I had to dress up for the party and I couldn't resist the red bra and panties to go under the red dress. Come here cowboy, let me take off your sport coat." Our clothes landed in a heap on the floor, then I picked Harper up and put her on the bed. I kissed her slowly from head to toe. Damn, I'd missed this woman, and I knew I was in love.

As we cuddled each other, I told her how much I had missed her. "I'm so glad I could get a last-minute flight from Chattanooga. Bob has arranged for Tucker, me, and a new drummer to go on tour with Garth Brooks. We start on January 19."

"That's so exciting for you. I read that Garth Brooks is an up-and-coming country music star. Exposure on tour with him should put your music career on fast forward."

"It won't all be glamorous like Nashville. We'll be riding from town to town on a tour bus. We'll be staying in cheap motels or sleeping on the bus, nothing like this luxurious place. I wanted to treat me and you and for a weekend."

"It's lovely. Can we walk on the beach tomorrow since I have the day off? Al was really pleased with how well the party turned out."

"We can do whatever your little ole heart desires. Right now, I want to make love to you." As I kissed her hungrily and stroked her smooth skin, I thought about how much I loved the taste and smell of her.

We slept with our arms around each other for the rest of the night. In the morning as the sun shone in the sliding glass doors, I walked outside to view the gorgeous beach. There were a couple of dolphins jumping and playing off the second sandbar. It didn't seem cold to me, must have been about sixty-five degrees. Harper came up behind me and put her arms around me.

"Good morning," she said. "What a view to wake up too. Thank you for treating us to this."

"You are so welcome. We may not see each other for a few months, and I wanted this weekend to be special. Do you want to eat breakfast in our room or go downstairs?"

"Let's eat here and then shower and go to my house. I need more clothes, not just a red party dress."

"I'll order room service. You get a shower. Then we can go to your house. I'd love to see the kids, but I must admit, it's nice they are at your parents' house."

Harper grinned at me before she went into the bathroom. As soon as I heard her turn on the shower, I called downstairs to order pancakes, coffee, and bacon.

She came out of the bathroom wrapped in a terry-cloth robe and sat at the little table in the room just as I answered the knock on the door. It was the bellboy with our breakfast. I was famished, and so was Harper. It didn't take us long to finish all the food.

I laughed as Harper put the red bra, panties, and dress back on. "If we go now, not too many people will be in the lobby," I said.

"I hope not. You know what this looks like? A hook-up," she said. "It's called the walk of shame."

"There is no shame when I'm with you." I laughed. "Oh, that sounds like a song. I must tell Sawyer."

We walked out with our heads in the air as an older woman gave us an odd look. We ignored her. "Drive your car home. I'll follow you. I have to return this rental car to the airport on Sunday and I can drop you off at your house on the way. We don't need two cars at the hotel."

"Good idea. See you there."

Harper unlocked the door to her house, and as we went in, I noticed she kept it spotless. It was quiet with the kids gone. "I'll wait in the living room while you pack an overnight bag." Her house was charming with the rattan furniture that had green and white vinyl cushions. I loved her plant room too; it must have been a porch at one time. Her place was comfortable. One day, I hoped we could be together and live in a larger home. At that moment, I was worried that the distance between us while I was on the road would be difficult.

She came out wearing jeans and a sweatshirt. "You look more comfortable now. Let's go back to the beach. Did you bring the red dress? There's a New Year's Eve party at the hotel. I made reservations for us."

"You didn't tell me. Let me get it. That should be fun."

We drove back to the hotel together. I was so excited to have Harper with me for three days.

Chapter 21

As I was driving home to get clothes for the weekend, my thoughts went back to last night. I was in heaven. Cade surprising me at the Christmas party was a fantastic end to an outstanding event. Being in his arms and making love with him, in an actual bed with the sound of the waves from the Gulf of Mexico, was sensational. Of course, the *walk of shame* in my red dress the next morning was horrific. That older woman gave me such a *look*. I was so glad I didn't know anyone at the hotel.

I pulled into my driveway, and Cade was right behind me. "Come in, honey. I'll just be a few minutes. Do you mind if I water the plants? Last week was hectic with all the party work."

"Let me help you. I can do it while you get your clothes together," Cade replied.

"Okay, let me get you my watering can." I filled it up and gave it to him. How thoughtful of him. I would have Cade all to myself for the next two days. Cade finished watering the last plant as I came into the room.

"Thank you so much. We can go now."

"I like plants too, and you know my mom loves plants. Your plants are so pretty in this garden room. Your house is friendly. Are you hungry? I'm ready for lunch," he said. "Where can we get fried fish?"

"One of the most popular places is the High Tide Restaurant and Oyster Bar, just over the Fort Walton Beach bridge. Me and the girls go there sometimes for lunch. Everyone who is anyone is there at lunchtime during the week. Joey Roberts owns it. He's one of our bank customers. You'll love it."

"Tell me where to turn when we get close," he said as we set off in his rental car.

"Look down," I said as we were driving over the bridge and the inter-coastal waterway.

"This is our inter-coastal waterway that goes all the way from Pensacola in the west and Destin in the east. The closest way to go into the Gulf of Mexico, like we did when we went fishing, is through the Destin Pass. That was such a fantastic day."

"I loved it too and was so glad you could go with me, Green Eyes." My heart swelled at his words.

When we went into the restaurant it was dark because we'd come in from the bright outside light. The bar for late night drinking and dancing was to the right; and the restaurant was on the left. It was typical of the seafood restaurants in our area. Photos depicting the old days when Fort Walton Beach had been founded adorned the walls. There were stuffed fish on the walls and the tables had vinyl tablecloths and paper coloring sheets for the children. The hostess greeted us and seated us by the window.

One of the regular waitresses came to our table. She'd been working there for as long as I had been going to eat there and probably longer. "Hi y'all, good to see you today. What can I get you to drink?"

"I'll have a Budweiser in a bottle. What about you, Harper?"

"I'll have a Coors Light."

When she returned with our beer and to take our order, Cade was smiling. "I want a dozen oysters first and then a fried grouper sandwich." He smirked at me. "I may need those oysters."

I tapped him playfully on the hand and gave him a dirty look. Then I waited until she had left. "I come here for lunch often and the waitress knows me. I can't believe you said that about the oysters."

"Well, it's true I will need them. I plan to make love to you as much as possible this weekend."

"Okay, I forgive you. I want to make love to you too. Can we go back to the Holiday Inn, walk on the beach, and take a nap after we finish eating?"

When the waitress brought the oysters, Cade inhaled their smell. Then our sandwiches came with French fries. Of course, they were perfectly fried and so good. I could tell Cade loved the food because he ceased talking.

As we went to pay the bill at the cashier's stand, Joey Roberts, the owner, was there. "Hi, Harper. That was a fabulous party the bank hosted. Al told me you planned it." Joey was an ordinary-looking man about five feet eight. He had sincere eyes and everyone I knew liked him.

"Thank you. I think everyone had fun. Joey, this is Cade Fox from Nashville. He surprised me last night by showing up at the end."

"Hello, I've heard your song *Green Eyes*. It's good. If you ever want to come and play here, I also own the Seagull Bar next door by the water. We get a sizeable crowd on the weekends, and especially on holidays. I'd love to have you."

"Thank you. I'm getting ready to go on the road with Garth Brooks. Maybe I could convince him to get in touch with you." Joey handed Cade his business card and they shook hands.

As we drove across the Eglin Reservation back to Destin, I pointed out the damage the hurricane caused in 1986. "You should have seen these sand dunes before the hurricane. They were gigantic. The one on the left is the Matterhorn. When I was married to Mike, our friends used to gather here, have a bonfire, and slide down it. Now it's half the size. It'll take years for the dunes to build up again. You can see the pine trees, broken and ugly. I wish they'd cut them down so we can see the beach on both sides of the road

"I've heard about the hurricanes you have in Florida, but never seen the destruction they cause. Do they worry you?" Cade asked.

"No, we're used to them. When Mike and I were married and living in our first home in Fort Walton Beach, Hurricane Betsy hit. We went for two weeks without electricity. Sean was still in diapers, so I had to hand wash them. My dad and my brother came over to help cut the fallen trees in our yard. Lizzie and I walked to the end of Okaloosa Island, where we just ate lunch, and collected buckets of shells. Betsy was in 1974, and Charlie in 1986."

"We have ice storms and tornados in our part of Tennessee. They can be bad too."

Cade held my hand as we ran to the hotel doorway. As soon as we were in our room, Cade threw me on the bed and started kissing my neck. Then he snuck his hands under my sweatshirt and stroked my breasts through my bra. "Wait, do you want to take a walk on the beach first?"

"We can do that later. The oysters are working their magic on me," he murmured in my ear. We fumbled to get out of our clothes as fast as we could. When Cade nibbled my neck, then moved down to my breasts, I began to tremble. As I arched up to receive him, he kept kissing me. Then before I knew it, it was all over. Short, but oh so sweet. When he enfolded me in his arms, I knew I was smiling. We had been apart for too long and our hunger for each other couldn't wait. My body tingled all over in places I never knew existed.

We woke up at 4 p.m., rested and happy. I smiled at Cade. "It was worth waiting to take a walk on the beach. The sunset should be between 4:45 and 5:00 today. Would you like to catch it?

"Yes, let's put our sweats back on and watch it. Then we can take a long shower together and go out for dinner or order in."

As we walked over the dunes, holding hands, I couldn't stop smiling. I knew I had fallen in love with Cade. There was no point in worrying about the future. I was just going to enjoy it day by day. It wasn't too cold as we walked, and I enjoyed the sand and sun. We got to the Holiday Inn's beach just in time to sit and watch the sun slowly sink into the west. The round orange globe dipped below the water. As we sat with our arms wrapped around each other, I felt so peaceful.

Cade kissed me yet again. "Thank you for being with me." A sense of calm came over me when I heard his words.

We walked back and punched the button in the elevator for our floor. I slipped into the bathroom and turned on the shower. After dropping my clothes, I stepped into it. My eyes were closed, and I was lathering my hair with shampoo when Cade snuck in. His arms came around me and lingered as he soaped me all over, then I turned and he handed me the soap so I could wash him—all over. His cries of pleasure were music to my ears. Then lifted me, backed me against the wall of the shower; it was fast and furious, as if there were no tomorrow. Cade got out and I finished washing my hair. I still needed conditioner in the red tangled mess. As I stepped out, Cade wrapped me in a large, heated towel. Oh, that warm towel was so good. I enjoyed him toweling me dry before I slipped into the terry-cloth robe the hotel provided. Cade put on the other terry-cloth robe. "Want to stay in tonight and order off the room service menu?" he said.

"That sounds fantastic to me."

He ordered a bottle of wine for me and appetizers. He drank the whiskey in the small bottle in the minibar. We cuddled on the sofa and watched the movie *Pretty Woman*. "You look as beautiful as Julia Roberts in your red dress," he said. Then he took my hand and pulled me toward the bedroom. We were both sleepy, but neither of us wanted to miss the chance to make love again before falling asleep with our arms around each other.

Chapter 22

What a treat it was to wake up next to that gorgeous redhead. I hoped I hadn't worn her out making love. I couldn't get enough. We had the whole day ahead of us. When I stroked her face, she woke up and smiled at me.

"Good morning. We have the whole day to do whatever you want to do."

She stretched. "Would you like to drive into Destin, walk along the docks and eat lunch at Harbor Docks?"

"That sounds perfect. You know I want a charter boat one day. It would be fun to see all the boats and talk to a boat captain. I remember Harbor Docks; we had a drink there after the fishing rodeo. Do they have a good lunch?"

"Yes, Miss Ann cooks the best food. Stevie, the bartender, is a friend of mine. You'll like him. We can eat at the bar so you can get to know him."

We jumped into the shower together. I tried not to get excited, but it was impossible with her in there with me. My member was standing straight up. She laughed at me and then dropped to her knees. I closed my eyes and leaned against the shower wall and enjoyed the extreme pleasure she gave me.

"You didn't expect me to do that, did you?"

"No, but it was heaven?"

"I wanted to please you."

"Let's get dressed, have some coffee and a donut, and drive to Destin," he said.

The drive over the Destin bridge was gorgeous. The sun was shining, and the water was crystal clear. I stopped at the docks beside The Boat House. As I held open the door for Harper, she was laughing.

"What's so funny?"

"Seeing the Boat House reminds me how much I didn't want to come that Sunday night you were playing. I'm so glad the girls insisted I go with them. If I hadn't gone, you would never have seen me and sent me those beautiful roses."

I took her hand and kissed her on the neck. "Yes, Green Eyes, you captured my heart that night."

Most of the charter boats were out fishing, but I saw one with the captain and first mate cleaning the deck. The captain looked young, about twenty-five. I walked up to him. "Hello, do you have time to talk?" I asked.

"Sure." He jumped off the boat and extended his hand. "I'm John Holley. This is my boat. You look familiar to me." John looked young to be the captain of such a fine boat. I wondered how he could have afforded it.

"I'm Cade Fox from Nashville. I played at the Boat House a few months ago."

"Right, I was there and this must be Green Eyes."

Harper blushed.

"Yes, this is Harper. She lives in Fort Walton Beach. She got my attention right away with her gorgeous red hair and green eyes. You are young to have a charter boat. How did you do it? If you don't mind me asking."

"Well, it wasn't easy. I was unhappy at the University of Florida. I didn't want a college education. I wanted to fish. My dad is a doctor and he insisted I finish school. So, I took a few business classes and Dad financed this boat for me. I'm getting to indulge my passion every day and Dad is proud of me now. I've won a few tournaments and have been paying him back."

"How awesome is that? I can't do it now, but after I'm famous and have some albums under my belt, I want to fish too."

"You need to apprentice for three years before you can get your captain's license. But you could buy the boat and get one of the local guys to be your captain. Come back and see me when you're ready. Maybe I can help you find a boat." John handed me his business card.

"Thank you so much. It was a pleasure to meet you. I wish you more success." I took Harper's hand, and we strolled down the docks and enjoyed the sunshine.

We arrived at Harbor Docks at noon. They had the fire going, and the place was toasty warm. Stevie saw Harper and came from behind the bar to hug her. He was slim and had long blond hair. He was wearing a cool-looking Harbor Docks shirt. I wondered about buying one for Sawyer.

She introduced me and Stevie said he'd seen me on the Opry show and heard I had been at the Boat House. We sat at the bar, where Harper seemed to know lots of people. She told me lots of business people came out to eat at Harbor Docks. We ordered snapper, with ginger rice and a cucumber salad. I ordered a beer, and Harper just wanted iced tea. The food was delicious. As we were getting ready to leave, the owner, Charles Morgan, stopped by, and Harper introduced me. Charles said he sponsored good bands out on his deck. He asked me if I had a band together yet. He was another young owner of a business. Charles couldn't have been any more than thirty-five.

"Almost, I'm waiting for my younger brother to graduate. My other brother, Tucker and I are going to tour with Garth Brooks early next year."

"Well, good for you. Keep Harbor Docks in mind when you finish the tour."

"Gee, you could play at the Seagull and Harbor Docks one day. I'd love that," Harper said, and I loved her enthusiasm.

"Let's finish up here and go back to the hotel and walk on the beach. It won't be too cool if we put on sweatshirts. Then we can get ready for the New Year's Eve party tonight."

Just before we left, I bought Tucker and Sawyer the good-looking Harbor Docks T-shirts.

Chapter 23

I got in the shower first, so there was no distraction from Cade. As I stepped out, once again, Cade wrapped me in a large, heated towel.

I took my time with my make-up and hair. I wanted to look spectacular for him. Once he was out of the shower and in his robe, I asked him to zip up my red dress.

"Love that dress on you, Babe," he said. "I know you want me to zip up your dress, but I'd rather take it off you."

"Thank you, honey, but you bought tickets to the New Year's Eve dinner and dance and we are going."

Cade was dressed in a navy-blue suit with a red tie. I thought it looked great on him. We were ready to go and there was a surprise for him in the restaurant. I was sure he didn't know about it. We stepped out of the elevator where the maître d' greeted us and took the tickets from Cade.

"Follow me, sir. Your seats are by the window."

"Is this room moving? I feel like I'm on a boat." As we sat down by the window the room revolved slowly. Cade's mouth dropped open and I laughed at him. "It's a revolving room. We'll see the Gulf and the Bay. Our tickets are the best seats in the house."

"Well, I'll be darned. This is terrific. I'm sure my brain will get used to going around in a circle soon."

"It will. Look at the menu, the four-courses look divine and champagne comes with the dinner too." The server poured us each a glass of champagne and water on the side. I raised my glass and we clinked glasses.

"Here's to your success in the music business."

"Here's to our love lasting forever," said Cade.

We had finished the champagne when the server introduced herself. "I'm Norma Calhoun, Phil's wife. I heard you played at the Boat House, and I'm so pleased to meet you in person. Norma, like her husband, was tall for a woman. She was pretty with blonde hair pulled into a bun. She had a charming southern accent. A short time later, she served salad along with olive bread and oil and vinegar dressing. We ate quietly and enjoyed the view as the restaurant continued to revolve. The second course was fresh Gulf grouper, sautéed and topped with fried jumbo soft-shell crab, hollandaise sauce, and honey-roasted nuts with steamed green beans on the side.

"This is delicious. I've never had grouper with a fried soft-shell crab on top before."

"It's one of my favorites," I told him as Norma filled our champagne glasses again. "This should be my last one. I'm getting a little buzzed," I said.

Cade laughed. "This is a special night. If you drink too much, it'll be okay. I'm here to look after you."

From then on, I drank water and left the champagne untouched. And there was no way I could eat all the fish. I left some on my plate.

"Your fourth serving is dessert. We're serving moist chocolate cake filled with creamy chocolate ganache or homemade key lime pie with a graham cracker crust," Norma said as she cleared our plates. I rolled my eyes at Cade.

"I'm so full I don't think I can eat another bite."

"Bring us one of each. We can dance and eat them later. Did you like the food?" Cade said.

"It was fabulous. Let's enjoy the view and let our stomachs settle."

When Norma came back with the dessert, Cade ordered Jack Daniels on the rocks. Champagne was probably not his favorite. I sipped my water and relaxed as I watched the moonlight dancing on the water. We talked about Cade's upcoming bus trip with Garth Brooks. He told me he still didn't have the itinerary, but he would be meeting Garth Brooks when he got home.

Eleven p.m. arrived and the dance band was ready to perform. We'd been listening to slow background music while we ate. Four good-looking black men in tuxedos were standing on the bandstand. They were the Four Tops. Their big hits were in the sixties and they toured the United States in the eighties. *Baby, I Need Your Loving* was the first song they played. Then came *It's All in the Game*. At that point, Cade took my hand. "Dance with me," he said. Cade held me close. "I'm in heaven," he whispered in my ear. I felt the same way. We danced for the rest of the hour and sat down just before midnight. Norma freshened my champagne, and I ate a piece of chocolate cake while Cade ate the key lime pie. He ordered another Jack Daniels on the rocks. At the start of the evening when we'd first arrived, they had given us noisemakers and confetti. We let loose when the band played *Auld Lang Syne*, then we danced beside our table and held each other tight. The countdown began and everyone was waiting until the stroke of midnight. When it came, Cade kissed me long and hard and I felt dizzy.

"I can't wait to tell Phil I got to be your server tonight. It was a pleasure to meet both of you and I wish you good luck in 1991," Norma said as she bade us goodnight.

Chapter 24

The evening couldn't have been any better. Harper looked gorgeous in her red dress. The food was outstanding and to top it off; we danced together for the first time. It was a wonderful way to bring in the New Year with the woman I loved. I'd never felt this way about any woman. The moment I saw her emerald-green eyes in The Boat House, she fascinated me. Harper didn't know it yet, but I had booked a photographer to photograph her on the beach in that red dress. Not only did I want a photo of her to take with me while I was on the road, but I had another use for her photo.

When we left the restaurant the elevator was empty and I was able to kiss her some more.

"Oh, Cade! This was the best New Year's Eve ever. I loved every minute and I love you."

"I enjoyed it too, but dancing with you was the best. We are enjoying so many firsts together. I hope there will be many more."

Inside our room, Harper turned for me to unzip that gorgeous dress again. I put her on the bed and took off my suit. I knew I'd better give her two aspirin, or she was going to have one hell of a hangover the next day. I filled a glass with water and brought them to her. She looked at me and smiled. "Oh! You've thought of everything. I'll need those. Are you taking any?"

"A couple. I want to enjoy our last day together."

Our lovemaking was quick. I could tell Harper was ready to sleep; so, I didn't prolong it. There was always tomorrow. She fell asleep in a flash. I didn't know anyone who could fall asleep as fast as she did. That was okay because I enjoyed looking at her sleeping as I stroked her face. I was going to miss her while I was on the road. I was torn between wanting a successful music career and just moving to Destin to be near her. If we were truly in love, we could wait to be together. I wondered if she'd consider moving to Nashville once I became famous. Her children might enjoy living on a farm. They didn't appear to be close to their father, so maybe it would be an option. I'd have to wait and find out.

I woke to being kissed on my neck. Harper was tracing my tattoos with her finger. It electrified my senses, and, of course, my member was awake with one thing on his mind. I took my time arousing Harper. Then the inevitable happened because we had such a hunger and thirst for each other. One that I doubted could ever be satisfied.

After I collapsed on the bed beside Harper, I drew her on top of me. I wanted to hold her as close as I could. She stroked my face and then lay quietly. We lay like that for a few minutes and enjoyed being close. I could have dozed off, but I didn't want to sleep. I wanted to enjoy my last few hours there with Harper. "Let's have a shower together, then eat breakfast. I have a surprise for you at noon."

"You do. Tell me."

"I found a friend of yours. David Shea is coming here at noon to take photos of you. Do you mind putting the red dress back on for the photo shoot?"

"Oh, that is so sweet. You want photos of me? This dress was well worth the money, but I feel like all I have done is wear it for days," she said and laughed. "Let's get in the shower. No monkey business. I have to put on my make-up and fix my hair."

I behaved in the shower and just enjoyed touching her beautiful body as I lathered it with soap. I dried Harper and wrapped her in the hotel robe. "I'll order room service while you fix your face and hair."

I ordered pancakes and bacon, then regretfully packed my suitcase. After the photo shoot, we would have to leave. Harper came out of the bathroom looking fabulous. We devoured our breakfast; lovemaking sure made me hungry. Harper said she was missing her kids but reassured me she'd had a wonderful weekend. She was an excellent mother, but mothers need time off too.

At 11:45, I told her to put on the red dress. We were meeting David in the lobby, so we might as well take our things and check out.

"Okay, I hate for this magic weekend to be over."

David greeted us in the lobby. He was a little older than Harper, had his camera slung around his neck, and a cigar in his mouth. "Hello, Harper, and you must be Cade," he said. He gave Harper a wink and shook my hand. He had told me previously that his best friend, Michael, had been married to Harper for ten years. "What kind of shoot do you want? The beach, the sand dunes, or there's a fabulous, twisted oak tree down the road that would make a great prop," David said.

Harper looked at me with excitement in her eyes. "David is the best. Just turn him loose. You can pick which photo you like the most."

"Let's drive a couple of miles back toward the Eglin Reservation. I know a perfect spot. Harper will look fabulous sitting on the curve of that old oak tree with the beach in the background."

We followed David to the spot and parked. Thank heavens it was a nice day for January the 1st. The sun was not too bright, so David could take a wonderful photo. We walked over to the tree. He was correct. The old oak tree was gnarly and twisted, with just the right curve to sit on. I picked up Harper and put her in the curve. David took photos of us the whole time. Then he told me to take Harper out of the tree and for both of us to recline against the dune. Harper knew how to pose as if she were a model, while I was kind of gawky.

"David, can we have one by the water? It's so gorgeous today," Harper said.

"Sure, let's walk over there. I want you to hold hands, then I'll take a close up of Harper with the waves in the background." He knew what I was planning, but I had told him not to tell Harper.

"That's a wrap. I got some fabulous shots. I'll send them to your home address Cade, and you can pick the ones you like best," David said.

"David, you better let me come by your studio and see the proofs. I want one of Cade and me. He's going to be on the road for the next few months. Please call me at the bank and tell when they're ready."

"I will. Nice to meet you, Cade, and good luck with your tour."

We got back in the car and drove toward Harper's house. Neither of us spoke. I could tell by the forlorn look on her face that she was sad too.

When we arrived, her mother and father's car was in the driveway and the kids rushed out. "Mama! Mama!" they shouted. "We're so glad you are home." So much for kissing Harper again.

"Come in, Cade. I want you to meet my parents."

Her father greeted me with a handshake and her mother hugged me. "We've heard so much about you. I'm glad we are here to meet you in person," she said in her English accent.

"It's a pleasure to meet both of you. Thank you for letting Harper spend the New Year with me. We've had a fabulous time."

"Cade can't stay. He's got to return his rental car and catch the plane back to Nashville," Harper told them. As I walked her outside, tears glazed her eyes.

"Don't cry baby, time will fly, and we can be together again soon." I hugged her and gave her a chaste kiss on the lips. Her family were peeking out the window. I waved as I drove away. My heart was breaking.

Chapter 25

As I lay in bed on New Year's Day morning, I felt so many emotions. Three nights alone with Cade had made me fall more in love with him. To be alone with just him, no children, no family, had been terrific. It gave us both time to get to know each other better. Who would have thought I would fall in love with a country music singer with tattoos? Not me. I loved tracing the tattoos from his neck down his arms with my finger. Then my thoughts went to being in the shower with him and I knew I would it. There was so much I would miss about him.

Tears ran down my face as I waved goodbye to Cade. Mom hugged me and just let me cry. Dad tried to crack a joke, but it fell flat. They'd brought sandwiches for lunch, so we sat at my kitchen table, and I told them all about my exciting weekend. Lizzie said Dad had taken her horseback riding at the stables behind their house. She couldn't stop going on and on about the palomino mare she had ridden. "Papa rode the black stallion," she said. Her next comment wasn't really a surprise, although I didn't tell her that.

"Mom, can I get a horse? Papa says we can keep it at the stables behind his house."

"Well, that's a surprise. Let Papa and I talk about it. He would be the one who'd have to feed it every day because we live forty-five minutes away," I replied.

"I think we need to wait another year or two until you're a little older before you get a horse. We can always go riding when you come," he said.

"Oh, okay," she said with a downcast expression on her small face. Dad gave me a *sorry* look. I think he knew that would happen. She'd been so carried away after her riding experience. I remember when he took me to meet Maude. She was scrawny, needed feeding, and looked downright pitiful. I told him I wanted a feisty Quarter Horse, not an old nag. He made me understand that my first horse needed to be calm and not feisty. Maude surprised us all when we fattened her up. She had several gaits—she could walk, trot, canter, and gallop, and she could pull a wagon, jump a ditch, swim and was always the lead horse on my trail rides. My whole family loved her.

Mom and Dad wanted to get home before it got dark. They hugged us and kissed us goodbye. "I can't thank you enough for having the children this past weekend."

The children left the house to go play with the neighbors. I put my red dress in the closet and unpacked the rest of my things. Clothes went in the washer, chicken came out of the freezer for dinner and I moped around. I was glad I'd be going to work the next day so I could keep myself busy. When I got in bed, I let thoughts of the past few days flow through my head.

As soon as I arrived at work the next day the girls surrounded me before I could even put my purse down.

"I saw you leave with Cade. You didn't even say goodbye. Did you realize he was coming? Tell us all about it," Kate said.

"Whoa! Can you all wait till lunch? Then I'll tell you all about my fabulous weekend. Right now, we need to get to work." With a secret smile, I turned and went into Al's office to see what he wanted me to do.

He was grinning at me. "Your surprise date impressed Dorothy," he said.

"He surprised and impressed me also. Thank you for letting me have Friday off. We had a wonderful weekend. Cade is going on the road, so he won't be distracting me for a while. Do you have letters to dictate to me?"

"Why don't you send thank you cards to all the customers who came to our Christmas party? The auditors are coming back this week to audit Doodle Harris some more. Poor Doodle. He sure is in a mess."

I wrote out thank-you cards, and when it was time for lunch, the girls came to get me.

"Let's go out for lunch. Not everyone needs to know the details," Suzanne said.

We walked over to Pizza Hut and got a table in the back. They were all ears as I told them what we got up to. Needless to say, I left off mentioning the fabulous sex.

"That's all? How was Cade in bed?" Melody said.

I laughed. "I won't give you any details, but he was amazing." They laughed, and we carried on eating our pizza.

Back at the bank, the auditors had arrived, and I became busy gathering the information they wanted on Doodle. When Mike and I were first married, Doodle had offered us a lot on Holiday Isle. It was $25,000 we didn't have. Mike was never good at saving. It was such a relief when I divorced him and could save my own money. It was such a relief not to be embarrassed by his overdraft at the bank. In the end, I told him to move his account.

I was glad when the day at work finished, and I could home, feed the children and go to bed.

Chapter 26

I dozed on the flight home; my mind was full of memories of making love to Harper. It was going to be awhile before I would lay eyes on her again.

Regardless, I was excited about the prospect of playing with Garth Brooks at Hee Haw. I hoped Tucker and I would like the new drummer, Richard Boone. Playing with him would be so different from just playing with my brothers. Tucker would be waiting for me when the plane landed and I was eager to find out what was in store for the new year.

I walked to baggage claim where Tucker was standing by the carousel keeping an eye out for my bag.

"Hey, brother, so glad you're here to pick me up. We don't have to meet Bob and the new drummer for a couple of days so we can go by the house and visit the family," I said once we'd had a brief hug.

"Glad you're home. Mom and Grannie are cooking meatloaf for dinner. Here, let me take your bag. The truck is outside." Once we were in the truck, the questions poured out of him. "Tell me all about your trip. How was Harper? What did you do?"

I filled him in on all our fun. "I'm afraid I'm in love. I've never felt this way about a woman before. She's not only gorgeous, but so easy to be around. I had a local photographer take photos of her on the beach in a fabulous red dress. I haven't told her, but I want to use one on the cover when we do the album *Green Eyes*. The album cover will be a surprise. Has Sawyer been writing more songs?"

"Yeah, he's written two more. One's a fast song, *Riding Down the River*, and the other one is slow, *My Tennessee*."

"Great, we can jam with him when we get home."

"Right, it'll be great fun," he replied, grinning from ear to ear.

Mom, Grannie, Sawyer, and Dog were waiting on the porch and I could smell the meatloaf cooking. I gave everyone a hug and took my bag to my room while Mom got me an iced tea.

"Come out to the porch. We want to hear all about your trip," she said.

We settled on the porch, and I told them about surprising Harper, the hotel with the revolving restaurant, the New Year's Eve party, and the places and people I met.

Mom gave me a wink. "Is that all?" she said.

"No, Mom, I think I'm in love. It'll be hard while Tucker and I are on the road. Harper says there is no one else in her life and we'll have to see how our long-term relationship goes." Grannie smiled, and I could tell she was glad I was happy.

"I hear you've written two more songs. I can't wait to hear and play them after dinner," I said to Sawyer.

"Hope you like them. We need to have an upbeat one like *Riding Down the River,* whereas *My Tennessee* is more of a ballad. I've got a couple of ideas for faster ones."

"I thought of the name of a song when I was in Destin. *There is no shame when you are with me.* It could be a quick-step tune. Think you can come up with some words?" I asked Sawyer.

He nodded and looked thoughtful.

Just then, Grannie stood up. "Let's eat, boys. I can't wait to listen to you play Sawyer's new songs. He's been humming them for days," she said.

As always, the meatloaf and vegetables were delicious. After dinner we got out our instruments and Sawyer used only one drum to keep the beat going. His songs were good, real good. They should be a hit too. We practiced for an hour and then went to bed. Tucker and I needed to be back in Nashville to play for Garth Brooks at the Opry.

Two days later, Bob arranged for us to use a practice room at the Opry. He brought along the drummer. Richard Boone was tall, about six feet two. His skin was dark, so dark it made me wonder if he had Cherokee blood. His black hair matched his dark eyes, and I noticed he had tattoos on his fingers. He shook our hands. "Good to meet you, Cade, and Tucker. I like the two songs you have playing on WXFM radio. I've been practicing them and some of Garth's songs," he said. I liked him and felt we'd be compatible if his drumming was up to par.

We played for an hour. Richard was good, and I felt sure we'd combine well. I could tell by the smile on Bob's face that he was pleased. He told us we could use the room again the next day and Garth would come and watch us.

The following day, Garth showed up with his tour manager. He must have been around our age and wore a large white cowboy hat that curled up around the edges. He had a clean-shaven face except for a little bit of hair on the cleft of his chin and he wore a T-shirt under his shirt, and, of course, cowboy boots. Bob was there to represent us. We played five songs and he clapped and stomped his feet to one of the faster ones.

"Good job, guys. You play well together. I want you to join me at Hee Haw and then on the tour," he said when we stopped playing. "I've got to leave now, but John Davis is my tour manager. He'll stay to explain the details and give you the agenda."

John differed from the country stars. He wore a black suit, white shirt, and a black string tie. Although he was wearing the traditional cowboy hat, it was black. He looked to be around fifty-five or sixty, and I could tell he meant business when he talked to us.

"Let's go to the bar and find a table where we can talk," Bob said. There was a small bar in the Grand Ole Opry, so we went there. Everyone got a beer and we made plans. John said he had an older bus that would sleep six. The three of us could use it, and anyone else from Garth's bus who had nowhere to sleep. He explained how he would pay us, and what he expected of us. There was to be no missing a show, and no rowdy behavior, or women on our bus. He gave us the itinerary for fifty shows. When there was a week or more in between, we could leave, provided we were back in time for the next show. Then he left. We had another beer and looked at the places on the itinerary. We would start in St. Petersburg, Florida and end in Charlotte, North Carolina. We'd get on the bus in Nashville on January 18 and drive to St. Petersburg.

"Wow! We sure are going to see the USA," said Tucker, who was overflowing with excitement.

"Yep, we never would have had this opportunity if it weren't for you, Bob. Thanks so much you are a fantastic manager—the absolute best."

"Thanks. You make it easy. I'm looking at the schedule and seeing you have a break between March 6 and April 13. Come back here and let's cut the new songs Sawyer is writing. We have time now to record the two new ones he has written before you take off to St. Pete. Can you get Sawyer over here? Let's go to The Barn and record *Riding Down the River* and *My Tennessee.* This will give you four of your own songs to play and get exposure."

Mom let Sawyer miss school on Friday. He drove over in her car and we went to The Barn to record. Bob told us everything looked good, and he would work with Owen Bradley again to get them finished before we left. That night we took Sawyer to The Blue Bird Café. Amy greeted us as we came in the door.

"Who's this good-looking guy?" she asked.

Sawyer blushed and we introduced him. "He's our youngest and our songwriter," I replied.

"Well, he's a damn good one. White Stetsons is playing tonight. Do you guys want to sit in? Did you bring your instruments with you? They'll probably let Sawyer use their drums." She left to go ask.

We listened to the band, then I got a whiskey at the bar and brought Tucker a beer. Sawyer had a coke. Mom would kill us if we let him drink beer. The White Stetsons agreed that we could play our new songs while they were having a break and Sawyer could use their drums. Sawyer was so nervous, but we calmed him down.

"Just play like we just did at the Opry," I said to him.

"Hi Folks, we are so glad to play for you while the band takes a break. I'm Cade Fox and these are my brothers, Tucker, and Sawyer. Sawyer is our songwriter. These are his two new songs we just recorded over at The Barn. Hope you like them." We got a standing ovation. Sawyer was grinning from ear to ear.

"I can't wait to tell Mom and Grannie," he said.

After we finished playing, we went back to the bar where Cindy was bartending. "Hey, who's the cute one with y'all?" she asked. We introduced her to Sawyer and ordered cheeseburgers. "Cindy, pour me a shot of Jack. Tucker, you want another beer? Sawyer's drinking coke. He has a few more years before he can drink with us."

Amy came over. "You wowed them again. Sawyer, your new songs are super. I'm sure they'll be hits. Cindy, put their order on the house," she said.

"Thanks, for arranging for us to play, Amy. We're getting ready to go on tour and be the front band for Garth Brooks. I know he was discovered here last year. We hope you're good luck for us."

"You guys give yourselves good luck. Come back and see me when you get a chance. You're always welcome."

We left feeling excited and on a natural high as we drove back to the apartment. The guys decided to watch TV, so I called Harper. She sounded happy to hear from me and listened to all our plans. God, I missed having that woman by my side.

Chapter 27

My life was back to normal, getting the kids off to school and going to work. Thank heavens the auditors had finished looking into Doodle's bank records. I missed Cade. That weekend was a fabulous time. Al and my girlfriends teased me about him for some time.

I was typing letters for Al when my phone rang. It was Pat Champion. "How are you?"

"Doing great. Can you meet me for lunch today? I know it's short notice, but I'm not as busy today and I want to talk to you. How about we have lunch at Mother Earth's Café at noon?"

"Sounds wonderful. I'll meet you there."

As I walked into Mother Earth's Café, I saw several clients already eating, and I nodded at them. Pat was already there waiting for me at a table. Mother Earth's was a small restaurant with only twenty tables, which was why we got there early. It had a green and yellow theme to go with the natural food they prepared. They were known for their smoothies, avocado and chicken salad, and they served sprouts on all the salads. It was popular with locals. Pat stood up to greet me and invited me to sit next to her. I knew what she had on her mind, but I let her talk.

"I want to offer you a position as my administrative assistant. As I told you when we last met, I want you to get your real estate license and I'll pay for you to take the course. I think you and I would make a good team. You have all the qualities to be a great realtor. I am also a general contractor, as you know. It would be a wonderful opportunity for you to learn more about the building industry too."

"Gosh! That's an exciting offer. Please, tell me how much I could expect to make. I support my children on my own. I get by, but raises are few and far between at the bank."

"Your salary would be $30,000 a year. Once you're selling homes and condos, we'd need to get another assistant for both of us. You'd be on straight commission, same as me. My days start early and are sometimes very late before they end. Are your children old enough to stay by themselves if we have to work until seven or eight p.m.?"

"Yes, Lizzie is very responsible and can take care of Sean. Their grandmother Hamilton lives down the street if they need help quickly. Tell me how and where I can take the real estate class. I'd need to give the bank two weeks' notice."

"There's a class starting in two weeks' time; it's taught by Anthony Hart. He's an excellent teacher and you should pass easily. Once you finish his class, then you need to go to Panama City Beach to take the State test. What do you think? Would you like to be a realtor and make more money than you do at the bank?"

"I sure would. I know you do very well, as do many other realtors who bank with us."

"Super, here's the form to apply for the course with Anthony. I'll give you a check to pay him. They hold the class in the back of the Emerald Coast Realtors Association on Hollywood Avenue. It starts at 9 a.m. and goes for a week."

I laughed. "So, you brought the package knowing I'd want to do this?"

"Yes, always have a contract with you when you sell real estate, or you're hiring an assistant." Pat chuckled.

We ate our chicken and avocado sandwiches and drank iced tea. Then Pat asked me about the stranger who showed up at the Christmas party and my fast exit. I told her about Cade and not to worry about me being distracted, because he was away on tour, and he'd be gone for a year. We might get to see each other twice during the year, but that would be all. I would be her dedicated assistant and I was ready to learn about the real estate industry. As we shook hands and I left, my heart was beating fast. It was really happening, and I knew I could do it. I watched Pat drive away in a flash car and I climbed into my Chevette and went back to the bank to tell Al I was leaving.

I walked into his office timidly. "Boss, can I talk to you for a minute?"

"Sure, come in."

I closed his door and sat in front of his desk. Tears were sliding down my face. I loved the people at the bank, but I needed to grow and make more money for Lizzie and Sean.

"What's wrong?" Al asked. Obviously, he had seen my tears even though I had dashed them away with my hand.

"Nothing, except that I've just had a job offer from Pat Champion. She wants me to come and learn the real estate business after I have taken the course and sat the exam. She's offering a good salary. I need to grow, and there's not much future with the bank."

"Well, I'm glad there's nothing wrong, although losing you isn't something I want. But I know you support your kids on your own and you have to think about the future. I'm proud of you, and I know you'll be a terrific realtor."

"Thank you so much for supporting me. I can give two weeks' notice and then the real estate class starts. Who do you want me to train to replace me?"

"I think Suzanne would be perfect. She's not you, but she'll be a suitable replacement. So, begin training her now."

I left Al's office and walked over to Suzanne and told her to follow me to the break room. She looked puzzled but came with me. "How would you like to be Al's assistant? Pat Champion has asked me to work with her and learn about the real estate business. He wants you to replace me."

She put her hand on her heart. "Me! Yes, yes, I'd love that."

"Fabulous, go tell your supervisor to find someone to replace you and I'll begin training you immediately." I gave Suzanne a big hug. "I'm going to miss you girls, but I'll continue to bank here, and we can still be friends and do things together."

As we came out of the break room, everyone was staring at me and Suzanne, clearly wondering why we went in there. I would tell them when we were getting ready to go home. Melody already had an excellent position. Perhaps Kate could take Suzanne's place as a teller and get off the switchboard.

Just after five, they were waiting in the parking lot. Suzanne was so excited, she started babbling. I stood back and let her enjoy the moment. Then she told them my exciting news. Everyone hugged before we left the parking lot. I couldn't wait to get home and call my mom and dad.

I gave the kids a big hug and picked up the phone. Mom answered. "Hello, Mom, I have some exciting news. Can you put Daddy on the extension?" Dad got on the extension.

"What's up?" he asked.

"I got a great job offer today. My bank client, Pat Champion, asked me to be her assistant and learn the real estate business. She thinks I'd be a terrific realtor and is going to pay me $30,000 a year until I earn my own commissions."

"You're leaving the bank? You've been there for ten years. That's steady work, not commission based," Mom said.

"I can do it, Mom, I know I can. Besides, she's going to teach me and pay for my real estate course and the test. I've seen her deposits and she makes a lot of money."

"Harper can do it. She's smart, well liked and works hard," Dad said. "This is a fantastic opportunity to learn from her friend. I'm proud of you. Have you told your boss at the bank?"

"Yes, he thinks it's a good move, and he's excited for me. I'm going to train Suzanne to take my place. There are two people here who want to say hello to you both," I said before Mom could come up with any more objections.

Lizzie and Sean got on the phone and chatted. Lizzie did most of the talking, and Sean just answered with one or two words. I started their dinner and poured myself a glass of wine. What a great day it had been.

Chapter 28

Tucker and I packed our bags and drove to meet the guys at the buses on January 18. Garth's bus was nicer than ours, of course. Ours was older. It had three reclining seats in the front and three in the back. In the middle, there was a kitchenette with a sink, a hot plate, and a small fridge. Across the way was a small bathroom. We grabbed the first three seats before anyone else arrived. Moments later, two guys walked over—Steve and John. They were the set-up boys for the concerts. Both were rather scruffy, with unkempt beards, wrinkled clothes, and tattoos on their fingers, as if they had been in a gang. Since they were the roadies, I guessed it wasn't important for them to look good. Just then, the bus driver arrived.

"Hello, I'm Gus. Let me show you where to store your instruments and suitcases. I could tell Gus was a no-nonsense kind of guy. He looked to be about eighty but was probably in his sixties. Many years in the sun had wrinkled and tanned his face. He wore wire-rimmed glasses and a khaki uniform. He had a long white beard and white hair to go with it. It would be interesting to learn more about him.

It was almost time to leave when Richard showed up. He arrived on time, but for some reason Gus wanted him to arrive earlier. Gus gave him a look and then made an announcement. "One, be early and on time." He glanced at Richard. "Two, respect the bus rules: no fighting or cussing. Three, if you're late, I leave without you, and you'll have to find your own way to the next concert." Then he climbed into the driver's seat and started the engine.

Our bus followed Garth's bus with his musicians. We left Nashville on Highway 65 south toward Montgomery, Alabama. When the buses turned into a truck stop, we were told we could eat lunch there. "Forty-five minutes and be back here ready to roll," said Gus.

After leaving Montgomery, we took Highway 231 to Dothan and on to Tallahassee. We parked for the night in a campground about thirty miles south of Tallahassee. Gus built a fire in a pit and grilled us hotdogs and heated beans. We sat around the fire drinking beer and telling stories. Getting to know each other was crucial for a year-long bus journey. I strummed my guitar and Tucker played his banjo. After a few beers, Gus recounted how he started driving a bus for musicians.

"I joined the navy at eighteen to get off the farm in Tennessee. I was on a destroyer when the war in Nam started. We sailed there, dropped soldiers off at port, and anchored away from the fighting. We had a small infirmary on board and sometimes they brought the wounded over by helicopter. Those poor guys were a gruesome sight. My rank and position increased from starting as a kitchen hand to becoming head chef. After a two-year duty in Nam, they transferred me to Hawaii. Now that was a damn good duty. What an island. Lots of great music, fruit, and surfing. As the head chef, I served both the off-duty and on-duty personnel. I retired from the navy after thirty years and returned to Tennessee, but I got bored, and then this job became available. So, I took it."

Everyone was yawning by then. I pulled Tucker up out of his chair. "Let's get some sleep. I hope those reclining seats make good beds," I said to him.

In the morning, Gus fixed breakfast over the campfire. There was coffee, scrambled eggs and bacon. We were lucky he knew how to cook outdoors.

The bus drove south down Highway 98. I had my map out and tracked our route. Highway 98 would take us along the west coast of Florida. Just after Perry, we saw thinning pine trees and glimpses of the Gulf of Mexico. The bus rolled into Tarpon Springs, where Gus suggested we explore the Greek fishing village. In a few hours' time in St. Pete, we'd be getting ready for the concert. Showtime was eight p.m. The bus would depart at one p.m.

Tucker and I wandered down to the old fishing village, where we saw the huge sponges that were sold in the stores. Greeks first arrived there during the 1890s to work in the sponge industry. They wore hard hats, deep-diving suits, and hooked the sponges on to a fishing boat. Many Greeks stayed to raise their families. The town along the Anclote River docks was bustling with bakeries, restaurants, and shops.

"I'm hungry. That restaurant and bakery look inviting. Let's go eat there," Tucker said. We walked into Hellas to the best smells besides fried chicken. A sign said seat yourself, so we did. A gorgeous young woman with long dark hair and sparkling brown eyes came to take our order.

"Hello, I'm Anastasia and I'll take your order. What would you like to drink?"

Tucker was dumbstruck as he stared at her. I spoke up. "Bring us two sweet teas and tell us what you recommend. We've never eaten Greek food."

"My favorite is our Gyro. It's a blend of beef and lamb, finely seasoned, broiled and served wrapped in pita with sliced onions, tomatoes, and tzatziki sauce."

"How does that sound?" I asked Tucker and he nodded. "We'll have two of those with French fries."

After she walked away to place our order, Tucker found his voice. "Man, she is gorgeous. Did you see her dark eyes? I get how you felt when you saw Harper for the first time."

Anastasia brought our tea and food. It was as delicious as it smelled. When we paid the bill, we left her a good tip. She stared at Tucker as we left. Perhaps she had sensed his interest. Or maybe she was attracted to him.

Before we got on the bus, I called Harper. It went to voicemail, and I left her a message that tonight was our first concert. We napped on the bus while Gus drove us to St. Petersburg. By the time we arrived at the Florida Suncoast Dome, we had been on the road eleven hours and traveled 728 miles. The Dome is an impressive venue for concerts and sporting events. We were told that Kenny Rogers had performed at its grand opening on March 30, 1990. Playing to a sell-out crowd in this enormous dome would be thrilling. Steve and John got off the bus and joined the rest of the set-up crew who would set up the lights and electronics. We freshened up in the bathroom at the Dome. Tucker, Richard, and I were wearing white shirts, black string ties, jeans, and boots. We were all nervous. I sneaked a few swallows of Jack from my flask in the toilet backstage. Richard's eyes looked a little glassy. He must have smoked a joint.

On stage, the lights faded, and the MC announced us as the Foxes from Nashville. Our first song was *Green Eyes,* since the crowd was already familiar with it. Then we played our other three songs. The crowd gave us roaring applause and then it was over for us. Garth and his band played for another hour.

Gus had arranged for us to stay in a motel room for the night. Tomorrow we would drive to Rosemont, Illinois. We sat around the motel room. It was a simple room with three twin beds, one chair, and a rack for hanging clothes. The shower was so small I wasn't sure I would fit inside. Richard and Tucker were drinking beer, and I fixed a Jack and water. Everyone was happy with our first big performance together. I walked outside to call Harper. It was midnight, but I wanted to share my excitement with her.

"Hello. I'm so glad you called. Tell me all about your first big concert," she said in a sleepy voice.

I gave her all the details and told her how much I missed her. She told me she had the proofs of the photos David had taken.

"They're wonderful. I can't wait for you to see them."

"Come to Nashville when we have a break in March. We'll be cutting more records there. We still have our apartment."

"Oh, that would be wonderful. I'm sure I can manage a quick trip to see you in March. I love you, honey. I need to go back to sleep now."

"Love you too, sweet dreams."

Chapter 29

My two weeks' notice at the bank had ended and Al had invited everyone to go to Liollio's for drinks and appetizers for my going-away party. I appreciated so many of the bank employees coming to say goodbye and I assured them I would remain a customer. "In return, I hope you all will use me and come to me for your real estate needs. Of course, Melody can assist with your mortgage requirements."

The real estate class started at nine a.m. at the real estate office on Hollywood Boulevard. Thirty people were signing in and getting workbooks when I arrived. After I sat down next to a cute blonde girl, I introduced myself. "Hello, I'm Harper Hamilton."

"Cathy Harrison. Nice to meet you."

The instructor, Anthony Hart, welcomed us and told us not to be nervous, that we just needed to read the book and take notes and we would pass. I sure hoped so. I wanted to be active as soon as possible. Then he started explaining all the legal terms the State of Florida used. He frightened me when he detailed the penalties and fines for not following the ethics and rules.

When Cathy and I sat down together to eat the lunch that they had provided I asked her if she was worried too. She agreed he scared her to death.

"Do you find the instructor attractive?" she asked.

"Yes, in a preppy sort of way. He's older than us. I can tell you think he's cute." Then I laughed and told her I was in a long-distance romance.

"Really," she said. "You don't look like the country music type."

I told her I wasn't, but he had grown on me, and I explained how we met.

She subsequently followed through with her plan to flirt with our instructor.

We both passed the basic course. On the last day while we stood talking in the lobby, Anthony asked her on a date and she accepted. They left for drinks, and I left for home. It had been hard on the kids while I was in class, so I took them for pizza. I told them that I only had one more test to take before I could start selling real estate. Lizzie, as always, was positive. "I know you'll pass and we'll be rich," she said and I laughed.

"Thank you for your positive words, but it takes a long to time to get rich selling real estate."

The next day, I started as Pat's administrative assistant. She welcomed me to her attractive office at Century 21. "Today, I'm taking you on a listing appointment to see a couple in Shalimar. They built their home three years ago, and he's being transferred to another air force base. You can listen as I talk about the current sales prices in their neighborhood. I'll compile a list of all the listings, pending and sold."

We drove in Pat's Cadillac. A luxurious car with leather seats, a sunroof, power items, and a mobile phone stand between the driver and passenger seats. I hadn't seen anything like it. I hoped one day I could trade in my Chevette for a nicer car.

"Just watch and listen so you understand how I find out what they think the price for their home should be."

We knocked on the door and a handsome man of about forty-five greeted us. Pat introduced me, and we walked in to greet his wife. Her golf outfit was cute, and she was well put-together.

"I know I built your home, but would one of you please give Harper and I a tour?"

"I'd love to," the husband said. "Darling, please put on all the lights for Pat and Harper?" He was obviously the one in charge. As we walked through the home, he reminded Pat of the extras he had added. Colonel Johnson pointed out the trayed ceiling and the extra moldings around the windows and doors and he pointed out the bedroom and exquisite fireplaces. He reminded Pat about the costly cabinetry in the kitchen and bathrooms. He opened the garage and showed us how he'd had it painted. It looked like you could eat off the floor. As we walked to the patio, he pointed out the professional landscaping.

Pat turned to me. "Do you understand Colonel Johnson's house will be worth much more now that he has made so many improvements?"

"This home is perfect in every detail. You have a lovely home. It will be an honor to help Pat sell it," I said.

"Thanks, ladies. As Pat knows, I like everything in its place and keep my home manicured. Let's sit at the kitchen table and review Pat's comparable list."

Once we sat down, Mrs. Johnson brought us iced tea and cookies. Pat took out a colored folder with all the different properties she'd selected to show them. She knew them and figured theirs would be the most expensive one to sell that year. When she gave him the figure of $450,000, he looked pleased.

"Right on the money. This is what I think too. I'm confident mine is worth $30,000 more than the one down the street that just sold."

"Yes, it is. Someone is going to appreciate all the extras you and your professional landscaping. When is your transfer to the Pentagon?"

"I have to be there in a month, but my wife will only go once the contract is complete."

Pat took the listing form out of her folder and wrote in the amount of $450,000 as the listing price. She had also prepared a seller net sheet for Colonel Johnson in advance. Both signed the listing agreement since they were both on the title deed. Then she discussed the seller's disclosure. There were no problems. She also handed him the neighborhood homeowner's association document. He filled in the current quarterly dues for Lake Lorraine.

Pat told them she would have a sign put up the next day and would advertise the home as soon as possible. "When would you like us to do the first open house?"

"We can be ready by the weekend. Is that convenient for you?" Colonel Johnson replied.

"That would be excellent. I'll bring Harper with me; I'm training and mentoring her. We'll be here Saturday morning at ten and leave around four. Is that good for you both?"

"Perfect. We'll go play golf and have drinks at the club afterwards."

"Wow! That was smooth. I hope someday I can handle a listing like you just did," I said once we were in the car.

"You will. Let's head back to the office and I'll show you how to list on the MLS. I have a sheet that tells you in numerical order what steps are next. This will be your responsibility. If you have questions, you can ask me. This is a great listing; we should sell it quickly. Be ready to work this Saturday. On Friday, we can sort out the open house signs and print the flyers."

As I drove home that evening, I felt sure I was going to like the real estate industry.

Chapter 30

It was great to sleep in an actual bed and shower in the hotel. We took turns showering and then headed to breakfast. Everyone ate quickly, and we were soon ready to get back on the bus. Gus told us to load up. It would probably take two days to reach Rosemont, Illinois. Gus drove us through the cattle farms in Florida and Alabama and back to Nashville. He dropped us off late and said we will leave again on January 30. Being back in our apartment for a day or two was wonderful. Florida was warm, and it was thirty-five degrees in Nashville. I knew I'd better tell Tucker to pack warmer clothes before we left for Illinois and Michigan.

Tucker and I called Grannie and Mom the next morning and told them about our first large concert and how exciting it was that the crowd loved our performance. We couldn't go home as we had to be back on the bus the next day. While Tucker did our laundry, I called Harper's cell phone. It rang and rang and then went to voicemail. A new message was in her voicemail and it tickled me.

"This is Harper Hamilton with Century 21 Real Estate. I'm away from my phone and will call you back as soon as possible. Have a great day." Good for her, she got the real estate job. I hoped she'd call me back that night.

I bought food at the grocery store so I could cook for Tucker and me. There was no point in spending money eating out. Money went by fast when we were on the road. I was cooking a pot roast when my cell phone rang. It thrilled me to see that it was Harper's number. "Hello, honey."

"Hi, I'm so glad you called. I was with Pat at an open house in Shalimar. It was super. We had ten people come through and two seemed interested. I'm thrilled to have this job; it's the best in the world," she blurted out.

"Wow, slow down, Babe. It sounds like you are super excited and loving your new job."

"I am and apologize for being self-absorbed. I want to hear all about what you've been doing and the tour."

"That's okay, and it's great that you are thrilled and excited. Riding the bus is boring, but the concert in St. Petersburg was amazing. We have today and tomorrow here in Nashville before we leave for Rosemont, Illinois, next. Right now, I'm cooking dinner for me and Tucker."

"That's good. Training myself to cook ahead of time for the kids is tough. This weekend was my first time working. If we get a contract on this house, we won't do more Saturday open houses on it."

"Well, I'm proud of you for stepping out of your comfort zone. When do you take the final real estate exam?"

"Next weekend. Cathy, who took the class with me, and I are going to Panama City Beach and spending the night, then taking the test at 8 a.m. the next day. This coming week, I'll be working with Pat and learning more. The kids are hungry, so I better feed them. I miss you."

"I miss you too, honey. Give the kids my love." I hung up; I was missing her so much. I just prayed we could keep talking and keep our relationship going while I was on tour. At least she was busy too.

Tucker and I enjoyed the pot roast, watched TV, and went to bed. Our song, *Green Eyes,* was going through my head as I went to sleep. How I wished she was there to make love to me.

The next day, our tour group met with John Davis, our tour director and we went over our last trip. He voiced his pleasure with the turnout at the Sun Coast Dome. He told us that Garth's songs were charting higher on the radio. Touring was the sure way to succeed in the music business. "Keep up the good work and be ready to leave tomorrow," John said.

We ate a late lunch with Bob at The Blue Bird Café. Everyone was glad to see us, and Amy asked how we enjoyed touring with Garth. Tucker and I both spoke at the same time. "It was outstanding." Not long after, we left to go home and pack. Six a.m. the next morning would come soon enough.

Richard Boone showed up just in time. Everyone else was already on the bus. We rolled out behind the fancier bus on Highway 165 toward Illinois. We camped just south of Rosemont and Gus told us we had traveled 1215 miles from St. Pete to where we were. He kept tabs on miles and time. Must have been his military past. He cooked us a stew over the fire. Everyone was drinking and strumming their instruments. Tucker stared at me every time I took out my flask. Later in the evening, Boone and two others left and came back with glassy eyes.

We arrived at the Rosemont Horizon in the late afternoon and checked out the stage and the dressing rooms. Not bad, just not as fancy as the new dome in Florida. I snuck into the toilet to have a couple of quick slugs of Jack from my flask and avoided Tucker until it was time to go on stage. The audience was very supportive of us and Garth's band. As we were leaving, Boone asked me if I wanted to smoke with him. "Naw," I told him. "I have my own poison."

The scenery along Lake Michigan was a pleasant change from farmland as we drove from Rosemont to Auburn Hills. It only took five hours, and we had time to look around the Detroit Pistons' home basketball court.

While the roadies were putting up the basketball hoops and getting the lighting ready for our concert we grabbed some fried chicken from the restaurant next to The Palace. Again, I snuck my two swigs of Jack when Tucker wasn't around. I needed it to calm my nerves. I wasn't used to performing for large crowds.

We jumped on the bus as soon as the performance was over. Gus told us it was eight and a half hours to The Fabulous Fox Theater in St. Louis. When we arrived, we could shower at the motel. Everyone slept except Gus. That man was a driving machine.

When we woke, we had arrived at a small motel outside of St. Louis. Gus told us to take a shower, grab something to eat and come back in two hours to leave for the performance. We did. When we arrived at the Theater, Tucker and I asked Gus to take our photo in front of it. After all, we were the Fox brothers. He did and laughed at us. The inside of that place was amazing and gorgeous, like a real Byzantine palace. They told us the same architect built one like it in Detroit. The hall had stained glass windows. The ceiling was a round dome inlaid with tiles and a fabulous light fitting hung in the center. It had balcony seating surrounded by more seats. Everything was contained in the dome. We would get a classy group of fans for the performance.

Playing at that theater was a completely unique experience. Our music sounded so much better with their acoustics that I wished someone had been recording us. As we left, fans asked for our autographs. Tucker was enjoying all the cute girls running up to him and begging. Several took photos of us. Even Boone was having a good time. The girls seemed to like his dark good looks. We went to the motel with big, swollen egos.

Chapter 31

I'd been studying every night for the real estate exam, even so I was concerned. Many people had to take it multiple times to pass. Yikes! I needed to pass it the first time.

We had a hotel reservation in Panama City on Friday evening, and the test was at 8 a.m. on Saturday. Cathy and I would check in together. I picked her up at her condo and as we talked while I drove she sprang a surprise on me.

"Anthony and I have been seeing each other and I think I'm falling in love with him. I hope you don't mind that he's coming to Panama City."

Well, that was a shock. Luckily, he wasn't in charge of the test; the State of Florida administered it. I guessed he wanted to come and support Cathy. We were eating dinner in the restaurant at the Holiday Inn when Anthony walked in. Cathy was thrilled to see him.

"Hello, girls, I thought I'd surprise you," he said. "I know you'll do well in the test so don't be nervous."

After dinner, we were having a drink in the bar when Anthony whispered in my ear. "Can I take Cathy to the room while you stay here?" Oh no! He wanted me to stay and drink. The test was too important for me to get drunk. I sat by the window, ordered soda with lime and reviewed the glossary.

Two hours later when they finally came back. Cathy was sporting a gorgeous diamond ring and beaming. "Look! Anthony has asked me to marry him."

"Congratulations, I'm so happy for both of you. Now, if you'll excuse me, I'm going to bed." I slept like a rock and woke up to the phone ringing; my wake-up call to get ready for the test. Cathy was missing. I guess they got a room.

When I walked in Cathy was seated at the front of the meeting room and there were fifty people taking the test. I took several deep breaths and opened the exam paper. I answered all the questions that I could with answers which I knew were correct, then I went back to the other ones. I finished just before the timer said, *turn in your tests.*

While the results were being compiled, we had coffee and donuts. My result was seventy-seven. I was thrilled. Only one point above being failed. Thank you, Lord, I passed. Not a great score, but I didn't care. I could pay my dues and become a realtor. I walked outside and called Pat to give her my good news. Anthony was taking Cathy home so I drove home alone, tired but elated.

While I was away, Pat had received an offer on the Shalimar listing. She and the seller would negotiate it with the buyer's agent. She told me to come into the office on Monday and she would explain how she expected it to play out. I spent Sunday with my children, working in our yard where we planted bulbs for the upcoming spring. I enjoyed a relaxing day after the stress of taking the test. That night, Cade called to tell me about the Fabulous Fox Theater they had played at in St. Louis.

Chapter 32

We left St. Louis on February 3 in a vicious snowstorm. Gus had to drive carefully back to Nashville. We were all tired but elated with our performance at the Fox Theater. Because the trip was only four hours and thirty minutes, we didn't have a break for lunch. When Gus stopped at the parking lot, he told us he would see us on the 27th for our drive to Texas. Garth and his band were going on to the 33rd Grammy Awards in New York. Tucker and I were glad to get back to our apartment. We washed our clothes and threw a frozen pizza in the oven. It was a relief not to have to perform and be able to relax at home. Being on tour had worn me out.

The next day, we surprised Grannie and Mom when we arrived at their house. Sawyer was outside playing ball with Dog.

"Well, look what the cat drug up. We didn't know you were coming. I know Mom and Grannie will be happy to see you," Sawyer said. We walked into the kitchen where they were baking. It sure smelled good.

"Boo," said Tucker and they both jumped.

"Stinker, you shouldn't scare an old lady like that," Grannie said. Then she hugged us both as hard as she could. Mom waited and gave us both a swat on the butt and hugged us too.

"To what do we owe this surprise?" she asked.

"Garth is playing at the 33rd Grammy Awards in New York; so we got a few days off. We can stay for a couple of days if it's okay."

"Of course," said Grannie. "We're baking bread and a pound cake. I know that's your favorite, Cade. Tucker, I'll bake you a chocolate cake tomorrow."

After dinner, we wanted to watch the Grammies, which I knew we'd both enjoy. Before dinner I went to the barn to see Satan and Suzie. Satan smelled me as soon as I walked in the door and he whinnied loudly and pawed at the stall door. "Relax, I'll put on your bridle and we'll go outside, but it's too cold for a run today." My thoughts went back to the last time I was home and Harper was there. That's when I knew she was the woman for me. Those green eyes, her red hair and, oh, that body. I felt a hard-on coming, just thinking about her. I fed Satan a carrot and stroked his ears and muzzle. It was cold, so I took him back inside to his stall. He wasn't happy and tried to avoid going in.

"Come on, boy, if it warms up we can go for a run tomorrow. Now get in your stall." He did. Suzie, always the patient one, whinnied to me. "I didn't forget you, girl." I gave her the other carrot and rubbed her head. She nuzzled me as if to say, *I missed you too.*

After a wonderful dinner of pork chops, potatoes, gravy, and field peas, we settled in the living room to watch the Grammies. It was exciting to see Bette Midler sing *From a Distance.* Mom really liked her songs whereas Grannie preferred Tony Bennett singing, *When Do The Bells Ring for Me?* None of us liked MC Hammer. Garth Brooks and his band played *Friends in Low Places.*

"I hope we can be at the awards one day. Keep on writing more songs, Sawyer. We need ten to cut an album. We'll have a break in March and will be ready to do some recording," Tucker said.

"I've written a couple more. We can play them tomorrow and see if you like them."

"That reminds me," Mom said. "Cade, you got a letter from Harper and the envelope says don't bend. I'll go get it for you."

Inside were the photos David Shea took of us in Destin. "Wow! Look at Harper." I passed them around and everyone thought they were great. There was also one of her and me by the beach. "What do you think about the one with beach background for our album cover? Or do you like the one in the crooked tree?"

"The one in the crooked tree is perfect. Her eyes are sparkling," Mom said. Tucker said he liked the one with her hair blowing by the beach and Sawyer liked them all.

"I guess it'll be up to our production company to decide. Oh, look, Chet Atkins and Mark Knopfler are playing now. They've won Best Country Vocal Collaboration. We sure have met some amazing artists in Nashville this year. Just to go on tour with Garth Brooks and his band is fantastic," I said.

"Mom, did we tell you about Gus? He's our bus driver and keeps everyone in line. He cooks, finds us hotel rooms, and can drive for hours. I think he's at least eighty. Should we introduce him to Grannie?"

"Don't you be trying to fix me up, you young whippersnapper. I had all the men I wanted with your grandpa. He almost put me in my grave and so did your daddy. I'm proud of you boys and want you to be successful, just don't let it go to your heads or get you in trouble."

"Yes, ma'am," we all said in unison. When the awards show was over we were all ready for a good night's sleep.

The next morning, it wasn't so cold and I took Satan for a run. He was jittery and impatient, but I needed to blow the cobwebs out of my head.

After lunch, we sat on the porch with our instruments. Sawyer introduced us to his new songs. The first one, *A Coal Miners's Son,* featured Tucker's banjo as the primary instrument. The next one was for my electric guitar and had a fast beat. Sawyer called it *Running on Country Roads.* They both had good drum licks and a steady beat. We played them each three times and the more we played, the more we liked them.

We left the next morning, and I called Bob to see if we could play the new songs for him. He said to meet him at The Barn. Chet Atkins and Garth Brooks were still in New York. Bob was excited about their awards. After we played the new songs for him, he called Owen Bradley in to hear us play. Owen was younger than most of the record producers. He looked about my age. He wore old blue jeans and a faded striped shirt. His hair was long and pulled back into a ponytail. When Owen got excited, he stuttered, waved his hands around and talked loudly. "Duh, duh, damn, those songs are excellent. Your brother Sawyer is gonna win an award one of these da, days. Let's record those in March when y'all have a break. That makes eight for your album. He needs to write two more and we can produce it."

We left with smiles and went to The Blue Bird Café for burgers.

Chapter 33

As early as possible on Monday morning, I was at Pat's office. We sat with two copies of the offer on Shalimar in front of us. Pat was yellow magic marking the items to which she thought her seller would not agree. First, the offer was not $450,000. It was only $430,000. Second, they wanted him to leave his expensive golf cart.

"Okay, now we make him a seller's net sheet to show him what he would net from this offer of $430,000. Men like the Colonel are numbers' guys. He wants to know the bottom line. So, we'll prepare a net sheet to go on top of the contract. During our meeting, we'll discuss the contract terms and show him the net proceeds' figure."

She had me open an excel spreadsheet. First, I put the offer at the top, then subtracted our 6% commission. Next, I deducted the State documentary stamps and what his taxes would have been for the months he had been in the house that year. I came up with a net of $422,190. I didn't deduct a pay-off because there was no mortgage. Then Pat called the Colonel.

"I have an offer to present to you. When can Harper and I come over to discuss it?"

"That's great. How about five p.m.? I'll be home from the office by then."

"Okay. See you then," Pat replied. When Pat hung up the phone, I asked if she was nervous about presenting a lower offer to him. "No, this is part of negotiating. I know he left some room to come down. We'll find out what he wants and then present a counteroffer. Print a counteroffer form and leave the price blank. We'll fill that in when we meet with him."

She picked up the phone and called the buyer's agent. "Good morning," she said. "Thank you for the offer on Colonel Johnson's home. We are meeting with him at five p.m. today. You might like to tell your buyers that a counteroffer will probably be coming. I'll call you when I know what it will be."

That was so smooth. I couldn't wait to see what the Colonel's response would be.

I ran to pick up sandwiches for me and Pat. She had lots of phone calls to make. Then I left at three to meet the kids after school and fix them something to eat.

"I'll be home later tonight. Pat has an offer on the house she has listed and I need to go with her to present it."

"Okay, Mom," Lizzie said. "We'll do our homework and get ready for bed. Good luck."

I met Pat at the house in Shalimar at 4:45. One thing I learned quickly about Pat was that she was always early or right on time. She drove up and we rang the doorbell.

"Come in," boomed the Colonel. "Let's sit at the kitchen table so you can show me the offer. Mary, come here. You need to know the details too," he said to his wife.

Pat showed him the net sheet first. He looked it over. "Don't you think $430,000 is too low?"

"Yes," Pat said. "But they always come in lower than the listing price. Remember the other homes in your neighborhood sold for around this price?"

"Right. I want to counter at $440,000, and he can't have the golf cart. I have my insignia and name on it."

"Will you be using that golf cart at the Pentagon?" Pat asked. "How old is it?"

"Well, no. It's ten years old. But I've maintained it every year."

"We can have the insignia and your name removed. Don't let something like an old golf cart, which you can't use, stop you from selling your house. You know we have to work hard on the first offer. You've heard the saying, 'The first offer is the best'. Well, in my experience, this is often true."

"Okay, did you bring a counteroffer form?"

"You know I did. We just need to fill in the price then you and Mary need to sign it."

Once it was done, we got up, shook hands, and left.

"You go home to your kids. I'll drop this off with the selling agent for her client. I'll see you in the morning," Pat said and off she drove.

Chapter 34

We packed and got on the bus for College Station, Texas. Tucker and I had never been to Texas. Maybe we would find new cowboy hats. The drive was long, twelve hours and 774 miles, Gus told us, and too far for him to drive in one day, so we broke up the trip and stayed in a crummy hotel in Texarkana, next door was Fat Jack's Oyster and Sports Bar. Everyone went over to check it out, even Garth's band. When we walked in, Jack Mills, the owner, greeted us.

"Welcome, you boys on tour?" he asked. Jack was a jovial guy with a big smile. I could tell he had been an athlete even though he was old. He had a white muscle T-shirt on under his faded overalls and worn-out cowboy boots. He fitted the image of his bar.

Garth shook his hand and told him we were on route to College Station.

"Their first beer is on me," Jack said to the bartender.

Sports memorabilia covered the walls. Jack had played semi-pro ball for the Texas Titans. He had signed photos of several other ball players too. After we ate, the pool tables were calling us to challenge everyone. Tucker beat me, then we sat at the picnic tables to watch the others. I was drinking Jack and water and Tucker had a couple of beers. It wasn't long before I heard yelling, cursing, and pool sticks flying. Richard Boone had tangled with a guy who was heavily tattooed. It looked like he was beating the hell out of Boone. Boone was on the floor being pummeled. I jumped in to help and got whacked over the head with a pool stick. Tucker pulled Boone away and several others grabbed the other guy. Boone's face was bleeding near his eye. Tucker asked the bartender for a wet towel just as Big Jack came over.

"That's enough! Don't make me call the cops," he bellowed. Everyone backed off and we took Boone back to the room. He had a swollen eye and a couple of cuts. We all took some aspirin and went to bed.

When we got to the Rollie White Coliseum early the next day, I had a hangover from the night before. All I wanted was a greasy hamburger and a beer. Tucker frowned at me.

"Brother, you hit that Jack Daniels pretty hard last night. I bet you have a colossal headache."

"Not too bad. I just need a greasy hamburger and fries. I'll be fine by concert time."

Not long after we arrived we discovered that Texas A&M began in 1876, as an agricultural and military college. Students were officially nicknamed *Farmers,* but the moniker *Aggies*—a common nickname for students at schools focused heavily on agriculture—gained favor and became the official student-body nickname in 1949.

I bought Sawyer a T-shirt. We looked at straw hats and got two with Aggie Logos, which we would wear that night at the concert. We showed up early at the Coliseum, which was another unusual theater. Although it was nothing special, just a college gymnasium. We sure saw lots of different concert venues. Everything went well and none of us went out that night.

Gus greeted us the next morning at seven a.m. "Heard you boys got in a little trouble the other night. Everyone okay to travel?" Everyone nodded and he drove off toward the Temple Theater for the Performing Arts in Meridian, Mississippi. Texas seemed to go on forever until we finally arrived in Louisiana. The scenery changed to swamps and bridges as we drove to the lower end of Louisiana. The tour director must have been worried we would get in trouble in New Orleans, so they didn't stop. As we had left early, Gus drove straight through to Meridian. It was getting warmer, in the high sixties, so he decided we could sleep on the bus. The theater had dressing rooms and showers, so we went there early with our gear to clean up. The dressing rooms were fancy and matched the theater's Moorish revival style. Tucker and I were tired, so we didn't explore Meridian. Gus had lawn chairs, and we sat outside, plucked our instruments and napped.

I called Harper around six p.m. She was home and answered quickly.

"Well, hello, stranger. Where are you today?"

"Meridian, Mississippi, for the concert tonight. We just left College Station, Texas. How's the real estate business?"

"I love it. We just put that Shalimar house under contract. Pat is teaching me how to negotiate. There's never a dull moment."

"That's awesome. Playing for crowds is exciting, but driving on this bus is boring."

"I'm sure it is. I couldn't do it. Where are you going next?"

"We play at the Strawberry Festival in Plant City, Florida. Is that anywhere near you?"

"No, Babe, that's very central Florida. Too far for me to drive and I have no one to take care of the kids."

"When's their spring break? We'll be back in Nashville on March 6 or 7 for more than a month. Perhaps you could come up to see us."

"Let me find out the dates and check with Mom and Pat. I could probably come for a weekend. I miss you so much."

"I miss you too. I can send you a plane ticket if you can come."

"I'll let you know in a few days. I need to run. Pat has me showing a condo for her this afternoon. I love you."

"Bye, Green Eyes." Well, at least she said she still loves me. I was glad she liked her new job.

Chapter 35

I watched my children get on the school bus before I dressed in navy-blue slacks, a white blouse, and navy-blue pumps. At the last minute, I added a colorful scarf. As I drove to the office I was eager to see what Pat had planned. When I arrived, her white Cadillac Escalade was in the parking lot. She must have gotten there early.

"Good morning. What exciting things will we be doing today?" I asked her.

Pat waved a piece of paper over her head. What in the world?

"Look, you are officially a realtor now. Here's your license," she said. "You need to set up your license with the Board of Realtors on Hollywood Boulevard. They'll show you how to use the multiple listing service, how to add a listing, and teach you about contract forms. Don't sign up for lots of classes though because I'll teach you as we go. Those classes can take up a lot of time."

"Fantastic! I'll do that right now." I called the board and signed up for orientation on Thursday. After I finished my call, a tall woman in a red business suit opened our office door. She looked as if she knew where she was going and what she wanted.

"Hello, Susan. Come in. Meet my new assistant, Harper Hamilton. She just got her license today," Pat said.

When Susan walked over to my desk, I stood up and shook her hand. She was definitely attractive with long brown hair, hazel eyes, and a creamy complexion. She had a firm handshake. "Where do you want to review the inspection report on my sale in Shalimar?"

Pat motioned us over to the round table. Susan took the report out of her alligator briefcase and put it on the table. She and Pat looked it over.

"This is terrific. Only three issues that need to be addressed," Pat said.

"Yes, your listing was in excellent condition. Just as I thought it would be when I saw Colonel Johnson was the owner. There's a little wood rot on the door out to the pool. The dryer vent needs to be cleaned, and so do the gutters," Susan said.

"We can have that done in less than a week. Are you ready to close? Do they have their financing in place and their down payment ready to wire to the title company?" Pat asked.

"They do. Just send me the final bill to repair these items so I can show my buyers and we can close next week. It's been a pleasure working with you. Bye for now." Susan stood up, turned and walked out.

"Colonel Johnson will be pleased. Harper, please call my handyman and tell him we need him at the house tomorrow."

"Yes, ma'am."

Pat was on the phone with Colonel Johnson, and I could tell by her grin that he was happy. The handyman said he could be there at 9 a.m. the next day.

Pat stood up. "Let's go to lunch to celebrate. I'll drive."

We got in her Cadillac. Someday I intended to have a car like that. She drove us to Liollio's Restaurant. The parking lot was packed. As we went in the front door, a small man in a black suit, white shirt, shiny black shoes, and slicked back hair greeted us at the door. He had a Greek accent.

"Come in, ladies. Who is this attractive lady with you?" he asked Pat.

"This is my new assistant, Harper. She's just become a realtor. We're here to celebrate. Harper, this is John Georgiades, the owner of Liollio's."

"Follow me to a special table by the water and I'll send out an appetizer," John said. As we followed John through the restaurant, I took in the Greek paintings on the walls, large potted plants, and white tablecloths. It was my first time eating at Liollio's. It had not been on my previous banker's budget.

The appetizer was Greek pita bread with yogurt. We ordered Greek salads with Kalamata olives, feta cheese, cherry tomatoes, and sliced cucumbers. The salads were served with red wine vinegar dressing and we ordered iced tea.

While we were eating the pita bread, a thin man with blondish-brown hair, graying temples, dark brown eyes, and a square jaw, sat down. He was wearing a faded shirt, blue jeans, and work boots. Pat welcomed him. He was staring at me as if he knew me.

"Hello, Bob, have you met my new assistant, Harper Hamilton?" Pat said.

"She looks familiar," he said as he reached across the table and shook my hand. "I know. You were Al McLeod's secretary. I saw you at the Christmas party. I guess you're working with Pat now. Congratulations. She's the best in three counties. She lists lots of properties that I build. Have her bring you to see my newest one in Mary Esther." Then he got up and was gone in a flash.

Pat laughed. "That's Bob Bonezzi He's always in a rush to be somewhere and rarely takes time for lunch. He's great to work with though, and I'll take you over to see the new town homes he's building on the Gulf."

We finished our lunch and went back to the office. Pat made phone calls, and I ordered my business cards and signs for my car. "When can I order a gold jacket like yours? I want to look like a Century 21 agent too."

"We'll do that tomorrow. Now go home. It's almost five-thirty. I'll see you tomorrow."

Off I drove in my little Chevette. It had been a good day.

Chapter 36

Bright and early, Gus banged on our hotel room door. "Get up, you lazy fuckers! It's time to rock and roll to Plant City, Florida."

I rolled over, stretched my arms and legs. Thankfully, I didn't have a hangover. Tucker was already up and dressed and Richard was groaning. He still looked rough from that fight he got into in Texarkana. There was a huge discolored blue circle around his eye. I cleaned up hastily, grabbed my backpack, and headed for the bus.

Gus had bought us biscuits and coffee from McDonalds. "You're a lifesaver, Gus."

"You boys are a royal pain in my ass, but I love you. Now get on the bus. We have a long drive of nine or ten hours to Plant City. We'll stop for lunch somewhere in Florida, then I'll park on the Strawberry Festival grounds. You'll have a motel room for two nights; so you can shower when you get there."

As the countryside rolled by, I daydreamed about Harper. We would be in Nashville for a month. Surely, she could fly up for a weekend. I wanted her to watch us record the new songs Sawyer had been writing while we were on the road. As soon as I got back to our apartment, I would call her and see if I could buy her a ticket. She should have been able to fly from Pensacola to Nashville. I fell asleep dreaming of her green eyes and red hair.

We stopped for a quick lunch in Gainesville, home of the Florida Gators. Everything in that town was orange and blue. We wouldn't be opening for Garth because there were so many other artists playing at the festival. We would be in the back on stage with him. Richard wouldn't be able to play his drums because Garth would use his own drummer, but me and Tucker would play our instruments.

When we arrived, we were all impressed with the 325 acres of outdoor activities. There was a small circus, all kinds of rides, and a Ferris wheel. We walked past the covered outdoor stage and then inside. A cute strawberry blonde with lots of freckles greeted us. She looked to be in her thirties. She was short, had on overalls and a checked shirt with a straw hat.

"Hello boys, I'm Patsy Brooks, no relation to Garth. We're glad to have you here. You'll join an impressive lineup of other musicians. For the next eleven days, we have Reba McEntire, George Jones, Charley Pride, the Oak Ridge Boys, Carl Perkins, Ray Stevens, Mickey Gilley, and Lee Greenwood entertaining our crowd. We're excited that Garth and y'all have joined us. If you need anything, you can find me in that cute building with the sunflowers and strawberries painted on it. Here's a box of our delicious Florida strawberries for you to enjoy."

As we walked away, I goosed Tucker. "Can you believe we are here with all these amazing country musicians? I hope we get to meet a few of them."

"I know," Tucker said. "This is so exciting. It's a shame Sawyer isn't here."

"He will be one day. We'll come back and the Fox Brothers will be a headline act too."

"Come on boys," Gus said. "Let's check into the motel. You have the night off and need to play tomorrow at 8 p.m. Richard, behave yourself. No fighting or drinking too much."

The motel was just outside the fairgrounds. The outside was painted yellow, the doors were strawberry red, and the windows had flower boxes with red geraniums. We needed our photo taken in front of the motel for Mom and Grannie to see the cute place.

We showered and shaved, then roamed the fairgrounds. A group of Seminole Indians was dancing. Children were riding in dragon trains and whirling saucers that looked like an open strawberry. Teenage girls were selling strawberries from open wooden porches. I sure wished Harper could have brought her kids to see everything. The weather was refreshing, a pleasant seventy-six degrees. No wonder people liked to live in Florida. Tucker and I cleaned up the bus while Richard was sleeping in his bed. Then we looked around the fairgrounds again. It was 6 p.m. We ate at a barbeque joint a lot like the one we have in Dunlap. We enjoyed ribs, baked beans, corn, and sweet cornbread. "What do you think of this sweet cornbread?" I asked Tucker.

"Well, it's different from the kind Grannie makes. They must put sugar or honey in the batter. We'll have to tell Grannie about it when we get home. Do you think we'll have time to visit during the month we are home?"

"Sure, but I hope Bob has some gigs for us and has us booked into The Barn to record. Let's go watch Reba McEntire sing. She starts at seven." As always, Reba was fantastic. I loved her songs, *Fallin' Out of Love* and *For My Broken Heart*.

The next day we practiced with Garth's band and played the songs he was going to play that night. Garth praised us and told us he was glad we had joined his tour. Afterwards, we rode a few adult rides and bought souvenirs. Strawberry jam made in Plant City for Mom, Grannie, and Harper. A T-shirt for Sawyer that read *We Grow Them Sweet in Florida*. It had a big strawberry on the front with the writing across it.

Garth's band didn't dress up, so we didn't either. Jeans, T-shirts, and boots, so we wouldn't stand out. We were on the covered bandstand that was open to the outdoor seating. It was huge and there had to be around seven thousand people watching us that Saturday night.

The first song we played was *The Thunder Rolls*. We received a standing ovation and then everyone sang along with *Friends in Low Places*. We also played the songs from *No Fences,* the album he cut in 1990. By the time Garth finished, he was soaking wet with sweat and so were we. What a night! What a performance!

I cooled off outside the motel and had a couple of swigs from my flask. It didn't take me any time to fall asleep.

Chapter 37

When I attended orientation at the Board of Realtors, at least I wasn't the only newbie. Cathy was there and we had lunch together. She and Anthony were planning a wedding in a few months, and she had gone to work with him in his office. He sold mostly commercial real estate and was training her to sell residential. I told her about working for Pat Champion as an assistant and how she was a great mentor.

I stayed for the afternoon session and then went home to the kids. It thrilled Lizzie and Sean that I was home early and I sat at the table with them while they did their homework. Sean was having trouble with his reading, so I helped him with his phonics. Lizzie had always been an excellent reader, but math. That was another story.

I settled into my comfy chair in my plant room. I needed a break from learning real estate, so I picked up Glamor Magazine from the coffee table. I was behind in reading my subscription and looked through January's issue. Christy Brinkley was on the cover. How could anyone be that naturally beautiful with her long blonde hair, turned-up nose, and green eyes? Okay, I had beautiful green eyes, but sometimes my red hair made it hard to find colors that looked good on me. I perused the magazine to study the latest fashion. As I looked at the pink Chanel suit with black trim, I shook my head. Not that color, maybe if it were blue with black trim. Next, I saw a long jacket with larger buttons over a short pencil skirt. To pull it all together, the model had on a large chunky bead necklace and an alligator purse. Oh my, the jacket was $285. And the skirt was $105. I knew I needed to make serious money if I wanted to dress like a model. I had been wondering why Cade hadn't called, so I got up to retrieve his schedule. He was in Plant City and should be back in Nashville by Sunday. Was he waiting to call me when he got home?

The following morning I was at the office bright and early, eager to begin my day.

"We're going to do an open house at Crystal Beach in Destin. Bob has a new home that's finished. He's building cottage-style homes a couple of blocks walk to the beach. We'll spend the day in one of them. Print some flyers for number 80 Crystal Beach Drive, load the open house signs into my car and grab a bunch of my business cards. I'll meet you in the car," Pat said.

Pat drove to Destin and when she turned into Crystal Beach, it surprised me. I hadn't been to that neighborhood with picket fences and pastel-colored homes with metal roofs. We pulled into the driveway of a pale yellow house with white shutters. Pat showed me where to put the open house sign, then she gave me the code to the lock-box before we walked inside.

"This is cute. How much are these?"

"This one is three bedrooms, two bathrooms, around 1,460 square feet and priced at $159,000."

"You're kidding me, right? Who would pay this much money for such a tiny house? It's not even brick."

"You'll see. And don't let Bob hear you say that. Let's get our folders out and put them on the counter along with my business cards. Then we'll turn on all the lights and sit where we can see the customers walk in. Watch me, for the first time or two, and then I'll let you practice on the third one who comes in."

Around ten a.m., a middle-aged couple arrived. Pat greeted them, shook hands, and started asking questions. They said they were from Michigan, snowbirds who were thinking of buying a second home in Destin to get out of the cold weather for the winter. Pat showed them all the home's features and walked behind them. They liked the large master bedroom that had a door to the wrap-around porch. They hadn't seen imitation marble bathrooms before and were impressed, but the price shocked them. They thanked Pat for showing them the house and left.

"You are going to get lots of snowbirds from January to March 15th. I spend time with them, because one in ten will buy here. It takes him a while to get used to the fact that their large homes in Michigan are the same price as our cottages," Pat said.

"I see. I guess those aren't bad odds." We sat around chatting for the next hour until the doorbell rang. Joe and June Batson looked to be around forty. Pat showed them the house and I trailed behind again.

"We have a condo and I'm tired of having a condo for a second home. I told Joe we need a cottage like one of these," June said.

"Where's your condo?" Pat asked.

"Sun Destin in Destin. It's a one bedroom and we want more bedrooms so the grandchildren can come in the summer and spring breaks."

"Sun Destin sells well in March. Lots of the snowbirds who stay there decide to purchase before they leave. Where are you from?"

"We're not snowbirds," Joe said. "We live in Montgomery and like to come down on weekends and holidays. I'm not ready to retire yet, but in a few years I will."

"One of these cottages would be perfect for you. Would you like to have one built to your specifications? I'd be happy to list your condo and then you'd have the money ready when yours is completed."

Joe looked at his wife. "I like that idea, do you?"

"Yes, that sounds wonderful. I want a light lavender one and I think a little bigger."

Pat invited them to sit at the table where she spread out the plat map for them. She showed them the vacant lots that were available and gave them a packet of cottage plans.

"This is great. We'll go back to our condo, look through the plans and then drive around and see the vacant lots. Will you be here again Saturday?" Joe asked.

"I sure will, after ten. Do you want us to come and preview your condo, so I can offer an opinion on the listing price? We'll be here until four but could come by on our way back to Fort Walton Beach."

"That's a lovely idea," June said. "Our unit is number 1002 on the tenth floor."

"Perfect, we'll see you then," Pat said.

When they left, Pat high fived me. "See, you never know who will walk in that door. We'll go see their condo, go back to the office, and do the comparable for their condo. Let them study the plans overnight and see which one June likes. She'll be the decider on the plan. He'll be more interested in the numbers I give him on Saturday."

We previewed their condo, had one glass of wine with them, and then excused ourselves. "We'll see you Saturday. I'll have all the numbers for you and when you know which plan you want, I can give you a price," Pat said.

"I'm worn out from the excitement and learning. I can't wait for Saturday," I said to Pat.

"You'll get used to it. Nothing is easy when you first start. Get a good night's sleep and I'll see you at the office at nine tomorrow."

Chapter 38

We were glad to be on the bus and going back to Nashville. Gus told us we would stop halfway to spend the night. If we drove straight through with no problems, it would be eleven or twelve hours before we got back to Nashville and he didn't want to risk it. We stopped outside of Perry, Georgia. Gus knew about some cabins with bunks by a lake. He got out the charcoal grill and told us to start the fire. Tucker put the coffeepot on the small grill with the charcoal and lighter while Gus and I went across the street to a small market that sold meat and sundries. "What do you want me to cook? I can do hamburgers and beans quickly," he said.

"That sounds good. You pick out the meat. I'll get buns, the beans and ice. Meet you at the cash register."

A little old lady who looked to be Grannie's age in a cotton dress and apron was at the cash register. She gave Gus a big smile. "Where you boys comin' from?"

"We've been to Plant City for the Strawberry Festival and we're on our way back to Nashville. I can't drive that far anymore without a stop in the middle. I parked us across the street at the cabins." He winked at her and paid for our groceries.

"You still got it, Gus. She was flirting with you. I didn't see a wedding ring on her finger. Why don't you go back in there and invite her to eat with us?"

"Don't be silly, boy. I don't have time for a woman."

Tucker had the paper plates, mustard, and catsup out. Richard looked like he'd already had his evening weed smoke. I got out the glasses, filled them with ice and poured Gus, Richard, and I a Jack Daniels and water. Tucker was already drinking a beer. It was nice and relaxed around the campfire. We were all hungry since we hadn't stopped for lunch. The hamburgers were tasty and juicy, the meat was excellent, and the beans were beans, but the meal was filling and satisfied my hunger.

Gus told Richard it was his turn to clean up, then he lit his cigar. I didn't like smoking but enjoyed the smell of the cigars Gus smoked. I fixed another drink and wandered off to call Harper. I found a stump to sit on behind the cabin near the lake and dialed her number. It would have been seven p.m. her time. As the phone rang, I realized I hadn't called her in several days. It was Sunday night and I hoped she was home. I was listening to the wind in the trees when she answered.

"Hi, Babe. It's your worn-out boyfriend."

"Well, so you didn't forget me. Just teasing. I know you were at the Strawberry Festival and you would've been busy. I'm glad you called. How was the concert?"

"We played on the stage with Garth. Then we wandered around and listened to the other bands. The festival is really something. I would love to take Lizzie and Sean one day. There are lots of rides for kids, plenty of games and great music too. We should be in Nashville from the 7th of March until April the 10th or so. Would you be able to come?"

"Let me find my calendar. Here it is. Easter vacation for the schools is from the 29th through the 31st. I'm sure Mom and Dad would have the kids for me. I could fly up for a long weekend. How would that fit your schedule?"

"Well, no matter what I'm doing, you can come along with me. We hope to be recording at The Barn and hopefully Bob will have a gig for us. I'd love to take you to The Bluebird Café."

"I'd love to see the café and you. I've been busy with Pat and keeping up with her real estate business. But at night I fall asleep thinking of you and wishing your arms were around me."

"I'd like to do more than just to put my arms around you. I'm getting hard just talking to you. I'd like to lie you down in the grass by this lake. Kiss you all over until you beg for more."

"You're making me blush. I'm not used to phone sex. You've made my knickers wet."

"Good, you'll go to bed thinking about me. I'll send you a ticket after your parents agree to have the kids. One day, I want them to come with you. I think they'd like Grannie's house."

"I know Lizzie would love to ride Suzie and Sean would love Dog and listening to you and your brothers play on the porch. He's been asking about learning the guitar."

"We'll have another week's break in July. If I don't come down to Fort Walton Beach, then you can bring them up here. I'll teach him a few chords on my old guitar ... I love you."

"I love you back. Good night."

Chapter 39

I had a restless night's sleep. I kept thinking about going to Nashville, planning my talk with my mom, and about that sexy phone conversation. Then without warning, Lizzie was leaning over me.

"Get up Mom or we'll all be late."

I rubbed the sleep from my eyes and went into the tiny bathroom we shared. I knew I'd better get a move on, so the kids wouldn't be late to school. When I walked into the kitchen, Lizzie was feeding Sean cereal with bananas and milk. They were both dressed. What would I do without her? She was so responsible.

"Thank you for feeding your brother. I'm so proud of how you take care of him. Come here, let me brush your hair." She loved it when I brushed her hair; it was a way to let her know I loved and appreciated her. Sean's hair was short, so he didn't need any brushing. I got out their lunch money and walked them out the door to catch the bus. As I waved goodbye, my heart swelled with love for them. I finished my muffin and fixed a coffee to go. Let the excitement at the office begin.

"Good morning, sunshine," I said to Pat. "What's up for today?"

"Well, good morning to you. Why is that grin on your face?"

"Cade called last night and he wants me to fly to Nashville over Easter weekend. Do you think it would be a problem?"

"No, you go. I can handle the listings for a few days. What are the dates so I can put them in my planner?"

"The 29th to the 31st of March. I have to call my mother and make sure she's okay with the kids going to Milton. I'm sure she'll be fine, she loves to have them."

"Okay, pull your chair up to mine so I can show you how we figure out the best price to sell 1002 Sun Destin for the Batsons."

Pat showed me how to find the condos that had been sold in the last year and how many were pending and active. Their condo was nicely furnished with coastal sofas, two chairs, a king-size bed, and it was in great condition. It would be above average price. She printed out everything so we could take it to the model home the next day.

"I can't give them a price difference until I see which plan they want to build. But I'll encourage them to list and get theirs sold now. It'll take Bob about six months to build the new one. By next September, it should be ready to move in."

"That's exciting news. I mailed all my sphere of influence letters on Friday. I hope to hear from some of my people this week."

"Good job. Let's work on a postcard mail out for the Crystal Beach homes. Look up all the vacant lots in the area and add them to an Excel spreadsheet. We can mail out a card offering original floor plans from our builder."

"I'll do that now. There are 350 properties in total. I just need to see which ones are vacant. Then do you want me to do a template?"

"Yes, I have lots of calls to make so you can do that today," said Pat.

As I looked at the tax record, copied and pasted it into the spreadsheet, I wished I could buy one of them and build a home. Perhaps one day it would happen. It looked as if people were paying $15,000 to $25,000 for the lots. Pat taught me the lot needs to be 25% of what the final home will cost. I found out if the lot was paid for, that could count as the 20% down for financing. There was so much to learn, but I loved it.

At three o'clock I took a break and called my mom. She said she would be happy to have the children at Easter if I wanted to go to Nashville. I left a message on Cade's phone. I'd never been to Nashville. It would be exciting to see the places he had told me about. We had almost finished for the day and were ready for the Batsons on Saturday when my cell phone rang. It was Cash Moore. "Hey, Harper. You want to list a lot I have in downtown Fort Walton Beach?"

"I sure do. Where's it located? I'll go look at it this afternoon." Cash told me where it was and I told Pat.

"See, I told you those sphere of influence letters would get you customers. Find it on the tax records and then go over and walk the lot."

I left to go walk the lot. Glad I was wearing flat shoes. The lot had lots of vegetation, but it was in a good part of downtown. It would be an excellent listing. I went back to the office. After looking at what had sold in the area, I came up with a price of $150,000. I sat with Pat and showed her my findings.

"Good job. That's what I'd price it at too. Now fill out the listing agreement, the vacant land disclosure and make an appointment to see Cash to get everything signed."

When I had finished, I called Cash. "I have all the documents ready for you to sign, can I come over this afternoon?"

"Sure, come to the Faux Paux liquor store. My office is upstairs."

I arrived at the liquor store on Okaloosa Island. There was a black wreath on the door and a sign that said. *Open unless Cash is dead or married.* That was too funny. I walked up the stairs and went into the office. His receptionist, Patti Baker, greeted me. Patti and I had been friends for many years; we were both in the American Business Women's Club.

"Hi, Harper. I'm glad to hear you are in real estate now. Cash is waiting for you in his office. Go on in."

Cash gave me a hug. "Nice to see you. So, you are going to be a realtor now. Good for you. How are your kids?"

"The kids are great and I'm excited to have a new career. Thank you for giving me this opportunity to list your lot." Cash sat down behind his desk. He was quite a character with his short, curly hair, round face and stocky body. Not a good looker, but I'd heard the women chased him. He had stacks of money on the desk and was counting it into piles. His office had lots of Auburn College flags, photos, and statues. It was obvious this was his college of preference.

"Here's the listing agreement. Pat and I both think $150,000 is the best price to list it. You only paid $50,000, so you'll make a nice profit when it sells."

"I agree with you. Where do I sign?" He signed, I thanked him and turned to leave.

"Great to see you. Now get to work and sell that lot for me."

I said goodbye to Patti and left the office. One of Cash's famous cars was out front. It was a gold Mercedes convertible with flashy wheels that didn't come from the factory. The tag on the back said, *I'm nuts.* Only Cash could get away with something that crazy.

Chapter 40

Tucker and I were so glad to be home. Our apartment looked like the Taj Mahal after our time on the road. We put away our suitcases and instruments and called Mom.

"We're home and it feels good to be here."

"I know you are. How long for?"

"Around thirty days. I'm sending Harper a ticket to come to Nashville for Easter weekend. I know you want me to come home, but I think this is necessary to keep our relationship going. Did I tell you she's selling real estate now? She loves it."

"I understand. Send Tucker home so you can have some privacy with Harper. I hope you can come home for a day or two. We miss you."

"I'll plan on it. I'm going to talk with our manager and see if he can get us a couple of gigs while we're here. Can Sawyer come over on weekends?"

"Yes, but he needs to finish his last quarter of high school. He should graduate in May."

"Oh no! We'll be out west when he graduates. We might not be able to come home. Our tour will take us to Washington State, Oregon, Idaho, Utah, Wyoming, South Dakota, and Oklahoma."

"You two sure are seeing the USA. Are you enjoying the tour?"

"Yes and no. We're homebodies, but the excitement of performing in some of the most amazing venues is great. Do you want to talk to Tucker? I need to run to the store for groceries." I handed the phone to Tucker and told him I'd be back soon.

I cranked up the old truck and drove a couple of blocks to Bruno's Grocery Store. I was going to make beef stew. I picked up yellow onions, carrots, celery, small potatoes, and stewing beef. We could eat that for a few days. We also needed milk, cereal, bread, and lunchmeat for sandwiches. And I decided to get spaghetti fixings too.

Then on impulse, I drove to the Ford truck lot. As I pulled in there was that same sales agent, John Reinhold, at the curb. He saw me and waved. He walked over wearing another loud leisure suit. This one was maroon with a pink shirt and striped tie.

"Hey, Cade. Where've you been? I read that article about y'all in *The Tennessean.*"

"We've been on tour with Garth Brooks. We're home for a month. Do you still have a black Ford Lariat 4x4 on the lot?"

"I sure do and it has your name written all over it. Come with me. I'll get the keys and we can take it for a test ride."

"Wow! This truck is a dream machine." John Reinhold laughed as I floored it up a hill.

"What do you say? Are you ready to get a new truck? You must be making good money on a tour with Garth Brooks."

"I've been putting money away for a down payment. Can we figure out what my payments would be if I put $5,000 down on it?"

"Yes, let's go in and see the finance manager. You can fill out a credit application and he can give you the payment figure."

We walked through the lobby to the finance office. I don't know how they worked in those glass offices where everyone could see what they were doing. When George Simmons worked out the figures, the payment was $199 a month. I knew I could afford it because I was making good money.

"Okay, let's do it. You get it ready and Tucker and I will come back tomorrow to pick it up." As I left, I couldn't wait to surprise Harper, Mom, and Grannie.

I walked in with a big smile on my face. I put all the groceries on the counter and looked around for Tucker. He was in the laundry washing our clothes from the trip. I waited until he came into the kitchen. "Would you like to have my old truck?"

"Sure, what have you done? Did you go by the Ford dealership?"

"Yep, and guess what? I can afford the black 4x4 Lariat. We can pick it up tomorrow."

"Fantastic. You've been wanting that truck, and I'll be glad to have yours for a while. When I get a new one, we can give Sawyer your old one."

I cooked the beef stew and we ate as if we were starving. Tucker cleaned up the kitchen and I called Bob.

"We're back and ready to work in Nashville for a month. Have you lined up any gigs for us?"

"Yes, Tootsie's wants you to play this Friday and Saturday and so does Skull at the Rainbow Room the weekend after. Kathy at The Blue Bird Café asked if you want to sit in on Wednesdays this month. I'll set it up and get back to you tomorrow. Glad you're home. Get Sawyer over here with his new songs and let's record them. You should have ten by now and we can cut an album."

As I drifted off to sleep, I kept seeing that big black truck waiting for me to come get it. I would call the airlines and buy Harper a ticket too. She was going to be surprised when I picked her up in my new truck.

Chapter 41

Pat and I met the Batsons on Saturday. They picked out an 1,860 square foot three-bedroom, three-bathroom home to be built on Lot 30 in Crystal Beach. The price came to $195,000 with changes. Pat told them we could get $99,000 for their condo in Sun Destin International. That would leave $100,000 for them to finance or pay in cash. I could tell by the grin on their faces they wanted to proceed.

June picked out the lavender color with white trim and white shutters and Joe wanted a carport. They signed the listing to sell their condo. Pat said I could put it into the Multiple Listing Service and she would give me part of the commission when it sold. It would be my job to put it on the agent's tour, advertise it, and work on any offers we got. I was thrilled.

We sat at the open house in Crystal Beach for the rest of the day; however, here were no more visitors to our cottage. When I got home, my business cards and car signs had come in the mail. The kids thought they looked cool on my yellow Chevette. I took them out to Pizza Hut to celebrate my new listings. Sean was especially excited. I let him pick what kind of pizza he wanted and he ordered a large with pepperoni and sausage. We ended up taking home several pieces.

"Can we stay up later tonight and watch a movie together? *Little Dracula* is on at eight," Lizzie said.

"Okay, we'll watch it together." We cuddled on the couch and turned on *Little Dracula*. Sean loved it, but Lizzie not so much and I just absent-mindedly watched it. My mind was full of learning real estate and excitement about seeing Cade at the end of the month.

It was late when Kate called and talked about getting together on Sunday. The girls were going to The Back Porch in Destin to watch a duo sing. Suzanne was bringing her son, David. Did I want to come and bring the kids? I said I'd meet them for lunch.

We met everyone at the restaurant. The Back Porch was right on the beach in Destin, on what used to be the main highway, but it had a dead end at the park. The building was colorful with lots of beach and drink signs. My favorite drink was a frozen daiquiri. All my girlfriends were there:

Melody, Kate, and Suzanne. Lizzie was friends with David and Sean liked him too. They headed for the beach to play on the swings. We ordered strawberry daiquiris and watched the kids, then we listened to the duo play eighties' music. The weather in March can be variable. It was sunny and seventy-six degrees. Warm enough to get a tan if you could stay out of the wind. The kids were digging holes in the sand and making a castle.

Our conversations ranged from what was going on at the bank to how I liked real estate. "Have you heard from Cade?" Kate asked.

"Yes, he called the other night. He's back in Nashville for a month and he's sending me a ticket to visit over Easter weekend. I can't wait."

"Aren't you glad we dragged you to The Boat House on Melody's birthday?" Kate said.

"Yes, thank you. So far, our long-distance romance is working."

We called the kids up to the porch and ordered lunch. I switched to iced tea. One daiquiri was enough for me. All of us ordered fried shrimp baskets with fries and coleslaw. The kids wanted chicken fingers with fries, and, of course, 7UP.

The Gulf of Mexico was rough because of the March wind and I was glad the kids didn't ask to go in the water. After we ate, they snuck the remaining bread from our sandwiches and fed the seagulls. Suzanne and I made them fill in the hole they had dug and wash the sand off their feet, pick up their shoes, and come back to the boardwalk. It was nice to be with my girlfriends on a Sunday afternoon. We said our goodbyes and went home.

"Do you know why we had you fill in the hole you dug in the sand?" I asked Lizzie and Sean while we were driving home.

"Yes, Mama. If baby turtles fall in the hole, they can't get to the sea to grow up and be big turtles," Sean replied.

"That's right. Never forget."

That evening I called Cade. "Good news. Mom said she would have the kids so I can come to Nashville."

"That's fantastic. I'll be at Nashville Airport to pick you up. Bob has us booked for a couple of gigs at Tootsie's and The Rainbow Room and Amy has asked us to sit in on Wednesdays at The Bluebird Café. Plus Bob has us scheduled at The Barn to record our album."

"Wow, I would love to see you and Tucker do that. Will Sawyer get to come over too?"

"Only if Mom lets him skip school. I'm working on her."

"The kids and I had lunch today with my bank buddies. They asked how you were doing and said to tell you hello."

"That's nice. I'm glad you are doing some fun things. I can't wait to see you."

"I'll be there soon. I need to get the kids in the bathroom. They have school tomorrow. Love you. Bye."

Chapter 42

My phone rang at 9 a.m. As I rubbed my eyes with one hand, I answered it with the other. "Hello."

It was John Reinhold to say they had approved my credit, and I could pick up the truck.

"Bring a cashier's check for your down payment. We can call your insurance company from the dealership. Can you be here this morning?"

"I sure can. See you soon." I rolled out of bed, put on the coffee, and woke Tucker. "Let's go get my new truck." We ate a quick breakfast of eggs and toast. I put my checkbook in my pocket and we drove to the bank. The pretty teller, Mary Jane, attended to us. She batted her eyes at Tucker and he blushed. As she was printing the cashier's check, I nudged Tucker. "Get her phone number, dummy. She thinks you're cute," I whispered.

"Okay." All of a sudden he got brave. "Mary Jane, would you like to go out sometime? We're home for a month."

"I'd love to." She wrote her phone number on a piece of paper. As we left, Tucker turned around.

"I'll call you tonight."

"Good job, brother. It's about time you had a date. You can always invite her to come watch us this weekend or to The Bluebird Café."

We laughed and joked all the way to the dealership. John was out front with the black truck all clean and ready for me. We shook hands and went into the finance office and sorted out the paperwork.

"It's full of gas and ready to go," said John. "Are you guys playing anywhere while you're home? I'd like to come hear you play."

"Come to Tootsie's this weekend. I'll buy you a beer. If they ask you for a cover charge, tell them you're my guest."

"I sure will. Thanks, guys. See you this weekend."

Tucker drove my old truck home and I loved every minute of driving my new 4x4 Ford.

When I arrived at the Blue Bird, Amy greeted me at the door. Tucker was picking up Mary Jane.

"It's good to see you home again. How's the tour so far?" She walked me to the bar and ordered me a Jack and water. We sat down and I gave her the short version of our trip.

Tucker walked in and came to the bar with Mary Jane who was wearing a slinky dark blue dress that complemented her black hair. She was holding Tucker's arm, and he had his banjo in the other. Tucker introduced her to Amy.

"Welcome, Mary Jane. You're in for a treat. These two are skilled musicians and I love it when they come to play for us."

We found Mary Jane a front-row seat, got our instruments out and tuned them. Of course, our first song was *Green Eyes*. The crowd clapped and sang along. It was still early. There would be more in attendance at the second set. Next, we played *When I Saw You* and *Riding Down the River*. Then we played a couple of Garth's songs and took a break. Tucker went over to sit with Mary Jane, and I walked up to the bar. Cindy was bartending, and she gave me a big smile.

"If it ain't my favorite country music singer." She put a Jack and water in front of me. "Where've you been? I've missed you."

"On tour with Garth Brooks, we're home for a month. Good to see you too." It was time for our second set when Richard Boone walked in with a couple of rough-looking guys. He waved and they went to the bar. We played our new songs, *My Home's* in *Tennessee,* and *A Coal Miner's Son.* The café had filled up and everyone clapped. Then we played Garth's songs. Everyone knew those words. It was a good evening and it felt great to be back in Nashville.

Tucker and Mary Jane left to go out to eat. I stayed and had too many drinks with Boone and his friends. I was in the bathroom when Boone walked in. He offered me a line of coke. I thought about it, knew I shouldn't, but the temptation was too great. Wow! What a high.

Chapter 43

The office phone rang and I answered it because Pat was out meeting her builder. The caller wanted me to show him and his wife 1002 Sun Destin. Before I hung up, I asked if they would like to see more than one condo, perhaps the two bedrooms that were listed. They agreed it would be a good idea. I told them I needed to make appointments. Could we meet at one o'clock in the lobby? They should look for the redhead.

I called the Batsons and told them I had prospective buyers who wanted to view their condo. Then I called the rental department and asked if 1004 was vacant. They said it was and I could pick up the keys in the lobby. The new couple found me in the lobby. They were from Atlanta and were dressed in casual clothes. They introduced themselves as Sue and George Bennett. "We want a rental investment and a place to come with our children a few times a year," George said.

I picked up the keys to 1004, then I showed them the restaurant and the indoor swimming pool that opened to the outside, and the arcade before we walked to the beach. After touring the property, we caught the elevator to the tenth floor.

First, I showed them our listing, number 1002. Sue thought it was well decorated. George said the kids could sleep on the sleeper sofa. The one bedroom was $20,000 less expensive than 1004, the two-bedroom condo we were going to see next.

They liked the décor in 1004, and just as they commented on it I noticed the master bedroom door was shut. *That's odd. Why would the door be shut?* I opened the door and a man sleeping on the bed. He sat up, startled. He was dressed in overalls and had a name tag on his shirt.

"Oh, my God. I'm sorry. I was fixing the toilet and just lay down to rest. Please don't tell the front desk," he said before he got up hastily and left.

"Is this how they run their condo maintenance? I'm not sure I want a condo here," George spluttered.

"Everyone makes mistakes. I'm sure it horrified him when we opened the door," Sue said.

I didn't know what to say. It had horrified me too. "Would you both like to go downstairs and get a drink? We can talk." We went to the restaurant and I ordered a Diet Coke. Sue ordered one too, and George had a beer. George calmed down while we were talking about whether to buy a one or two bedroom. He told me he was an accountant in Atlanta, and Sue said she was busy with her young twins and wasn't working. I offered the information that a one bedroom had the best cash flow for rentals for the price. Buying a two bedroom was a convenience. They decided they would talk it over and call me the next day. I paid the bill and we left. George didn't look happy. Sue would have to do some real convincing if she wanted that two bedroom.

I drove back to the office. Pat was at her desk and I told her what had happened. "Well, at least no one was in the bedroom making whoopee," she said with a laugh.

"Well, it horrified me. They're going to think it over tonight. George is an accountant and Sue stays home with their twins."

"An accountant, oh dear. Accountants are a tough sell. They run the numbers up and down and around. If he buys one, it'll be the one bedroom."

"Oh! I learn something new every day from you," I replied.

The next morning, the phone rang at ten. It was George. "I've decided we want to put in an offer on 1002, the one bedroom. Where can we meet you?"

"I can meet you at Sun Destin. They have a small meeting room. Would that be convenient?"

"Yes, meet us at one o'clock. Bring a contract with you."

"Yes, sir. See you then."

I looked at Pat. "He wants to make an offer on the one bedroom."

"I told you. You'll learn to read your clients. It takes about a year. By then, you'll have them figured out."

I met them in the meeting room, took out my contract and addressed George. "How much would you like to offer?"

"$10,000 less than the asking price of $150,000. I brought my checkbook and I'll put 10% down and pay cash for the rest," George said.

I wrote up the offer and had them both sign it. "I have to present it to the Batsons and will call you as soon as I can. Will you still be here in Destin?"

"Yes," Sue said. "I sure wanted that two bedroom, but George is right. 1002 makes better financial sense. He knows best. The twins can sleep on the pullout sofa."

After they left, I called the Batsons while I was still in the lobby. They said to come on up. We sat down at the dining room table and I presented the offer for $140,000. Joe wasn't happy. He told me he would take $145,000, but no less. I reassured them I would speak with the Bennetts that afternoon. I went down to the meeting room and called George Bennett.

"Mr. Bennett. They countered your offer. They will sell you the condo for $145,000."

"Let me speak to Sue. Hold on." He left the phone, talked with her and came back. "Okay, she wants it. Are you still at the condo? If so, we'll meet you there and sign the counter."

I didn't have a counteroffer form with me. I called Pat. She told me to strike a line through the $140,000 on the contract and put $145,000 out to the side and have all the parties initial it. Since it was a cash offer, it wouldn't matter. The Bennetts came and initialed the changes. I congratulated them, told them I would make a copy and mail it to them.

Then I took the elevator to the Batson's condo. When they opened the door, as usual, the view of the Gulf of Mexico from their unit thrilled me. But especially on that day when I had made my first real estate sale. They both initialed the price change and I congratulated them. June was so excited.

"Thank you. Now get Bob Bonezzi busy building our new cottage." Even Joe smiled and shook my hand.

I drove back to the office. *I just might be good at this job.*

Chapter 44

Tucker woke me. "Brother, get up. Breakfast is cooked and ready."

Lord help me, my head was killing me. I should never have hung out with Boone and his friends. I washed my face and ran a brush through my hair. It was sticking up like I'd had a fight with my pillow. "It sure smells good. Thanks Tucker." I poured a cup of coffee and sat down with him. "Your breakfast has hit the spot. Now if only you could learn to make biscuits like Grannie. Tell me about your date."

"Mary Jane is cool. She lives with two other girls from the bank in an apartment uptown. She's originally from Memphis and went to Nossi College of Art and Design here in Nashville. She's an artist although she works at the bank. She paints and sells her work at a small studio. Her family is small, only her and her sister Beth. Her mom is an art teacher in Memphis and her dad is vice president of a bank. And I really like her."

"She sounds interesting. We should go see her artwork if she has an event. You know Harper is coming to see me at Easter. I told Mom I couldn't come home that weekend. Are you going home for Easter?"

"Yes, I'll go so you and Harper can have the apartment to yourselves. Mary Jane is going home to Memphis. I already have a date with her in the middle of this week. She said she'd bring her roommates to watch us play at Tootsie's this weekend." Then Tucker whacked me over my aching head with the dishtowel. "I'll do the dishes. Then we need to go over to Tootsie's and talk to Steve Smith."

I called Boone and told him to meet us at Tootsie's around noon. I couldn't wait to show Harper Tootsie's Orchid Lounge. She had probably never seen a lavender painted bar. Steve greeted us. "Hi guys. Glad you're home. Did you enjoy touring with Garth?"

"We sure did. Garth can draw a crowd. We've seen some great show venues. But it's always good to be home. We're about the record our first album."

"That's great news. You'll be on your way to stardom soon. I want you to play this weekend on Friday and Saturday. The band I booked canceled on me. Can you help me out?"

Boone walked in a few minutes after one p.m. He must have had an aversion to being on time. "We'd be glad to. Steve, this is Richard Boone. He's our drummer for the tour."

"Nice to meet you, Richard. I'll put your names on the billboard to say you'll be playing this weekend."

We left and went down the street for a late lunch at Jacks's Riverfront Bar-B-Que. It was nice to see the area being renovated. It used to be an area of homeless people and empty buildings. Some people even say it was Jack's that started the current revitalization of lower Broadway Street. Inside we found a wooden table and high-backed banquet seats by the window. We ordered Budweisers while we looked over the menu. Everything made my mouth water.

"What are you guys going to eat?" asked the server. He was six feet two with a baby face and he wore blue jeans and a red and white checked shirt.

"I'm going to have the Texas beef brisket plate and another beer," I said.

Tucker ordered the smoked Boston turkey plate and Boone the Tennessee pork shoulder plate and another beer. It took no time for our server to bring it out. The smell was tantalizing. We dug into the sandwiches, corn on the side, cornbread, and greens. No one talked. The food was delicious. When we had finished our server came back.

"Are you guys musicians?" he asked. "Mr. Cawthon gives a discount if you are. He's encouraging the musicians who play at Tootsie's to come eat here."

"Well, thanks, that's much appreciated," I replied. "We'll be playing at Tootsie's this weekend. Come see us." We threw our cash down on the table and left him a good tip. I was sure we'd be back and we wanted him to remember us.

The weekend was upon us before we realized it. We met at Tootsie's at seven and the show would start at eight. Boone's friends came in and joined us at the bar. Boone slipped me a small packet of coke while Tucker kept turning around looking for Mary Jane and her friends. I had to tease him about her. They showed up about fifteen minutes before we were about to play. As soon as they arrived I slipped off to the bathroom to enjoy my poison. Tucker got up, greeted the girls and sat down at a table with them.

Couldn't say I blamed him. Boone's friends looked rough and unsuitable to meet those sweet girls.

We started playing at eight. Steve Smith was a stickler for his shows starting on time. For an hour we played all our songs and some of Garth's. The crowd's reception was wonderful. When we took a break at nine, Tucker joined the girls and Boone and I went to join his wild friends. After a Jack and water, Boone asked me if I wanted to go to the bathroom. Inside, he passed me another small packet of the magical white stuff. I rolled up a bill and snorted. What a rush.

We finished our last hour playing other country musicians' songs. Steve came over and thanked us for a great show. I joined Tucker at Mary Jane's table and met her girlfriends. All of them were cute and friendly, just like Mary Jane. They were drinking girly drinks, cosmos, and daiquiris. Tucker ordered a beer and I ordered my usual. The girls were ready to go home, so Tucker walked them to their car. I waited for Tucker in the truck. He had the biggest grin on his face.

"Okay, why the grin?"

"She let me kiss her goodnight and I asked her out on Sunday since we won't be playing anywhere and she agreed."

"Good for you. I like her."

It was only eleven, so I called Harper. She didn't answer, so I left a voicemail. I hoped she wasn't out with some other guy. I tossed and turned in bed.

Chapter 45

Pat and I went out to dinner at the Coach-n-Four to celebrate my first sale. It was close to my house, so I didn't get a babysitter. Lizzie could watch her brother for a few hours. We knew the Coach-n-Four for their delicious steaks. We both ordered a filet, baked potato, salad, and a bottle of Merlot. As we ate, Pat went over the next tasks to be done in relation to the condo.

"Your buyers will want an inspection to be safe. You never know what minor issue can kill a deal. We don't need a survey for a condo, or in this case, an appraisal since it's cash. Call Wayne Cole and get the inspection set up for next week."

We enjoyed our steak, and I took my leftovers home to the kids. I was glad it was a few short blocks to home because I felt a little tipsy. I'm not used to three glasses of wine in one sitting. Never mind, it was fun to celebrate and I enjoyed Pat's company.

The kids were asleep by the time I got home and I didn't even wash my face. I fell into bed exhausted from excitement and the hard day's work.

The next morning, I had to remove my make-up. Yikes, it was all over my pillow. I knew I'd better wash my sheets. The kids were watching cartoons, but Sean was clamoring for pancakes. I made bear pancakes for Sean. Hearts for Lizzie and regular ones for me. I cooked bacon too and filled glasses with orange juice. I loved Sundays with my children. We didn't have to rush to do anything.

As I was cleaning up, I saw the red light blinking on my answering machine. It was a message from Cade. I guess I slept through his phone call. I'd call him back later.

"What do you kids want to do today? It's not beach weather. How about we ride our bikes and go play goofy golf up on the highway?"

They both turned away from the television. "Yes!"

"Okay, bring the laundry and put on some bike-riding clothes, plus a light jacket."

We rode through our neighborhood and then took a right up to the highway and the Goofy Golf place. It was one of their favorites and we played for an hour. Lizzie got a hole in one and won a free round of golf next time we were there. Sean was annoyed because he didn't get a hole in one. I ignored his complaining. We rode home and put our bikes in the garage. I told Lizzy to read a book to her brother, and I called Cade.

"Hello, Babe. Missed you last night," he said when he answered. His voice sounded a little odd, could he have been concerned about where I had been?

"Sorry, Pat and I ate at the Coach-n-Four to celebrate my condo sale. We drank a little too much wine. I was sound asleep when you called. What have you and Tucker been doing?"

"We played at Tootsie's Friday and Saturday night. Tucker met a nice girl at the bank and went out with her. She brought her girlfriends to hear us play on Saturday night. He's excited about her."

"That's nice. He needs a girl in his life. The kids and I went bike riding and played goofy golf. We're back now and I'm doing laundry."

"Wish I was there with you. You could wash my clothes too." I laughed. "I'm hanging around the house today too. Just a couple more weeks and you'll be here. I can't wait to give you a kiss and make love to you."

"I'm excited too. I can't wait for you to show me all the places you talk about in Nashville. Please don't talk phone sex. The kids are in the other room and they could walk into my bedroom at any moment."

"You're no fun. Just kidding. I understand. I'll ravish you and talk dirty when you get here. I love you."

"Love you too." I ended the call. Easter weekend couldn't come soon enough.

Chapter 46

The two weeks before Harper was coming to Nashville flew by. We played at Tootsie's again and then at Skull's Rainbow Room. I avoided Boone unless we had to play together. His drug habit was enticing me way too much and I knew Harper would not approve.

Mom let Sawyer skip school on the 22nd so we could record our album. He drove over Thursday after school with his drums, then we went to The Barn, twenty miles outside of Nashville in the town of Mt. Juliet. The real name is Bradley's Barn. It's named after Owen Bradley, who owns it. But we just call it The Barn. At one time, it was a real barn with cattle, horses, and feed. First thing in the morning we got Sawyer's drums set up before we rehearsed all our songs. We would record at three p.m.

"You guys sound great," Bob said. "I can't wait to see the album put together. We'll use photos of Harper on the beach in Destin. That'll make a terrific cover. I think the name of the album needs to be *Green Eyes.*"

"Yes, we all agree that's the best name. Tucker and I are so proud of Sawyer." I tousled his hair and his grin was as wide as his face.

"Thanks, brothers. I can't wait until I can be part of the band. Mom has agreed I can tour with you."

"Let's break for lunch. My treat," Bob said.

We drove to Snow White Drive In with Bob. He pulled up, and we went to the order window before we sat at one of the picnic tables. Everyone ordered hamburgers, all the way, with onion rings and chocolate milkshakes. The car hop brought the food out to us. Those onion rings smelled delicious and the hamburgers were so moist, I had to use several of the napkins on the table. Sawyer was enjoying listening to our chatter. It was all new for him.

We took turns in the outside bathroom. My hands smelled like onions and I didn't want any juice on my guitar when I played. I washed my hands three times to make sure there was no onion smell left and joined the rest of the group in Bob's car before we drove back to The Barn and got ready to record.

I was nervous and felt the need for a swig of Jack. I needed to be upbeat for the recording. I took a bathroom break, locked the stall door, sniffed some coke and knocked back a couple of swigs. I was ready to play.

The recording studio was comprised of one room called the studio, or live room. They had equipped it with microphones and stands for our performance. Sawyer's drums were behind the mics for me and Tucker. In front of us was the control room, where the audio engineers were, along with the record producer. The audio mixing consoles with effect units were behind the glass shield. We were all nervous and had to do a number of takes. It was a long, drawn-out performance and we didn't finish until 8 p.m.

"Whew, that wasn't so easy, I'm exhausted." I rubbed my eyes. "How about you two?"

"Yeah, I'm worn out too," said Tucker.

"I'm not," replied Sawyer. "That was the most exciting thing I've done in my life."

"You're younger than us. Let's go to The Blue Bird Café when Bob drops us off at our apartment," I said.

Bob congratulated us on a great day before he dropped us off at the apartment. When we walked up to my new truck, Sawyer couldn't contain himself. "When did you get that?"

"A couple of weeks ago. Wait until you ride in it." As we drove to the Blue Bird, Sawyer couldn't stop talking about the truck.

It was Friday night and as usual the place was packed with nowhere to sit. We wandered over to the bar. Cindy was working. "Who's the cute guy with you two?" She poured a Jack and water for me and a Budweiser for Tucker. "What will the cute guy have?"

"This is our youngest brother, Sawyer. Give him a root beer. He's not old enough to drink whiskey yet."

"Hello, Sawyer. Nice to meet you," she said as she poured him a root beer. "What have you guys been doing today?"

"We just finished recording our first album at The Barn."

"How exciting. I know it'll be great. Sawyer, I hear you're the songwriter in this family."

"Yes, ma'am."

"Well, I'll make sure I get your album. I love your brothers and am pleased to meet you."

We sat at the bar and listened to a new singer, Kenny Chesney. His boyish face had no facial hair. He had dark, longer hair and hazel eyes; he didn't look any older than Sawyer. I hadn't heard any of his songs, *The Tin Man, Whatever it Takes, and I Finally Found Somebody*. But we agreed his music was entertaining. I paid the bar tab and drove back to the apartment. It had been an exciting day that had whipped us.

The next day, we showed Sawyer around downtown Nashville. The excitement in his eyes was worth the time. We walked down to the river and got tickets to ride the Music City Queen Riverboat down the Cumberland River. The paddle-wheel boat was three stories high and we climbed the stairs to the top floor and enjoyed the scenery along the river.

We took Sawyer to eat at the Belle Meade Cafeteria which had been in business since 1961. We chose meat and two side dishes. I had grilled chicken livers with onions, dressing, greens, toast, and egg custard pie. Tucker chose salad, fish and salmon cakes, fries, dressing, a roll, and chocolate pie. Sawyer had fried chicken breast, creamed corn, a roll, and chocolate cake. There was so much to eat, we wouldn't have to eat supper.

Once we finished our meals and drove home each of us took a nice nap. When I woke it was dark. I looked at my watch. It was nine p.m. When I walked out of the bedroom, my brothers were watching television.

"Hello, sleepyhead," Sawyer said.

"Guess I was tired, and all that good food put me to sleep. Did y'all eat any dinner?"

"Yes, we warmed up that soup you made the other day."

"I'm not hungry. I'll just watch television with you two."

The next morning we said goodbye to Sawyer and he went back to Dunlap. "I've got a geometry test on Monday. I better go home and study," he said.

"Give our love to Mom and Grannie." We both hugged him and he drove away.

Chapter 47

When I got home from the office, Lizzie waved an envelope in front of my face. "Mom, Mom, it's from Cade." She was hopping around the room. I tried to grab it, but she kept hopping away from me.

"Okay. It must be my plane ticket. Do you want to open it?"

"Yes, a letter and a plane ticket." She handed them to me.

I sat at the kitchen table and read the short but sweet letter.

I can't wait to see those green eyes. I'll pick you up at the airport. Love, Cade.

I fixed grilled cheese sandwiches and soup for dinner. Then I reminded the kids that we would be going to Milton Thursday after school, and they would stay through Easter.

"Will the Easter Bunny come to Milton?" asked Sean.

"Of course. He always came when I was little. He'll find you and Lizzie."

"Okay, then I guess I can go."

After the kids were in bed, I called Cade.

"Hello, Babe. Did you get the ticket?"

"I sure did, and it's just a few days away. You won't believe what Sean asked. He wanted to know if the Easter Bunny would come to Milton."

"I'm sure you reassured him."

"I did. What have you been up to?"

Cade told me all about Sawyer coming over to record the album. How good he thought it was going to turn out. How excited he was that I was coming, and that Tucker was going to stay with Mom and Grannie while I was in Nashville.

"-Oh, nice. We can stay in bed all day. But I want you to show me the sights too."

"I will. I'll pick you up at the airport at noon on Friday. Love you."

"Love you back." Just three more days and I would be on that big bird to Nashville. It was going to be difficult to concentrate at work for the next two days.

I dressed in a suit for my closing on 1002 at Sun Destin. As I drove to the title company, I was so excited. It was my first closing. I went in early and Delys Dearmon and Alison Etheridge were waiting for me. They both greeted me and showed me to the boardroom.

Ten minutes later, the Bennetts showed up to sign the buyers' side of the closing. Sue was so excited, her eyes were glistening. Always the calm one, George just sat down. Once the formalities had been completed I handed them the keys and hugged them both. Alison handed them a folder with all the documents inside. I walked out with them and gave them my closing gift. I had found a cute sign that said, *Always have a shell in your pocket and sand in your shoes.*

Joe and June Batson came fifteen minutes later. I greeted them both and introduced them to Delys and Alison. Delys showed them the closing statement for the seller's side. Joe looked it over and agreed it was correct. June told Delys that they would meet her again after the completion of their cottage in six months.

"How wonderful," Delys said. "Is Bob Bonezzi building it for you?"

"Yes," said Joe.

"He's a wonderful builder. You'll be pleased. Thank you for your business, and I look forward to seeing you in the future."

We all shook hands and I walked out with the Batsons. "I'll be in touch throughout the building process. Thank you again for letting Pat and I list your condo."

Alison ran out to catch me at my car. "Wait, Harper. I have your check for the office and the closing papers for your file."

"Oh! I'm sorry. This is my first closing and I didn't know the correct procedure."

"You'll learn. Pat likes her check on the day of closing if the deal is cash."

"Thank you. I appreciate you and Delys making this transaction so smooth."

"You're welcome. We'll see you again."

I grabbed a hamburger from McDonalds' drive through and then went to the office. Pat was working on a new listing. I handed her the folder from the title company. She opened it and grinned at me.

"Congratulations. We make a good team. I'll have the broker process these checks and hopefully you'll get paid before you leave for Nashville," she said.

"Thank you. This has been a great learning experience."

Chapter 48

Harper was flying to Nashville. I showered and shaved, then I bid farewell to Tucker before he left for Dunlap. I inspected the apartment for clothes on the floor, changed my sheets, cleaned the bathroom, and hung up clean towels. There was a bottle of white wine and snacks in the fridge. We could eat eggs, bacon, grits, and toast for breakfast. Oh yes, I remembered to put a pack of Diet Coke in the refrigerator.

As I traveled to the airport ten miles away, *Green Eyes* was playing on the radio of my new truck. I parked and walked in. Nashville's airport is much bigger than the one in Chattanooga. I stood in the hall outside baggage claim and waited for Harper to walk my way. There she was. I ran toward her, grabbed her, and swung her around in my arms.

"Welcome, my love. Hope your flight was good."

"Yes, it was smooth and right on time. My bag should come off the carousel soon."

I took her hand and walked to the baggage claim. I wanted to kiss her but knew it would embarrass her in front of strangers. I picked up her bag and we left the airport. The look on her face was priceless when I opened the door to my new truck.

"What is this? It's gorgeous."

"I wanted to surprise you. Do you like it?"

"Yes, it's stunning. Are we going four-wheeling?"

"Perhaps, but we have lots of other things to do while you're here." I kissed her at length after I'd pulled her close. We held hands all the way to the apartment. We were both quiet, as if we were getting to know each other all over again. I carried her bag up the stairs and opened the bedroom door. Then I couldn't wait any longer. I held her, kissed her neck, her throat, her eyes, and her lips. She moaned with pleasure.

When I removed her silk blouse and skirt and let them fall to the floor. She was wearing a lacy pink bra and panties.

"Wait, this isn't fair." She unbuttoned my shirt and unzipped my jeans. "Step out of those jeans," she said. "Now come here and let me see what's causing that bulge in those boxer shorts."

We were both breathing rapidly when I scooped her up, pushed back the covers and lay her on the clean sheets.

"Oh, I have missed your loving so much. I want to look into your eyes," she said.

"Beautiful Harper, I've wanted to kiss every inch of you for the past few months."

It was every bit as amazing as the first time I made love to her by the lake. At that moment *she* was my addiction. I couldn't get enough of her. It was an energetic session and we both collapsed from exhaustion before we slept.

When we woke, it was five p.m. Oh my! We had slept the afternoon away. "Come here, Babe."

"Give me a moment. I need the bathroom," she said.

When she came back I was already hard. Such was the effect she had on me constantly. And then it happened all over again. Delicious lovemaking with the beautiful woman of my dreams. She called my name over and over before she rolled off me and cuddled up close. I wrapped my arms around her. I had a need to keep her safe. "I love you," I whispered in her ear. *You will never know how much.*

"I love you too and I missed you so so much."

I stroked her hair and kissed her. "This is going to be a wonderful weekend. Would you like to go to The Blue Bird Café, have a hamburger, and listen to some music?"

"That would be wonderful. Can I take a shower and put on fresh clothes before we go?"

"Of course, we have plenty of time. They play late into the night." Harper rose to go to the bathroom. I'd give her a few minutes and then join her.

Chapter 49

As I went into Cade's bathroom, my heart was still pounding. He was a great lover, I couldn't get enough of him. I turned on the shower to warm up as I found my shampoo and conditioner in my make-up bag. As I stepped into the shower, I closed my eyes and let the water wash over my body. Just then I felt Cade slip into the shower and stand close to me.

"Stinker, did you miss me already?" I said.

"Yes, but I promise to behave and just wash you. Which one is your shampoo?"

Cade started washing my hair and it felt so good. Only my beautician had ever done that for me. "That feels wonderful. Don't stop."

Cade laughed at me. He was enjoying it also. Mercy, he was hard again. His appetite was insatiable. It was then that I decided his member needed a name. "Can I call him *Rocky* for being rock hard?" I asked as I looked down at his soapy member.

"Hmmm, that's a good name, but you don't think you're getting out of this shower without *Rocky* playing with *Baby*? Do you?"

"Who's *Baby*?" I asked.

"*Baby* is where your beautiful legs and tummy meet."

I laughed. It was a special moment as we teased each other. "Hmmm, that's a good name for my special place. Come closer, Rocky," I said as I drew him toward me. Being joined to the man I loved was beyond amazing. I loved it that our bodies were becoming tuned to each other.

As we toweled off, I told Cade to get dressed in the other room. I didn't trust Rocky not to get excited again. I dressed in my mid-length slinky green dress. Put on my cowboy boots, finished my make-up, and exited the bathroom. A wolf whistle greeted me.

"You look gorgeous, and that's the perfect outfit for Nashville. I can't wait to show you off at The Blue Bird. Are you ready to go?"

"Yes, handsome, take me anywhere you want." Cade helped me into the truck. It was too high for me to climb up by myself. We drove downtown and I enjoyed the neon lights, the people, and the restaurants lit up at night.

When we arrived at The Blue Bird Café, Cade parked down the street and we walked hand in hand to the café. There was a long line out front.

"Wait here, Babe. I'll slip in and get Amy to let us in." Moments later, he and Amy arrived at the door.

"Hello folks, this is Cade Fox, one of our favorite musicians. So, I'm going to let him and his girlfriend in ahead of you. I'm hoping we can get him to play his number one song, *Green Eyes*."

Cade reached for my hand and drew me inside. "Amy, this is Harper from Fort Walton Beach, Florida."

"Hello, I've heard a lot about you. So glad you could visit us in Nashville. Cade, go get your guitar. I want you to play for Harper in the break."

Cade looked surprised but left to get his guitar. Amy led me to the bar and pulled out a barstool. "What would you like to drink?"

"How about a Cosmo?"

"Good choice. Cindy, this is Harper. Please bring her a Cosmo and put a Jack and water on the bar for Cade. The drinks are on me."

Cade returned and stood behind my barstool.

"Is this who's been keeping you from asking me out?" Cindy said with a twinkle in her eye as she brought our drinks.

"Yes, I presume Amy introduced you two." He slipped his arm around me in a possessive way that let Cindy know I was his girl.

"She did. You're beautiful. Is that song Green Eyes about you?"

"It wasn't when my brother wrote it. But it is now," said Cade. I smiled into his eyes and he gave me a kiss on the forehead. "Can you order us hamburgers and French fries? We're starving."

"Coming right up," Cindy replied.

I was feeling loved and glad to know that Cade wasn't dating Cindy because she was cute as a button. The burgers came and we devoured them. Amy came over and asked Cade if he would play a couple of songs. He picked up his guitar and sat down behind the mike.

"Come with me, I have a seat saved for you at the front," Amy said as she took my hand and showed me where to sit. Cade was strumming his guitar and when he saw me, he announced to the crowd that he would play *Green Eyes* for a special lady in the audience. The crowd looked around, wanting to see who it was. My face heated up and I looked down. I didn't want anyone to see my green eyes. As he played and looked into my eyes, a couple of tears escaped down my cheeks. I dashed them away with my hand.

Cade played *When I saw You* next, then when he'd finished he stood up, reached for my hand and made me stand next to him. The crowd stood up and gave him a big round of applause. It embarrassed me, but Cade looked proud and hugged me tightly. We walked back to the bar where Cindy had drinks waiting for us.

"Great job. Has Harper heard you play before?" Amy said.

"Yes, at the Boat House in Destin. However, she wasn't impressed, and she left before the set was over. It took some doing to get her to go to the Rodeo dinner with me."

I blushed and Amy laughed. "I guess it worked. She's here with you now."

We finished our drinks and I yawned.

"Are you worn out? Ready to go home?" Cade asked me.

"Yes, please take me home. I need to sleep."

Chapter 50

Nothing felt better than waking up with Harper beside me. I lay there watching her sleep. She must have been dreaming as her eyelashes were fluttering. I stroked her face to wake her up gently. Her eyes opened and shut until she was wide awake. "Good morning, my love."

"Good morning to you too. Did you sleep well?" she said.

"Like the dead. Shall I make you some coffee? I have frozen biscuits that Grannie sent and homemade strawberry jam."

"Mmmm, that sounds delicious. Can I take a shower while you fix breakfast?"

"Okay." I left to start the coffee and breakfast and take a swig from my flask. I ate a piece of bacon, so Harper wouldn't smell alcohol on my breath. I wondered if she would like to go to the park and walk across the pedestrian bridge and I could show her around downtown. Harper came out wrapped in her bathrobe with a towel around her hair. That woman looked gorgeous just like that. I didn't know why she bothered with make-up. I served her coffee while the biscuits were baking, then I set the table. "You're going to love the strawberry jam. Mom buys it at the local grocery store. It's made in Dunlap."

"Wonderful coffee. I slept well too. Thanks for bringing me home early. I loved hearing you play. It's obvious that Amy likes your singing too, and the crowd adored you. I can't wait to hear the album."

We ate breakfast, then I told Harper I had a surprise for her. I went into my cabinet under the TV and pulled out the finished album. When I held it up, Harper gasped.

"Oh my God! Is that me on the cover?"

"Yes, I wanted to surprise you. We all voted and decided on this one of you by the water with your hair blowing in the wind. Do you like it?"

"Oh, yes. It's wonderful. Can you play it on your record player for me?"

I put it on to play and took her hand. "Sit on the couch with me." We held hands and listened to the whole album. Neither of us said a word and when the album ended, Harper kissed me so passionately it took my breath away.

"The album is wonderful. Sawyer has written some amazing songs and y'all played them so well. I'm honored you have me on the cover."

"I want you to take this home with you. Play it often, show it to your girlfriends and your parents. I love you, Harper, and want us to be together one day."

"Oh, Cade, that is so sweet. I love you too."

"Would you like to walk downtown on Broadway, visit the shops and then go on a walk across the river on the pedestrian bridge?"

"That would be fun. I'll get dressed."

We drove downtown and parked on 5th street. I took her hand and turned left at the corner to Broadway. I explained that Broadway was the major road running from the south-west to the north-east through the heart of downtown. It extended from 21st Avenue south to First Avenue and connected neighborhoods such as the Gulch and Music Row with the Cumberland River waterfront. I had never seen a city with so many neon and bright lights. It was exciting and I was proud to live there.

"It's nice they mark the streets east to west. At home ours are north and south and end at the Gulf of Mexico," she said. "This is an interesting city. Much larger than Pensacola, which I'm used to. What are the banners on the light poles for?"

"They call this the District. It links Second Avenue, Broadway and Printer's Alley. Nashville is trying to attract more tourists now that country music is popular." We walked past Jacks, Stags, and the Nashville Store. "Want to go in and buy a souvenir?"

"Oh yes, I want to get the kids a T-shirt each."

"Here's some with guitars on them. Sean wants to learn. Let's get him one of these. What would Lizzie want?"

"Look! Here's one with Dolly Parton on the front. She'd love this."

I took them both to the counter and bought them. When Harper protested I shushed her. "Let me treat them. They let their mama come to see me. It's the least I can do."

"Thank you. I'll make sure they know you bought the T-shirts."

We walked over to Rhinestone Western wear just off 5th Street behind the Ryman Auditorium. Harper rolled her eyes.

"I've never seen so many clothes with rhinestones in my life. They look so heavy. How do the music stars wear them?" she said.

"I don't know. They must be hot under the lights when they're performing. I'm glad we don't have to dress up. Do you want a fancy western shirt?"

"I don't think so, but thanks for asking. I think you should get one for when you're famous." Harper laughed.

"Let's hope they're out of style by then." I hugged her tightly. *Maybe we should go home and get into bed. Better not, I want to show Harper more downtown.* "Let's get something to snack on at Tootsie's and have a drink. It's right down the street."

"Oh my! It really is painted orchid. Did you say a man owns it?"

"Yes, Steve Smith, I'll introduce you. We've played here a few times. He draws a large crowd. In the early 1990s, Steve Smith and a partner bought Tootsie's Orchid Lounge after Hattie Louise 'Tootsie' Bess died. He and his partner bought it for under $10,000, despite warnings about crime in the area. The area is improving, but there's a pawn shop nearby."

Steve was standing at the bar having a beer. "Hello, Steve, I want you to meet my girlfriend, Harper from Florida." Steve was a large man in his thirties with a short beard and a mustache and he always wore a golfer's hat and sunglasses. He was always ready with a manly handshake. Steve turned around.

"Hello Harper. Welcome to Tootsie's. We love to have Cade and his brother play here. Would you like something to drink?"

"I'll have a Jack and water and Harper likes Cosmos. I'm glad she could meet you."

"Well, it's my pleasure."

"Would you give Harper a brief history of the bar while I hit the bathroom?" I asked Steve.

"I'd love to. Well, it all started with Tootsie Bess taking care of the artists," Steve began. "Tootsie Bess bought the bar—originally named Mom's—in 1960, and for the next fourteen years, the lounge was in a position to accommodate several up-and-coming stars who appeared on the Grand Ole Opry. At the time, the Opry was only an alleyway away. The Ryman Auditorium behind Tootsie's Orchid Lounge was home to the

Grand Ole Opry from 1943 to 1974, before it was moved to the Opryland complex. However, there wasn't a lot of room backstage, so performers headed to Tootsie's before and after shows. They sat upstairs at Tootsie's, to drink and hang out, swap music and pick guitars. And Tootsie ran a tab for every one of them. Whenever they had a hit and they made a little money, they would square up with her.

"Tootsie Bess, who sang in her husband's band, Big Jeff & The Radio Playboys, was known for her generosity toward other musicians. It was said that she had a cigar box behind the counter full of IOU's, which Opry performers would pay at the end of the year so she wouldn't lose money.

"And they worked around there. Willie Nelson and Kris Kristofferson were known to sweep and mop the floors and help pay their bar tab in other ways. In fact, it was a couple of painters who owed money on their bar tabs who gave the bar its name. Tootsie Bess offered to *call the tab* even if they painted the building, but when asked what color, she said, 'Whatever you can come up with'. They painted it, she went down there the next day, looked at it and said, 'Oh my gosh. It's Tootsie's Orchid Lounge now'. That's how she named it.

"Roger Miller was rumored to have written *Dang Me* in Tootsie's, and Hank Cochran, Waylon Jennings and Patsy Cline are just some of the other well-known performers to have spent time there. Dolly Parton and Loretta Lynn also sang for crowds at Tootsie's, which was a filming location for the 1980 biographical film *Coal Miner's Daughter,* which told the story of Lynn's life, from her early teen years to her rise as a country artist.

"What has come to be known as *Tootsie's Wall of Fame* still contains many of their photos. As the years have gone by, we've added several new photos to the wall, but there was a time when the future of Tootsie's looked grim. By the 1990s, Broadway had taken a real turn for the worse. They boarded up businesses and only a few customers were coming through the door. Tootsie Bess had passed away about a decade earlier, and the beloved honky-tonk was in danger of closing. When we bought it, there was a 200-watt light bulb hanging in the center of the room and you could smell the bathrooms from the street. They were doing about $500 a day. Homeless people were sleeping on mattresses and cots in the backroom. As you can see, we've revamped downtown, and we're proud to be part of the restoration. If you two will excuse me, I have a business appointment upstairs," Steve said as he stood up and left in a hurry.

"That's an interesting history," I said to Cade. "I sure am glad downtown is getting better and hopefully safer. I know you must leave late after playing your gigs."

"Don't worry, we're careful and park behind the bar and I have a pistol in my glove compartment. Would you like to eat here? They have good sandwiches."

"Fine with me. Whatever you want. I'd love a good grilled cheese sandwich with French fries and a Diet Coke."

I ordered our food and another Jack and water. I'd cut down on my drinking and other activities since Harper's arrival. We ate, paid the bill, and walked down to Riverfront Park where I guided Harper to a bench. We sat and I put my arm around her. We were both full and just enjoyed the March sun and the glistening water on the Cumberland River.

"Would you like to go to a fine dining restaurant tonight?"

"Not really. Let's go home to make love and then decide if we're hungry."

"I can't think of anything else I'd rather do." I held Harper's hand, and we walked back to the truck.

Chapter 51

As we drove back to Cade's apartment my heart was full of love for him. What an enjoyable day. I dreaded going home the next day. The weekend had gone by so fast. We raced up the stairs and Cade threw his arms around me.

"Alone at last." He opened the door and we ran for the bed, stripping off our clothes as we went. "Wait, I want to take that red bra and panties off you. They're my favorites."

We tumbled onto the bed and I admired his tattoos and the well-defined muscles on his arms. It was then that I began to tingle deep down inside. Making love with Cade was beyond compare. At that moment I began to believe he was the love of my life. The thought scared me and I tried to calm my thumping heart. Cade was lying on his back, smiling. He took my hand and held it. We lay close together for several minutes. As soon as we climbed under the bed clothes, my eyes closed and I fell asleep immediately.

When I woke a few hours later, Cade was snoring quietly. It was still dark outside. I got up and sneaked into the bathroom. A quick shower would revive me. No sooner had I wet my body when Cade joined me. Rocky was hard as a rock again, but this time Cade just held me gently and hummed *Green Eyes* as the water flowed over us. It was a superb romantic moment in the half-light before dawn—one I would never forget. We stepped out of the shower, and once we were dry Cade bought me my robe.

"Are you hungry, Babe?" he asked.

"Do you have any ice cream and chocolate cookies?"

"I do. I'll fix us a bowl. You dry your hair and come to the living room when you're ready."

Cade had a Garth Brooks album playing on the stereo and the ice cream and cookies were on the coffee table. "Yum, this will hit the spot." We sat together and enjoyed our dessert. As soon as our bowls were empty Cade appeared with two snifters of Grand Marnier.

"A toast to us and a fabulous weekend." We clinked glasses, then I took a sip.

"That warms me right to my core." It felt good. I took another sip, and another until it was almost gone. Cade took the glass out of my hand and we sat there with our arms around each other.

"Look what you do to me," he said.

When I looked at his boxer shorts, *you know who* had found his way out. I laughed and punched him lightly on the arm.

"I want to continue living in this apartment indefinitely," I said.

"We will someday. Let's go back to bed."

Chapter 52

Today was going to be a tough day. I hated saying goodbye to Harper. I wanted a drink, but I knew she would smell it on my breath. She was already up and packing her suitcase. She turned and smiled at me with those gorgeous green eyes.

"Good morning. Did you sleep well? I sure did," she said.

"Yes, would you like to go out for breakfast before I take you to the airport? I know a cute place nearby."

"That'd be nice. I made some coffee already. I'll get you a cup."

"No, I need to get up. Give me a minute and I'll join you."

As we drank our coffee, I knew I'd thought of the perfect place to take Harper. "I'm going to take you to The Loveless Café, you'll love it."

We both got ready, and I put Harper's suitcase in the truck. We could go to the café and then on to the airport. Her flight was at 2 p.m.

The restaurant was packed. After parking behind the café, I helped Harper out of my truck and we wandered hand in hand to the café. As we walked in, the hostess spoke to me. "Aren't you Cade Fox? I saw you play at The Blue Bird Café."

"Yes, I am. This is my girlfriend, Harper."

"How cool is that? Let me put down your name. As you can see, we have a full house. Take her to the shops in the old motel while you wait. Check back with me in thirty minutes."

"Come on, Babe, you'll love their barn. It used to be a motel as you can see by the sign. It sells lots of goodies and they have a catalog business too. You might want to take home some biscuit mix and jam."

"This is such a neat place. I love that they saved the buildings and are reinventing them. Oh, look blackberry jam, my favorite. I must get some. My kids will love the biscuit mix. I wonder if they're as good as your Grannies?"

"We'll find out when we eat. Let me buy those for you."

"Cade! You spoil me."

"That's what I want to do. Having you here is the best thing that's happened to me since Thanksgiving." I pulled Harper close and kissed her. I could tell it embarrassed her when people stared at us.

The restaurant still had that old country cooking feel with red and white checked tablecloths and I could smell the bacon sizzling. The cute hostess, with her hair in braids and freckles on her nose, seated us at a small table for two. "Your server will be right with you. Please, could you autograph this menu? I know you're going to be famous soon," she said to Cade.

"You're the first person to ask for my autograph. I'd love to sign it. Our first album *Green Eyes* is going to be for sale soon."

"Oh goodie," she squealed. "I'll definitely buy it. I love that song."

Harper gave me a pat on my back. "You're on your way, my love."

We ordered scrambled eggs, biscuits and bacon, along with sweet tea. We both ate like we hadn't eaten in days.

"That food was delicious," she said. "The biscuits were almost as good as your Grannie's. I love the blackberry jam and I'm glad you bought me some to take home."

We left and drove toward the airport, which was about twenty-seven minutes away. There was an hour or so before Harper's flight and as we drove north on Highway 251, I looked for a country road to turn off on and I found one.

"Want to go four-wheeling? This new truck can go anywhere."

"Sure, that'd be fun."

I turned north-west on a dirt road, put the truck into 4-wheel drive, found a steep hill and off we went. When Harper held on for dear life, I laughed. At a spot under a big oak tree, I pulled her toward me and kissed her. I remembered the time we made love in my old truck when I took her to the Chattanooga airport. It was time to christen the new one.

"Cade, you're torturing me."

I pulled town my boots and jeans and boxers in such a hurry. I couldn't get enough of her and yet again she called my name as we reached the height of our passion.

"You're a naughty boy. Look how wrinkled my skirt is?"

"No one will notice. It'll straighten out and you can always blame it on the seat belt squeezing you when you meet your parents. We better get going." There was just enough time to catch her plane. Harper was quiet, and so was I. As we pulled into the airport, she wiped her eyes. I took her bag out of the truck bed and opened her door. She hugged me tight and tears cascaded down her face.

"Don't cry, sweetheart. I'll see you again before the tour is over."

"Sorry. I loved being with you and now it's back to my normal life. I'm going in now. Bye." She walked away trundling her bag behind her. At the airport entrance, she turned and blew me a kiss. I drove down the road and watched the plane leave then headed for my apartment.

Tucker wasn't back from Mom's yet, so I poured myself a double Jack and water and found the little packet of cocaine Richard had sold me. Just a little something to keep me from being depressed.

Chapter 53

The plane trip was only an hour to Pensacola. When I walked to baggage claim, everyone was there waiting for me. The kids hugged me tight, and Mom and Dad were next.

"Did you bring us anything?" Sean said.

"Sure, but I can't open my suitcase until we get to the house. What have you done this weekend?"

"Papa took me horseback riding again," Lizzie said. "He let me ride the black one who was spunkier than the horse I rode last time."

"Nana took me to the movies while Lizzie was horseback riding. We saw *Ernest Scared Stupid.* Ernest unleashed an evil troll upon a small town on Halloween night and helped the local children fight back. Nana laughed a lot during the movie, and I ate popcorn."

"I'm glad you had so much fun. One day I want to go horseback riding with you. I'm afraid we can't stay the night in Milton as you have school tomorrow. We'll have to leave soon. Have you had lunch?"

"Yes, we took them to Woolworth's and sat at the counter. They had hot dogs, fries, and milkshakes," Mom said.

"What fun! I loved it when you took me there, Mom. Thank you both for having the children. I had a wonderful time in Nashville. Cade took me to all the famous places. I'll tell you all about it on the ride back to Milton." I told them all about the fun things Cade and I did. We arrived back in Milton and put the kids' suitcases in my Chevette. I kissed my parents goodbye before we drove down Highway 87 to Navarre. The trees were still bare and there was no sign of spring yet as we drove to Fort Walton Beach. It was nice to be home even though I knew I would miss Cade.

We ate cheese sandwiches with a can of Campbells chicken and rice soup for dinner. The kids took their baths and I tucked them into bed. Sean wanted me to read a book, so I did, but he fell asleep before I finished. Lizzie was reading Black Beauty. She had the horse bug. One day, I would take them to Chattanooga and let her ride Satan. She was good enough to handle him.

It was back to normal on Monday. Breakfast, lunches made, and the kids off to school. When I drove to the office Pat was already there.

"Hey, girl. Did you have fun?"

"I did. Cade showed me all the famous spots. Nashville is so different. It has its own vibe. Music is everywhere you go. He took me four-wheeling in his new black truck on our way back to the airport and he gave me a copy of their first album." I held it out to show her.

"Is that you on the cover?"

"Yes, David Shea took the photo. The boys surprised me and used this one on the cover."

"It's gorgeous. Tell me when they're available. I want one."

"Okay. So, what's on today's calendar?"

"I have a new listing for you to put into the computer. Then we're going out to Crystal Beach to view the town homes Bob Bonezzi is building. He's calling them Green Reef and I want to buy one."

"Okay, I'll get started on the listing."

As we drove in Pat's car to Destin, her mouth was downturned and her expression was bleak. The usual gleam in her eyes was gone. "What's wrong? Can I help?"

She sighed. "My husband cheated on me again while you were gone. It's usually with a flight attendant, but this time, it was one of our neighbors. She kept stopping by the house we were building in Indian Bayou and he told me she was trying to sell him insurance. He already has plenty of life insurance."

"I'm sorry. I understand how being cheated on feels. Michael cheated on me from the time we moved to Tallahassee until I divorced him ten years later."

"Well, I'm sick of it. Our son is graduating from high school this year and going to college, so it's time for me to live my life without his father. That's one reason we're going to see the town home on the beach. I want one. He can figure out what to do with our family house."

"Who are you going to use as a divorce attorney?"

"Don Dewrell is the best one in Fort Walton Beach. He won't let my husband get away with hiding any assets. I make enough money selling real estate, so with some from him, I should be fine financially."

"One of my best friends, Anna, works for Don. Have you met her?"

"Yes, she's a cutie with those big brown eyes and she has a lovely outgoing personality. How do you know her?"

"I met her on one of my first dates with Michael back in 1965. She was married to Johnny, one of Michael's friends. We became closer when Michael and I moved to Fort Walton Beach. She has two boys. One is Lizzie's age and the younger one is two years older. She lives in Indian Bayou too. When Johnny cheated on her she got divorced. Don was her attorney, and then she went to work for him."

"Wow! What a great location. Wish I could have one of these," I said when we arrived at Green Reef.

"You will one day. Keep working hard. You know I've been doing real estate since I was twenty-one. There's Bob. Let's walk through the town homes with him."

I remembered meeting Bob with his dark brown eyes and squarish jaw when we were in Liollio's.

"Hi, girls. Are you here to view the town homes? The first five are almost ready to sell. Come on, let me show you."

Pat took the lead and I followed. She and Bob talked about the construction, the finishes, and appliances while I listened and learned. They had four bedrooms, two bathrooms and two stories and the Gulf views were spectacular. And I just loved the huge soaking tub with a window overlooking the beach on the second floor off the master bedroom.

"I want one of these for myself," Pat said to Bob.

"As an investment? You have a gorgeous house on the bay."

"Just put my name on one. I'll explain later. I'll draw up the contract when I get back to the office. Are you ready to list the other four?"

"I will be next week. Get the paperwork ready. Let me finish and clean everything before you list them."

As we left to go back to the office, I could tell Pat was excited about the town home.

"That makes my decision final. I'm going to divorce my husband and move to the beach. I can just see myself walking on the beach and drinking wine in the tub. Although I might have to wait until my divorce is final to close. Anyway, I'm going to see Don Dewrell tomorrow."

I completed the listing paperwork for the town homes and Pat wrote herself a contract on number three. She was a determined woman. I couldn't blame her, there is nothing worse than a cheating husband. I remember the time I saw her husband on a payphone at the Junior Store, just a block away from her home. Something triggered in my mind and I knew he must have been cheating on her. He was a good-looking airline pilot who must have been well paid, so why would he be on a payphone?

I thought about the time in Marianna when Michael called and asked me to put his golf clubs on the Greyhound Bus to Pensacola. He wanted to play golf with his friends in the liquor business. I was a dutiful wife and as I reached into the side pocket for the head cover a bundle of letters fell out. I grabbed them, put them in my purse and shipped the golf clubs. When I got in my car, I read the lot. He was having an affair with a teacher in Atlanta, and he had a private post office box where she sent him letters. I was enraged and immediately drove back to the bank and banged on the back door.

My boss opened it. "What on earth?" he said.

"Let me in," I said to him. "Look at these letters from another woman. Michael's been cheating on me. I need a safe deposit box and we need to transfer my last paycheck to a different account."

"Slow down. We can do this in the morning. I can't get into the vault tonight. Put them in your desk and calm down."

"Calm down! How am I supposed to calm down? He's been cheating on me since we got married. Can you get me a bank job in Tallahassee? I'm going to divorce him and move there."

Michael knew I had found the letters when he his golf clubs arrived in Pensacola. He called and called. I refused to answer. Then he came back to Marianna and begged me not to get a divorce; he cried and pleaded with me to let him stay. I gave in. The rest is history. It took me ten years to feel confident enough to leave him.

Chapter 54

Tucker and I met Gus at the tour bus on April the 12th. Richard, of course, was almost late. He came dragging up, looking like death warmed up. He must have really been into the coke while he was in Nashville. Coke doesn't make you look ten years older in a month. His skin looked gray and his eye sockets were dark. His hair was long enough to put in a ponytail. I wondered if he was doing other drugs.

"Boys, I hope you had a wonderful month off. Come on! It's time we hit the road." Gus was driving us out west to Texas, Washington, Oregon, and California.

"Cade and Tucker, I heard you cut your album. Proud of you two. Richard, you look rough. What was your vacation like?"

"Nothin' special. Hung out, played music."

The months of April and May flew by. We played Bell Country Expo Center, Tacoma Dome, McArthur Court, Pacific Coliseum, then back to Oregon to Portland Memorial Coliseum, Yakima Valley SunDome and Spokane Coliseum. It was darn cold in all those places. Our sheepskin coats, gloves, and boots kept us warm. Tucker and I called home twice. Mom said Grannie was taking the winter weather hard and she sat in front of the fire all the time. We told Mom we would fly home for Sawyer's graduation. Our break was between May 27 and June 14. She told us Sawyer's graduation would be on Thursday, May 30, 1991. I called Harper several times. There wasn't much to tell her, except that I loved and missed her.

The old hotel rooms were chilly and damp. I knew I'd be glad when it warmed up. Gus drove us to Boise, Idaho, Salt Lake City, Utah, Missoula, Montana, Casper, Wyoming, Rapid City and South Dakota. Ten states in less than a month. We liked Casper Events in Casper, Wyoming. They had built the arena in April 1982. It seated 8,395 for ice hockey and indoor football games, plus 8,842 for basketball games, and up to 9,700 for concerts. It had a large stage and was warm inside. The crowd cheered us as we finished our songs and went wild as Garth took the stage. We finished up in Oklahoma City at the Myriad Convention Center on May 26. We booked a flight home to Chattanooga at Will Rogers World Airport. It would take Gus two days to drive back to Nashville from Oklahoma City and we needed to be home for Sawyer's graduation. The tour would continue on June 14. It would be nice to have a break. We hoped Mom would let Sawyer come with us on tour.

Sawyer picked us up at the Chattanooga Airport at 3 p.m. When I saw him waiting in baggage claim, I swear he had grown five inches. He was as tall as me. We both hugged him. He was glad to see us and picked up my bag before we got into Mom's car. I let Tucker sit up front, and I stretched out in the back seat. When he pulled in the gate and parked in front of the house Dog came running out along with Mom. Grannie was in the kitchen fixing fried chicken, vegetables, and cornbread for dinner. I walked into the house and put my arms around Grannie and hugged her. Mom made us tea and we sat in the kitchen where we were surrounded by the smells of chicken frying and cornbread baking. Mom got up to serve us and had Grannie sit down.

"Lord, it's good to see you two. You look tired. Are you okay?" asked Grannie.

"Yeah, we just play late at the venues. It takes an hour to unwind, and we sleep in uncomfortable single beds with lumpy mattresses," I said. "We miss your cooking something fierce."

"We sure do," said Tucker. "We miss all three of you and Dog." Dog perked up at the mention of his name and lay his head on Tucker's lap. Tucker had been slipping him pieces of fried chicken. As always, the dinner was delicious.

"Go sit in the living room with Grannie while Sawyer and I put the dishes in the sink to soak. I'll do them later," Mom said.

We cuddled up to Grannie on the sofa. "Are you okay?" I asked Grannie.

"I could be better. This winter has got my bones hurtin', and my arthritis is acting up. I guess I'm getting old."

I had our album on the coffee table, ready to surprise Mom.

"Oh, my God! Is that your album?" Mom shrieked. She picked it up and couldn't take her eyes off it as she ran her fingers over Harper's photo on the cover. "She looks stunning. Has it been released?"

"Not yet, next month. They gave us four copies."

"Well, it's wonderful. I am so proud of all three of you." She put it carefully back on the table with seeming reluctance and told Sawyer to go get his ukulele and play his new song for us. He surprised us with *No Fun Being a Traveling Man,* a fast melody that mentioned long roads to nowhere, playing in saloons, and losing at cards. It had a great beat and would be an excellent song.

"Nice one, Sawyer," I said and Tucker nodded.

We played Grannie's favorites for the next hour, then she surprised us and went to bed early.

"Is Grannie okay?" I whispered to Mom.

"I'm not sure. She refused to see the doctor despite her failing heart. She's tired, can't catch her breath and goes to bed early every night."

"That's not good news. I pray nothing happens to her while we're away on tour."

Tucker and I said goodnight too. The tour was tiring and the plane trip was tiring. And I wanted to ride Satan the next day.

I was up early and took carrots out to the barn. Dog followed me and both horses nickered when they saw me open the barn door.

"Good morning, Satan and Suzie. I sure have missed you." I rubbed their muzzles and fed them the carrots. "Satan, you want to go for a ride?" I was sure he did because he pawed at the door and did a little dance in the stall. I put on his bridle and then his saddle. He could hardly contain his excitement. I led him into the pasture and opened the gate. Once I was on his back, we took off with Dog following us. We slowed to a trot as we approached the big oak tree and the lake where Harper and I made love for the first time. I slipped off Satan and led him down to the lake for a drink. I sat on the ground and enjoyed the breeze off the lake, the rustling leaves and the peace. Dog was panting and drank from the lake before he lay in the shade. I dialed Harper on my cell phone.

"Guess where I am?" I said as soon as she answered.

"I don't know. You move around so much. Tell me."

"I'm at the lake where we first made love. Tucker and I flew home for Sawyer's graduation. I've just ridden Satan out to the lake before everyone wakes. If only you were here beside me."

"I'm so glad you made it home for Sawyer's graduation. How are your mom and Grannie?"

"Mom is great. Grannie not so good. Mom thinks her heart could give out."

"Oh no! Y'all love her so much. I hope she'll go to the doctor."

"Mom has tried. She might be ready to call it *a life*."

"I'm sorry, I hope she'll be okay. She's such a lovely lady. Listen, I'm afraid I have to go to work now or I'll be late. Please give everyone a hug and send my love to your family. Wish I was there. Don't forget I love you."

"I love you too."

I was feeling stressed, and there was nothing for it but to take out my little packet of cocaine. I couldn't drink at Mom's house, but she wouldn't know what I had in my pocket for a pick me up.

We spent the next two days getting Sawyer a new suit, shoes, and a tie in a men's store in downtown Dunlap. Graduation was in the high school gym at 5 p.m. on Thursday the 30th. Sawyer drove there earlier; I let him drive my new truck. The rest of us went in Mom's car and I sat in the front. There were seventeen graduates and Mom took photos as Sawyer threw his hat high in the air at the end of the ceremony. Then we drove to our favorite barbecue restaurant for a celebration dinner. The rest of the graduation group and their families must have had the same idea because the place was packed and everyone was in a lively mood.

Not long after we sat down, I asked Mom if Sawyer could join us on tour. Her reaction was not good and there was a scowl on her face.

"No. Let Sawyer work this summer and save his money for a truck. He can join you on the weekend when you're in Nashville. I don't want him on the road yet. He's just turned eighteen and that's too young. Sorry," she said in a firm voice. I knew there was no arguing with her. When she made up that mind of hers, you didn't challenge her decision and she was probably right.

"I'm saving my money for a truck like Cade's," Tucker said to Mom. "When I buy one, I'll let Sawyer have the one Cade gave me."

"We'll be back in Nashville in October and December. Please let him come to play with us then. The tour will be over," I added.

"We'll see," she said.

Chapter 55

When I went with Pat to Don Dewrell's office, Anna greeted us and introduced us to Lee, Lloyd Blue's paralegal. Lee was our age and raising her children by herself too. She had lovely brown eyes and long, brown hair. Her beautiful, wide smile made you want to know her better.

Pat went into the office with Don, and I stayed in reception and chatted with Anna. I filled her in on Pat's cheating husband.

"I guess they all cheated, Michael, Johnny, her husband, and Lee's ex-husband. Don will fix Pat up good. We should all go out for a drink this evening," Anna said.

"That would be fun. Where should we meet?"

"There's a great little bar behind Staff's Restaurant that most people don't know about. Meet us there at 5:30."

"Okay, I'll tell Pat."

Pat came out smiling, and Don came out to say hello. Don had a way with all women. He was tall, had sandy hair, wore a white shirt, blue dress pants, a belt with a huge gold horse buckle and ostrich cowboy boots. His southern voice was commanding and everyone said he was amazing in court, not only with divorces but criminal cases too.

"Well hello, Harper. Good to see you. That was a grand Christmas party the bank threw."

"Yes, it was, thank you. Glad you enjoyed it. Guess what? Pat is teaching me about real estate. I'm a realtor now." I couldn't wait to give him my news.

"You couldn't have a better teacher and I know you'll be great."

"Thanks. It's good to see you."

We left and since we were downtown, we went to lunch at Joe and Eddie's Restaurant. It was open twenty-four hours a day, seven days a week, and many a late night of revelry concluded there with a plateful of eggs and lots of black coffee.

Pat ordered fried chicken, lima beans, cornbread, and sweet tea. I was hungry for a Mother Tom omelet with hashbrowns, biscuits and sweet tea. Good ole southern cooking was their specialty.

"Anna has invited us to meet her and Lee after work at the bar behind Staff's. Would you like to go?"

"Yes, that sounds like fun. I could use some laughs and a drink. My husband is going to be in for a surprise when Don gets through with him."

"I was stupid not to use Don, but Michael said he'd kill me if I used him for my divorce. If I had, I could still have been living in our house on Pocahontas. Instead, I had to sell it and split everything with that jerk. My attorney warned me, but I was trying to be fair and I never thought he wouldn't pay me child support."

We went back to the office and worked on details for Pat's closing that was coming soon. Then we freshened our make-up and drove to the bar where the girls were already waiting for us. It was dark, but the name outside was clearly visible: Docie's Dock. The sign said it was the oldest bar in Fort Walton Beach. There were a few business executives drinking at the bar. I knew them from my bank days. The girls were at a table in the corner.

"We're glad you could join us," Anna said. "Pat, this is Lee. She works for Lloyd Blue in our office."

"Nice to meet you, Lee," Pat said. "What are you girls drinking? I'm a little out of practice."

"We are having Cosmos. Vodka and cranberry juice with a twist of lemon."

"Sounds good. I'll get us a couple," I said and went to the bar.

When I got back to the table, Pat was filling them in on why she was divorcing her husband. Anna gave her a brief history of her divorce and Lee chimed in to. We made Pat laugh and decided we were the best detectives in town. We had all caught our husbands, who were too stupid to get away with their antics.

"We should start a part-time detective agency and call ourselves The Catch Cheaters Detective Agency. We'd make a fortune," I said.

"I'd love to do that on the weekends," said Lee.

"Me too," Anna said.

"Me three," I replied.

"I'm too busy with real estate, but I'll support you girls. You can work out of my office on the weekends," Pat said and laughed.

We shook hands and ordered another round of cosmos. All too soon I had to get home to the kids and fix supper. Nothing fancy, hot dogs and macaroni and cheese.

That night, I dreamed I was in dark clothes, driving around, catching cheating husbands for my clients.

Chapter 56

Gus drove us to Noblesville, Indiana, where we wouldn't be playing, because Trisha Yearwood was the opening act for Garth. She was a new country artist who was talented, attractive, gracious, and humble. The show began at eight and Trisha played a forty-minute set. There was a set change and Garth went on stage at nine and played a seventy-five-minute set. When he played *Friends in Low Places,* the audience of 8,000 went crazy. Then he said he would be available to meet and greet after the show. He asked those who wanted to see him to step to their right and line up and be kind to each other. The show ended at 10:15 and so many people got in line. Fortunately, the crowd was patient and orderly. They had set up a table with a chair for Garth so he could sign autographs and shake hands. Tucker helped keep the line in order. Meanwhile, Richard and I had snuck back into the bus where we smoked some weed, did a few lines of coke, and drank. By the time Tucker joined us we had passed out. He shook me hard.

"What the hell have you been doing? We're leaving for Fort Payne, Alabama."

I mumbled something and went back to sleep. Gus drove us down Highway 65 through Louisville, Nashville, and Chattanooga. We were so close to Mom and Grannie it would have been nice to get off the bus. I slept the whole eight hours and woke up just before Fort Payne, Alabama, just in time to see the beautiful views and waterfalls between Lookout Mountain and Fort Payne.

By 1991, the June Jam event was bringing 67,000 fans to Fort Payne, which resulted in one of the most well-attended country music events across the nation. The event made over $15 million for charities and had performances by popular artists such as Dolly Parton, Garth Brooks, and Willie Nelson. There were fifteen gigs that Saturday in June and we got to be back up for Garth. I cleaned up my act for June Jam. We played outside, and I didn't need drinking or drugging. Tucker gave me an odd look when I showed up to play.

"I'm okay," I said.

"I hope so. I don't know what the hell you're doing to yourself? You're drinking too much, not sleeping and I think you're buying cocaine from Boone."

"Bullshit, you don't know anything about what I'm doing."

"I'm your brother for God's sake. You don't think I can tell what you're doing? Mom has already asked me what you're up to and she's worried sick. You need to stay away from Boone and his extra-curricular activities."

"Oh, so now you're blaming Boone. Shut the fuck up!" I walked away. The last thing I needed was an argument with my brother. I knew I had better try to stay clean.

It was ninety degrees when it was our turn to play and I could smell the alcohol dripping out of my pores. My head was pounding with a big headache. It served me right for what I got up to the other night. I needed to stay away from Richard, but the question was, could I?

Gus drove us back to Chattanooga, and Mom picked us up at the bus station. We spent a few days with her and Grannie before we had to leave for California. Sawyer had written more songs. We jammed on the porch, ate good food, and I rode Satan several times. I needed to get back to being myself. I couldn't believe I was getting hooked on cocaine.

"Can we take Sawyer with us to California? Let it be his graduation present. He can fly back on July 1st," I asked Mom at breakfast one morning.

"Please, Mom?" Sawyer said. "I'd really like to see California and it would be good for me to watch Garth Brooks perform and I could write more songs."

I could tell Mom was thinking it over as was evidenced by her pensive expression and wrinkled brow. "Okay, you're right, he should go."

All three of us jumped up and hugged Mom. Grannie laughed at us.

"I agree he should see the Pacific Ocean and the mountains of California," Grannie said.

I called Harper that night. "Hello sweetheart. Guess what?"

"I don't know."

"Mom is letting Sawyer come to California with us on the bus. He'll fly back on June the 30th."

"How exciting for him. I'm glad. Wish I could go."

"I wish you could too. We're halfway through the tour. It'll end in November.

"How's real estate?"

"I sold another cottage last week. It was exciting and should be a good commission."

"Good for you. I'm glad you're enjoying it."

"Yes, there's something new every day. When are you leaving Dunlap?"

"Tomorrow. We need to get back to the apartment and get ready to leave on the bus. Mom has washed all our clothes, but we need some cooler ones for the next few months ... I love you."

"I love you too. Have fun out there."

Before we left the next morning, I walked to the barn and gave Satan and Susie carrots. I knew Mom would feed and take care of them while Sawyer was gone. He was so excited he had the truck packed for all of us when I got back from the barn.

Mom hugged each of us and Grannie gave us kisses. "You behave, Sawyer. Don't give your brothers any problems. *He's not the problem.*

"Who's this young whipper-snapper?" Gus asked when we arrived at the bus.

"This is our younger brother, Sawyer. He writes our songs and has just graduated from high school. Is it okay if he comes with us?"

"Sure, what's one more fox on the bus," Gus said and chortled.

The drive to Costa Mesa took thirty hours and it was 2,017 miles via the I-40. We passed through Arkansas, Oklahoma, Texas, New Mexico, Arizona and into California. Our first stop was just before Oklahoma City. Gus pulled into Ann's Chicken Fry House so we could all have a good meal. The old sign had a picture of a blonde woman who must have been Ann, and the historic sign was for Route 66. It was an ancient weatherboard restaurant with an old gas pump and a gorgeous 1959 pink Cadillac outside. The fried chicken and biscuits were as good as Grannie's.

Gus found an old budget motel for that night. Sawyer bunked with Tucker, and I bunked with Richard. He was out of cocaine, but we enjoyed a few Jacks with water. The next morning, we ate the biscuits Gus had bought from Ann's, so we didn't have to stop.

"Hey, guys," Gus yelled. "You want to stop in Winslow, Arizona?"

"Absolutely," I said. "We might be country musicians, but we all love the Eagles." I pulled out my guitar and started playing *Peaceful Easy Feeling* and *Take It Easy*. Everyone sang along and by the time we got there, we had sung our hearts out. We drove to an old brick building downtown and Gus parked the bus. We brought our instruments out and played. Sawyer was in heaven as he played his ukelele. I had my guitar and Tucker had his banjo.

"Take a photo of us, please, Gus?" I said and we laughed so hard. I swear a girl in a flatbed Ford drove by, looked at me and wondered what was so funny. We stayed at Earl's Motor Court, a typical classic-style Route 66 motel, reminiscent of the type built all along The Mother Road in the 1940s and 50s. Many buildings were closed and had been bulldozed, but Earl's slice of Americana had survived because of the resurgence of historic Route 66, as a result of international trippers, cruisin' the Mother Road & perhaps because of the Eagles. After we had eaten supper, we walked to the famous Prairie Moon Restaurant with our instruments. It was an old block building with a large neon moon sign. An older-looking waitress with red lipstick, lots of mascara and eye make-up along with a red silk dress waited on us.

"Hey, y'all. Watcha gonna have tonight?"

"Bring me a Jack and water and two beers for my brothers."

"You think it's okay for Sawyer to have a beer?" Tucker asked.

"Sure, why not? He's on vacation." Sawyer grinned at me.

A local guy came up to shoot the breeze with us. He said the bar continued to be popular as long as Route 66 went through downtown. He said that 'ladies of the night' lived and serviced the travelers and truckers in the houses behind the bar. There was plenty of illegal gambling and plenty of alcohol.

Sawyer rolled his eyes. "Mama would have a fit."

The owner of the bar noticed our instruments. We didn't want to leave them in the motel. He asked us to play, and, of course, we did. All the Eagles songs and our ten from the album *Green Eyes*. The bar had filled up by the time we played. We were given a round of applause and a few tips. It was a fun night.

Chapter 57

Cade called last night. He sounded a little drunk, but happy. I hoped he wasn't drinking too much. He told me all about Winslow, Arizona. I knew it was exciting for Sawyer to be with his brothers. Even so, I wondered how they managed to sleep in shoddy motels and put up with traveling on that old bus across the country. It was a good thing I wasn't a musician. I couldn't have coped with a lifestyle like that.

I had an exciting day ahead for me. The previous day, a couple who were looking for a beachfront home had walked into the office. I pulled up several on the computer and they said they would ring to let me know which ones to show them. The one in Destin was $1,500,000. They also wanted to drive down 30A and there were three in that area.

I dressed in my burnt orange spandex suit. It had buttons down the front of the jacket, which was long and came to my thighs. The skirt was the same color and short. I put on a chunky bead necklace and wore my brown heels. I couldn't afford clothes like that until I got my first commission.

"Wow, aren't you a sharply dressed woman?" Pat said.

"Thank you. I love this new suit. I thought I should look professional when we look at the Gulf-front homes today. The clients are calling with a list of the ones they want to view.

I was settled at my desk studying the multiple listings I had pulled up for them the day before when the phone rang. It was Mr. Thompson.

"Good morning, Harper. Martha and I have decided which homes you can show us. The ones on Scenic Highway 98 in Destin, Blue Mountain drive and the two in Pelican Circle. We can meet you at your office at noon. Do you think you can set up appointments for this afternoon?"

"Yes, sir. I'll get right on it now and be ready to take you to see them by noon."

I called the agents and got lock-box codes and instructions. They wanted to come and meet me, but when I told them I worked for Pat Champion, they said I could go by myself with my buyers. I circled each home on the multiple listing map and sorted them into the best order. I would give that folder to the Thompsons and keep the agent's copy.

The Thompsons walked in right at noon. Mr. Thompson was the epitome of a southern gentleman from Memphis, Tennessee. He was six feet tall with gray hair at his temples. His blue eyes were piercing and he wore tidy pale brown pants, a white shirt, and loafers. Martha Thompson was gorgeous, with blonde hair, green eyes, and flawless skin. I wondered if she'd had a facelift. They were both in their seventies, but she looked fifty-five. Her outfit, a turquoise-blue pant suit with silver sandals, was superb and expensive. She wore a gold Rolex watch on her left arm, a diamond ring that had to be three carats and her ears held diamond earrings.

"Good afternoon. I want you to meet my broker, Pat Champion. She's been selling real estate for many years and is my mentor."

Pat walked toward them and shook their hands. I was sure their attire impressed her.

"Take the Thompsons in my car. Leave me the keys to yours in case I need to go somewhere," Pat said.

I was thrilled. I didn't want to drive them in my Chevette or ask Mr. Thompson to drive.

Our first stop was the homes on Scenic Highway 98. All three were new and had not been occupied. We went into the least expensive one, Casa Palmas, which had five bedrooms and five and a half bathrooms. The price was $1,495,000. Pat taught me to always show the least expensive home and then move up if the client didn't like it.

"This one is lovely," Martha said. "The doors and windows show off the beauty of the Gulf. Do we need over five bedrooms?" she asked her husband, John.

"If we end up with more grandchildren, we could use six bedrooms. The one next door has six. Let's see it next."

It was named *Bougainvillea,* and a mass of bright red bougainvillea covered the entrance. It was an inviting Mediterranean style. Soaring ceilings greeted us in the foyer, while the living area had columns and old-world light fittings. The kitchen was state-of-the-art, with the latest appliances and maple cabinets that complemented the cream walls.

"Oh! I adore this one," Martha said. "Just look at the view and the large deck for entertaining."

"Yes, this one is more like what I had in mind," John said. "What's the price?"

"It's $1,575,000. Do you want to see the third one? It's priced at $1,500,000 and has seven bedrooms and six and a half bathrooms with a two-car garage and a garage apartment. It also has a heated pool, a large deck and comes furnished by Sugar Beach Interiors."

"Yes, let's see it. If Martha approves of the furnishings, it'll save a lot of time. We could start using it right away," he said.

I could tell when we walked in that Martha loved the house. She enthused over the furniture and the heated pool while John said he loved the idea of the garage apartment for their son's family. They sat on the white couch and gazed at the sparkling Gulf of Mexico. Pat taught me to keep my mouth shut and listen to what they were saying. While they exchanged looks and expressed their love for it, I tried to remain calm.

"We like this one best of the three, but we still want to see the ones on Highway 30A," John said.

On the way to 30A they talked about their children and grandchildren and how excited they would be when they surprised them with a beach house. I turned off Highway 98 onto 30A and drove to Blue Mountain Beach and as I did, I recounted the story of why it was called Blue Mountain. "Back in the 1840s, the sand dunes were covered with blue lupines. The early sailors spotted the blue from a distance and named it Blue Mountain. The white dunes were so high back then, at an elevation of sixty-five feet, they could be seen from a long distance away." Then we saw the sign that said, *Welcome to Blue Mountain established in 1948.*

Martha turned to speak to John. "This is a little farther away from the stores, restaurants and activities that our children would love, isn't it?"

"Well yes, but this one is only $900,000. It's older, but what a charming area," said John.

"But it only has four bedrooms and four bathrooms," Martha replied.

"Let's go in and see. It might not work, but I like it," he said.

I could tell John liked everything. The home was older and had a nautical flair. There were old beams on the ceiling, rattan furniture with white cushions, simple beds with bright comforters, and lots of pillows. They had painted the dressers green and blue in the colors of the Gulf.

There were fishing rods in the dining room for easy access to surf fishing and it had interesting art that complemented the furniture, including a painting by one of the 'Highwaymen' in the master bedroom.

We sat down in the living room. "Do you think there's room on this lot to build a two-car garage and an apartment above it?" he asked.

"I can ask the listing agent, when we get back to the office. So far, which are your favorites?"

"I like *Bougainvillea* in Destin the best," Martha said.

"I like that one too, but this one speaks to me," John said. "Find out if we can build a garage apartment and we'll decide tomorrow."

I turned off all the lights and locked the house. When we were in the car, I asked if they wanted to see the ones on Pelican Circle.

"No, it's between these two. Let's drive back and we'll go out to eat. Call me when you find out about the garage apartment, then we'll make our decision and make an offer on one of them."

I thanked them for their time and we shook hands. They left in a Cadillac Escalade. Thank heavens Pat had let me drive her car. I bounded into the office.

"Well, how did it go?" Pat asked.

"Oh my God! It was fantastic. She likes the one in Crystal Shores and he likes the one in Blue Mountain. I have to find out if they can build a garage apartment on the one in Blue Mountain.

"Great, now call all the agents back first and give them feedback. They'll be waiting to see what your clients thought."

"Okay, they didn't want to see two of them."

"That's okay, just tell the agents the truth. They'll respect you."

I called all the listing agents, then I called Sandi Nichols to inquire about building a garage apartment on her listing. She said yes and it would cost about $100,000. Next, I called the Thompsons and relayed the information.

"Okay. Martha and I have a lot to discuss. We'll meet you tomorrow at your office at one o'clock and give our decision," John replied.

I had a difficult time sleeping that night. I was too excited.

Chapter 58

We finally arrived in Costa Mesa, California around 4 p.m. on June 22. Sawyer was clamoring to see the Pacific Ocean. We offloaded our gear into a tiny motel and changed into shorts and T-shirts. We called a cab, which took us to Huntington Beach, known as Surf City, USA.

"Pick us up at the pier at 10 p.m.," I told our cabbie. When we arrived at the pier, it was uninhabited because a storm had destroyed it in 1988. We ran down to the beach, took off our shoes and socks and jumped into the water.

"Oh my God! It's freezing," I said. "The Gulf of Mexico is warm."

"I don't care, I'm getting wet," said Sawyer.

"I'll go in up to my knees. It's too cold for me," said Tucker.

Tucker and I watched Sawyer having the time of his life. He was a Tennessee country boy who had seen little of the world and he stayed in the water for twenty minutes. We didn't bring a towel, so we walked to the souvenir shop and bought him a beach towel. He also needed another pair of shorts and a T-shirt. He wanted the one that said, *I surfed Huntington Beach,* so I bought it for him.

Once he was dry and dressed, we strolled along the boardwalk for about two miles. Girls were roller-skating in tiny, short shorts and crop tops and guys were running and racing. We were hungry by then, so we walked downtown to Main Street to find a place to eat. Downtown had colorful buildings, some old and some new. We found Longboard Restaurant and Pub. The sign outside said it had been built in 1904. A sure sign it was a good place to eat was all the bicycles outside. True to its name, it had dozens of long surfboards hanging on the walls and ceiling.

A girl about eighteen with straight, long blonde hair, brought us our menus. She wore cut-off short shorts that were ragged and a white crop top that exposed her tummy. Her dark tan showed off her white teeth. Sawyer's mouth dropped open when she put the menus in front of us.

"Hi guys, I'm Bunny, your server. Do you know what you want to drink?"

"Bring us all a beer, whatever is the favorite here in California," I said.

"Well, craft beer is all the rage. I'll bring you each one. My favorite on the menu is our lobster sub. They deliver lobster every day from Maine, so they're very fresh."

"Yum, that sounds fantastic," said Sawyer. He blushed when he looked up at Bunny.

Tucker and I both nodded. "Yes, we want that too."

The place was rocking by 7 p.m. with lots of tourists in family groups. It was summer and the kids were out of school and a few older surfers with long, bleached hair were drinking at the bar. Our table was close to the bar and I heard them talking about the enormous waves that they'd had the previous week. It was an enjoyable place to eat and the lobster subs were delicious.

Back in the motel Tucker and I lay on our beds and talked about how cool California was; we were so glad the tour had taken us there.

We arrived at the amphitheater in the afternoon. It was an all-day affair in the warm California sun. Several bands were playing including Naomi Judd. We were lucky to meet Naomi and her daughter, Wynonna. They were both gracious and beautiful women. Naomi wore a short, bright red dress with a wide skirt. Her red hair hung down the back of her dress. Wynonna had on black pants and a black top and boots that matched her black hair and guitar. The audience loved them. I asked Naomi why it was her last tour.

"I'm wearing out. It's time to stop touring and enjoy the rest of my life," she said.

Joe Cocker sang his favorite songs including, *Cry Me a River*, *Unchain my Heart* and *You Are So Beautiful*.

We backed up Garth and his group. Sawyer was backstage, watching, and he wanted so badly to be out there playing the drums. I hoped one day he would be with us. At the end of the concert, Garth spoke to the audience.

"Thank you for this. Nights like tonight are why I love music and all of you. Awesome weekend. We love you!"

It was a long day and I was exhausted when we finally got to bed. I walked out back and took a swig or two from my flask to calm down. I knew Tucker wouldn't approve with Sawyer here. I wanted to call Harper, but it was too late.

"Do you want me to rent a car and we'll take a short road trip down the coast?" I asked Tucker and Sawyer the next morning once we'd woken up.

"Oh, my gosh, can we?" said Sawyer.

We hired a rental car at one of the downtown hotels and picked up a map. The drive was worth it; we drove down Highway 1 to San Diego. Two hours later we stopped in La Jolla, a beautiful coastal area with a rugged dramatic coastline and views of expansive beaches, rocky cliffs, pine trees and sandstone canyons. I took photos to send back to Mom.

Our next stop was Coronado. We took the ferry across to Coronado Island, home of the famous Hotel del Coronado. It was worth the visit to see the amazing white Victorian structure with the red roof that had been built in 1888. Several United States presidents had stayed and dined at the hotel. There were photos of them, and, of course, Marilyn Monroe, Jack Lemon and Tony Curtis had filmed *Some Like It Hot* there.

We carried on and drove to San Diego, home to many attractions. We visited Old Town San Diego before it got too late. It had a vibrant Spanish community and historical buildings from the 1800s. The Bazaar Del Mundo marketplace was filled with Mexican restaurants and bars. We stopped in Las Cuatro Milpas, the oldest Mexican restaurant in San Diego where we ordered a few beers and ate authentic Mexican food. It was difficult to decide between fresh tortillas, rice, stewed pinto beans, and beef tacos.

"This is the best Mexican food I have ever eaten," I said. "It'll be hard to enjoy it anywhere else after this fine meal. Sawyer, you or Tucker will have to drive us home. I'm beat." I heard Tucker and Sawyer talking to each other as I fell asleep in the back seat.

As soon as we got settled in the hotel, I walked outside to call Harper. She answered on the second ring.

"Hi Babe, are you busy?"

"Not right now. How are you? Where are you?"

"We're in Huntington Beach, California. We played last night and today we rented a car and drove south down the coast. It was a glorious trip.

I want Sawyer to enjoy his few days in California. I'm so glad Mom let him come."

"That's wonderful. I know he loves being with you both. Wish I was there too."

"One day, I'll bring you here. It is so different from Florida. The Pacific Ocean is freezing. I prefer your Gulf of Mexico. I miss you so much."

"I miss you too. So glad you can call once in a while. It's late. I need to sleep. Love you, good night."

Chapter 59

I couldn't wait to get to the office to hear from Mr. and Mrs. Thompson and at ten o'clock he called.

"I have a problem," he said. "My wife wants the house in Crystal Shores and I want the one in Blue Mountain. Do you have an opinion?"

"Oh my! I'm new at selling real estate, but I asked my mentor, Pat, which one she would buy. She's been a real estate investor for several years. She said, Blue Mountain, because it has more opportunity for appreciation. The ones in Crystal Shores are already at the top of their appreciation and have been for a year or more."

"Hmm," he said. "I agree. Let me take Martha for brunch and I'll call you back."

I turned to Pat. "I'm on pins and needles. He wants Blue Mountain. She wants Crystal Shores. He's going to call me back after he takes her for brunch."

"That's a good sign," Pat said. "Usually the woman wins, but after meeting them, I have a feeling Mr. Thompson will prevail."

I fiddled around and tried to find some paperwork to do until Mr. Thompson called back. Finally, an hour later, he rang.

"We're coming over to your office. Get a contract ready on the house in Blue Mountain and include $100,000 for the builder to build a garage apartment. Martha's a little disappointed, but I told her she could refurnish it any way she wanted."

"That's exciting. I'll have everything typed and ready when you arrive."

I hung up. "Oh my God! They're going to buy the Blue Mountain house."

Pat grinned at me. "I told you so."

I prepared the contract and called Sandi Nichols.

"I'm going to bring you an offer on the Blue Mountain house. Can I have the name of the builder you recommended? Mr. Thompson wants to build the garage apartment and meet with him before he goes back to Memphis," I said to her.

"Great news. I knew you could do it. You have the best teacher in Pat Champion." She gave me the builder's name and contact details..

At exactly noon, the Thompsons walked into the office. I jumped up to greet them and shake their hands. Once we got past the pleasantries, I put the contract on the table in front of John in the conference room. "I haven't put a price on it yet. The builder is Jim Howell; he has lots of references and I have his contact details. Sandi highly recommends him, and Pat says his reputation is excellent too."

"That's good to hear," said John. "If they accept our offer, I want to meet with him tomorrow."

"Yes, Sandi said he's happy to meet with you at the property and show you where the garage apartment can be built."

"I want to offer $850,000 for the house and I'll pay the builder $100,000 for the garage apartment. If we do any upgrades, I'll pay him out of pocket."

"Are you going to finance it?"

"No, I'll pay cash and put $500,000 down now with $50,000 going toward the garage apartment, and I'd like a separate contract with the builder for him to complete the garage apartment."

I added those items to the contract and had them both sign it.

"I'll take your offer to Sandi Nicols as soon as you leave. Hopefully, she'll have a contract or a counter for me quickly. I'll call you as soon as possible."

"Thank you. We'll wait to hear from you."

They left, and I gathered up my things then called Sandi to tell her I was on my way to bring her an offer. When I arrived at her office, she was all smiles.

"Sit down. Let's see what you have for me." She read the contract.

"Okay, let me call me the seller. Why don't you go next door and get something to eat? I bet you haven't had lunch."

"You're right. I've been too nervous to eat. I'll go eat and let you work your magic on your seller."

Next door at The Blue Mountain Café I ordered a wonderful homemade chicken salad sandwich and a Diet Coke. I sat and enjoyed my sandwich and the atmosphere of the cute café. On the walls were sweet sayings such as *Always have a shell in your pocket and sand in your shoes.* Another one said, *Relax, you are on beach time.* I loved it out there on 30A. There wasn't much traffic, smaller homes, and, of course, the gorgeous Gulf of Mexico.

When I went back to Sandi's office, she grinned at me. "Guess what? They accepted the offer."

"Oh! That's fabulous. Can we make an appointment with Jim Howell to meet him tomorrow morning? We can meet at your office. Will you have the signed contract back by then?"

"Yes, I'll fax it to them, get their signatures and have it ready when you meet Jim. Let's make the appointment for 10 a.m."

"Super, I'll call the Thompsons and meet you here tomorrow. Thank you, Sandi. I'm so excited. This job is sure more fun than being a banker."

"You're going to be very successful. I just know it."

I sat in my Chevette and called Mr. Thompson to give him the good news. Then, since it was already getting late in the afternoon, I drove home. The kids were getting off the bus when I arrived.

"Hey, Mom, what are you doing home so early?" Lizzie said.

"I have great news. I sold an expensive home out on 30A. I thought we'd go out to Tony's Restaurant and celebrate."

When we arrived, Tony greeted us. "Look who's here to eat with us." He hugged me and the children. We had not been there in a while, and he knew us and my ex-husband. We used to eat there a lot when I was married.

"We're celebrating," I said. "I just got a real estate contract on a gulf-front home on 30A."

"Good for you. Desert is on me. Congratulations. What do you want to eat?"

"The kids want a pepperoni pizza, and I would love your lasagna with a house salad. Sprite for both of them and I'll have a glass of red wine."

During dinner, we talked about what the kids had been doing in school. Lizzie had a report to write on the latest book she was reading: *Harry Potter and the Philosopher's Stone.* Sean was learning multiplication tables, not his favorite. The food was delicious and at the end, Tony brought us tiramisu. We went home, full and tired.

Chapter 60

After we played at the Shoreline Amphitheater in Costa Mesa, we left for Los Angeles with Gus on the bus. We would stay at the motel in Huntington Beach and return after our performance in Los Angeles. The amphitheater was in the center of Universal Studios and when it had been an outdoor theater, it was used for stuntmen.

The event was the 1991 Academy of Country Music Awards. We were only there to cheer Garth Brooks and see all the celebrities. We had fantastic seats at the side of the theater. We saw George Jones, George Strait, Robert Duval and Johnny Cash, to name a few. Sawyer was in complete awe and I must admit, so was I.

When Garth received his award for Entertainer of the Year, he thanked the musicians who had influenced him and Chris LeDoux for showing him it pays to be a nice guy offstage. Garth Brooks was always a nice guy. I couldn't imagine being that successful and winning the award.

During the day, we roamed around Universal Studios and saw some of the movie sets. On July 1 we hailed a cab and took Sawyer to the airport. We hated saying goodbye to him, and he hated leaving.

"I can't thank you enough for this last week together. I've seen so much and I loved California. I can't wait for you to come home so I can play with you on stage," he said before we hugged him goodbye and went back to meet Gus. We were leaving for Tucson, Arizona, that afternoon.

From then on, the tour wasn't as much fun as when we were in California, and I began to drink more and more. I missed Harper. I missed home. Maybe I wasn't cut out to be a famous country music star. By the time we reached Dallas in September, we had been on the road and in nine states from Tucson to Syracuse, New York. The tour was getting to me. I was snorting too much coke and Boone wanted me to try heroin. So far, I had resisted, but I felt myself spiraling down. Was I going to be an alcoholic like my dad? Tucker was furious with me and would barely talk to me. I called Harper less and less. I didn't want her to guess what was going on.

After our performance in Dallas at the Reunion Arena, Boone and I went to the famous honky-tonk, Billy Bobs. It was a huge dance hall with memorabilia from bull roping to all the stars who had played there. Boone and I rolled up to the bar and ordered our regular Jack and water. Then we turned to watch the dancers. We had several more drinks before I had the guts to ask the cute blonde next to me at the bar to dance. We two-stepped for several songs and returned to the bar. Over the noise, she told me her name was Nancy. She was drinking straight shots of Cuervo tequila.

"Let me buy you a shot," she said.

"Why not?"

We danced and her large tits rubbed against my chest. I was aroused. When we returned to the bar, she grabbed my face and kissed me. Wow! It felt good to be kissed. I returned her kiss. Then she took my hand and pulled me out back. We kissed and hunched over each other until I was so horny, I thought I might come in my pants. I unzipped her jeans and thrust my hand inside. She was so wet, and I knew she wanted me. I pulled her closer to the shed, which hid us from being seen from the bar, undid her jeans and pulled mine down.

"Hold on, cowboy," she said. "I need to get a condom out of the back pocket of my jeans. I want you, but I don't want a disease."

It was a fantastic release as I plunged into her and she whimpered as she climaxed. When it was over, I took off the condom, pulled up my jeans and threw the rubber in trash can nearby. She grinned at me.

"Good job, cowboy. I needed that and I guess you did too."

We walked back into the bar and all of a sudden, I thought about Harper. Oh shit! What had I done? I had let the moment and everything I'd had to drink overcome me. I found Boone.

"We need to go," I said. He was so drunk he agreed and we caught a cab back to our motel. It was four in the morning. Tucker was awake.

"What the hell did? You're so drunk you can't stand up. You disgust me. You're just like Dad. I'm ashamed to call you my brother. And don't think I didn't see what you got up to with that slut out the back."

I fell on the bed in my clothes and passed out. I was so drunk I didn't take in what he said. I registered his anger but not much else.

Chapter 61

The Thompsons closed on their Blue Mountain beach house in July. Jim Howell was still building their garage apartment. What a nice guy. I think he was attracted to Pat, but she ignored his advances. He was a large man, six feet tall, well-built with muscular shoulders, dark hair and smiling eyes. If I hadn't been in love with Cade, I might have been interested in him.

Cade hadn't been calling as much. The last time I heard from him was after he put Sawyer on the plane to fly home from California. He'd left a few voicemails, and we'd only had one long chat when he was in Syracuse. He told me how beautiful the woods and mountains were, and how they reminded him of our time in Tennessee. I missed him, yet I had a feeling something wasn't right.

With the commission I received from the sale on Blue Mountain, I decided to trade in my Chevette. I called my dad and asked him to come over and go car shopping. We'd always done that together when I was younger. Of course, back then we'd brought home the 1957 two-door, yellow and white Chevy. Mom was not happy with us.

Dad and Mom came over on Saturday and while Mom took the kids to a movie, Dad and I went to the Pontiac dealership. On the way over, he asked me what I wanted. I told him I had seen a four-door Pontiac LeMans GT that I liked.

We drove to the dealership, and I took Dad to meet David Lee. David was the son of my old boss, Gary Lee, at the bank.

"Hello, Harper. It's good to see you," David said. "Is this your dad?"

"Yes, David meet Paul." They shook hands.

"I need to trade in this Chevette on a four-door sedan. Now that I'm selling real estate, this Chevette doesn't give me the right image."

"I can see that, but it looks like a nice trade-in. Which Pontiac model are you thinking might fit you?"

"Well, I love that blue LeMans on the showroom floor. Can we see if I can afford it?"

"Sure, I'll take your trade-in over to the used car lot and let my manager put a price on it. Buddy will take this one off the showroom floor and let you test drive it."

Dad and I got in and Buddy rode in the back.

"I like it," Dad said. "I wouldn't mind one of these for myself. It's sporty looking with these fancy chrome wheels and it even has power windows and locks."

"It drives real well, Dad. Let me pull over and you drive it too." We changed places.

"It's super to drive. You should get this one. I like the color and the leather seats. If Sean spills something on them, they'll clean up easily."

We pulled into the dealership and left the car at the curb.

"Don't put it back," Dad said to Buddy. "If Harper can't afford it, I want it." Then he laughed.

"Dad, that's not fair. Let's see what David says."

David led us into his office. "I can give you $5,000 trade-in for your car and I'll discount the list price of $15,749 for the LeMans down to $14,749. That leaves you a difference of $9,649."

"Can you tell me what the payments would be on that?"

"Yes, I'll be right back as soon as I've spoken to the finance manager."

"What do you think?" I asked Dad.

"That's a fair price. Now that you're making more money, you should be able to afford it. Let's see what David tells us about the payments."

"Your payments would be $241 a month for 48 months."

Dad looked at me. "Can you afford that?"

"Yes, now that I'm selling real estate, I can. I couldn't last year."

"Okay," said David. "Follow me and you can talk to Chris in the finance department. I told him to give you the best interest rate."

Dad and I went to see Chris and I filled out a loan application. Chris checked my credit rating and said they would approve my loan. I signed all the papers and gave him the ownership papers to the Chevette.

Dad and I drove away in the gorgeous new blue LeMans. When we drove up to the house, the kids came running out.

"Mom, whose car is that?" asked Sean.

"Mine. I traded the Chevette for a bigger and better car because I need it to sell real estate."

"Can we go for a ride?" asked Lizzie.

"Let Papa take you. I want to visit with Nana," I said.

Mom and I talked about my real estate sales. Mom, the cautious one, wanted to make sure I could afford the new car.

"Have you heard from Cade lately?" she asked when we had exhausted the subject of my new car.

"Not much. I guess he's busy traveling. The last time he called, he was in Syracuse and they had been to nine states." Mom pursed her lips but said nothing.

Dad and the kids came back, and as the two of them spilled out of the back seat, they couldn't stop saying how much they loved my new car. Shortly after that, Dad and Mom got ready to leave so they could be home before dark.

Chapter 62

I woke up with my head pounding. The shame hit me hard in my heart as I remembered the girl. What had I done? How could I have had sex with her? I loved Harper, didn't I? At that moment Gus banged on the door. I didn't have any more time to dwell on what I had done.

"Get up, you lazy shitheads. We have to leave for Ottawa in five minutes."

I threw on my clothes and woke up Boone. "Hurry or Gus is going to leave us behind."

There was no time for anything but dragging our backpacks to the bus. Tucker was already there with a disgusted look on his face. Clearly he wasn't speaking to me. I slunk on the bus with my head low and found my seat. Thank heavens there was a Coke in the refrigerator. I drank it and went back to sleep. I didn't want to think about what an idiotic thing I had done the night before.

We played in Ottawa that night. I don't know how I performed; I was still so hung over. Boone slipped me some coke when Tucker wasn't around. That helped.

It was a long ride back to Nashville. Gus dropped us off at our apartment. It was so good to get into my bed and when I woke, Tucker had a stew cooking on the stove.

"You better eat. You look terrible and Mom is going to be worried when she sees you." These were the first words he had spoken to me for some time.

"Thanks. It smells delicious. I need a shower, then I'll eat." As the water ran over me, I thought about Harper and how I had cheated on her. I needed to see her. I'd call and see if I could send her a ticket. We would be in Tennessee until November 15th.

Tucker's stew was fabulous and I felt much better. I needed to wash my clothes and clean my truck if we were going to spend the weekend with Mom and Grannie, which I knew it would be good for me. At least I hoped so.

It was wonderful to be back in Dunlap on the farm. Sawyer was glad to see us, and Grannie cooked our favorite fried chicken, field peas, macaroni and cheese dinner. We were sitting on the porch, playing a few songs when Mom stood up. "Take a walk with me, Cade." *Oh shit, that tone of voice meant trouble.* "You don't look good," she said. "I know you've been drinking too much. Tucker told me about the late nights you've been keeping. He says you've been hanging around Boone too much, probably doing cocaine."

"No," I stuttered.

"Don't try to fool me, boy. You look terrible; you have dark sunken eyes and you've lost at least twenty pounds. Tucker told me you cheated on Harper with a slut in a honky tonk. How could you? That woman loves you so much. If she knew, she would quit seeing you permanently. She had a cheating alcoholic husband. You think she wants another one? I'm disgusted with you. I can't let you break her heart or mine for that matter. I watched your dad drink himself to death. I know about cocaine and other drugs that are available to you. You don't get sunken eyes and a gray cast to your skin from just drinking. Neither can I let Sawyer come to Nashville and have you influence him. Thank heaven Tucker is stable. He's furious with you and I wouldn't blame him if he found another group to play with. He and Sawyer are too talented to waste their time and their careers with you. If you keep it up, stay away from them and me. I've had enough heartache in my life. I can't sit by and watch you do what your father did to himself and us."

"Dad had a heart attack."

"Yes, but the drinking led to it. You have your whole life ahead of you. Don't ruin it."

"I understand, Mom," I said in a quiet voice as I pushed my hands deeper into the pockets of my sweat pants and clenched my fists. *She thinks I'm an addict like my father. I'm not, I'm me, not him. I just need help to get through this tour and when it's over I'll kick this habit—the drugs and the booze. I can do it. It won't be hard because I am NOT an addict.*

We went back to the porch where Tucker gave me a look that said, *I told you so.*

The next day, I went for a long ride on Satan. I needed to clear my head. When I got back, I called Chattanooga Airport to book a ticket to Fort Walton Beach. I needed to see Harper. We were playing at Charles

Murphy Athletic Center in Murfreesboro on November 7. If I flew there for a three-day weekend, I could be back in time for our concert.

"I want to go spend a few days with Harper. Should I surprise her or tell her I'm coming?" I said to Mom.

"I wouldn't surprise her. She's busy selling real estate now, so you better see if she has time for you."

I slipped into my bedroom and made the call. "Hello, Babe. Would you like me to come down for a three-day weekend?"

"Of course. When would you like to come? Halloween is coming up. Sean would love it if we went trick or treating."

"That would be lots of fun."

"Let me check the calendar. Halloween is on Thursday. Could you fly down Wednesday so we could trick or treat on Thursday? The school Fall Festival is on Saturday."

"I can do that. Do I need a costume?"

"Yes, I'm always a witch. Would you like to be Dracula? I have an old black cape and we can paint your face white. Wear black clothes and an old white shirt so that I can put blood on it."

"Okay, I can do that. Is there a hotel or motel close to your house?"

"Yes, there are some cute cottages in Mary Esther that you can rent for a few days at a time. Let me call and see if I can book one for you."

"I can't wait to see you. It feels like forever since I've had you in my arms," I said.

"I'll call you when I find a cottage. Do you want to bring your brothers? They might like to see where I live."

"I'll ask them, but Tucker might want to go back to Nashville and see that cute banker he was dating."

"Okay. Bye ... love you," she said.

Chapter 63

I told the kids the good news that Cade was coming for Halloween weekend. "What do you want to be this year? We need to decide."

"I want to be a ghost, like Casper," said Sean.

"Can I be a witch like you, Mom?"

"Okay. I'll go by the pattern store and get material so we can make your outfits this weekend. Lizzie, it's time for you to learn to sew."

"That'll be cool, Mom."

The next morning, I stopped by JoAnne's Fabrics. It was at Elgin Parkway, just across from where we lived. Everything in the store was Halloween related. I wandered over to the patterns and found Casper the Ghost and Little Miss Witch patterns. Then I picked out the material and thread. On the way out, I saw a smaller witch's hat for Lizzie. Mom had given me her witch's outfit and Dad's black cape when she retired. My mom had so much fun being the secretary of Berryhill Elementary. She led the Halloween parades and had dozens of costumes. She knew all the children and parents by name for twenty-five years. They loved her. When she retired, they put on a special party and gave her a big write-up in the *Press Gazette.*

When I arrived at the office, Pat was writing a contract on another of the houses in Crystal Beach.

"Come outside. I have something to show you," I said.

"Oh! That is a great car. When did you get it?"

I told her about my dad coming over and how we traded the Chevette.

"You'll be much happier driving clients around in that fine car. I'm proud of you."

"Thanks. It was time to trade. And guess what? Cade is flying down for Halloween weekend to go trick or treating with us and come to the Fall Festival. I hope you won't need me to work that weekend."

"No, enjoy your children and Cade. You've been working hard and deserve time off."

That night I cut out the material for the costumes. Lizzie watched and I showed her how to pin the pattern on the material. They were both excited about their costumes.

On Sunday, I got out the sewing machine and put it on the kitchen table. "Come sit next to me. We'll sew the ghost outfit first. I'll let you stitch the straight lines. Once we have it stitched, we'll put it over Sean's head to see where the eye holes need to be," I said to Lizzie.

"Let's see if it fits and how long it needs to be, so you don't trip," I said to Sean. He stood still while we marked the location for his eyes. Then I showed Lizzie how to pin up the bottom before I took it off him and lay it on the table to mark and cut the eye holes.

"Watch, Lizzie, I'll cut the holes and then zigzag around them with black stitching. That'll make them stand out." Sean was thrilled with it and ran around the neighborhood to show his friends. While he was outside, we sewed Lizzie's witch dress. "Well, we are ready for Halloween," I said when her costume was finished.

I called Cade and told him I had found the cutest cottage in Mary Esther by the inland waterway. Since it wasn't summer, he could rent it on a daily basis. I gave him the phone number of the rental agency and told him to call and reserve it.

The week went by slowly. I couldn't wait for Cade to arrive on Wednesday afternoon. I was in the kitchen making my special broccoli and cheese casserole when the doorbell rang. Sean answered it. "Mom! Cade is here."

I ran to the living room and he hugged me tight.

"I thought I'd surprise you. I got an earlier flight out of Atlanta, rented a car, and here I am."

My heart was thumping in my chest. When I kissed him in front of Sean, he laughed and Sean jumped up and down.

"Lizzie, come here, they're kissing," Sean yelled.

"Hi, Cade. Don't mind Sean, he's goofy," said Lizzie.

"Come into the kitchen. Do you want some sweet tea?" I said.

"What's that I smell? It's heavenly."

"My best dish, sure to cast a spell on any man who eats it."

"I think you've already cast a spell on this man."

"The casserole is almost done. I need to make a salad and then we can eat. Then I'll take you over to the cottage."

As we ate, Cade told us about California and what fun they had there. Lizzie told him how we made the Halloween costumes and she had learned to use the sewing machine.

"This casserole is delicious. I've never eaten anything like it before. Mom and Grannie fry a lot of their food."

"I love their cooking, but I never learned to cook the southern way. I learned to cook most of my meals out of the *Betty Crocker Cookbook*. When I married Michael, I couldn't cook anything. His mother taught me many dishes, and I experimented with the cookbook. I'm so glad you like it."

Sean got up from the table and came running back in his ghost costume. "Boo," he yelled as loud as he could. Cade laughed and tried to grab him.

"Come here, you little ghost. I'll fix you for scaring me," Cade said as he succeeded in catching him and then tickled him.

"I need to show Cade where he's staying while he's here. Lizzie, will you clean up the kitchen and put Sean to bed, please?"

"Yes, Mama."

Cade backed out of the driveway, and I backed my new car out of the garage. When I got near his car, he rolled down the window.

"Nice car. Wow! So nice. I know you love it."

"I do. It's so much better for showing homes and making myself look more successful in front of my clients. Follow me. I'll show it to you when we get to Mary Esther." As I drove, I worried about how tired Cade looked and he had lost a lot of weight too.

We pulled up to the cutest white-block house on the south side of Highway 98. There were ten cottages on a single-lane road that lead to the Intracoastal waterway. The cottage Cade had rented was right by the water. The key was under the mat. Cade had a backpack with him and he put it on the floor inside the door before he turned and kissed me. I responded passionately. Before we knew it, we were on the bed and Cade was unbuttoning my blouse. Oh, how I had missed him. I pulled up his T-shirt and stroked his chest.

"Stop, let's do this right. Take off your clothes and get into bed with me," he said.

I pulled off my jeans and blouse and Cade un-hooked my bra. Then he brought his mouth down on mine again. It was all over in a flash. We had been apart for too long. I flopped on my back and he lay next to me with his arm across my chest. He was still breathing as rapidly as me.

"Oh sweetheart, I have missed you so much," he said.

"I'm so glad you flew down to see me." We lay there quietly and let our breathing return to normal.

"Have you lost weight?" I asked him.

"Only a little. We don't always eat so good on the tour."

"Honey, I can't stay tonight. I have to go back to the kids and get them off to school in the morning. We'll have tomorrow together and then we can go trick or treating."

"I know. I understand. Call me in the morning after the children leave. I'll come over. We have the whole day to be together."

I put my clothes back on and kissed Cade goodbye. I felt so peaceful driving home.

Chapter 64

I woke up struggling to remember where I was. Did I dream Harper was here last night? I shook my head. I was in Mary Esther in a rental cottage. My head was confused from sleeping in so many hotels. I made myself a cup of coffee in the coffeemaker that was on the counter near the sink, then I took a shower. As I showered, I reminisced about how much fun her kids were, and how happy I was to be with Harper, Lizzie, and Sean. Playing music was my first love, but being away from her was so hard.

I took a swig from my flask and then brushed my teeth. I wouldn't be able to drink much in front of Harper. I put a small packet of coke in my back pocket just in case I needed it.

When Harper knocked on the door a short time later, I swept her into my arms and kissed her neck. "Good morning, sunshine."

"Good morning. I got the kids off to school. They're so excited about trick or treating tonight. So, what would you like to do today?"

"I'd like to go down to the docks and look at the charter boats. Then we can eat at Harbor Docks."

"Perfect, it's a beautiful day to walk the docks. We can see who's winning the rodeo. Today is the last day."

"Let's go. Do you want breakfast?" I said.

"No, let's stop at The Donut Hole."

We drove in Harper's new car. It smelled so new. She pulled into the restaurant and I ran in and bought two chocolate cake donuts for her and two cream filled ones for me. I grabbed another cup of coffee and brought her a Diet Coke.

"Perfect choices. Thank you. We can go down to the harbor and eat on one of the benches," she said.

We sat and watched the water while we ate. Most of the boats were already out fishing. I felt so relaxed and happy to be with Harper that I was determined to own one of those boats one day. I wondered how long it would take me to save up enough money to buy one.

When we finished our food I took Harper's hand and we walked down the dock to view the leader board. A tanned guy with a scruffy beard came over.

"Hi, welcome to the weigh station. I'm the weigh master. Didn't I see you at the Rodeo dinner last year?"

I shook his hand. "Yes, sir. I'm Cade Fox and this is Harper Hamilton. How's the rodeo going?"

"Good. They caught lots of amberjacks and some large groupers. Today is the last day."

Then we drove over to Harbor Docks. Stevie was at the bar and greeted us.

"Look what the cat's dragged in. Good to see you, Harper and Cade. Are you here to eat?"

"Yes, we're hoping for fresh fish," I told him.

Our waitress came to the table. She was smiling and wore a Harbor Docks T-shirt and short shorts.

"Good to see you, Harper," she said. Stevie told me you were dating Cade Fox. I love your song, *Green Eyes*. I'm a big country and western fan."

"Cade, this is Kitty, a friend of mine."

"Nice to meet you, Kitty, and thank you for the compliment. What's your favorite food here?"

"I recommend the snapper with artichoke hearts and a cucumber salad. If you like fried fish, get the grouper special with French fries and coleslaw. Let me get your drinks while you decide. What can I bring you?"

"I'd like a Budweiser and bring Harper a glass of white wine."

We discussed the selections and when Kitty came back with our drinks I ordered the snapper for Harper, and the grouper special for me. The food was delicious. We passed on dessert.

"We better go home and get ready for Halloween tonight," Harper said.

I paid the bill, we said goodbye to Kitty and Stevie and Harper let me drive her new car. It was sporty and drove well. I preferred my truck, but if I had to drive a car, that would have been a good choice.

Chapter 65

Today was fun showing Cade off to Kitty and walking the docks. When we arrived at my house the kids were already dressed in their costumes and waiting for me to do their make-up. I painted Lizzie's face white and put powder over it. Then I drew eyebrows and a big wart on her chin. Next was red lipstick.

"Yikes! Mom, I look frightful," she said.

"You're supposed to look frightful. I'm going to make my face look just like yours." Sean was waiting for his make-up. All I did was circle his eyes and mouth in black eyebrow pencil.

"Okay, Cade, you're next. Put on your black T-shirt and jeans. I have the cape ready and the fake teeth." He stood still while I made his face white, drew black eyebrows and drips of blood from his mouth. "Look in the mirror. You're scary too."

"I sure am. I haven't dressed up in years. This is fun."

I put on my witch's dress and made up my face like Lizzie's. Then we put on our witch hats and picked up our plastic pumpkins for collecting the candy, and off we went round the neighborhood. Hardly anyone recognized us and the kids collected way too much candy. When we were back home, they emptied their pumpkins onto the kitchen table. They sorted the candy and did some trading.

When we cleaned our faces it took forever to get off the white make-up. I'd have to bleach my washcloths and towels. The kids were so tired I told them to go to bed without a bath. Cade was slumped on the sofa. I was tired too.

"Do you want anything to drink?" I asked. "I want a rum and coke. Should I bring you a Jack and water?"

"Please. That was exhausting but lots of fun." We kissed and cuddled on the couch. There would be no love making. Little ears would be able to hear everything in my small house. Then I walked Cade out to his car and gave him a big hug and a long kiss.

"Come over early and I'll fix breakfast. We have to go to the school festival and then we'll be free to do whatever we want. Kate is coming over to babysit tomorrow night. She wants to see you."

"I guess I can spend the night without you. Love you, Babe."

I slept like a rock. I was exhausted along with everyone else. I woke to find the kids eating candy. "No, you can't have candy before breakfast." They looked at me with guilty faces. "Put it back. I better work out how many you can eat each day."

I whipped up pancake mix, fried bacon and told Lizzie to pour four orange juices. I had just finished cooking when Sean let Cade in.

"Good morning. How did everyone sleep?" he asked.

"Great!" The kids said in unison.

"Me too," I replied. "Are you ready for pancakes?"

"I sure am."

As I told Cade what I found the kids eating when I got up, I had to laugh.

"I can't blame you kids. I would have done the same thing. I love chocolate candy," he said. "Are we still going to the school festival?"

"Yes, it starts at noon," Lizzie said.

"They have a dunk the principal booth. Can you throw a softball?" I asked Cade.

"I sure can. We'll buy tickets and dunk him." He laughed.

At Lizzie's school, Bruner Middle School, they held the festival on the large soccer field where there were booths, items for sale, and the dunking booth. It was a good thing the temperature was seventy-six degrees because the principal and vice principal both got soaked. I bought tickets for Cade to throw the softball. As he was getting in line, Suzanne and her son walked up.

"Hi, you two. Look who's visiting. He's going to dunk the principal," I said.

"Oh! Glad he's doing it and not you or me. I get called in often enough when David gets in trouble," Suzanne said.

When Cade pitched the first ball and missed, the crowd booed. The second pitch came close but missed too. More boos. The third one hit the mark and Mr. Massey. He dropped into the water and came up spluttering.

He had only been at Bruner for a couple of years and this was his first time in the dunking booth. He took it like a good sport.

Once we got home, Cade took Sean and his baseball to the neighborhood park. Lizzie went down the street to visit one of her girlfriends and I got in the shower before I got ready to go out with Cade.

Kate came at five and was happy to see Cade. "Hello, cowboy. Who let you off the tour bus?" she asked.

"Hello to you, Miss Kate. We have a month's break."

"It's good to see you. I love your album and bought it as soon as it came out."

"Thanks, my brother Sawyer has talent. Good to see you, Now if you'll excuse me I have to go clean up for tonight. Thanks for babysitting. I'll be back in thirty minutes."

Chapter 66

What a wonderful time I had with Harper's children. Perhaps it would be nice to be married and have a child with Harper. Of course, babysitters would be a necessity to keep our love life going. I appreciated Kate saying she would stay with the kids so we could go out by ourselves. Once I'd showered and shaved, I was feeling shaky so I snorted a line of coke before I drove back to Harper's house.

Sean opened the door. "I saw you coming," he said.

"Thanks. Are you going to play Chutes and Ladders with Kate?"

"She said we could and Mom has ordered a large pizza. Want to stay and eat pizza with us?"

"No, I'm taking your mom to a fancy restaurant in Destin. Is she ready?"

"Mom!" he yelled. "Cade's here. You better come into the living room."

Harper walked out in a gorgeous, knee-length, green, silk dress that matched her eyes. She had on black high heels and gold earrings. I wished I had a camera.

"Hello. You ready to go?" she asked.

"I am. We have reservations at Marina Café in Destin at seven."

"Fantastic! I love Marina Café and don't get to go there too often."

I kissed her and told her how gorgeous she looked. We held hands as I drove to Destin. Neither of us talked much on the way. I wondered what she was thinking. She would tell me if she wanted me to know.

The maître d' led us to a waterfront table set with a white tablecloth, a candle, and a vase with a rose. The view of the harbor and sailboats moving in the wind was spectacular. It wasn't dark yet because Florida was on daylight saving until the first week in November.

"This is nice. Did you make a special reservation?"

"I sure did. Nothing is too good for you, my love," I replied.

We glanced at the menus. I wanted a steak and when I ordered a vodka martini with olives, Harper said she wanted one too. When our drinks came, we toasted each other.

"The last couple of days have been fun with your children. You've done a great job raising them."

"Thanks, they're well behaved and I don't know what I'd do without them. I'm glad their father has moved to Atlanta and I don't have to share them too often."

"What do you want to eat? Everything looks wonderful, but I want a large steak. How about you?" I asked her.

"A filet would suit me, not too big though. They have asparagus as a side dish, and I'd love a baked potato."

We placed our order when the server came back. One martini was enough for me and we both switched to Pinot Noir. The food was superb. They cooked our medium-rare steaks to perfection. The vegetables were steamed with a light butter sauce and the baked potato was served open with butter and sour cream. We both ate every morsel on our plates.

"We must have been starving," Harper said. "Everything was delicious. Please don't order dessert unless you want one. I'm stuffed."

"I couldn't eat another bite. I'll get the bill." I paid and took Harper's hand. We walked onto the deck to look at the boats, the water and the moon rising. It was so romantic. I wished I could ravish Harper right then and there.

"Can you come back to the cottage with me for a while?"

"Yes, Kate told me to take my time coming home."

We went into the cottage, and I couldn't wait to take that emerald-green dress off Harper. I kissed her slowly and she responded with a sigh and then pulled away from me.

"Babe, is something wrong?"

"No, just realizing this is our last night together."

"I know that long-distance dating is difficult. Come closer and let me love you." I took it slowly as I removed her dress and put it on the chair. Then I lay her on the bed and removed my clothes. She was wearing a silver-gray bra and panties. I took my time caressing her. I knew she needed more romance and cuddling rather than wild sex. I pulled her close.

"I love you," I whispered in her ear." She wrapped her arms around me.

"Do you want to make love or just cuddle?" I asked.

"Make love to me."

It was different—we reached a plateau where we had never been before and I knew she felt it too. Afterwards, I held her for a long time.

"That was just what I needed. I love our frantic sex, but this was so much more loving," she said after a time.

"I know, honey. Sometimes I just can't wait to ravish you. Tonight was different and wonderful."

We lay hugging for a while longer until Harper got up, picked up her clothes, and went to the bathroom. She came out dressed.

"You better take me home. I don't want to take advantage of Kate."

Neither of us talked until we reached her house. "I have an eight o'clock flight back to Nashville. I need to be at the airport by seven and I have to return the rental car. We better say goodbye tonight."

"I guess that's the best idea. We're usually rushing to the airport, and it leaves me feeling empty once we part."

"It's been a wonderful weekend with you and your children. I have nine more concerts on the tour. Then I should be home in Nashville and Bob will set up gigs for us. We're hoping Mom will let Sawyer come to Nashville. We need to record a second album."

"I know touring is hard on you and Tucker. Can't you make a living playing around Nashville?"

"Yes, I don't see why not. We're selling lots of albums and after touring with Garth, we should be more in demand. Hopefully, we can see each other more and you can spend some time in Nashville."

"That sounds good to me. I better go inside."

I kissed Harper and walked her to the door. My heart was heavy and I saw tears slip out of her eyes as she waved goodbye.

Chapter 67

Kate woke up as soon as I came in the front door. She rubbed her eyes and looked at her watch. "It's only midnight. I thought you would come dragging in here in the morning."

"Cade has an early flight and I didn't want to keep you up late. It was our last night together and that always makes me sad. I was ready to come home."

"Are you in love with him?"

"Yes, but I'm worried my emotions are getting out of control. I think I better pull back and see how things go when he is off the tour."

"Better to be safe than sorry," said Kate.

"Thanks for staying. You're a great friend."

"I enjoy your children. You know we miss you at the bank. How do you like selling real estate?"

"It's challenging, but I'm learning so much. The money is good too. Did you see my new car?"

"Yes, it's sporty. Maybe when you're successful, you can teach me."

"I'd love to; you'd be a good realtor."

Kate left and I went into the bathroom to wash off my make-up and hang up my dress. I hoped I could sleep. Saying goodbye to Cade was becoming more and more difficult.

I slept fitfully and tossed and turned all night. When I woke, Cade had left a sweet message on my voicemail. Then it was then that I decided I needed to go see my mom. The next day, we stopped for donuts and then drove to Milton. My parents were just coming home from church.

"What a surprise," said Mom.

"Hope you don't mind that we came to visit you."

"You can always visit us. Come inside," Dad said.

The kids and Dad got out the Sunday paper. The kids looked at the funny pages and Dad read the news. Mom invited me into the kitchen and made us a cup of tea.

"I know something's on your mind. Do you want to talk about it?"

"You can read me like a book, Mom."

"Of course, I'm your mother. You'll do the same thing to Lizzie when she's older. There's something in a mother's intuition. Tell me what's going on."

"I'm afraid of my feelings for Cade. His career is unnerving me. This tour has been hard on him, and he didn't look so good this weekend. He's thinner and his face had a worried look on it often."

"I'm sure his music business is stressful. There's lots of driving on that tour and so many places and beds to sleep in."

"He says it'll be different when he's finished touring. His manager will be lining up places for them to play around Nashville and the surrounding areas. He's hoping Sawyer can move in with him and Tucker in January. His mother doesn't want Sawyer on the tour. She's protective like you."

"She sounds like a smart mother to me. I know you like her and his grannie."

"I do. You know what a planner I am. I can't imagine leaving you and Dad and moving up to Nashville. My real estate career is taking off. What would I do up there? I wouldn't have family or friends."

"You'd survive. I followed your father from England to America without knowing anyone. Luckily, his mother was so kind and I loved being with her. Then we moved several times while Dad was in the Navy. I made new friends everywhere we went. You could do the same."

"Thanks, Mom. I just needed you to reassure me. I guess if it happens, I can sell real estate in Tennessee. The kids would love to live on a small farm. Lizzie could have a horse and Sean could have a dog. Am I worrying too much too soon?"

"You probably are. Being single without a good husband to lean on is difficult. It's been so wonderful for me to have your father. He's a rock of stability. Perhaps not the most romantic man in the world, but always there when I need him."

"Cade is very romantic. I hope he'll be steady as a rock like dad. They only made one Paul Hamilton. I could use a clone of him."

"Take your time and see how things are when his tour is over. Don't rush into anything," she said and then hugged me. "Come on, let's see what everyone wants to do. I bet Lizzie would like to go up to the stables and ride."

When Dad heard us talk about riding horses, he looked up from the paper. "Great idea. Let me call and arrange for four horses. Sean can ride with me. Mom, go change out of your church clothes."

We got in dad's truck and drove north down the dirt road to the stables where four horses were waiting for us. They were all different shades of brown, tan, and two had white socks on their legs. Lizzie ran up to the one she had ridden before and stroked her muzzle. Dad gave each one a carrot. The stable boy helped us to mount and led us onto the road. We walked down the path under the power lines. From then on the horses seemed to know where to go and we trotted most of the way. Dad told Lizzie and I we could gallop to the river and he and Mom would catch up. Lizzie's hair was flying and the smile on her face was delightful to see. I loved it too. I remembered riding my horse down this trail when I was in high school. She always had to be in front on trail rides.

Lizzie and I dismounted and let our horses drink in the river. I had swum here many times and let my horse swim too. The ride was just what I needed to get my mind off Cade. Dad, Sean, and Mom trotted up several minutes later. Mom didn't like to gallop. When she rode my mare, Maude, she was always getting off and on to see why Maude was stumbling or if she had a rock in her hoof. Dad and I told her Maude was fooling her. She never did that to us. Mom was a sucker.

Once everyone's mounts had drunk, we got back on for the ride home. It was brisk, about sixty degrees, and perfect for riding. No flies and no sweating as we rode back to the barn.

We had a late lunch. Mom made macaroni and cheese with tomatoes on top. Everyone's favorite.

It was three o'clock when we drove home. The kids needed an early night early after their busy weekend. We'd had trick or treating, the school fair, and horseback riding. They must have been worn out.

Chapter 68

When I arrived back in Nashville, I went into a depression. Tucker teased me and said I had it bad. Yes, I did.

"How's your romance coming with the banker girl?"

"Her name is Mary Jane, and we had a couple of dates while you were in Florida. I really like her, but we still have a couple of months left on the tour. I'm tired of traveling and I'm sure you are too."

"Yes, we need to meet with Bob and make sure he has some gigs for us in December. Our last place is Amarillo, Texas, then we'll be home for good. Have you talked to Sawyer? Is he writing more songs for us to record?"

"Yes, he has at least five more finished."

"Great. Another five and we can cut another album."

"He can drive over to Murfreesboro on the 7th when we play at the Charles M. Murphy Athletic Center. Would Mom and Grannie like to come too? I'll call and ask."

I sat on the couch and called Mom. "Hi Mom, I'm back from Florida."

"Did you have a good time?"

"Sure did. You need to meet Harper's children. We had so much fun trick or treating and going to their school festival."

"I'm glad you like them. Wouldn't you like to have one of your own someday?"

"Yes, I'd like a boy, but a girl would be fine too. Harper can still have children. We haven't gotten that serious yet. I rang because Tucker and I are playing in Murfreesboro on the 7th. Would you like to come and hear us play? Sawyer can drive you."

"That would be fun. I'd like to see Garth Brooks and you two on stage. I'm not sure Grannie could make the trip though. It would be uncomfortable for her to sit on the bleachers."

"I know, but I wish she could. I'll get you two front row tickets. Come early in the afternoon, so we can get together and I can give you the tickets."

"We will. Can't wait to see you two. I love you both."

I turned to Tucker and gave him the good news, then I needed a nap.

When I woke up, Tucker was gone. He left me a note to say he had a date with Mary Jane.

I called Boone. "You going out tonight? I need to buy some coke from you. I'm all out."

"Sure, a couple of us are going to Whiskey Bent Saloon tonight. Hank is playing. Meet us around eight. I'll save you a barstool."

"Okay, see you then. I'm having trouble sleeping. Do you have any Xanax?"

"You know I have everything. When are you going to try some smack? You don't know what you're missing."

I drove down to meet Boone and his friends, walked into Whiskey Bent and found them at the bar. The bar was always full on any night. It wasn't where I usually went, but it was Boone's favorite. I ordered a double Jack and water. Boone grinned at me.

"Glad you're back. Have fun in Florida?"

"Sure did."

"That Florida girl sounds like she's a little too good for a guy like you. You ain't planning on marrying her, are you?"

"Naw, just having a good time." *What am I saying? I love Harper. And it's not any of his business.*

Hank Williams Junior performed his favorite songs, including *A Country Boy Can Survive, Family Tradition, Outlaw Women, All My Rowdy Friends are Coming Over Tonight.* He always wore dark sunglasses and a cowboy hat during his shows. After intermission, he played *Whiskey Bent and Hell Bound.* The audience went wild as they hooted and called out his name. The dancers were already drunk, but this song got them back on their feet.

"Let's go play pool down the street. I'll meet you in the bathroom and give you your order. I've missed that money from your pocket," Boone said.

I walked into the dungy pool hall, saw Boone and waved him to the back and the men's room. I waited for him to come in and locked the door when he arrived.

"Worried, Fox?" He laughed sadistically. It was unnerving and I shuddered. "Here's your coke and ten Xanax."

We played a few rounds of pool. Boone beat me twice until I rallied and beat him. His friends were stumbling drunk, and some guy pushed one of them out of his way. And oh shit! That's when the fight started. Boone jumped in to help his buddies. I stayed back and tried to stay out of it. The fourth guy must have figured I was one of them and he came for me. I ducked, but his second punch hit me in the eye. I fell and he jumped on me. Boone pulled him off and I scrambled up and got the hell out of there. I was in no condition to drive, but I needed to get home. I drove the back streets and fell in the apartment door. Thank heavens Tucker wasn't home. I looked in the mirror. I had the beginning of a shiner on my left eye. I found a bag of frozen peas and took them to the bed with me. I took a Xanax and fell on the bed. After a while I finally passed out.

At noon, Tucker woke me. "What on earth happened to you?" he asked.

"I don't feel like talking about it. Just in the wrong place at the wrong time. Can you bring me a glass of water and a BC Powder?"

Tucker grudgingly brought both and put them on the bedside table, then after shaking his head and giving me a dirty look, he left me alone. I woke about three and made myself a Bloody Mary. That helped. I drove to the hamburger place down the street and ordered one with French fries to go. I hoped Harper didn't call. I just couldn't talk—to anyone.

Chapter 69

I woke up thinking I couldn't believe it was almost Thanksgiving, and soon it would be Christmas. My real estate job sure kept me busy. My next appointment was to show houses in Crystal Beach. The Batsons had referred the Armstrongs, from their hometown. I had to get ready and get the kids off to school. The couple were meeting me at the office at ten.

"I'm Phil and this is my wife, Charlene. The Batsons have wonderful things to say about you."

"Thank you. I love referrals. It makes getting to know my clients so much easier. Do you want a coffee or a soft drink?"

"I take mine black," Phil said. "And I know Charlene will have a Diet Coke."

They looked to be about fifty. Phil was tall and solidly built, like an ex-football player. He had very black hair and brown eyes—no gray in his hair yet. Charlene was an attractive brunette with hazel eyes. She had on a navy-blue pantsuit with a bright scarf around her neck. It was obvious they were from Alabama with their southern accents.

"You said in your email that you'd like a cottage near the Batsons and one similar to theirs. Do you want a brand new one built, or do you want to look at the ones that are currently for sale?"

We'd like to see what you have that's available now," said Charlene. "It would be so good to celebrate Christmas here in Destin with our grown-up children."

I looked at Phil, and he nodded.

"We can drive over there now, and I can show you the three that are available. There's a three bedroom and two four-bedroom ones available on Clipper Cove.

"Don't you agree we should get a four bedroom? The kids will get married and hopefully we'll have grandchildren," Charlene said to her husband.

"Yes. Let's have Harper show us the two with four bedrooms. I'll pay cash, so we can close soon if we find the right one," Phil replied.

"That's great. Cash is quick for closing. Shall we go? Do you want to ride with me?"

"No, we'll follow you. If we like one, Charlene is going to want to look for furniture."

I drove up to 4452 Clipper Cove. It was a four bedroom with three and a half bathrooms and a garage. I hoped they'd like it. Charlene was smiling when she got out of the car. The house had white siding with a black door and shutters. The floors were beige tiles and the kitchen was white.

"I like this one for sure," said Charlene. "What do you think, Phil?"

"Very nice. Let's go upstairs. I like the fact it has a single-car garage. Are golf carts allowed?"

"Yes, sir. Although they just must be street legal." I followed them upstairs and could told they loved the house.

"I like it, but we should see the second one too," Phil said.

We walked past the pool down to 4475. I explained it was a heated community pool with low homeowner's association dues. Then I showed them the fenced walkways to Crystal Beach drive that went to the beach.

I opened the door and let them go in front of me.

"I don't like this kitchen and living room layout as much," was Charlene's first comment.

"No, I don't either. Take us back to 4452, please. That may be the one," said Phil.

I pointed out the walkway down Hutchison Street to the beach. They liked how close it was to the house. They spent a good hour talking and deciding where to put furniture. I told Charlene that Karen Waterfield at Sugar Beach Interiors had the best selection of coastal-style furniture and would take good care of them.

"This is the one," Phil said. "Is there any negotiating on new homes?"

"No, but I can get Bob to give you the blinds. He also pays the title insurance, and you pay the documentary stamp tax."

"Do you want to go meet Karen at the furniture store? I can introduce you," I asked Charlene. "I have a contract for this home in my car. I can fill it out while you two look at the furniture. Karen has an office I can use."

"That's a great idea. We'll follow you to the furniture store," Phil said.

I called Karen and was pleased that she was free and could meet with them immediately. We drove up to her soft pink store where she always had inviting outdoor furniture out front. She was waiting at the desk by the door and stepped forward to greet us.

"Karen, I'd like you to meet Phil and Charlene Armstrong. They're buying 4452 Clipper Cove and want it furnished. Can you show them around while I use your office to write the contract?"

"Of course. It's so nice to meet you both. I know you'll love working with Harper, and I promise to take excellent care of you. I know that house is a four bedroom. Do you want bunk beds in the smaller bedroom?"

"Yes, that will be for future grandchildren. Phil and I like a king-size bed in our bedroom, and you can put queens in the other two."

I left them in Karen's capable hands and went to her office to write up the contract. I was thrilled they were paying cash. My children would have wonderful Christmas presents.

I called Pat to tell her to put 4452 pending in the Multiple Listing Service and that I would be back at the office after they had signed the contract.

After an hour and a half, Karen led the Armstrong's into her office. "They've picked out everything they need," she said. "I can even do the linen, TVs, and the kitchen package so they can be in before Christmas."

Charlene was bubbling with excitement. Phil looked serious and wore a small frown. They both sat down and I explained everything. They both signed the contract. When Phil asked how much deposit, I told him $10,000. He wrote a check.

"Charlene overspent a little on the furniture. She's going to pay for that out of the inheritance from her mother," Phil said.

"I don't mind. I love everything that Karen found for us. It'll be fun to have all new furniture for a new house," Charlene added.

I shook hands and congratulated them. I told Phil I would email him a copy of the contract and be in touch when the title agency had everything ready to close. They thanked me and left. Karen was delighted and gave me a hug.

Chapter 70

I stayed close to home for the next few days to let my black eye fade and heal. Tucker was angry with me and refused to speak to me again. I hoped it would go away before we played on Thursday the 7th at the Middle Tennessee University auditorium.

When Mary Jane came over to the apartment to see Tucker and brought us chicken and rice soup that she'd made, it was inevitable that she would notice my eye.

"What's wrong with your eye?" she asked me.

"I got hit by accident. I wasn't even in the fight and this guy just punched me. Does it look awful?"

"Yes. Let me put concealer on it and see if that'll fade it. Don't you have to play tomorrow night?"

"Yes, Mom is going to have a fit. See what you can do with your concealer, please."

She dabbed it on and blended it.

"Go look in the mirror."

"That's much better. Can I borrow it for tomorrow night?"

"Yes, of course. You can give it back to Tucker when you're finished using it. My girlfriend and I are coming to watch y'all play at the auditorium."

"Thanks so much. Come meet us at Demos' Restaurant at 4 p.m. Mom and Sawyer will be there. Then you can follow us to the auditorium and sit up front together."

"That would be super."

I called Mom on Wednesday night and told her I had tickets for her and Sawyer and to meet us at Demos' Restaurant at four. Then we would go to the auditorium.

Tucker and I dressed in our jeans, white shirts, black string ties, and boots and I used Mary Jane's make-up to disguise the discoloration around my eye. You could still see it, but it wasn't as bad. We drove over to Demos' Restaurant and I asked the hostess for a table for six. She seated me and

Tucker waited out front for everyone else to arrive. I badly wanted a swig of Jack from my flask but knew Mom would smell it, so I abstained.

Moments later, Tucker arrived with Mom, Sawyer, Mary Jane, and her friend, Susan. I stood up and Mom gave me a big hug. I hugged Sawyer too and said hello to the girls.

"What happened to your eye?" Mom asked as soon as she'd sat down.

Oh, Lord, I knew that was coming. Why was I out with Boone and his rowdy friends? I should have known better.

"It wasn't my fault. I was in the wrong place at the wrong time. Some guys were fighting with Boone, and one of them thought I was involved and he slugged me."

She looked totally disgusted but made no comment. She hated that I went to bars, just like Dad used to.

The restaurant wasn't busy yet. Four was a little early to eat, but necessary on that occasion. There was good ole country food and a little Italian. Tucker, Sawyer, and I ordered country fried steak, mashed potatoes, and green beans, which was the special. Mom ordered spaghetti and meatballs. The girls wanted a salad with chicken breast on top.

"I'm so glad you and Susan came to eat with us and are coming to the concert. All I ever have around me are boys," Mom said to Mary Jane as she smiled at the girls. "Tucker tells me you're working at the bank and taking college classes at night. Good for you."

"Yes, ma'am. Susan and I work together and are roommates. I'm not sure what I want to be yet, I'm just getting through the basic college courses right now. The bank will promote me if I get a business degree and study finance."

Tucker put his arm around Mary Jane and gave her a squeeze. It was obvious he liked her a lot.

"That's a wonderful career for sure. What about you Susan?"

"I want to be a teacher. Tucker told me you taught elementary school. Did you enjoy it?"

"I loved it. It was a very rewarding career and I adored my students. Now that I'm retired, I miss them."

We ate quickly and didn't stay for dessert. Tucker and I needed to get to the venue. I gave Mom, Sawyer, and the girls their front-row tickets and passes to backstage.

"Sawyer, you know where to go. Take Mom and make sure Mary Jane and Susan are near you when your park. Come backstage after the concert and y'all can meet Garth."

The band members were arriving as we pulled into the parking area. Garth's fancy bus was already there. Gus was helping the group get the instruments into the auditorium. Tucker and I brought ours inside, and thankfully Boone was on time. They had enclosed the auditorium with glass and it held 10,000 fans. As Murfreesboro was so close to Nashville, the event was sold out.

"Are you guys ready to play your new songs? There's a full house and your album has been selling well. Make me proud," Bob said when he came into our dressing room.

"Don't we always?" said Boone with a sneer.

"Right Boone. Getting into fights in pool halls is not good for the band's reputation. And Cade, I see your shiner, luckily no one will notice it from the audience. You two need to clean up your act, especially when you're in Nashville. If you keep getting into fights, you won't be invited back to tour next year."

Boone shrugged and I tried to look remorseful. Bob was right. After he left, I went to the bathroom to have a couple of swigs from my flask and a hit of coke. The last lot I got from Boone had gone up in price and we'd had an argument when I complained.

"You fucker," he'd said before he snatched my money, stormed out the bathroom door and slammed it behind him.

I needed to be up to perform. It would be the first time Mom had seen us play at a big concert.

We played first and warmed up the audience. They clapped and hooted when they recognized our songs. *Green Eyes* was still in the charts, and *When I Saw You* had gone to number five on the local stations. We played for thirty minutes and then out strode Garth and his band. Everyone was screaming his name and lighting their lighters as if they were candles. They played for forty-five minutes and when it was over, Garth went out back to sign autographs. Mom, Sawyer, and the girls were waiting in line and they waved at us. We hung around and watched how Garth made everyone feel special. When it was Mom and Mary Jane's turn, I walked up with them.

"Garth, this is my mom, and Tucker's girlfriend." His grin was big. "Hello Mom, you have talented sons."

"Thank you, we sure enjoyed your concert," she said.

After they got their programs autographed, we left. "Get in everyone and I'll drive you to your cars. I know Mom wants to get home to Grannie. I sure wish she could have come," I said.

Mom hugged me and the expression on her face told me she smelled alcohol on my breath.

"I'm worried about you," she whispered in my ear. "I'm not dumb. I know what you are doing to yourself and we've already talked about this and I've warned you. You have such a bright future if you don't mess it up."

I didn't reply. I just got in my truck. Mom left with Sawyer and I figured I better go home. When I got back to the apartment, it was too late to call Harper. I took a Xanex and slept like the dead.

Chapter 71

Everything was ready for the title company to complete the Armstrong's contract when Karen called to say I had lots of *sugar bucks* from her furniture store and I should come and use some for Christmas presents. This was the lovely way she rewarded us when we referred clients to buy furniture. The Armstrongs had bought an entire house full of furniture and I couldn't wait to see what they had purchased. I was about to leave when my cell phone rang; it was Cade. I walked into our lunchroom so I could have privacy.

"Well, hello. How was the concert last night?"

"Fabulous. Mom and Sawyer came and ate dinner with us and she got Garth's autograph. I think she enjoyed herself. Mary Jane and her friend Susan came too. Tucker is besotted with her, I can tell."

"That's exciting. So glad your mom could see you both perform. Wish I'd been there."

"Do you think you could bring the kids to Atlanta on December 14? We'll be playing at the Omni that night. It's a Monday night. They'd have to skip a couple of days of school."

"That's just before they break up for Christmas on the 21st. Lizzie will have tests. I wish we could, but not this time."

"What about bringing them up to Mom's house before Christmas for a few days?"

"Let me check with Pat to see if we get busy then."

"You decide, Mom will be glad to have y'all anytime. I can get a couple of blow-up beds for Sean and Lizzie."

"Lizzie can sleep with me, but Sean would need a blow-up bed. Anyway, it's more than a month away. Where are you going next?"

"We leave for Houston in a week. Then to Gainesville, Shreveport, Atlanta, Charlotte and finish in Amarillo on the 15th of December."

"I don't know how you do it. I could never travel like you and Tucker do."

"Well, it'll be over soon and Bob is working on places for us to play in Nashville after that. Sawyer has more songs written and we need to cut another album."

"I'm glad you called. I need to go. I just sold another cottage and Pat is checking my paperwork. Love you."

"Love you too, Babe."

"Was that lover boy?" Pat asked.

"Yes, he's got one more month of the tour. He wants me to bring the children to his mom's house during the holidays. How busy will it be after Christmas?"

"Probably not too busy. Buyers spend time with their families. But don't go before Christmas. You need to be here when the Armstrong's cottage closes and they have all their furniture delivered."

"Right, I thought so. After Christmas would be better. Lizzie will be beside herself, riding Cade's horses. She has horse fever. I had it at her age too, all the way through high school."

"Looks like all your paperwork is correct. Can you verify with Bob that the punch list in the Armstrong's cottage has been completed?"

"I'll do it this afternoon. I'm going to see what they've purchased at Sugar Beach. See you tomorrow."

I drove to Sugar Beach where Karen was arranging furniture and greeted me with a smile.

"Come see what the Armstrongs purchased," she said.

"Wow! No wonder Phil said she'd overspent. What gorgeous furniture."

"Look at this round glass sphere filled with shells. He wouldn't let her buy it. It would look perfect on the dining room table."

"Do you think I have enough sugar bucks to get it for them as a housewarming gift?"

"Let's go to my office and see." Karen looked at her notes. "Yes, you have more than enough."

"Perfect. Can we wrap it up like a present?"

"Of course. You have more bucks left. We have gorgeous candles." When Karen showed me the selection I picked out one for my mom and one to take to Cade's mom too. I liked the idea of earning sugar bucks. Three presents and I hadn't spent any of my money.

Needless to say, Lizzie saw me carry them inside. "Who are those presents for?" she asked.

"The big one is for Mrs. Armstrong as a closing gift. The others are candles. One for Nana and one for Cade's mom. Would you like to go visit Cade and his family in Tennessee after Christmas?"

Sean jumped up and down and Lizzie looked excited. "That would be terrific," Lizzie said.

"I want to go too, as long as Santa comes to Nana and Papa's house for Christmas," Sean said.

"I'm sure he will. He's never forgotten you."

"Are you hungry? I have chili cooking in the slow cooker. I put it on this morning before I went to work. I didn't have lunch. Let's eat early."

The chili was perfect for a cool November evening. It always gets colder after Halloween. Time to turn on the heat and put warm blankets on our beds.

Chapter 72

When Bob arranged for us to record two more songs that Sawyer had written while we were in Nashville, we picked up Boone and drove over to The Barn. Boone looked as antsy as I felt. There was always a Xanax hangover the next morning. It took a few cups of coffee and a snort of coke to get rid of the sluggish feeling.

We had barely started when Bob called us out of the recording booth. "Cade and Boone, you're messing up. What's going on? You forgot some words and missed a few licks on the drums and guitar."

Boone just frowned. I didn't know what to say. I knew I was off. "Sorry. I'm feeling a little off today. Can we try again?"

"Yes, but you know we only have limited time to record. There are other musicians waiting. Play the song again."

We did and thank God it sounded much better.

"Brother, you and Boone better get your damn acts together. Both of you are drinking too much," said Tucker once the session was over and we were outside. "How many times do I have to tell you? No matter what I say you don't listen and neither do you listen to Mom. What the hell is wrong with you? What's it gonna take to make you wake up?" He glared at me, got in the truck and slammed the door.

"Sorry. I don't know what's gotten into me lately."

We dropped off Boone at his apartment and stopped to eat hamburgers at Rotier's Restaurant where they had the best burgers in the city for under ten dollars. The restaurant had opened in 1945 and was popular with local and Vanderbilt fans. It had old-school, pine paneling, well-worn lumpy booths, and was just in the university's shadow. The hamburger patties were large and hand made. Just what I needed for nourishment. I didn't get a beer because I knew Tucker would say something. We both ordered sweet tea and fries.

The next weekend when we played at Tootsie's, Mary Jane, came in with a couple of cute friends. At least she took Tucker's mind off me. Later that day, I called Harper to see if she was coming before Christmas. She said it wouldn't work, because she had a closing and had to be in Fort Walton Beach. She said she would try to come for a few days after Christmas.

We left for Houston on the 15th of November. It was hell getting up at 6 a.m. in the morning to get on the bus.

"Well, hello boys. You been behaving?" Gus said.

"I have," Tucker replied.

"What about you, Cade and Boone?"

"Same ole same ole," Boone replied. He was particularly sullen.

"Staying out of trouble," I mumbled. There was no fooling, Gus. He had seen it all. I slept the whole way to Houston. We arrived in plenty of time to set up the stage at The Summit. By then, many of our venues looked the same: big basketball stadiums that held concerts.

I was tired from playing late and drinking, plus I wasn't sleeping well. I found myself getting irritated with everything and everyone. I didn't feel like talking to Harper or listening to her being so upbeat about real estate or what the kids were doing.

"You want to get a cab and go to downtown Houston?" Tucker asked.

"Naw, I'm going across the street to eat and then back to bed. Wake me when you get back for tonight's concert."

We played one more night in Houston, then left early the next morning for Gainesville, Florida. You would think these tour people could organize their schedule so we didn't have to criss-cross across the country so much. If we had a fine bus like Garth, it wouldn't be so darn uncomfortable. Yet again, we traveled on the I10 through Texas, Louisiana, Mississippi, and into Alabama.

"You guys want to stay in Mobile tonight? We can go eat oysters at Felix's Fish Camp?" said Gus.

Everyone agreed that would be a change from barbecue. Gus left the interstate and parked downtown in a nearby bank lot. We bailed out, stretched, and walked over to Dauphin Street downtown. Gus was rambling on about some woman he had taken to Wintzell's when he was in the navy. "Best oysters in town, boys," he said. "My pecker was like a wooden rock that night." Gus had plenty of tall tales.

It was a bright glary day in Mobile and when we walked inside, I couldn't see in front of me. Gus was up front flirting with the hostess and when she seated us, I could see why. She was about twenty and had Mocha-colored skin, long black rasta braids and eyes that sparkled. All of us ogled her as she sashayed down the aisle.

We ordered six dozen oysters and six draft beers. Those oysters were very cold, fresh, and huge. I put horseradish sauce on mine and scooped them up with a Saltine cracker. Another round of beer came and we ordered fried shrimp dinners. It was the best food we had eaten in a while. After my belly was full, I looked around the restaurant. It wasn't a large place. There was a long wooden bar and several tables, and, of course, tile floors and brick walls. *Oysters Fried, Stewed and Nude* said a big sign over the bar. All the signs on the walls were hilarious: *A woman is as young as she tells you she is. An adolescent is a minor with a major problem* and *A silent wise man says more than a talking fool.*

When our cute hostess came back and asked if we enjoyed our food, Tucker asked her about the signs. She told us the original Mr. Wintzell loved collecting signs, and they had stayed intact since 1938. We each paid our own bill and Gus led us to the old hotel down the street—The Battle House Renaissance. Appropriately named, it had quite a military history. Built in 1852, the hotel was on the site of President Andrew Jackson's headquarters during the War of 1812. The hotel had also served as a makeshift Confederate hospital during the American Civil War. It amazed us to be staying there and even better, it was inexpensive.

Mobile is a city like New Orleans, with lots of history and beautiful old buildings. But we weren't there to enjoy it. The next morning, we were up again at 6 a.m. to drive to Gainesville, Florida to play at The Stephen O'Connell Auditorium. Tucker and I have always been Vanderbilt Commodores' football fans. At around that time they were playing the Florida Gators. As we drove in that Saturday, the town looked deserted. Gus told us that the game was at Vanderbilt, not in the Swamp, which was the nickname for Gainesville. Too bad, otherwise we could have gone to a ball game. Gainesville has always been a music town. Tom Petty and the Heartbreakers were local boys.

I hoped we'd fill the auditorium, and that not everyone would be out of town for the game. Luckily, we had almost a full house that night. It wasn't cold, so we slept on the bus and spent our hotel allowance on our last night in Mobile.

Lexington, Kentucky, was our next stop—twelve hours away. Gus announced we would drive straight through to a motel in Lexington. We could rest the next day and play on the 23rd at Rupp Arena. This was home to the famous University of Kentucky Wildcat basketball team. The convention center hosted some big-name entertainment. Guns and Roses had played in June and Rod Stewart just before us on November 6.

We spent the night in a cheap motel near the college. I was so wired up after the show, I took a Xanex so I could sleep and I drank nothing. I slept deeply. Early the next morning, Gus banged on our door.

"Get up, you lazy shitheads. Let's head to Nashville for the Thanksgiving holiday."

Tucker opened the door and let the chilly air blow in. "I'm up," he replied. "I'll get Cade and Boone up too. We'll be ready to go in ten minutes." He turned on the coffee pot and had a cup ready for each of us to take on the bus.

"Thanks, Tucker, just what I needed."

Boone mumbled thanks. He was never one to be very appreciative.

"Well, thanks, Boone, glad you are up and ready to go," said Tucker.

Gus was in a great mood as he sang along to one of Garth's songs on the radio.

"You sure are in a good mood," I said. "Have you got a hot date waiting for you at home?"

"You boys aren't the only ones who have a love life. There's a sweet woman waiting for me in Franklin. She's a fabulous cook and has invited me for Thanksgiving. I can't wait to eat her cooking."

"Well, good for you. Tucker and I will head to Dunlap. Our Grannie can cook some great Thanksgiving food too."

"Where you going Boone?" Gus asked.

"My mama lives in Dixon. It's about forty miles from Nashville. I'll go home. I haven't seen her in a while and my sister's family will be coming.

She has three little girls and a worthless husband. They'll probably hit me up for some Christmas money."

"That'll be nice if you give them some money. You've been making plenty on this tour unless you drank it all," said Gus.

Boone ignored Gus and looked out the window. He never talked about anyone close to him. Tucker and I were lucky to have our family.

Chapter 73

My phone was ringing as I walked into the house at 6 p.m. Lizzie answered it in the kitchen.

"Mom, it's Cade," she shouted then kept talking to him before she finally handed me the receiver.

"Hello, honey. What were you and Lizzie talking about?"

"I was asking her if she wanted to come to Dunlap for Thanksgiving and ride Satan."

Lizzie began jumping up and down in front of me. "Mom! Mom! Can we go? Please?"

"Calm down, let me talk to Cade first. I need to check the calendar and see if you have enough days off from school." I took the calendar off the wall and stared at it. "If I let them skip school on Wednesday for the drive to Dunlap and we came back the following Monday, we could come. Monday is a teacher's only day. It's a seven-hour trip, but probably nine because with the kids I'll have to stop a couple of times and we'll have to eat lunch."

"I hope y'all can come. Mom and Grannie are already asking if you will."

"Let me call my parents. They can always have Thanksgiving with my brother and his family. When did you get home?"

"Tucker and I just got back from Lexington. We'll go over to Dunlap on the Wednesday and wait for you. I'll pick up a blow-up bed for Sean at Walmart. You need to bring warm clothes for them. It can get cold around Thanksgiving."

"I will. Is there anything I can bring your mom and Grannie?"

"No, thanks for asking. Tucker and I will give them extra money for the turkey and food. They don't like to take it, but it's only good manners."

"Let me call my parents and I'll call you back. Are you going to be home tonight?"

"Yes, we have laundry and the apartment needs cleaning."

"Bye, I'll call you back."

I fed the kids leftover beef stew with a corn muffin, then I called Mom.

"Hi, Mom. Have you eaten dinner?"

"You know, we always eat at five. Dad is watching the news and I'm knitting and glancing at the TV. What's up?"

"Cade has invited the children and I to his mother's in Dunlap for Thanksgiving. Lizzie is dying to ride his horses and Sawyer has said he will teach Sean to play the guitar. There are enough days off from school that we could leave on Wednesday and come back the following Monday. Now that I have my new car, I'd feel safe driving that far."

"That sounds wonderful for you. We understand. We can invite Tony, Annette, and Jamie over and I can buy a smaller turkey. I'll tell your father. At least you're taking the children with you this time."

"Thanks. I'll talk to you before we leave. I better call Cade back and tell him it's okay."

Cade was thrilled and I was excited. I wondered if there would be snow in the mountains. The kids would love to see it. Lizzie was beside herself, knowing she would ride the horses and Sean was ecstatic that Sawyer would teach him some guitar chords. I went to bed dreaming about our trip.

It was very slow in the office for the next few days. Pat told me it always slowed down around Thanksgiving and that me being out of the office wouldn't be a problem.

I made sure I packed warm clothes for all of us including jackets, gloves and woolen hats. Then I watered all my plants and cleaned out the refrigerator. The car had a full tank of gas and blankets and pillows in case the kids wanted to sleep.

When we drove off at eight a.m., it was fifty-six degrees in Fort Walton Beach, but I knew it would get colder the further north we went. I got to Crestview, went to Georgianna and took Interstate 65. We stopped in Clanton at Durbin Farms Market. Clanton was the peach capital of the South and it had a huge water tower that was painted like a peach. The kids were starving, so we had ham sandwiches, chips, and drinks at the café. Then I bought chocolate-covered pecans and two jars of peach jam for Cade's family. Sadly, it was not peach season because I would have loved to buy them fresh peaches. As we continued our trip, the kids fell asleep, and I bypassed Birmingham. Then took Highway 59 north and stopped in Fort Payne, Alabama, for a bathroom break. I had been learning about country music stars and I knew this was the home of the group Alabama.

They were so popular in our area, and I'd heard they had bought a house in Destin. Instead of following 59 to Chattanooga, I took a westerly road on smaller highway 24. Then traveled north on highway 28 to Dunlap. When I stopped to call Cade, he said he would meet us downtown in Dunlap at the courthouse. It was almost dark and I knew I would never find the farm.

He was waiting there for us when I drove up. We all jumped out to hug him and stretch our legs. I smelled whiskey on his breath and he seemed antsy. Sean and Lizzie wanted to ride with him, so I followed. The gate was open, and all the porch lights were on when we arrived. I would never have found their home by myself. Tucker and Sawyer walked out to greet us and take our luggage into the house. Something delicious must have been cooking in the kitchen. I could smell it from the front door. Cade gave me a big kiss in front of everyone and Mom and Grannie were standing in the living room, ready to meet the kids. Dorothy gave them each a big hug before they met Grannie. Her eyes twinkled as she bent to give them a hug and a kiss on the cheek. She had on her cotton dress and her apron with a sweater around her shoulders.

"What beautiful children you have. I'm not surprised; I knew they would be handsome. Would you two like cookies?"

"Yes, Miss Grannie," Sean said. Then Lizzie piped up. "What kind did you bake?"

"I made chocolate chip, oatmeal and raisin," she said. "Want one now before dinner?"

"Don't you think it will ruin their appetites?" Dorothy asked Grannie.

"Just one. This is a special day for all of us. Come on, follow me into the kitchen."

Cade, Dorothy, and I looked at each other as if to say, *Let Grannie do what she wants.*

Dorothy poured me a glass of wine; she already had hers on the coffee table. Then we sat down.

"I'm so glad you could come. Grannie loves children, and she has talked about nothing else but wanting to meet your two," Dorothy said and I smiled, pleased that Grannie was happy.

"I'm surprised Lizzie hasn't dragged Cade out to the barn. She's so excited and she's an excellent rider now."

Grannie came back to the living room and announced that supper was ready. There were two extra chairs at the table for the kids. Tucker said the blessing, and we passed around the platter of pork chops, macaroni and cheese, field peas and cornbread. Sweet tea was at each place setting.

When Sean tried to talk with his mouth full, I glared at him. "Sorry, Mom. This macaroni and cheese is better than Nana's."

"It's his favorite. How did you know?" I said to Grannie.

"A little birdie told me they like it and you like field peas."

"I do too. They're my favorite. Thank you for making them for me." The food was so delicious. I wished my mom could cook like Grannie and Dorothy. I would have to remind Sean not to tell her we liked Grannie's macaroni and cheese better than hers.

I washed the dishes and Cade dried them while the others went to the front room. We had almost finished when he dropped a small glass and it shattered on the kitchen floor.

"Here, let me help you clean it up. Where are your mom's broom and dustpan?" I said.

"I can do it. You go into the living room with the others."

It was a rather quick retort from him and I wondered what was bothering him.

By the time I went into the living room, Sawyer had his old guitar out to show Sean how to hold the pick and strum it. There was lots of laughter before we all went to bed. As I fell asleep, Cade's short attitude in the kitchen was on my mind.

<h1 style="text-align:center">Chapter 74</h1>

That Xanex must have knocked me out, everyone was already in the kitchen when I woke.

"You slept late, sleepyhead," Mom said when I finally appeared. "Come eat some pancakes. Grannie has made special blueberry ones for the kids. You can have some too."

I better get my act together. I kissed Harper, Lizzie, and Sean on the head. "Did y'all sleep well?"

"We did," said Lizzie. "Can we go see Satan and Suzie after breakfast?"

"We sure can. Just dress warmly. It'll be fifty degrees when we go riding."

Sean came to the barn with Dog and Sawyer, but he didn't really care about riding. He wanted to go back to the house for more guitar lessons. Satan and Suzie were excited to see us. Satan was pawing the ground and pushing Suzie out of the way. As usual, he wanted to be first. I led him out of the stall so Lizzie could meet him. Harper stroked Suzie's muzzle and gave her a carrot.

"He's so beautiful," Lizzie said. Her eyes were glistening with excitement as she put her hand on his muzzle. He nudged her as if to say, *I've been waiting for you.*

"She's a natural," I said to Harper.

"I know. She's been riding with my dad at the stables behind their house."

"Let's brush him and put on his saddle and bridle. Do you know how to do that?" I said to Lizzie.

"Yes, but he sure is tall."

"Okay, let me get the stool out of the barn, then you can climb up and put his bridle on." She did a good job. I just had to fit the bit in his mouth. I picked up his saddle blanket and put it on his back. Then I handed the saddle to Lizzie. It was heavy, but she managed it. That girl was just like her mother; there was nothing she wouldn't attempt.

"Now get on his back." She did and I tightened the belly band. I didn't want her to slip off. "Okay, ride him around the paddock. I'll get Suzie saddled and bridled for your mom and me to ride." Suzie, always the patient one, stood waiting.

"Do you want to be in front of or behind me?" I asked Harper.

"I'm happy to ride behind you. That way, I can put my arms around you." She gave me a big smile. I put my feet in the stirrups and then reached down for Harper to swing up behind me. I opened the gate and told Lizzie to let Satan walk out. When I spoke to Satan in a firm voice his ears perked up. "Satan, we will not run. You have precious cargo on your back. So go slow." He snorted.

We rode down the road toward the lake at a slow trot. Then we dismounted. I gave Harper a grin and a kiss before we led the horses to drink and came back to the tree. "Okay, Lizzie, you and your mom ride Suzie. You can canter if you want to. I'm going to let Satan run ahead. He needs a good workout." As the girls cantered we passed them. Back at the barn I took off Satan's saddle and left on the bridle. When they rode up ten minutes later, the grins on their faces said it all. Lizzie looked overjoyed.

"That was the most fun ever. Next time can I gallop Satan? I know I can do it," Lizzie said.

"Yes, now that I've seen you ride, I know you're a real horsewoman." We settled the horses in the barn and walked back to the house. I could smell turkey cooking. We were in for a fantastic feast.

"What can I do to help?" Harper asked my mom.

"Nothing. You know this kitchen is tight enough with me and Grannie in it. You can help the boys do the dishes afterwards."

We sat on the sofa and watched the Macy's Thanksgiving Day Parade and I held Harper's hand. Sawyer and Sean were strumming the guitar. They were not interested in the parade.

"How are the lessons coming?" I asked Sawyer.

"He's a natural; he's learning so quickly."

"Can I get him a guitar for Christmas?" I whispered in Harper's ear. She nodded.

Chapter 75

It warmed my heart to see Lizzie so happy riding the horses and Cade was acting sweeter. He might just have needed sleep. The smells coming from Grannie's kitchen were enough to make my mouth water. I remembered how good her Thanksgiving food was last year. My children would be surprised by what they ate. My mom's cooking couldn't compare.

When Dorothy called us into the kitchen we stood around the table and held hands. Dorothy held Sean's hand and Grannie held Lizzie's. I could tell they liked my children. What a great feeling. Tucker said the blessing.

"Thank you, Lord, for this bountiful feast that Mom and Grannie have prepared to nourish our bodies and thank you for our guests, Harper, Lizzie, and Sean." Everyone said amen.

Once we all had food on our plates, we ate. "This is the bestest Thanksgiving meal I've ever eaten," Sean said. Grannie and Dorothy laughed and the boys chuckled.

"I told you he would fall in love with your cooking. Now Sean, remember not to say that to your Nana. It's not her fault she wasn't raised in the South," I said.

"Yes, Grannie and Miss Dorothy, this is the best turkey and dressing I've ever eaten. I like the squash casserole and the green beans too," said Lizzie.

I ate so much I had to unbutton my jeans. The boys and I put the leftovers away and the children went into the living room with Dorothy and Grannie. I could hear them answering questions. Thank heavens my children were polite. Once the dishes were finished we joined the others in the living room. Sawyer sat down and motioned for Sean to come close. Sean strummed and sang *Amazing Grace* with Sawyer. Grannie cried and wiped her eyes.

"How did he learn that so quick?" I asked Sawyer.

"He's a natural. While you were out riding we worked on the words."

"I'm so proud of you." Sean gave me a big smile.

Then Cade took out his guitar, Tucker got his banjo and Sawyer announced that he had two more songs for them to record. The boys had already looked at the words, but they hadn't played them together. The first one was *Girl of My Dreams*.

Grannie dozed off, but the clapping at the end woke her. "What did I miss?"

"We played Sawyer's new songs," Cade replied.

"Well, I liked Sean playing *Amazing Grace*. You know I like your religious songs the best."

The boys played a mixture of her favorite songs next, which made her happy. When Cade asked me if I wanted to go for a walk, Mom invited the kids into the kitchen for cookies and chocolate milk. Cade and I bundled up in warm coats, gloves, and scarves and walked down the road holding hands. When we got to the barn, he pulled me inside.

"I have to kiss you. I want to make love to you," he said.

"It's difficult with everyone around, but your mom is a doll. She must have known we wanted to be alone."

Cade kissed me and unzipped my coat, then he took off his gloves and reached under my shirt. I wanted to cry out with pleasure. "Don't you have a clean horse blanket?" I asked.

"There is a couple in the back. Come with me." He pulled out two woolen blankets and lay one over a hay bale. "This should work. Keep your jacket on; pull off your boots and jeans." He covered me with the other blanket, then took off his boots and jeans before he crawled under the blanket with me. It felt so good to have him on top of me. He kissed me again and by then Rocky was ready for Baby. We didn't waste any time. Both of us were so wound up. When it was over he rolled off me. We had to hold each other or we would have fallen off the hay bale. We both laughed.

"I needed you. Making love with you is always wonderful," I said.

"I've missed you so much. I can't wait for this tour to be over."

We got dressed and walked back to the house where I went directly to the bathroom, I sure didn't want Dorothy to smell sex on me. Grannie might not notice, but I'm sure Dorothy would. By the time I went into the kitchen, they were putting out desserts. How could I choose? There was pumpkin pie, pecan pie, and a chocolate cake.

"Yum. How do I choose?"

"Why choose?" Grannie said. "Have a slice of everything." So, I did.

"That reminds me, I have presents for you. Lizzie, get what we bought at the market in Clanton.

"How sweet of you. I love chocolate-covered pecans and imagine the peach jam is delicious. We can have some for breakfast with Grannie's biscuits tomorrow," said Dorothy.

That night, we watched the movie *It's a Wonderful Life,* with James Stewart. Then it was off to bed. I took my shower, so I'd be ready for whatever Cade had planned for us.

Chapter 76

I woke again with a Xanex hangover. I couldn't sleep if I didn't take one. I needed a drink. I felt edgy and anxious. It was an effort to go into the kitchen and put a smile on my face, even though I loved having Harper and the kids with us for Thanksgiving. I needed to stop drinking and taking Xanex and cocaine. Somehow I had to dry out when the tour was over.

"Good morning, everyone," I said as I tried to be my old cheerful self. "Those pancakes look delicious Grannie, are there any left for me?"

"You made it just in time. I was going to throw out the rest."

"Sorry, I haven't been sleeping well," I said and Tucker glared at me. "What shall we do today, kids? Do you want to see Lookout Mountain? Or the waterfalls?"

"I can pack y'all a picnic lunch to take," said Mom.

"That's a great idea," said Harper. "Cade can eat and then we'll get ready."

"Take them to Lula Falls. They have the upper ones and the lower ones," Mom said.

We drove down Highway 111 to Lookout Mountain first and stopped to admire the view.

"The local Indians used to use this mountain to send smoke signals to each other. Then later, the Union Army used this spot to send messages during the Civil War," I told them.

"Can we send a smoke signal?" asked Sean.

"Who would we send one to?" I asked.

"Nana and Papa in Florida."

"I don't think they could see the signal that far away. Plus, you need permission to start a fire. We could burn down the entire mountain if a spark got loose." That boy asked some unusual questions. I enjoyed his curiosity. I was feeling a little better since I snuck a couple of swigs from my flask before we left.

Harper laughed at Sean. Clearly, she was used to his unusual questions. Lizzie nudged me and asked if we could see the waterfalls next. We climbed back in the truck and drove down the mountain, crossed the Tennessee

River and bypassed Chattanooga. The road was winding and full of amazing scenery. Our trees in Tennessee were fantastic.

At Lake Lula we found a picnic table and Harper brought out the turkey sandwiches Mom had made, along with potato chips, pickles, and soft drinks. She suggested we eat before we hiked up to the falls.

"It's a little over a mile and a half to the top. Do you think y'all can make it?" I was sure they could. It was me I was worried about. I'd done no hiking since we went on the tour.

"I'm sure we can," said Harper. "We do lots of walking at Topsail Hill State Park."

We enjoyed the lush greenery on the old trail. The sign said it was shorter and easier for hiking. I was huffing and puffing by the time we reached the top. It was worth it to see the magnificent falls, and the kids loved it. I hugged Harper. "That was harder than I thought. How do you feel?" I whispered in her ear.

"I feel good, but my legs are going to feel it tomorrow. Hiking in Florida is much easier."

Going down was much less difficult, but we were careful not to stumble on the railroad ties. We all used the bathroom facilities, where I took advantage of the privacy and took another swig from my flask.

"Do you want to stop at Lookout Mountain on the way home?"

"Yes," said Sean.

When we stopped, I showed them the sign that said you could see Georgia less than a mile away. Alabama was 25 miles away. We were on the border of Tennessee. North Carolina was 50 miles away and South Carolina was 80 miles away. Kentucky was 120 miles away and Virginia was 120 miles away. As we stood taking in the sights snowflakes began to fall.

Sean started jumping up and down. "Snow! Snow!" he yelled. "Can we stay and make a snowman?"

"Wow!" Lizzie said. "This is astounding. I've learned something I didn't know. I'm so glad we stopped. The snow is beautiful."

"We can't stay. We need to be down this mountain before the snow sticks and we get stuck," I said to Sean.

As we drove home the hike had exhausted the kids so much that they fell asleep in the back seat. I held Harper's hand as we listened to the country music station. When *Green Eyes* came on, we smiled at each other.

The kids went down to the barn with Sawyer. Harper and I were tired and we fell asleep in the recliners in Grannie's living room. When the children came back, their voices were loud. I jolted awake, then Harper woke.

"We brushed Satan and Suzie," said Lizzie.

"I threw the ball for Dog," said Sean.

Tucker came into the living room. He'd been taking a nap. "Do y'all want to go to Sticky Fingers Smokehouse for dinner? I'm sure Grannie and Mom are tired of cooking."

"Great idea," I said. It thrilled Mom and Grannie that we were going out to eat. We took two cars. Tucker drove Mom's car and I drove my truck.

"Can I ride with Sawyer?" Sean asked.

"I want to ride with them too," said Lizzie.

"What are we, chopped liver?" I laughed. I was thrilled. I could get a few kisses before we got there. When they took off first, I kissed Harper passionately. Rocky went hard and Harper reached over and gave him a pat. He was throbbing in my jeans.

"We need to behave. They'll wonder about us if we are too far behind them. Can we take a trip back to the barn after dinner?" I said. "Are you wanting me as much as I want you?"

"You know I do. I love you," she replied.

When we arrived a few minutes after the rest of the family, Tucker grinned at me.

"We've ordered our usual with an extra slab of ribs. They're bringing cornbread, pulled chicken, deviled eggs, baked beans, and fries. I want the kids to try the Pretzel bites; I ordered them as an appetizer," Tucker said. The pretzel bites came to the table along with sweet tea for everyone. Sean and Lizzie loved them. The food was tasty and we had lots of leftovers to take home.

As soon as we arrived home, Mom and Grannie got in the recliners and Sawyer played his guitar and then let Sean play. I took Harper's hand.

"We're going down to the barn to say goodnight to Satan and Suzie," I told them. We gave the horses their carrots, and I found the blankets for the hay bale. Harper was already taking off her clothes and I did the same. Her skin was warm to my touch, and I took time to kiss her in all the places she loved.

"Please, make love to me now," she said as she arched her body toward mine.

We lay side by side and I tried to calm down and still my thumping heart. I kissed her. "I love you, Green Eyes."

"I love you too. We better go back before someone wanders down here looking for us."

"I wish we could stay here all night. But you're right, we better go back."

Chapter 77

Grannie said she wanted us to go to church with her after breakfast and I got up bright and early to dress the kids. I wondered why she was so adamant. She hadn't been on my last trip to Dunlap. Grannie had on a navy-blue dress with a white collar and her white apron. Dorothy was wearing a beige dress with pearls and earrings. The biscuits were already on the table.

"Are we dressed nicely enough for church?" I asked. I had put on a green A-line dress with a matching sweater and my black heels. Lizzie wore her red and green Christmas dress with black patent leather shoes and Sean wore navy blue pants with a white dress shirt and his brown church shoes. Thanks to my mom, they always had a pair of church shoes.

"Oh, yes. You all look just fine," Grannie said.

"Why are you so dressed up?" I asked.

"This is a special service for our family. On this date thirty years ago, we buried Papa Fox, Grannie's husband, and the boy's grandfather. We're taking flowers for his grave and giving a special donation to the church in his memory," Dorothy replied.

"Tucker, Sawyer, and I have our donation ready for the building fund. Papa would be proud that we can contribute," said Cade.

"That's so special. I'm glad we're here for this day. Our church in Milton is very special to my father. He's on the building committee and is very active in Saint Rose of Lima," I said.

This time, when I told the children to ride with me and Cade, there was no grumbling. We drove to the white church that had a red door and a white steeple. Cade shared the history of the church that dated back to 1853. Union troops partially dismantled the original church under General Crittenden in the summer of 1863, and the remaining structure burned in late August of that year. In October of the same year, General Wheeler's Confederate cavalry raided a federal wagon supply train on route to General Grant in Chattanooga. They buried many of the dead soldiers from both sides in unmarked graves.

We followed Grannie and Dorothy into the church. They sat on the right-hand side about halfway down from the front. The preacher had a black robe over his white shirt and tie. He looked to be Grannie's age, at least eighty. He had combed his wispy hair over his bald head, and his face was covered in wrinkles, just like hers. "Good morning," he boomed.

"I see we have the Foxes in attendance this morning, along with three faces I don't recognize. This is the thirtieth anniversary of the burial of George Fox. He was a faithful son of Christ and a member of our church. We are pleased y'all honor him today."

When it was time for the donation basket to be passed around, Grannie put an envelope in. Then Cade put his and the boys' envelope in next. I felt strange because I didn't have an envelope from our family.

The preacher was standing at the front door as we made our way out of the church. He hugged Grannie and Dorothy, shook hands with the boys, and then looked at me. Cade put his arm around me and introduced me and the children.

"Glad to have you. Come any time."

Grannie led us out back to the cemetery, past the unmarked graves of the Union and Confederate soldiers, to a peaceful place under an oak tree. She bent down and placed sunflowers on George Fox's grave. Dorothy was next with a white rose and the boys bent and placed arrowheads next to the flowers. Sean and Lizzie added rocks that came from the Lula Falls, and I prayed for peace. It was a special time for everyone. Next to George's grave was John Fox's, the boy's father. They kneeled in front of the headstone and said a prayer, although they didn't leave any tokens or flowers.

Back in the car, I asked about the arrowheads. "Did you and your grandfather collect arrowheads?"

"Yes, he took us everywhere in the area and we searched for them when we were young. He was the best Papa anyone could have."

"What about your father's headstone? You didn't leave anything for him."

"We do that on the anniversary of his death. Today was just about our grandfather." Cade's eyes were glassy and I thought I'd better keep quiet. It was a somber drive back to their home and I was glad the children kept quiet too.

For lunch, we ate leftovers from the barbecue we'd had the previous night. Dorothy and I cleaned up the kitchen. Sawyer and Sean were in the living room playing the guitar and Lizzie was begging Cade to take us horseback riding again.

"Okay, little miss horsewoman. We'll go riding. Put on some jeans and bring a jacket," Cade said.

"Why don't you and Lizzie go riding? I'll stay here and with your mom and Grannie. You and she can gallop. But please put her on Suzie. She'll beg to ride Satan by herself, but I would prefer she rides Suzie," I said to Cade.

"Mom! You're a spoilsport. I wanted to ride Satan."

"Come on, Lizzie, let's go to the barn," said Cade.

Dorothy made us each a cup of tea and we sat at the kitchen table. Their kitchen was a warm and cozy room, with soft yellow walls and yellow and green wallpaper. Flowery curtains graced the windows.

"We're so glad you brought your children to visit us," Dorothy said and Grannie nodded.

"They've loved every minute of our visit. We'll have to leave early tomorrow though. I'm so glad it's teacher planning day and they got an extra day off. I hope some time you'll come to Florida and visit us. That cottage Cade stayed in is inexpensive and has three bedrooms. Have your ever seen our white sand and emerald-green waters?"

"Lord no, child," Grannie said. "We didn't have money when George was alive to go visiting Florida. He worked in the coal mines and when he wasn't working, we couldn't afford to visit Florida, no disrespect."

"We just lived a different life," Dorothy added. "I went on a church trip when I was in high school. We took a bus to Panama City Beach and stayed in the Laguna Cottages. It was a trip to remember. There's nothing like your white sand. I'd love to come and visit you and the children one summer."

"I'm tired. Do you mind if I go take a nap?" Grannie said.

"Of course not. Go rest," I replied.

"Grannie is emotionally tired from this morning. The sadness of visiting her husband's grave wore her out," said Dorothy as she set about making us another cup of tea.

"We can have a girls' chat," she said. "You'll find out boys don't tell you how they feel as much as girls do. Cade tells me some things, but not much about how you and he feel about each other."

"We love each other and somehow we have survived the long distance between us. Although he seems different this time. Is there something wrong, do you know?"

"I can tell he's madly in love with you. But I worry about his drinking and hope that's all he's doing on his tour. His attitude and weight loss remind me of my husband, John, when he was the same age. Have you noticed him drinking more?"

"Yes, he keeps his flask full. I can smell it on him often. Then he puts mints in his mouth. My ex-husband was an alcoholic. Ten years of being married to him were so hard on me and the children, especially Lizzie. She adored her father but would run to me when he started shouting and tried to hurt me. I can smell liquor a mile away. I think Cade has been drinking more during the last few months. I'm very concerned about him. I couldn't possibly have a relationship with another alcoholic."

"I've noticed it too. I've mentioned it to him. Have you?"

"No. I'm hoping he'll stop after the tour. It'll be over soon. For the sake of my children and myself, I couldn't be with him if he is drinking, and God forbid, doing drugs."

"After you leave, I'll bring it up again. I don't blame you one bit. My life was hell when John came home drunk. That's why I haven't tried dating again."

When the front door slammed, Lizzie came running into the kitchen. Dorothy and I hugged and waited to hear what she had to say.

"We ran and ran. Satan always had to be out front, but Suzie kept up with him. I can't wait to tell Papa that I can gallop by myself now."

"That's exciting. Good for you. I'm proud of you," I said to her.

"She can really ride. I think she could have ridden Satan, but we didn't want to disobey your ruling," Cade said. Lizzie gave a huge smile as if to say, *I told you so.*

"Lizzie, go have your shower. You won't have time tomorrow morning. We need to leave by eight." Then I walked into the living room. Sean was singing and playing *Green Eyes* and Sawyer was grinning at me.

"Sean, that's fantastic. You've learned so much this weekend. We need to continue your music lessons next year."

"That would be stupendous! I hope Santa brings me a guitar."

"Well, you better put that in your letter to him when we get home."

Cade put his arm around me and kissed my forehead. "You're going to be a terrific guitar player, Sean. I just know it," he said.

Cade and I went out to the front porch. It wasn't too cold; he wrapped me in a blanket and we rocked in the rocking chairs. The sky was dark blue with no clouds and the stars seemed brighter than ever in the country.

"This has been the best Thanksgiving ever," he said. "Thank you for making the drive and bringing the kids. Mom, Grannie, and my brothers love them. It is so much more fun to have young ones around. I'm going to miss you so much."

"I'll miss you too, and your family. We come from different families, but I love yours and you too."

Chapter 78

Everyone got up early to say goodbye to Harper and the children. Grannie baked biscuits for their trip and Mom packed lunch. All of us had tears in our eyes. I could hardly stand walking them to their car. I hugged Lizzie and Sean with all my might and whispered, I love you in their ears. Then I kissed Harper as if it were the last kiss I would ever give her. Then they drove away.

I went down to the barn to give the horses a carrot each. I sat on the hay bale where we had made love and cried. I wanted a drink so badly, but I knew if I did, Mom would smell it and give me hell. I took a small snort of my coke to pick me up. Then I walked back into the house.

Tucker was waiting for me and gave me a hug. "Do you want to go back to Nashville today? Mary Jane will be back at work and I've missed her."

"Yes, let's get our things and drive back. Bob could have a gig for us. Why don't you tell Mom and Grannie instead of me?" I had a feeling Mom might want to give me a lecture so I avoided her.

Half an hour later, we both hugged Mom and Grannie, then gave Sawyer a hug too before he walked us out to the truck.

"I can't wait for y'all to be through with the tour. I'm hoping Mom will let me come play with you in January. In the meantime, I'll keep writing songs," Sawyer said.

"Let me drive, brother. You can sit and mope. Just kidding. I know you're going to miss Harper and her kids something fierce," Tucker said.

We arrived home a couple of hours later and I went straight to the store and bought more Jack Daniels. I took a couple of swigs straight out of the bottle as soon as I got back in the truck. Then I went shopping and bought hamburgers, spaghetti sauce and noodles for supper.

"I'm going to take Mary Jane out for dinner tonight. Will you be okay by yourself?" Tucker asked.

"I'll be fine. Go enjoy yourselves. I'll make spaghetti and we can have it for dinner tomorrow." Tucker left and the first thing I did was pour myself a large Jack Daniels and water, then I sat on the sofa and watched Dolly Parton in a Christmas show that was a rerun. I had another drink or two and then went to bed. I had forgotten to make the spaghetti, but I could do it in the morning. I took a Xanex and slept soundly.

The next morning, the red light was glowing on the answering machine. Harper had called when she got home to let me know they were safe. I called her cell phone. It was ten a.m. her time.

"Hi, honey, sorry I missed your call last night. I never heard the phone ring."

"I just know you wanted to know that we got home safe and sound. I was tired from driving and went straight to bed. I'm at work now, and Pat has plenty for me to do, so I have to go. I love you, bye."

It was probably just as well she couldn't talk. I sat on the sofa and hung my head. I was so depressed. Then I decided I'd better cook the spaghetti. Tucker was still asleep, which was good. When Bob called to ask if we wanted to play at Tootsie's for a couple of nights, I said yes. We had to be back on the tour on the 6th of December. Four more stops and then we would be finished. I felt as if I was ready for a nervous breakdown. If I stopped drinking, I would have to dry out and I couldn't do that on the road.

We played Tootsie's on Friday and Saturday night. Boone showed up late and looked like death warmed up. During the break on Saturday night we went into the bathroom together. I bought more coke from him. He asked if I wanted some smack. I said, hell no. When he rolled up his shirt sleeves before he washed his hands, I saw the needle marks.

"Boone, you're killing yourself slowly."

"Fuck off! It's none of your business."

"Sorry dude, I hate to see you do this to yourself."

"Who are you to talk? Leave me alone."

I stopped at the bar and had a shot of Jack to calm my nerves, then we finished our set. I was going straight home. Tucker was going out with Mary Jane. I would have the house to myself. I drank the rest of a bottle of Jack Daniels, took a Xanex and fell asleep on the couch.

Tucker woke me around 1 a.m. "Go to bed. What the hell is this? You're such a fuckin' mess." He held up the empty bottle. I was so groggy I had to hold on to the wall to get to my bedroom.

Chapter 79

It was an effort to get out of bed and get the children ready for school. We were all tired and a little grumpy. Lizzie didn't want to get dressed and Sean didn't want to finish his pancakes.

"Fine, hurry or you're going to miss the bus and I don't feel like driving you to school," I said in the end. They got on the bus, and I just had time to get myself ready for work. I dressed in beige slacks, a cream-colored pullover and leopard flats. I tied my hair in a ponytail and wore simple earrings. When I looked in the mirror, there were dark circles under my eyes. I found the concealer rubbed it in and hoped it would hide them. A couple of swipes of blush and lipstick and I was ready to conquer the real estate world.

Pat's car was parked outside the office. She always beat me to the office. Of course, she didn't have two children to get off to school. I walked in with a smile on my face. "Good morning, I'm back."

"I hope you had a good time. We have lots of paperwork to finish today. It's great to go on vacation, but we always pay for it when we get back. I listed two new homes while you were gone. Can you put them into Multiple Listing Service and get the flyers ready for open houses this weekend?"

When Cade called I told him I couldn't talk because Pat had lots of work for me.

"I'm on to it. Congratulations on the new listings." I took her folders and started entering the details. The first one was a resale of one she had sold two years ago in Mary Esther Manor. It was a three bedroom with two bathrooms, a two-car garage and a fenced backyard. She'd priced it at $99,000. I was pleased with the photos the photographer had taken, I uploaded them and used them for the open house flyers. "Here's the flyer for 481 Bryn Mawr. Do you want me to do an open house this weekend?" I asked her.

"Yes, call the owners, Jack and Barbara Townsend and set up the time with them."

We took a break and went to Mother Earth's for lunch. Pat didn't seem to be in her normal good mood.

"Are you okay?" I asked. "Did my trip cause any problems?"

"No, just dealing with this divorce. He's not making it easy. You'd think he'd want to be free to continue his romances."

"I think some men want their cake and ice cream. Michael didn't want a divorce, he just wanted to fool around with other women. When it was over, I had to find him a place to live. One of the owners of the Hog's Breath Saloon took him in. I was so thankful."

"Well, mine wants to keep the waterfront home in Shalimar. He's just having a hard time giving me money so I can buy the Green Reef town home from Bob Bonezzi. I met with Don Dewrell while you were away, and we subpoenaed J.T.'s financials."

"Don is the best. He'll get it sorted for you."

"How was your trip? Did the kids have fun?"

"Yes, Lizzie was in heaven riding the horses and Sean learned to play the guitar. Christmas is coming and I want to get him one. I can't get Lizzie a horse though. I hope she won't be disappointed."

When we got back from lunch, I worked on the other listing. It was 452 Ocean View in Crystal Beach with three bedrooms and two bathrooms. Pat had listed it at $132,900. It was a new home built by D. L. Gibson Construction. It was amazing how much more the homes were listed for near the beach in Destin. I printed flyers and as it was unoccupied, we were able to put a lock-box on the house so other realtors could show it.

The week went by fast, and on Saturday and Sunday, I had open houses at 481 Bryn Mawr. I put up my signs on the side entrance to the Mary Esther Mall and McDonalds. It was a high traffic area, and I had ten people through on Saturday and eleven on Sunday. On Saturday, one young couple seemed very interested. They said they would bring their children back on Sunday after church.

They came in at two and introduced themselves to me again. Sylvia and Steve Dixon were around thirty. He had a military-style short haircut, wore jeans and a preppy shirt. She had a blonde bob, blue eyes and wore navy slacks and a light-blue sweater. She introduced the children as Molly and Donny. They looked around eleven and seven. I showed them the features of the home and the took them into the backyard. The kids loved the fenced yard and reminded their parents that they could have a dog.

"Is this home something that would fit your family's needs?" I asked.

"Yes, I like the layout with the split bedrooms, the fireplace and the backyard," Sylvia said.

"I do too," said Steve. "I like the two-car garage and how close it is to Hurlburt Field. I fly C-130's at the base."

"Do you want to sit at the kitchen table and we can discuss price and talk about financing if you need it?"

Steve was a lieutenant in the air force, so he wanted a VA loan. They wanted to make an offer of $95,000 with 3% down. I told them that looked like an excellent offer and I gave them my favorite loan officer's business card.

"I have a contract with me. I can write it up and present it on Monday after you get Jean Jackson from Countrywide's loan approval. You could call her this afternoon, and with you being a lieutenant, she should be able to give you pre-approval over the phone."

The Dixons looked at each other and nodded. "Write it up," said Steve. "I'll call Jean when we get home."

They signed the offer and I told them I would get back to them by Monday afternoon. As they left, Molly began pulling on her dad's hand. "Can we get a dog for Christmas now? Please?" It tickled me to death and I loved it that they wanted a dog. I could get them a fancy collar and leash as a closing gift. As I was locking up the house, the Townsends pulled into the driveway.

"How did it go?" Jack asked.

"Great, we had eleven people through and the military couple who came through yesterday brought their children today. And I have an offer for you."

"Well, come inside. Let's review it," he said.

We sat at the kitchen table. "It's only $900 less than the listing price. They're getting pre-approved with a VA loan. He flies C-130's. I don't expect any financing problems."

"What do you think, Barbara?"

"It's a fair offer. Let's take it."

They signed the contract. I told them I would call on Monday after the buyers had their finance approval from the bank. I left and went over to McDonalds for a Diet Coke. Once I'd parked I called Steve and Sylvia.

"Congratulations, they've accepted your offer. Just get me that pre-approval letter and bring it and a 3% deposit to my office tomorrow. You can close after the first of the year. Let me know if you decide to get your children a dog for Christmas." They were thrilled. I drove home and ordered a pizza for dinner.

Chapter 80

It wasn't difficult for him to find her phone number. He had kept his ears open and he knew her surname and the town where she lived. He chose the time he would call her carefully. After dinner, but not so late that she would have gone to bed. He wouldn't have decided to do it if that fucker Cade hadn't kicked up a fuss about his prices going up, but what really made him decide was the behavior of his upstart younger brother. How dare he confront him and accuse him of messing up Cade's life? Cade was responsible for himself and it wasn't his problem if he couldn't control his drinking and drug taking. He was delighted when Tucker got carried away and confessed that he'd followed him and Cade and seen Cade knocking off that slut out the back of the bar. It was just the information he needed.

He'd already had several drinks when he decided the time had come to make the call. He'd chosen a bar that no one knew he frequented. And it was one that had a payphone in the hallway leading to the bathrooms, so his call couldn't be traced.

It was a dark, dingy corridor that he made his way along. Luckily, no one was using the phone. He stopped in front of it, hunched over as he took the thick scarf out of his pocket. Once he'd picked up the receiver he wrapped the scarf around it to make sure his voice was muffled. Although she wouldn't know his voice because he had never spoken to her let alone met her, and besides he'd already had a lot to drink and chances were his voice would be slurred anyway. She answered promptly and he imagined she thought it would be lover boy, Cade calling.

"Hello," was all she said and when he didn't reply she carried on. "Is that you Cade? Why aren't you speaking?"

"No, it's a friend."

"Who are you? What do you want?" Her voice had risen and she sounded uncertain.

"I just told you, I'm a friend ringing to warn you. That boyfriend of yours is an alcoholic druggie and he's cheating on you. If you don't believe me, ask his brother. He knows, he's seen him with her. You need to dump him. He doesn't love you. He never did. He's just using you. And you deserve better than him." He hung up. He'd said enough and knew he was on the verge of saying too much. He sauntered back to the bar with a twisted smile on his dark face. He needed another drink and then something stronger.

Chapter 81

Gus drove straight from the concert in Atlanta to Charlotte. We didn't get a hotel, just slept on the bus as Gus drove the 248 miles. We arrived around five a.m. Gus pulled up to a motel and as he helped us get our bags out of the bus, a little old woman who looked at least eighty and who was wearing a cotton dress with a red coat came out of the office.

"Hello, Gus. I've been watching to see when you'd get here. I've got coffee and biscuits for your guys in the office. Come inside. I'll get their keys for the rooms after y'all eat and relax."

"Connie, you are always so accommodating. Meet Cade and Tucker Fox and Richard Boone, they're the musicians and John and Steve have left to help set up the stage for Garth Brooks' performances."

We went inside the old motel that must have been built it in the fifties. Outside was white brick with a red brick porch. The old sign was green and had seen better days. The neon open sign in the window was bright and there was a window to check in without having to go into the office. Connie invited us into her kitchen, where she poured everyone a cup of coffee and put biscuits and grape jelly on the table. Her biscuits were almost as good as Grannies. They hit the spot. I ate three and so did Tucker. Boone nibbled at one, but he looked tired and worn out.

Connie gave us the keys to our rooms. Tucker turned on the TV and we lay on the single beds. I fell asleep for a few hours until Tucker woke me up and told me to take a shower. I took a long hot one and had a shave. We were hungry, so we walked down to the Bar-B-Que Drive In. We ordered pulled pork sandwiches, onion rings, and cokes. There was a concrete picnic table under the canopy, so we sat there to eat.

"You want to go next door and get a Dairy Queen?" Tucker asked me.

"Sure, I haven't had a soft serve this whole trip. I want chocolate drizzled on mine." We ordered two and ambled back to the motel. It was three in the afternoon. We had to be at the coliseum by eight.

"I better go wake Boone. He looked rough this morning." I banged and banged on his door. No answer. I ran to Gus's door and knocked loudly on it.

"What the hell are you banging on my door for? I usually have to bang on yours."

"Boone won't wake up. Can you get the key from Connie and open his room?"

"Sure. Wait here."

Gus got the key and we unlocked Boone's room. He wasn't in the bed, so I opened the bathroom door. "Oh my God!" I hollered. Boone was on the floor with a needle in his arm. Blood was splattered everywhere—on his clothes and the wall. "Call 911. Let me see if he's still alive." I picked up his arm and felt his wrist. "There's a weak pulse. Hurry! Gus, hurry!" I was shaking so badly, yet I couldn't leave him even though he was inert and I couldn't do anything for him. *Dear God, don't let Boone die,* I prayed as I slumped down beside him on the cold linoleum floor. As the seconds ticked by, I was constantly aware that I could so easily have been in Boone's place. Bile rose in my throat and I swallowed to stop myself being sick.

"What's happened?" Tucker shouted as he came into Boone's room.

"In here," I called out. Moments later Tucker appeared in the bathroom doorway and then immediately recoiled in horror.

"Oh my God! I ... I can't look," he said as he tried not to stare at the blood splatters staining the white concrete block wall, or stare at the needle protruding from Boone's arm or Boone's dark waxy face.

"He must have overdosed. Gus has gone to call 911."

"Is he d ... dead?"

"No, he's got a weak pulse."

"Come out of there," Tucker said as he held out his hand obviously hoping to pull me up.

"No, someone should stay with him. I'll wait till the ambulance comes."

Tucker nodded, turned, and retreated to the bedroom. His face was the color of parchment, but no doubt mine looked just as bad. Yet again I looked at Boone. I was drawn to him in a macabre way as I imagined myself lying there instead of him. I picked up his arm again and felt for a pulse. His arm seemed cooler or was it my imagination? The pulse was still there, but erratic and hard to find. *Such a waste of a life not to mention his talent as a musician. He was an excellent drummer.* My head drooped, I let out a ragged sigh and dashed tears off my face with my shirt sleeve. *If only they can save him.*

Gus returned with Connie. She was wringing her hands and praying silently. Fifteen minutes later, we heard the ambulance sirens. Two big guys came flying into the room and went straight to Boone.

"Y'all go outside. We need room to get the stretcher in here."

We stood outside waiting and worrying while they put Boone on the stretcher.

"Gus, I'm going with Boone to the hospital. Can you get a hold of Bob and find out about Boone's next of kin? Somebody get his wallet and bring it to the hospital. I saw it on the dresser."

The ambulance attendants slammed the back door and we took off. I sat to the side and watched Boone's chest to see if he was breathing. The attendant said it was twelve miles to Mercy General Hospital. When we arrived at the emergency room, everything went quickly and they took him in immediately. One of the Sisters of Mercy came to see me.

"Son, I'm Sister Mary Margaret. I'll stay with you while they try to save your friend. Can you give me any information about him? I need his full name and address, along with details of his closest relative." Sister Mary Margaret was wearing a dark blue habit, plain black shoes, and a large black and white cross around her neck. In her fifties, she had a soft glow on her round face. Peace radiated from her—I needed it desperately.

"He's my band mate. We're on tour and we were supposed to play tonight with Garth Brooks. His name's Richard Boone, and he's from Clarkesville, Tennessee. Our bus driver is trying to reach our manager to find out about Boone's family. He never talked much about anyone. I don't know if he has insurance."

"Can I get you anything? A Coke, coffee, or something to eat?"

"No, ma'am. Just show me where to wait and I'll notify you when Gus arrives with the information. I prayed to God. I asked him to help me quit this journey I had been on—drinking and drugging. That could have been me lying on that stretcher. He'd tried to get me to do heroin. Thank God I never did.

Thirty minutes later, Gus and Tucker walked into the waiting room. I stood up so they could find me. Gus had Boone's wallet in his hand.

"I found his mother's phone number and I called and told her what happened. She's very upset and told me she has no way to get here from Clarkesville. She's been worried about his drinking. She didn't know he was doing drugs. I attempted to comfort her, but it's difficult without being physically present."

"How is he?" Tucker asked.

"Don't know. No one has come out to tell me. Sister Mary Margaret needs his identification to register him. Let me go find her." I found her in a little office behind the check-in desk. "Gus is here with Boone's identification. Do you want to come meet him?"

"Yes, I'll be right out."

We stood up when Sister Mary Margaret came into the room.

"I called his mother to tell her what happened. Here's his wallet with his identification. Do you have any news for us?" Gus said.

"Let me enter his information in our system and then I'll talk to his doctor."

"How did you get here? Did you drive the bus?" I asked.

"No, Connie, let me use her car. We have been friends for many years. I always stop at her motel if I have a group going to Charlotte. This is just terrible. I had to call Garth and tell him y'all wouldn't be opening for him. He sends his regards and hopes Boone will survive."

The doctor emerged an hour later, led by Sister Mary Margaret. Their faces said it all.

"I'm sorry. We lost him," the doctor said.

Sister Mary Margaret came over to take my hand. "He's at peace now. Let's go to the chapel and pray for his redemption." We followed her to the small Catholic chapel where she led us to the front pew. Gus, Tucker and I kneeled on the prie-dieu. She prayed aloud for God to forgive him and let him enter His kingdom. Tears poured from my eyes. Tucker and Gus were wiping their eyes too. We left the chapel and returned to the waiting room.

"You boys can leave. We'll handle everything from here on. Thank you for his wallet and his mother's phone number. I'll call her," Sister Mary Margaret said.

Gus drove us home in Connie's Chevrolet Caprice. No one spoke. When Tucker and I went into our motel room, we both sat on our beds and hung our heads.

"Brother, has this taught you anything?"

"Yes, I'm going to check myself into a rehab when we get back to Nashville. I don't see any reason for us to finish the tour. Do you?"

"No, we can't play without a drummer. This is so sad. It could have been you. It would break Mom and Grannie's heart if you had overdosed. I know you have been hitting the hard stuff."

"I'm done with that poison, but I'll need help to detox. Let's get a flight to Nashville. I'll make some calls tomorrow and find the best place to go."

Tucker got up and hugged me tight. I hugged him back. As I lay in bed, all kinds of thoughts went through my head. I didn't want to end up like Boone. I wanted a future. I was in love with Harper. God help me. I needed to call Harper, but I wasn't ready to tell her what had happened.

Chapter 82

I barely slept after the phone call. My mind went into overdrive. Who had called me and had what he said been the truth? I knew it obviously wasn't Tucker or Sawyer and the voice gave me no clue as to who it could have been. I tossed and turned as the hours passed. I was wide awake as I stared at the ceiling. What should I do? I thought about calling Cade but decided against it. I even thought about calling Tucker, but I didn't have his phone number and even if I did what would I have said?

Dawn was breaking when I finally made my decision. I would write a letter to Cade and post it to his Nashville address. I would end our relationship. It wouldn't be a long letter, just long enough to say what needed to be said. That I had found out about what he had been up to and that I could not continue my relationship with him and that I wanted no further contact with him. I could not entertain a permanent relationship with another alcoholic cheater. It was impossible. When I was ready I would tell Mom about the call, but no one else. I didn't have a best friend and frankly it was just too painful to talk about, and apart from that it was no one else's business. Given time I might share it with Pat but not straightaway. I was in no condition to talk to anyone. I would put a barrier around myself and just to take it one day at a time until I began to feel better. If Cade called, I would *not* speak to him. There was no point even if he called twenty times in one day. I had nothing more to say to him.

It was after breakfast, once the children had gone to school when I sat down and put pen to paper. Writing to Cade was one of the most difficult things I believe I ever had to do. Tears streamed down my face and my hand shook as I wrote the words that would end our relationship forever. When it was done I sealed the letter and took it to the post box at the end of the street. My hand was unsteady as I quickly pushed it through the slot. There could be no turning back. I could not have a relationship with another alcoholic cheater. As I walked home my face was awash with tears and once I was inside I stripped off my clothes and stood under the shower and blubbered.

That afternoon when I took the children Christmas shopping for presents for Mom and Dad my heart wasn't in it, although I did my best to appear normal in front of them. I had yet to decide what I would tell them about Cade. We stopped at the knitting store and bought Mom a new container for her knitting. The old one was on its last legs. The next stop was a fancy gardening store, The Farmer's Harvest in Navarre. For Dad we found a special mulching tool that would mulch between vegetable rows. By that time, I was tired and ready to go home to eat the chili I had in the crockpot.

It was evening and I had finished cleaning up the kitchen when my phone rang. It was Cade. I cut off the call, turned off my cell phone and took the landline off the hook. He would get my letter very soon. I let out a ragged sigh and decided to go to bed early. I was totally exhausted after having had no sleep the previous night. But sleep didn't come easily until in the end I was just too tired to stay awake. I knew my final thought before I finally crashed would haunt me for a long time. I loved him and I thought he loved me, yet I had it all wrong. I had made a giant mistake. I had to put it behind me and move on.

The next morning I listened to the voicemail Cade had left.

"Hi Babe," he began in a hesitant voice and when he continued he was stuttering. "I need to tell you I have issues and I am going to rehab in Nashville. I don't know when I will see you or talk to you next, but I want you to know that I love you with all my heart and I hope you will wait for me to become sober. I am so sorry about all this and I know you don't deserve it, but I know I am doing the right thing and I hope and pray you will wait for me. Please look after yourself for me and remember I love you," he said before he ended the call. I pushed the button and erased his message. Part of me was sad—so very sad as I mourned what might have been but now would never ever be. At that moment I recalled the voice who had called me and my hurt turned to anger. *If you love a woman, you don't cheat on her. From now on whenever you come into my head I'm going to erase you. Words are cheap. It's actions that count and yours have spoken volumes.* And besides, it was too late. I had already posted my letter. And even if I hadn't I could not change my mind. I had made my decision and I had to stick to it no matter what.

Chapter 83

When Harper didn't answer her phone, I left her a voicemail letting her know I was going into rehab in Nashville. I wasn't sure how I felt, but I knew I would begin the steps tomorrow to recover. I took a Xanex so I could sleep. It would probably be my last one.

The next morning as Tucker drove me to the Cumberland Heights Foundation I became more and more anxious. There was a white wooden fence with a stone archway at the entrance. Tucker reached over and gave my arm a pat. "It's going to be okay, brother."

The building was attractive, with a white country-style home that had a large front porch and three dormer windows. On the side was a white chapel with a steeple and bell tower. We parked and went inside. An older man with white hair, a florid face, a dark-blue suit, a pink shirt, and no tie greeted us.

"Good morning, welcome to recovery," he said. He shook our hands and introduced himself as Dr. Thomas Clark before he led us to the registration desk where I filled my details, my insurance, and gave them a check for $20,000. That would be enough to start the process of detoxification, in-patient care, extended care if necessary, co-occurring disorders and the twelve-step immersion into recovery.

"Our program enables a man to go back to the primary meaning of his life, so he can start over again," Dr. Clark said, then turned to Tucker. "You may go now. Thank you for bringing Cade. We'll take good care of him."

Dear God, Tucker was leaving me and I felt so alone and terrified. Yes terrified, but what exactly I was terrified of, I couldn't have said. Perhaps it was many things. My mom and Grannie? Would they stick by me or reject me? Tucker had said he would tell them I was in rehab. Then there was the detox process and whether I would cope and how difficult it would be. But by far my greatest concern was Harper. Would I lose her? I had no idea. At that moment I recalled what my mother had said to me about my behavior and my father's behavior and Harper's ex-husband. And then Boone's dying face filled my mind and I shuddered. I knew I couldn't blame Harper if she left me, but the thought made me gulp back tears. I took my handkerchief out of my pocket and blew my nose so the doctor wouldn't see the state I was in.

Dr. Clark took me upstairs to my room, which was sparsely furnished with a single bed, a small dresser, and a desk.

"Lunch is at noon in the dining room. It's on the first floor. See you then," he said just before he left.

I put my clothes in the dresser. I didn't bring much, just jeans, shirts and one white shirt and tidy trousers for Sunday. I lay on the bed on my side and talked to God. *Dear Lord Jesus, Please give me the strength to get through this and please help Harper to understand that I will become sober and that I love her. She is the only woman I have ever wanted and will ever want. Please keep her safe for me until I have recovered and can look after her.* Then my mind clouded in confusion and I just couldn't cope as too many thoughts crashed in on me. I turned my head into the pillow and buried my face to stifle my incoherent sobbing as I gasped and shook like a demented person. Some time later I woke, unaware that I had cried myself to sleep.

After lunch a nurse came and took me to the detox clinic. She gave me some meds and hooked me up to an IV. I slept, then went back to my room. I felt woozy and weird.

At 5:45, I got up and went to the dining room. There were seventeen men of all sizes and shapes around the table. I made eighteen. On the buffet table was meatloaf, mashed potatoes, green beans, and slices of cornbread. I served myself a small portion and took a glass of iced water. No one spoke. I tried to eat as much as I could, although I left half on the plate. I poured myself another glass of water. At the end of the meal, the counselor came in and asked us to go to the smaller meeting room. We sat around on chairs. Everyone introduced themselves and I followed their lead.

"I'm Cade. I'm an alcoholic and an addict." This was my first AA meeting. The counselor asked if anyone wanted to share their story. A fifty-something man, who was balding, had a pot belly and slouchy clothes, spoke up. He told a story about being at the top of his advertising career and losing everything—wife, house, and his money because of his drinking. After the meeting, I went back to my room. I was still shaking, anxious, and sweating. I took the tablets the nurse had left on my bedside table with a glass of water.

The next morning, I went back to the nurse's room for more IV to help me detox. Then Dr. Clark took me to the psychiatrist's office. Despite not being a physician, his desk sign proudly displayed his PHD in psychology. He asked questions. Why did I want to recover? What made me want to recover? I answered them all truthfully. I told him about Boone dying and that I didn't want that to happen to me. He explained my program for the next several weeks. I knew I could do it. I was determined to get through it, whatever it took.

Every day after breakfast we had a meeting, then lunch and another meeting, and after dinner, another meeting. The Foundation created a routine for us.

I found a couple of guys who I welcomed as friends. One was a black professional basketball player from Memphis. He had played for the Memphis Grizzlies. His coach told him he had to recover or be kicked off the team. He was a giant, six feet five inches tall, with a wide white smile. He told me he loved country music, and we would get better together. His name was Joshua Jones.

The other one was older, probably sixty. Every day he dressed as though he was going to work. Pressed pants, expensive shirts, and Cole Haan shoes. He had been a record producer and had heard our songs on the KSM radio. He told me about going through a terrible divorce, losing half the money he had made, and that his children were so angry they wouldn't let him see his grandchildren. His name was Barry Brown.

These two helped glue me back together. We sat with each other at breakfast, lunch, and dinner. After five days, I almost felt like the person I had been before drugs and alcohol. The detox was working. I was ecstatic. I felt sure I was on the road to recovery. But then the blow hit me and I thought I could so easily lose the will to live and end it all.

Chapter 84

I had trouble sleeping and getting the children off to school. I tried so hard to put Cade out of my mind, but it proved almost impossible. All I could do was pray for him. It was over and there was no turning back. Christmas was upon me and I needed to focus on my children and my parents. I pulled myself together and went to the office. The Armstrong's cottage was ready for the final walk-through. They were coming in the afternoon and I would meet them at the house. If everything was as it should be, we would close at 3 p.m., and their furniture could be delivered the next day. I ate a quick lunch, a Reuben sandwich and Diet Coke in the break room. Pat was out at a lunch appointment. I wasn't ready to tell her about Cade yet.

I met Phil and Charlene at the cottage. "Are you excited?" I said.

"Beyond excited," said Charlene.

"Me too," said Phil.

"Let's walk through the house. I've brought blue tape to mark anything that needs to be touched up with paint or cleaned. As we walked, there were a couple of spots on walls in the bedroom that needed a touch-up. I tagged them. Inside the AC closet, it was dusty and needed to be painted. It wasn't much. I'd call Bob and get it done while we are at the closing. I knew Charlene was excited and wanted the furniture in place the next day.

They followed me to the title company. Alison had all the papers ready and was waiting for us in her boardroom. While they signed the papers, I went out and brought my closing gift so I could surprise Charlene. As soon as I returned I set it on the table.

"I know you wanted this from Sugar Beach, so I bought it to go on your beautiful new dining room table."

"Oh, my goodness. I love it. How did you know?"

"Karen told me you wanted it. You've been wonderful clients and I wish you much happiness in your cottage." We hugged each other and they left. Delys complimented me on a smooth closing and said she wanted to go buy one of the glass globes with shells for the office.

"Merry Christmas!" I said. "I have no more closings this year. I look forward to many more with you in 1993."

I called my mom to tell her my good news about the closing. She was proud of me and no longer worried that I could make it as a real estate agent.

"When will you and the children come over for Christmas? We're having gumbo on Christmas Eve and then going to Midnight Mass."

"We'll come early on Christmas Eve and stay for a couple of days. I know Lizzie wants to show off her riding skills to Dad."

"Okay, sweetheart. We'll see you then. I'm so proud of you."

"Thank you, Mom. I love you." I hung up the phone and went home. It was already 4:30, no point in going back to the office. I intended to take the kids out to dinner at Coach-n-Four.

As I walked into the house, Lizzie was studying for her tests that would take place before school was out for the Christmas holiday.

"Do y'all want to go to Coach-n-Four for a celebration dinner? I just closed on the beach cottage." The unanimous answer was yes. We went early as they had a two for one that Lizzie and I could share and Sean could have the children's dinner. As soon as we were in the car, I reminded Sean that he had to be on his best behavior because Coach-n-Four was a fancy restaurant.

Lizzie and I shared the T-bone steak with twice baked potato and salad. Sean had the small children's steak with potato. He wouldn't eat salad. They had Shirley Temples and I had a glass of Pinot Noir." The food was superb and the children behaved perfectly. I was proud of them and told them so. We went home, full, tired, and ready for bed.

As I tried to fall asleep, I wished I could tell Cade my good news. Soon, I would have to talk to Mom about him, but it would have to wait until I could do it in person.

Chapter 85

I received a letter today that crushed me and broke my heart. Tucker forwarded it to me and the date told me she had written it a couple of weeks ago. I read it when I was alone in my room.

Dear Cade,

I hope this letter finds you well. I must admit, I was taken aback when you told me about your decision to enter rehab. It's a lot to process, and I need time to sort through my emotions.

I want to start by saying that I care about you deeply, and it hurts me to see you struggle with your addiction. I understand that entering rehab is a necessary step toward your recovery and I commend you for taking that leap. I truly hope that this journey brings you the healing and growth you seek.

However, I also need to be honest with you about where I stand. After living with an alcoholic for ten years, and finding out that you are also one, I am fearful of a relationship with you and for that reason I am ending our relationship. I must protect my heart and the emotions of my children. I must prioritize my wellbeing and the wellbeing of Lizzie and Sean.

I need space and time to heal. I cannot continue to talk to you on the phone or see you after you get out of rehab. Please understand that my decision is not intended to punish you or make you feel guilty. It is a necessary step for me to reclaim my happiness and find a sense of peace.

Please take good care of yourself. I wish you all the best on your journey to recovery.

Sincerely,

Harper.

I tried to pull myself together after reading her letter. That proved impossible and I collapsed on the bed and sobbed my heart out. I had held so much hope that she would wait for me because she loved me, yet there was no mention of love in her words. I fell into a deep depression. From then on I tossed and turned every night and, of course, I had no Xanex to help me sleep. Who could I turn to apart from God? And why had He dealt me such a cruel hand?

The following days of detox were grueling and painful. My body and my mind were consumed by the fact Harper wanted nothing to do with me. I couldn't control my overwhelming desire for her. If only I could see her and touch her. Then withdrawal symptoms took hold as they reduced my medication and I found myself in agony. At times, because it was so painful, I wished I would die. My body trembled with uncontrollable shakes; my muscles ached as if they were being torn apart. Waves of nausea crashed over me and left me weak and unable to keep down even a morsel of food. The pounding headaches felt like a thousand hammers relentlessly striking my skull. It was mental anguish that truly tested my resolve. Could I do it? The cravings for alcohol gnawed at my mind and whispered promises of relief and escape. The constant battle between my desire for the poison and my determination to overcome it left me emotionally drained and on the verge of despair. Sleep became a distant memory as I experienced vivid nightmares and restless nights. I dreamed of using cocaine to numb my sadness and despair. The nights stretched on, each hour feeling like an eternity as I fought against the relentless pull of addiction. Some days I found solace in the support of the rehab center staff and my fellow residents, especially Joshua and Bobby. They understood my struggle, offered words of encouragement and a shoulder to lean on. Together we navigated the treacherous path of detox and found strength in shared experiences.

The days went past in a blur. I don't remember how many and sometimes I didn't even know which day of the week it was until one day my shakes, anxiety and sweats began to recede. What a relief. There had been times when I didn't think I would get through it, but then a picture of Boone on the bathroom floor would come into my head and I gritted my teeth and forced myself to be strong. I didn't find it easy coping with the meetings either. Some of the men's stories were horrifying. A number had gambled away their paychecks each week, while others had been violent to their wives or lost their jobs and their families as well as the belief in themselves. I had a lot to be thankful for that I had caught myself in time. Regardless, the loss of Harper was still at the forefront of my mind. Not a day went by without me thinking about her. No matter where I was or what I was doing she was always in my mind.

I had started the first step in the twelve-step program. I had admitted I was powerless over alcohol and drugs—that my life had become unmanageable. Everyone in the room had to voice this affirmation. And there was definitely no doubt I was powerless to control my urges. Why did it take Boone's death to wake me up?

After one of the breakfast meetings, Dr. Clark called me into his office.

"You've been here for some time now. I'm sure you have questions and I want to talk with you about the first step we discussed this morning. Do you understand why you were powerless?" he said.

"No, sir. Not for sure. I just knew it made me feel good to drink and that the drink took away my anxiety before I performed and the cocaine gave me confidence."

"Alcoholism is a disease, just like cancer, heart problems and other things. It resides in our brain and tells us what to think and do. Your entrance papers said your father was an alcoholic. Do you realize this disease is hereditary?"

"My mother told me Dad was an alcoholic. She was also worried about me."

"Yes, she probably knew you had the gene. We'll teach you how to control it. How to talk to yourself when it rears its head and wants you to drink. The first step is to recognize you have the problem. You can't make it go away, but you can control it. As you learn more and go through the twelve steps, you'll get a better understanding."

"Thank you, sir. I look forward to conquering this disease." I went back to my room to study and reflect before lunch and our next meeting. After lunch, the team leader asked us to sit in the circle to share why our substance abuse had become unmanageable. I listened to the other stories. For my friend Joshua, it had been the pressure of his professional football career. He felt as if he was not achieving his potential, so he snorted cocaine before a game. His coach had told him to come here and get clean or his career would be over.

Barry had fallen into the same trap as me. The music business was full of addicts. Addicts are some of the most intelligent, attractive, and hardworking people, yet their disease tells them otherwise. They need to bolster themselves up with drugs and alcohol. Barry had lost almost everything. He would have to start over when he was out of rehab.

When it was my turn, I was shy about talking. I just reiterated what Barry said, that the influences in the music business were treacherous.

Back in my room, I was reading the *Big Book*. I missed Harper so much. It was tough not to be able to call her and discuss what I was learning.

The next morning there was a letter from Mom. I saved it to read until after the morning meeting once I was back in my room.

Dear Cade,

I am so proud of you for making the right decision. You have a promising future, with a loving girlfriend and a supportive family by your side. Grannie sends her love. Sawyer says to tell you he has written two more songs written. He feeds the horses and when it is warm enough, he rides them. I received a card inviting us to come to visit you on Christmas Day. Everyone is invited and it says there will be lots of food and entertainment. We can't wait to see you.

Love Mom.

That was fantastic news, but obviously she didn't know that Harper and I were no longer together. Then again, who would tell her when no one in the family knew. I wondered if Dr. Clark would let me, Tucker and Sawyer play for the group. I'd ask him at our next session.

Chapter 86

Pat and I exchanged Christmas gifts. She gave me a beautiful planner for 1992 and I gave her a gold and blue scarf that would go well with her Century 21 blazer. She said she would spend Christmas Day with her son and thankfully her soon to be ex-husband had an overseas flight. He wouldn't be back until the end of December. I asked if I could leave on the 23rd to go to my parents' home. She said yes, business was always slow before Christmas. The week after Christmas would be a good time to hold open houses in Crystal Beach and I agreed to do several. We had just finished exchanging gifts when the office phone rang and I answered it.

"Hey, Harper, it's Kate. We're getting together for a Christmas lunch tomorrow at the Pizza Hut. Can you come?"

"I'd love to. I miss my bank buddies."

The next day Suzanne, Melody, and Kate were sitting at a table waiting for me. We ordered two large pizzas, one with everything and one with just pepperoni, cheese, and sausage. It was a workday, so we drank iced tea. I wore my new burnt orange suit, a chunky necklace and brown heels. I wasn't trying to show off, but I did want them to know I was doing well.

"Look at you," Kate said. "That's a gorgeous suit. It looks straight out of *Glamour* magazine."

"Thanks, I bought it after I sold my first house. I got the idea from *Glamour* but didn't buy one that expensive. I was lucky to find it in T. J. Max."

"Well, I love it," said Melody. "It looks fabulous with your red hair."

"Thank you. I'm trying to step up my wardrobe. You should see what some of my clients from Nashville, Birmingham, and Memphis wear. Oh, to be rich like them. Anyway enough about my clothes, tell me what's been going on at the bank. How's Al?"

"Al is the best boss," said Suzanne. "I'm so thankful you suggested I replace you."

"Guess what? They fired Janice, that bitchy vice president you didn't like. She was having an affair with a guy in the loan department. It was quite *the* scandal," said Kate.

"Wow! I never liked her. She was so mean to me before Al came and saved me from the switchboard position to be his secretary. What happened to the guy?"

"They asked him if he wanted to go to another branch in Panama City. He couldn't afford to be fired because he had a pregnant wife."

"What a jerk. He's lucky they didn't fire him too," I said.

"Tell us about Cade," Melody said.

I really didn't want to tell them he was in rehab or that I had ended our relationship. "He's still on tour."

"I love his music. I love the album with you on the cover," said Kate.

I had to talk about something else in case they went on about Cade. "Thank you for inviting me to lunch. I miss our times together. It's just Pat and me at my office and all her real estate clients keep her busy. We don't get to socialize much, although I'm not complaining. I love real estate and I'm having a good first year. Merry Christmas to all of you and I hope you a wonderful next year," I added. I didn't stay long after that. Cade had got stuck in my head and I had lost my enthusiasm for being with my friends.

When I arrived home, I packed my suitcase for a few days in Milton. You never knew what the weather would be like in December. It could be fifty-six degrees one day and seventy the next. I'd take a good jacket, something to wear if I went riding, and a special dress for Christmas Eve. My parents always went to Midnight Mass and I wanted them to be proud of me.

We left the next morning after a quick breakfast—just a bowl of oatmeal. I loved driving up Highway 87, over the Yellow River, the Blackwater River bridge and into Milton. When I turned right, I passed through our historic downtown. The old Imogene Theater was still there. The Santa Rosa County Junior Miss competition was held on the stage there. My yellow brocade dress was handmade—oh, how ugly it was. The girls had bouffant hair and wore purple eyeshadow. My parents were thrilled when I won. I was shocked. I drove past Milton High School. It hadn't changed. The brick building still had the big sign: *Home of the Milton Panthers.* I drove on to my parents' home which was near the country club. That area in Milton was not the same as the one in Pensacola or the ones my clients belonged to in Atlanta, Memphis, Birmingham or

Nashville. It was not even gated, although it did have a clubhouse, one tennis court and an 18-hole golf course. My parents enjoyed playing golf there and Mom played tennis. I loved their home in Tanglewood. It was an acre lot, with a pool and it backed on to the golf course. The weather was fifty-six degrees, and it was no surprise that they were all inside watching Christmas movies. I snuck in the back door and went boo. Mom dropped her knitting, and the kids jumped up to greet me. My boo didn't faze Dad.

"You know better than to scare me like that," Mom said.

"Sorry. I couldn't resist. You looked so absorbed. I don't know how you knit and watch movies at the same time." I hugged everyone and sat down to watch the end of *The Muppets Christmas Movie* with them. It felt so good to be home with my family. I would make a concerted effort not to think about Cade.

Chapter 87

After our breakfast meeting, I asked Dr. Clark if my brothers and I could play during the Christmas lunch. I had been so despondent about losing Harper, I thought entertaining the group might help to take my mind off her. She was my first thought when I woke every morning and my last thought at night before I finally fell asleep.

"What kind of music do you play?" he asked.

"We can play anything from Christmas music, country, rock and roll and religious songs like my Grannie prefers. I play guitar, Tucker plays banjo, and Sawyer can play drums or a guitar."

"That would be a fine idea. You can set up in the large cafeteria where everyone will be eating. Are your family coming?"

"Yes, my brothers, Mom, and my grandmother. They're so happy I'm in recovery; they wouldn't miss it."

"Good. Consult with my secretary and decide with her about the number of songs you should play."

That afternoon, we worked on our fourth step to make a searching and fearless moral inventory of ourselves. It was difficult. I dug deep inside myself. Why had I turned to alcohol and then drugs? When did I start to drink? I know I started in high school and then it got worse when I played music. The cocaine was a stupid mistake—I had been trying to pump myself up before I performed. The tour might have been a mistake too. Too much free time and boredom on the bus.

Once the session finished, I headed to the serene chapel in the hope of finding solitude. Once I was done in rehab, I intended to prioritize attending church in Nashville instead of just in Dunlap. As I was thinking about leaving, Barry came in and sat next to me.

"We must have had the same idea," he said. "Working on my moral inventory was depressing. I made so many mistakes."

"We all have. That's why we're here."

"Yes. I'm glad you've figured it out so much earlier than me. You have much more of your life left than I do. I put my poor wife and kids through hell. I wonder if she'll ever let me make amends?"

"Try. If she turns you down the first time, try again. Her love for you must have been immense for you to stay married for twenty-five years."

"We were very much in love for a long time. My drinking, staying out late and getting a big head when I was successful hurt our marriage. Then she finally told me to leave because she couldn't live with my habits any longer. I'll start over when I leave the Foundation."

"No one is ever too old to start over. You can do it. Could we start over together? Tucker and I have been saving our money. You could help us produce our next album. Dr. Clark is letting my band play for the Christmas party. Let me know what you think of our songs. You should sit with my mom and grandmother."

"I'd love to have someone to sit with. You sure they won't mind?"

"My mom and Grannie are the salt of the earth. They both have loving hearts. I'll tell them to reach out to you."

The next couple of days went by slowly. Breakfast—meeting. Lunch—meeting. Dinner—meeting. Then it was Christmas morning and my family arrived at ten. I hugged them so tight.

"Wow! Easy brother, you're going to break a rib," Tucker said.

Tucker, Sawyer, and I set up our instruments in the large dining room while Mom and Grannie went on a tour of the Foundation. When they came back into the dining room, I introduced them to Barry. He looked good. He had on neatly pressed pants, a white shirt, a colorful Christmas tie, and he was wearing socks with his shiny loafers. Mom looked him up and down when I introduced her.

"It's a pleasure to meet you, Mrs. Fox. Cade has told me a lot about you." He seemed to enjoy looking at my beautiful mother. She wore a cream fitted dress with a tan and brown scarf around her neck, pearls in her ears, stockings and high heels. I must admit, she looked great considering she was almost sixty.

"Thank you. We don't get to talk to Cade much, so you must tell us about yourself. By the way, this is my mother-in-law, Helen Fox. We call her Grannie. And Tucker and Sawyer, Cade's brothers. Won't you sit with us while the boys play their music?"

"I'd be delighted," he replied with a big smile. They found a round table close to where we had set up our instruments.

The servers were setting up the long buffet table with turkey, gravy, ham, cornbread dressing, green bean casserole, sweet potato casserole, wild rice, cranberry sauce, and more. The last table had desserts: pumpkin pie, pecan pie, chocolate cake, fruit cake and sponge cake with strawberries and cream. The tables and chairs were arranged in a large circle and our band area and the speaker's podium were at the top of the circle.

Dr. Clark went the podium and urged everyone to take a seat. "All stand and our minister, Sam, will say the blessing."

We bowed our heads and gave thanks that our families were with us, and for the delicious food we are about to eat. Then Sam led us in the Serenity Prayer before Dr. Clark took the microphone again and thanked everyone for coming and told us to eat. That was our cue to play a few songs. We started with Christmas melodies and Christmas carols. Then it was time to take a break and eat.

When I sat down, I noticed Mom and Barry were having a serious conversation, so I sat next to Grannie.

"How was the drive? Did you sleep okay in our apartment last night?" I asked her.

"Yes and I wouldn't have missed this day for anything. You've made me proud over the years. This is the answer to my prayers—you learning how to stop drinking." There were tears in my eyes as she reached over, hugged me, and wiped them off my face. She was so sweet and my heart was full of love for her.

The servers cleared away the dishes, and that was our signal to play again. We sang the songs Sawyer wrote for our band and a few of Garth's songs from the tour. When we finished, the crowd stood and gave us a standing ovation. I couldn't have been more thankful to my brothers. Then Dr. Clark went back to the podium.

"Our entertainers are the Fox Brothers from Dunlap, Tennessee. They have recorded one album called *Green Eyes* and have another one in the works. Cade and Tucker just finished a year-long tour on the road with Garth Brooks. Give them another hand."

Once we had chosen our desserts we went back to the table to mingle. Josha came over with his beautiful wife, Delores. She had on a suede camel-colored dress, a gold necklace and high heels. She reminded me of the New York models on the cover of magazines. She took my hand and squeezed it, then she bent over to whisper in my ear. "Joshua is fond of you. Thank you for being his friend." Behind Delores were two of the cutest twins, dressed in identical Christmas dresses, white socks, and black patent leather shoes. "This is Macy and Tracy. Girls, say hello to the Fox family."

Mom motioned to the girls to come closer. "Tell me, was Santa good to you this morning?"

"Yes, ma'am. We got matching bicycles, lots of dresses, and bows for our hair. I'm Macy and this is my sister, Tracy."

"We also got Barbie dolls, a Barbie doll's house and lots of clothes for them. But the best present is getting to visit our daddy," said Tracy.

With a wide smile and a few tears, Joshua expressed his emotion. He hugged both his girls and said he was glad to meet my family. Then he took his wife's hand and pulled her into a big hug. What an emotional day it was for everyone. By then, it was three p.m.

"We're going to have to leave soon," Tucker said. "Let's pack up the instruments and we'll come back for Mom and Grannie." As Tucker and I packed the instruments in Mom's SUV, he spoke some touching words. "You know we're all proud of you," he said as he patted me on the back.

Mom was saying goodbye to Barry and I heard her tell him to call her when he was settled in Nashville. Grannie was looking a little tired. It was her nap time. I walked them to the car. Mom hugged me and held me close.

"I'm sorry Harper has decided to withdraw from your life. She wrote me explaining her reasons. I understand, but I'm sorry it had to happen. Be strong, work on yourself," she said to me quietly out of earshot of the others, then she got in the car.

"Thank you all for coming. It has meant the world to me. My love extends to all of you," I said as I swallowed my impending tears.

Back in my room, I lay on the bed and let them flow.

Chapter 88

It was peaceful at Mom and Dad's house. The golfers didn't disturb them unless they hit a bad long shot into their backyard where Dad raised luffa sponges that grew on his tall pine tree. He had saved one with a golf ball inside just for laughs. Once you clean and dry out the luffas, and remove the black seeds, they make wonderful body scrubbers. He had one ready for me to take home.

On the afternoon of Christmas Eve, Dad arranged for us to go horseback riding. The stable had a carriage pulled by a fat white mare called Dolly. Dad drove and Mom and Sean rode in it. Dolly was too fat to ride, but she pulled the carriage just fine. Lizzie picked a brown Quarter Horse with a white blaze down her face and two white stockings. I rode a red gelding with a black mane and tail. Both were spunky. We rode on the regular roads so the carriage could clip along at a fast pace. On Highway 87 we went past the cemetery then downhill to the river. On our way back, we made a stop for my parents to show the kids the location of their plots in the cemetery.

"I don't want you to die," Sean said. "Please live forever. We need you."

Mom hugged him. "Everyone gets old and dies. If they're good, they go to heaven. When you're an angel in heaven, you wait for the rest of your family to join you." That explanation did not make him any happier. He frowned and had a sad look on his small round face. I would have to spend time talking with him about people dying.

"Can Lizzie and I gallop back to the barn? She's dying to ride fast," I said to Dad.

"Okay, you two go ahead. We'll be there soon. Just rest the horses when you get back."

Lizzie and I galloped the three miles. Her hair flew behind her, she handled her horse well and I was proud of how well she rode. We led our horses into the barn to return them to their stalls and the stable boy came out to help us. I could tell he thought Lizzie was cute, but she didn't pay him any attention although she accepted his help to remove the saddle from her horse.

The others returned twenty minutes later and we went home in Dad's truck. By then it was almost five and everyone was hungry. Fortunately, Mom had a pot roast with carrots and potatoes in the crockpot. Once we had eaten, I helped her clean up the kitchen. Sean took a nap so he could stay up for Midnight Mass and I dozed on the bed with him for an hour. Then we got dressed in our Christmas finery. Mom had bought Lizzie a red velvet jumper and a white shirt and, of course, new shoes. Mom couldn't tolerate church shoes that weren't in good condition. She had bought Sean navy blue slacks, a white shirt and a red tie, along with new black shoes. I put on a red woolen dress with a green and red scarf, stockings, and black heels. Mom came out in a green woolen suit with a white silk blouse underneath, stockings, and heels. Dad wore his favorite brown suit, white shirt, and a Christmas tie. I hoped we could get someone to take our photo before church.

Our church, Saint Rose of Lima, was a small brick church. There were only a few Catholic families in Milton. In the back were classrooms for catechism and meetings, along with a room for bingo and potluck dinners. Mom served on the altar committee and helped wash and starch the vestments. Dad was in the Knights of Columbus, who kept the grounds and carried out maintenance on the church.

We walked down the aisle and sat on the right side about five rows from the altar which looked festive with lots of poinsettias. My parents had always sat in that spot. The organist played Christmas music. Mom always teared up, which made me tear up. Thank heaven she carried Kleenex in her purse. I kneeled and prayed for Cade's recovery. We took communion and sang Ave Maria for the closing prayer.

It was lovely to see our church friends and everyone wished each other Merry Christmas. Then Dad finally encouraged Mom to go home. She loved to chat longer than he did. We drove home, drank hot chocolate and ate a piece of Mom's fruit cake. She read the children *The Night Before Christmas,* then it was off to bed, to dream of reindeer on the roof and Santa coming down the chimney.

When we opened our presents before lunch, everyone was happy, especially Sean. Dad had bought him a BB gun.

"That has to stay here with you," I said to Dad.

Lizzie loved her make-up kit and *The Black Stallion Returns,* the book I gave her. Mom had knitted her an Angora sweater and Mom gave Dad a leather bomber jacket. She said it reminded her of what he had worn when she met him in London. Dad loved his gardening tool, and we thrilled Mom with her new purse.

"Wait," said Sean. "What else did Santa bring me? There are a couple more presents under the tree."

"Let's open them. You first," I said to Sean. Wrapped in shiny gold paper was a large box that he tore into. I couldn't wait to see the expression on his face.

"It's a guitar! Santa knew I wanted one. Can I show everyone what Sawyer has taught me?"

"Yes, but let Lizzie open her present from Santa first." It was wrapped in shiny gold paper too. She opened it carefully. Her present was inside a jewelry box.

"A silver charm bracelet with horses on it," she shouted. "I love it! Please put it on my wrist, Mama."

Then Mom went to the kitchen and warmed up the gumbo, cooked the rice and baked garlic bread. I had already set the dining room table with Mom's green wine glasses, her special dishes and silverware. I'd brought a bottle of Chardonnay which I poured into the adults' glasses. The children had Sprite.

We held hands around the table while Dad said the blessing. Gumbo was our Christmas tradition. It was so much easier than turkey and all the trimmings. After we'd eaten, Sean went outside to search for the neighbor's orange cat, a frequent visitor. Dad turned on the television to see if there was another Christmas movie or a parade. Lizzie helped clear the table and sat in the kitchen while we washed and dried. No one could wash the green wine glasses except Mom. They had come from Grannie Michigan after she passed away and they were antiques.

At the end of a lovely family day I fell asleep in front of the television, and I think Dad did too. Sean and Lizzie played a board game in the bedroom. When I woke up, Sean was playing his guitar for Mom and

Dad. I wanted to talk to Mom about Cade, but Christmas didn't seem the appropriate time, so when she asked about him I just said he was fine and didn't elaborate. Family meant so much to us and I didn't want Cade and his issues spoiling the good time we'd had.

Chapter 89

At breakfast the day after Christmas Day, everyone had frowns on their faces and looked depressed. I felt terrible and had to force myself to get out of bed and go downstairs to eat. I sat by myself and had a cup of coffee and a donut. That was all I could choke down. Dr. Clark saw the depression on our faces. Years of experience had taught him how difficult holidays were for his patients. He spoke to us at the morning meeting.

"I know y'all are feeling sad, depressed and probably anxious today. Yesterday was a huge high and today's a big low. It's normal to feel this way. Let's pray to God or your higher power to remove our character defects and beseech him to remove our shortcomings. I've been where you are now. I remember feeling despondent. You can overcome these feelings. It takes practice, daily practice, for the rest of your life. Let's all say the Serenity Prayer together."

After the prayer he carried on. "You are learning the tools to defeat your demons, whether it was drinking, drugs, gambling, pornography, or another vice. Who would like to tell their story today?"

Joshua stood up. "I started drinking after my football games to calm down from the stress of the game. At first, it was just a drink or two at home. Then later, I met guys at the local bar and stayed there too late. Delores was upset. Then the coach heard about my drinking, which had progressed into cocaine use, and he called me into his office. He mentioned the substantial amount I earned for being their tight end and said it was contingent on receiving the help I needed. So, here I am." I was proud of Joshua. He had so much to lose, but I was angry at myself. I knew my dad drank too much. Joshua didn't even know who his dad was. His mom had raised him.

"You want to go shoot some basketball, bro? Maybe you could use some distraction after telling your story," I said.

"I sure do. I'll meet you in the gym in five minutes," he said.

Everyone must have had the same idea because the gym was full. We played for an hour. Joshua's height gave him an advantage on the backboard and at retrieving the ball. He was an outstanding player. I could take the ball away from some players on the floor but couldn't do the lay-ups although I sank a couple of free throws and one, long, three-pointer from outside. We sat down on the bench, drank water and rested. Engaging in a game of ball had boosted our mood.

I tried to call Harper again; she didn't answer. She hadn't answered any of the calls I was allowed to make. I so needed to talk to her, yet it seemed she didn't want to talk to me.

Chapter 90

There would be no New Year's Eve celebration for me. Last year was fabulous with Cade surprising me at the Christmas party and then staying in the Holiday Inn for the New Year. Although I did want to have a party for my girlfriends on New Year's Day.

At the office, Pat and I were working on a new listing in Crystal Beach. One of her previous clients in Water's Edge wanted to sell their home. It was in the front row across the street from the beach and the views of the Gulf of Mexico were amazing. Pat was working on the price comparable, while I put it into Multiple Listing and waited for her to give me the list price.

When noon came, I got us sandwiches from Subway and we ate in the lunchroom.

"What do you think about me inviting a few girlfriends over for New Year's Day? Would you like to come? I could invite Anna, Lee, Kate, Melody, and Suzanne. We could drink champagne and have some finger food."

"What a great idea. I don't have any plans. I could bring a couple of bottles of champagne. I'm hoping Don will get this divorce over soon. The construction of the town home at Green Reef is almost complete. I can't wait to move in."

"Okay. I'll call the girls and invite them. Let's start about one o'clock."

We finished the listing in Water's Edge. The price for the one-of-a-kind cottage with deeded beach access across the street was $495,000. It was a beautiful three-story home with a games room and a large balcony on the third floor. The furnishings came with the house and it was rental ready. I told Pat that I could handle the open houses.

Agent tours were a great way to meet other real estate agents and see new listings. We met at nine a.m. in Destin on Seaview Drive. Country Wide bank was the sponsor and there was a great breakfast. I met several new realtors as we followed the tour director, Avon Longo, from house to house. Pat's listing in Water's Edge was the last one on the list. I handed out flyers as the agents came in the door and told them I would hold an open house for the next couple of days if they wanted to bring their clients to view it.

I stayed to do open house and ended up with two sets of prospects. One set was snowbirds just looking at homes to give them something to do. The other guy told me he was an investor and looking for rental property. I showed him the cash flow sheet with rental projections of $74,000 a year. He was vague and didn't want to sign the guest register. Regardless, I gave him my card and thanked him for coming. At five, I turned off all the lights, locked the door and drove home. The children were playing a board game on the kitchen table. I gave them each a hug and stuck a frozen pizza in the oven for dinner. I poured myself a glass of wine and called my girlfriends to invite them on New Year's Day. None had plans and they were glad I was hosting a party.

The next day I was holding an open house again at Water's Edge. I was pleasantly surprised when the man who said he was an investor came back. This time, he introduced himself as Dr. Witkind. He looked over the house again. "I want to make an offer," he said a short time later.

We sat at the kitchen table. "How do you want it titled?"

"Witkind Investments," he said and gave me his address.

"I remember you from Barnett Bank. I used to work there. Aren't you a neurosurgeon?"

"I am, but I'm also an investor. My brother and I have already bought one condo, and he agreed this cottage would be an excellent investment. I want to offer $450,000. We'll pay cash and close as soon as possible."

This is fantastic—cash and soon. I hope it'll impress Pat and get her sellers to make this offer work.

As he left, I looked to see if he wore a wedding ring—he didn't. He was handsome, if a little short. His hair was black and his eyes were dark brown. He was wearing black jeans, a cream-patterned sweater, and shoes with pointed toes. He must have been from Miami or somewhere else out of town. I drove back to the office and waved the offer at Pat.

"What have you got?"

"An offer on Water's Edge. Now it's your turn to do your magic with the seller." I went into the break room for a Diet Coke and let Pat look at the contract on her own. Then I heard her call her client.

"I have an offer for you. I'll fax it over now. It's not the asking price, but you know the first offer is always the best and it's cash. We priced it a little high so we could get offers."

I walked back in. Pat said we would have an acceptance, or the counteroffer the following day. All I had to do was wait patiently. That was the hardest part about this business.

I dressed in my navy wool dress and heels because I hoped to take a signed contract to Dr. Witkind's office near the hospital. When I arrived at my office, I steadied my nerves.

"Well, I will be damned. Bill accepted the offer. He didn't even counter it," Pat said.

"Fantastic. I'll call Dr. Witkind." I called and he asked if I could come over at noon. I told him I would be there on time. I asked if he wanted to have lunch and he suggested we could eat at the hospital cafeteria.

His office was next door to the hospital in a complex with many doctors. It was a modern office with black leather furniture, chrome and glass tables, a large black and white abstract painting on the wall, and mirrors behind the check-in counter. A woman of about sixty was the receptionist, and she looked similar to Dr. Witkind. I introduced myself.

"Bruce told me you were coming," she said. "I'm his mother and his receptionist. He and his David are excited about the house in Water's Edge. I'll tell him you're here."

"Don't you look lovely? Great dress," he said with a big smile. "Bring the contract into my office so I can write you an earnest money check."

I followed him into his office. The room had the feel of the waiting area, complete with bookshelves filled with medical journals. His medical degree was from the University of Miami and his specialist degree in neurology was from Emory in Atlanta. He wrote me a check for $20,000 and said he would wire the rest when it was time to close then we walked over to the hospital. The lunchroom was bustling with nurses and doctors in their scrubs as they selected their choices from the buffet. Dr. Witkind wore similar clothes to the ones he had on yesterday. Maybe he always dressed in black and white. We each picked a salad and chicken and rice soup. When we sat down, I asked him where he was from.

"My parents raised us in Miami. They left Cuba during the Mariel boatlift in 1980. They left everything in Cuba. Dad was a doctor there. The communists took the lot. He was never the same after that and died of a heart attack at sixty. My brother and I came with them, of course. We're twins. We enrolled at the University of Miami and later attended Emory Medical School. My brother is a dentist and still lives in Miami. When an option came up to open an office here, I brought my mother with me."

"What a story. I've read about the boatlift from Cuba, but you're the first person I've met who experienced it firsthand. So fascinating. Thank you for lunch. I'll order a home inspection on the house and get the paperwork off to Delys Dearmon to close for you. Thank you, Dr. Witkind." When I stood up and shook his hand, he held mine a little longer than necessary and startled me by asking me out.

"I'm flattered, thank you," I replied a little hesitantly. "Let me know when you'd like to do something. You can call me if that suits you." *That was a surprise. I need to go out with him to take my mind off Cade.*

Chapter 91

Joshua, Barry, and I ate lunch together. We were excited that we would soon leave rehab. As we ate, Joshua asked us what we were going to do when we got out. Dr. Clark had said it was better to take it slow for a few months and not jump right back into what we had been doing before we arrived at the Foundation.

"I wasn't doing anything, since I lost almost everything," Barry said. "I'd like to get back into record producing, but I'll have to find an investor."

"I'll go back to Nashville and play some gigs with my brothers. If Sawyer is to join us, Mom made me promise not to drink," I said.

"Football season is over, and I won't have practice for a few months," Joshua said. "I have some money put away. We could talk about me as an investor for y'all. We could go to AA meetings together and be accountable to each other."

"That's a great idea," I said. "You're in Memphis, so we need to find a group close to each other."

"Delores and I have a town home at Legends Golf Club in Nashville near Vanderbilt. She'd be glad to come and stay there while we go to AA meetings."

"I think we could work well together. I could get an apartment near Vanderbilt so I could be close. Joshua, you are a prince among men. I love you, brother," Barry said.

"I'll tell Delores what we've decided when I call her on Sunday. We can start small in the beginning. Let's record an album first, Barry, then focus on recruiting other musicians," Joshua added.

It was time to go to our afternoon meeting, so we didn't talk anymore that day. I felt good about working with Joshua and Barry. Bob could still be the Fox brothers' manager, but Barry could produce our albums instead of us going to The Barn.

I called Harper on Sunday. I wanted to tell her my good news. I was very sad when she didn't answer, but I left her a voicemail anyway.

Chapter 92

With Christmas over, I began to plan the New Year's Day party. I made cheese olive balls and froze them, then I rolled meatballs and froze them too so they were ready for my Hawaiian meatball recipe. I found a tasty fruit punch for the children to drink and at the party store, I bought New Year napkins, plastic cups, and small plates. I found a New Year's pinata for the children to break. I intended to hang it on the tree in the front yard.

New Year's Day arrived and my friends came over. I had the table set, the pinata hung, the punch out for the children and the cheese olives warming in the oven. The Hawaiian meatballs were in the crockpot, and I had just baked a batch of chocolate cookies.

Pat arrived first with two bottles of champagne. Melody brought eggnog and rum to go on top. Suzanne brought orange juice for mimosas. Anna and Lee were next to arrive.

"Happy New Year everyone. I'm so glad you girls came and brought your children to visit with Lizzie and Sean. I've set up a table for them in my garden room." The kitchen was crowded as we filled plates for the children. Suzanne handed me a mimosa which was just what I needed. We sat in the living room and everyone could mosey back and forth to the kitchen for more food. As I knew it probably would, the conversation turned to men and they asked about Cade. I took a deep breath before I told them he had been in rehab and that I had decided not to see him anymore. They looked surprised but agreed with my decision. We were on our second mimosas, when I realized the kids need to burst the pinata.

"Come on girls, grab the kids and let's go see what the New Year's pinata has inside." Sean and Beau were first, but they were too short. Then Lizzie, and she missed. David hit it, but it didn't break. Jake broke the corner. Kelle and Sam fought over the stick. Sam won when he smacked it hard and everything came tumbling out. There was candy, toy cars, fake candy lips, pencils, and erasers. An odd assortment, for sure.

"I'm ready for a piece of that gorgeous cake Lee brought and some eggnog," said Melody. "That champagne has made me tipsy."

Everyone left at five. I threw out the trash bags and lay down on the sofa. Next thing I knew, it was seven p.m. The party had been fun.

"Are you two hungry?"

"No," said Sean. "I ate lots of cookies."

"I liked the meatballs and the cake. It was so good I ate two pieces," said Lizzie.

We put on our Christmas pajamas. Sean was ready for bed and Lizzie and I climbed into my bed. She wanted to sleep with me. As I drifted off, I was thankful for my friends, family, and the exciting new career I had coming in 1992. When Cade came into my head, I shut him out. He had called a number of times and every time I resisted answering. I was getting better at it and I thought the pain associated with the whole episode was diminishing. At least I told myself that was the case.

Chapter 93

It was our last week at the Cumberland Heights Foundation. I felt anxious and I wasn't sleeping. Could I do this when I left? For more than six weeks I had stuck to a regime, undergone counseling, and worked through the steps. Once I was home, I needed to follow this program, find a sponsor, and locate a morning meeting nearby, and I needed to explain to Bob how I had to live. There would be no more frequenting places such as Tootsie's or Skull's Rainbow Room.

Joshua and Barry were as worried as me. Barry had no one to be accountable to, whereas at least Joshua had Delores and the twins. We agreed to meet at the end of our first week and discuss the future. I knew I would face obstacles and triggers along the way, but I was ready to confront them head on. I felt a sense of hope as I embarked on my path to redemption. There would be challenges and setbacks. With each step forward I vowed to stay true to my commitment to a life free from addiction.

My last phone call on Sunday was to Tucker when I asked him to pick me up at noon on January 15th. He said he will be here, and that Sawyer had moved into the apartment; they were working on new songs. He told me Bob had them play back-up at the Opry and Amy was ready for us to play at the Bluebird Café. That helped my confidence.

Tucker and Sawyer were outside waiting for me as they stood beside my black truck. I said goodbye to the receptionist and shook Dr. Clark's hand. My brothers hugged me before I got into the right-hand front seat. I let Tucker drive home. I hadn't driven in six weeks.

"You look good," said Tucker.

"Thanks for coming to get me. I have to admit I'm anxious about beginning this new lifestyle. I hope both of you will help me."

"We will," said Sawyer. "First thing we'll do is go see Mom and Grannie on the weekend."

"Yes, I've missed the horses and Dog. Joshua is looking for an AA group near downtown. I'll find out from him tonight where to go tomorrow and find a sponsor. I wonder if there's a recovered musician who will sponsor me? How's Mary Jane?" I asked Tucker.

"We're still dating. She went home for Christmas when we came to see you. We went to dinner on New Year's Eve at The Standard. It's on Rosa Parks Boulevard and you have to book in advance. It's in a fabulous old house built in 1843 and serves sophisticated Southern fare. There was a champagne toast at midnight. We loved everything about the place."

It felt as if the apartment welcomed me. Tucker had my favorite stew in the crockpot. I guess he learned to cook different meals while I was away. I unpacked and we ate dinner, watched some television, and I went into my room to call Harper. My heart was pounding. The call went to her voicemail. *Dear God, give me strength to conquer this disease.*

Chapter 94

I dressed in my suit to go with Pat to the courthouse in Shalimar where she would be granted her decree absolute, the final order that would conclude her divorce. I picked her up at the office. She was a nervous wreck and kept wringing her hands and fidgeting all the way to the courthouse.

"It's going to be okay. Calm down," I said. "It'll be over soon and you'll have your divorce."

"I know, but we have been together since we were nineteen. Should I just cancel the divorce?"

"No! You know this is the best thing for you. Maybe not for him. You could never trust him again. Life without trust is not love."

"I know. I just hate change."

"Think about the new town home on the beach that you're moving into this week. What a wonderful place to start over. Anna, Lee, and I will help you move your things. When your ex gets back from his overseas flight, you'll be out of the house in Shalimar."

Don Dewrell was waiting for us when we arrived at the courthouse. He had on his win-win navy-blue pants, white shirt, red tie, beige sport coat, his traditional large belt buckle, and ostrich cowboy boots.

"Good morning, girls. You look gorgeous, as usual."

"Thanks, Don," Pat said. I'm a nervous wreck."

"No need to be nervous. I've got this under control. Judge Barron is a fair judge and he won't let your husband take advantage of you."

Don took Pat's arm and led her into the courtroom. I followed. We sat in the front row and waited for Pat's name to be called. I spied her soon-to-be ex sitting on the opposite side of the courtroom with his young female attorney, Sandy Hatton. She had on a charcoal gray power suit, a white silk blouse, and gold jewelry. She was attractive, probably thirty, with a blonde bob, a straight nose, and a prominent chin. I couldn't see her eyes from my seat. The soon-to-be ex-husband had on his airline uniform because that afternoon he was leaving for a week on an overseas trip. There were three other couples getting divorced before it was Pat's turn. By then, she was red in the face and wiping away tears. *Don't back down now, for*

God's sake. She and Don stood before the judge, with her husband and his attorney next to them. Along with her power suit, the female attorney had on those $2,500 Christian Louboutin high heels with the red soles. She probably drove a Mercedes too.

The judge read Dan Champion's argument about him not wanting to split his retirement fund from the airlines when he retired. Judge Barron told him that he would have to split it with Pat and he needed to make her the beneficiary of the whole fund if he died before her.

Then Don said he could keep the house and give Pat half of what it was worth. The expectation was he would pay her in the next few days. The look on Dan's face was priceless. He was so angry he was shaking and he looked as if he was about to explode. His attorney took his hand, whispered in his ear and he seemed to calm down. I thought he was probably sleeping with her.

Pat asked Dan to pay for their son's college education and buy him a new car to use for the four years while he was studying for his degree. She said she would pay the insurance on the car and give him spending money while he was in school. Thankfully, their son was not in the courtroom. He was off at Auburn.

Then the judge called Don and Sandy up to the bench without their clients. Once he had conferred with them, they returned to their clients. After further discussion, Dan agreed to Pat's requests and said he would have a cashier's check ready for her at the bank that afternoon. She would have to pick it up as he had a four o'clock flight to France.

Then it was over and Don took Pat's arm and we walked out of the courtroom. "Don't discuss anything in front of the courthouse. Meet me at the Garden Café for lunch," he said.

Pat was still shaking when she got in my car. "That was a nightmare. I can't believe he agreed to give me half of what the house is worth in a cashier's check today. I don't have to use my savings to purchase the town home now." She burst into tears. I patted her arm and let her cry. We were so different. My reaction to getting my divorce was as if someone had lifted an enormous weight off my shoulders.

Then we joined Don at the café, which was relatively close to the courthouse. It was where all the attorneys, clerks, and people who worked at the courthouse ate. Don was sitting at a table off to the side. The hostess walked us over to him. In a bucket was a bottle of Perrier-Jouët champagne that had been already been opened. Three glasses were on the table next to it. The special glasses matched the beautiful, well-known, flower-adorned bottle of champagne.

Don stood up just before we sat down and poured each of us a glass of champagne.

"To one of the best divorces I've enjoyed winning. A toast to Pat and her new life," he said.

"Thank you. You did a fantastic job getting me that money for my town home. The look on Dan's face was priceless."

Don had already ordered the café's special of a prime rib sandwich and French fries for us. He was a take-charge man. We enjoyed the food, the champagne, and the laughter. We hugged Don goodbye and returned to the office.

"I'm taking the rest of the day off to go to my town home and plan where everything will go. They'll deliver my new furniture from Lovelace Interiors tomorrow. Could you meet me at my house in Shalimar and we'll start packing? Thanks so much for being there for me."

Chapter 95

Joshua called to tell me he had found an AA meeting at 154 Representative John Lewis Way and the corner of Church Street at the Downtown Presbyterian Church. The meetings were at 8 a.m. in the mornings and 5 p.m. in the evenings in the basement. I met Joshua and Barry in the morning. It was a group of twenty and we sat in a circle and recited the Serenity Prayer before we shared our first names. After the meeting, everyone came over and shook hands and there was coffee and donuts. I looked around and wondered if anyone else was a musician, but I was too shy to ask. However, there was still time to find a mentor, even though it had been suggested we did it the first week after rehab.

The meeting had concluded when Bob called my cell phone and asked us to meet him for lunch at Jack's Bar-B-Que. Apparently, he had already called the apartment and talked to Tucker. When I arrived, my brothers and Bob were already waiting at a table. Bob got up and gave me a big hug.

"I'm so glad you're back. Come, sit, and let's talk about the future for the band," he said. Just then, a young server came to take our order. She had pigtails, rosy cheeks and bright blue eyes and must have been Sawyer's age. He noticed how cute she was right away. She smiled at all of us but lingered as she took Sawyer's order of a pulled pork sandwich and French fries.

"My favorite," she said.

I ordered ribs. I knew how good they were, and Tucker and Bob ordered smoked turkey sandwiches. We all ordered sweet tea; I guessed they were considering me. Yes, a beer would have been nice, but my craving had gone. After we finished eating Bob got down to business.

"I've been making phone calls to place your band. Several of the performers who have booked into the Grand Ole Opry are looking for back-up musicians and it would be a well-paying job. And, of course, Amy wants you to play at the Blue Bird Café at least once or twice a month. There are some spring and summer jams in Nashville and the surrounding areas which would give you exposure for the next album you cut."

"Thanks. That's great news. What do you think?" I asked the others.

"Sounds good to me," said Tucker.

"That would give me time to write more songs," Sawyer added.

I turned to Bob. "I met Barry Brown at the Cumberland Heights Foundation. He was a record producer before his divorce and fall from grace. Joshua Jones, one of the football players with the Memphis Grizzlies, was there too and wants to help Barry get back on his feet. He's willing to back him to help him start with our next album. Can you find a small place for him to set up as a recording studio?"

"Sure, I think I know an older building that's vacant. You made some useful connections there."

"The three of us sort of fell in together. They're great guys."

"I'm sure they'll miss you at The Barn, but as long as the album is top-notch, it'll serve you well to work with your friends."

"We have lunch together every Friday, so if you find a building, Friday would be a good day for us to see it."

"I'll get to work and see what I can do and hopefully meet you Friday. Starting tomorrow, we expect you all to be at the Grand Ole Opry for the next two weeks. I'll meet you there at 5 p.m. tomorrow."

As soon as the cute server came over to clear the table and bring us the check, Bob grabbed it. She smiled at Sawyer. "Are y'all music stars?"

"I'm not. I write songs," Sawyer replied. "When we play, we call ourselves the Fox Brothers. I've just moved to Nashville. Are you still in school?" Sawyer asked her.

"I just graduated. This is my summer job before I go to college in the fall. I could show you around Nashville. I'm Brenda by the way," she said.

"I'd like that. Can I call you?" She gave Sawyer her phone number and when she left to process Bob's credit card, we laughed.

"Way to go Sawyer. She's cute and you need someone your age to show you the sights," I said.

We drove home full of good food and happy that we had a job straightaway. I would tell Joshua and Barry the good news about the possibility of a place to record after the next meeting. The three of us fell asleep in front of the television. We wouldn't need dinner. Just an ice cream.

Chapter 96

When I got to the office, my cell phone rang.

"Hello, Harper, It's Bruce Witkind. Do you have plans for this Friday night? I'd like to take you to the theater in Pensacola. *A Street Car Named Desire* is playing at the Saenger Theater."

"No, I don't have plans. I'd love to see it."

"Good, I'll pick you at 5 p.m. We can get a bite to eat and then go to the show. What's your address?"

'I live near the Barnett Bank at 231 Greenbriar Road. I'll look forward to it. See you then."

Well, that was exciting. I needed something to take my mind off work and Cade. I was not over him. Regardless, I knew I'd made the right decision to break off our relationship.

Pat was not in the office because she was busy moving house. I was glad the chaos of her divorce was over and she was getting settled in her new town home. I spent the next couple of days doing open houses in Crystal Beach and mailing out more postcards to my sphere of influence.

When Friday finally came I went home early to get dressed for the theater. I wore my green silk dress, black high heels and pearls around my neck and pearl earrings. I had my black pashmina shawl with a small black purse. It could be cold in the theater.

When Bruce arrived he had on an expensive black suit, a white shirt and a blue bow tie. I welcomed him and invited him inside.

"It's cozy. I like the way you have the living room decorated," he said a few moments after he came in the door. "You look fabulous, by the way. That dress captures the emerald green in your eyes."

I blushed. "Thank you. I am ready to go if you are." I didn't tell him I had two children who were at their other grandmother's home. I wasn't ready to expose them to another man so soon after my break up with Cade. They had both taken my decision hard. Lizzie was so in love with Cade's horses and Sean loved having guitar lessons with Sawyer.

Bruce held the passenger door of his black Porsche convertible open for me. Thank heavens the top was up. He sure loved everything black.

"I thought we'd eat at Jamie's Restaurant. I love the atmosphere and you will too."

On the way to the restaurant we chatted about the house he had bought. He was in the process of redecorating it and had put his mother in charge.

The restaurant was downtown at 424 East Zaragoza Street in the Seville Quarter. He told me the house had been built in 1878 and only seated fifty people. Lights were twinkling on the front porch and the cottage looked different to the usual ones. Bruce took my hand as we walked up the steps. The maître d' greeted him.

"Good evening Dr. Witkind, so good to see you. Who is this lovely lady with you?" he said in his French accent.

"This is Harper. She hasn't been here before. Do you have my special table ready?"

"Of course. Follow me." It was a lovely corner table with a window that faced the garden. The maître d' pulled out my chair and placed a white napkin on my lap. Then he handed Bruce the menu, but he didn't give me one. I thought that was odd.

"I'd like to order for both of us if you don't mind. Chef Libbey Dasher knows my favorite dishes." I nodded. Just then the waiter came up and addressed Bruce.

"Good evening, Dr. Witkind. So nice to see you again. Will you be having your favorites tonight? The chef has it ready to prepare if that's what you'd like. I told her you were coming to dine with us tonight."

"Yes, we'll both have the caille farcie." Then he turned to me. "That's quail stuffed with mushrooms and Italian sausage served with a Madeira sauce. Do you like crab cakes?" he asked me.

"I do. Whatever you decide is fine with me."

"Then bring us the crab cake entrée and a bottle of Chassagne-Montrachet. Thank you."

"Gary Serafin has been the headwaiter here since the restaurant opened. Jamie's is one of my favorites in Pensacola. I hope you like the food."

Gary poured our wine. It was delicious and I'm sure it was expensive. The appetizer was very rich and tasty. I could tell Bruce loved it. I wasn't used to fancy French food, but I was beginning to like it. We didn't talk much during the meal. I was so full by the time we'd eaten the quail and drunk two glasses of wine had my head was buzzing. Then Gary brought out the house favorite dessert, lemon ice-box pie. I thought I couldn't eat another bite, but it was so smooth and creamy I ate it all.

"Did you enjoy your meal?"

"Yes, it was absolutely divine," I replied. "Everything you chose was perfect. Thank you, dining here was a real treat."

"I wanted to spoil you on our first date. We can walk to the theater from here." He took my arm as we walked down Zaragoza Street to South Palafox. The weather was perfect for a walk through historic Pensacola. I had been to the Saenger before with my parents when I was younger. The Spanish Baroque architecture was magnificent. Pensacola has a lot of Spanish history and the setting was superb.

The acting was excellent. The story was about Blanch DuBois, her sister Stella, and Stella's husband Stanley and what happened to Blanche when she fell from grace in Southern society and had to live with her sister and her husband. As an independent woman, I found the treatment of women during the transition from the old to the new South offensive. I had read the book, so I knew what to expect, even so it left me with an unpleasant taste in my mouth.

Bruce and I walked back to his car and as he drove me home, I asked him what he thought of the plot.

"You know, I respect my mother and what she went through when we left Cuba. I'm glad she wasn't brought up in the old South. My father adored her, and my brother and I were taught to respect women. What did you think?" he asked me.

"I enjoyed the acting. I was glad I'd read the book, so I knew what was coming. I too am glad I wasn't born years ago in the old South. But I love all kinds of literature and have had a love of reading since high school."

When we arrived at my house, Bruce came around and opened the car door before he walked me to the front door. I wondered if he would try to kiss me. He took my hands in his and kissed me on the cheek.

"Thank you for tonight. I had a great time and I hope we can do it again," he said. Then he smiled, turned, got in his Porsche, and drove away.

I was relieved, I wasn't ready to be kissed by him.

Chapter 97

I attended the 5 p.m. meeting at the church. After we recited our prayer and introduced ourselves to a small group of new arrivals, I noticed a guy sitting across from me with a droopy mustache, dark hair and black, brooding eyes. He glanced at me across the room. Then it was my turn to tell my story of drink and drugs while I'd been on the tour. I ended it by saying I didn't want to suffer the same demise as Richard Boone.

After the meeting, the guy with the brooding eyes came over. He offered me his hand and introduced himself. "I'm Robert Black. Everyone calls me Blackie. Your story is similar to mine. Do you have a sponsor?"

"Not yet. I was hoping there would be a musician or two in this group."

"Well, I've been a musician all my life and I've had my difficulties. Thank God I found the AA program twenty years ago. It saved my life. We should have coffee or lunch sometime and see if we'd be a good fit."

"I'd like that. What about lunch tomorrow? My treat."

"Yes, I could meet you at the Tin Angel at noon. Do you know it?" he said.

"Yes. I look forward to it."

When I got home, I told Tucker and Sawyer I thought I had found the right person to be my sponsor. They were happy for me.

"Bob called and we need to be available at the Opry for the taping of the CMA's 35th anniversary. It starts on the 10th and ends on the 13th. Several performers are going to need back-up. You need to be home by four so we can go over there tomorrow," Tucker said.

"Great news. I'll be home in time."

The next day, I met Blackie at the Tin Angel. I hadn't been there before. It was on the corner of 32nd and West End Avenue. The sign inside said they had named it after a restaurant in Greenwich Village and a song Joni Mitchell sang. It had a large tin sign and underneath the name it said *Warm Restaurant Cool Food*. Blackie was already waiting for me at a table in the front and he stood up to greet me.

"Good to see you. Sit down, let's order and talk while we eat. The signature dish here is hot chicken. That okay with you?"

I nodded.

"You'll love it. They fry the chicken breast, cover it with hot sauce and serve it over a special slice of bread with pickles."

It was delicious and moist and he was right I loved the unique spicy tang created by the sauce and the pickles.

Blackie told me the story of his fame, losing his wife and children, and his stint in rehab. He too had been to the Cumberland Heights Foundation. His children were grown up and had families of their own. He'd spent this Christmas at his daughter's home in Memphis with her husband and two little girls. He was still trying to reconcile with his son. Express how I felt, say what was bothering me, ask for help, were his words of wisdom. He then offered to be my sponsor and I accepted.

"I appreciate your friendship and you offering me sponsorship. I was beginning to worry that I wouldn't find one. I'm not as concerned about doing drugs as I am that I might want a drink. I succeeded in staying sober during all my nervousness when my brothers and I played back-up at the Opry last week. It was hard not being able to fortify myself with a drink, but I did it."

"That was an excellent test. Just take it one day at a time. You'll be tempted many times from now on. Just keep going to AA, working the steps, and one day you'll be someone's sponsor. That's how we get through life and conquer this problem. And I'll be there to support you, so just remember, ask me if you need help. Here's my phone number and my address. Don't lose them."

I found his words reassuring and I thanked him from deep in my heart. It was as if he was giving me a lifeline and I so appreciated it. By the time lunch was over I felt a lot happier, stronger, and empowered.

I picked up my brothers, and we drove to the Grand Ole Opry. Ronnie Milap, Patti LaBelle, Bob Dylan, Clint Black, Delbert McClinton, Vince Gil, Lee Roy Parnell, Pam Tillis, Trisha Yearwood, Alan Jackson, Wynona, Reba McEntire, Brooks & Dunn, Emmylou Harris, Alabama, Dolly Parton, together with Kenny Rogers and Willie Nelson were entertainers there during the taping and performing. We played back-up for a few of the stars who didn't bring their bands and it was exciting to watch so many outstanding performers. Television crews were everywhere. The lighting was superb and the actual show on the 29th went off without a problem. Watching Dolly Parton perform with Kenny Rogers gave me goosebumps.

My brothers and I were tired when the show was over and we didn't get home until midnight. I made hot chocolate and we ate left-over pizza. I wanted to call Harper and tell her about the show, but I knew there was no point because she wouldn't answer the phone. I tossed and turned and wished I could take a Xanex. I had thrown them all out. Sleep came around two in the morning.

The next morning, I called Harper again in the hope she would answer. No luck.

Chapter 98

Pat was in the office working on a new listing when I arrived.

"Good morning, I got tired of putting everything in its place at the town home. So here I am," she said.

"Good, this office seems empty when you aren't here. What are we working on today?"

"Bob wants a realtor tour of the three remaining town homes as soon as possible. We can plan a luncheon there or a happy hour around five. Which do you think would get the best attendance?"

"Everyone likes a free lunch. At least I do. How about we order from Mother Earth's? We can plan for twenty at least, give a door prize and gift certificates to Mother Earth's. I can send invitations in an email blast to all the realtors in our area."

"Great idea. What day of the week do you think would be best?"

"Either Wednesday or Thursday. Some realtors don't go to their offices on Friday."

"Okay, you're in charge. See how much she'll charge to cater the food. Buy napkins, and anything else you think we need."

I stopped in at Mother Earth's, where Betty Campbell, the owner, was still working. She was glad to see me and asked me to sit with her and have a glass of her special mango tea. I told her what we wanted to order for our realtor's open house.

"That's a great idea," she said. "Thank you for asking us to plan it. The only extra I'd add would be a tray of brownies. Everyone likes a little dessert. We can have it ready for you to pick up early, say ten a.m. on the day you decide to hold it. Just call me the day before."

"Thank you. I know all the realtors will be happy when they find out the food is from your café. I also want to purchase a gift certificate for $25.00." I told her I'd call her soon to set up the event, and then I left.

Pat was glad I had it all planned, and we settled on Thursday of the following week. I sent the emails. Then I got to work printing the floor plans along with an attractive handout. I would take the flyers to Destin the next day and hand them out to the different offices. Pat said she would take the ones to the Fort Walton Beach offices and put one on the Emerald Coast Association of Realtors' bulletin board.

I drove to Destin the next day and distributed flyers to several realtors. They said they would be there and looked forward to seeing the new town homes and eating lunch. I left Destin just as the sun was going down on the beach and as I crossed the Destin bridge to Fort Walton Beach, it dropped like a ball of fire. I wished I'd had a camera. I needed to remember to put mine in the car.

Chapter 99

I was adjusting to my AA meetings every morning. Blackie was such a good sponsor and so helpful. He understood me and offered good advice.

Our band had made good money playing at the Opry and royalties had come in for *Green Eyes*. I was happy my bank account was flush. My brothers and I went back to the Ford dealership to see John Reinhold. Tucker was itching to buy a truck. As we drove up, John came out to greet us. He had on a light blue leisure suit, navy-blue shirt, blue checked tie, and navy-blue shoes. The man had style.

"Well, if it isn't the Fox Brothers plus one. Whose turn is it now for a new truck?"

"Mine," said Tucker. "I want a red one like Cade's black F150."

"One came in yesterday. It's out the back and hasn't been serviced yet. Want to walk around back and see it? Who's the tall drink of water with you?"

"I'm Sawyer. The youngest Fox."

"He's living with us now in Nashville. He gets the credit for all the songs and a new album will be coming soon," I said.

"That's good news. Nice to meet you, Sawyer."

The red truck was in line to go into the service department, so John opened the doors for us to look inside. It had a gray leather interior, power windows and locks and a cassette player. I could tell Tucker liked it.

"I wish I could drive it. Will it be ready tomorrow?" Tucker asked.

"Yes. Do you want to get the paperwork and loan application done today? That way, you can drive it out of here tomorrow."

"Sure, let's go get it done."

Tucker was grinning from ear to ear and Sawyer was happy too. He would get my old truck.

We left and went to meet Bob downtown. He wanted to show me the building he had found for a recording studio before Joshua and Barry saw it on Friday. It was on 9th Avenue, about three streets over from Broadway, in a large building that had previously been a recording studio along with other offices. It had been vacant since the crash of '87 which caused a major business downturn in Nashville.

"Come on in. The electricity isn't on, but you can still tell if the space will work," Bob said.

There was a corner office in the front for a manager. A bathroom in the back and an open space for musicians to play. The glass wall was still intact between the open space and where the soundtrack guys could sit. It was dusty, moldy, and smelly from lack of activity.

"It'll need the air-conditioning ducts cleaned; the air conditioner is old. We can get it serviced and see if it'll work for a while before it needs replacing. There are lights in the studio for musicians, but all the recording machines will need to be replaced. I can get the rep to meet us Friday to give Joshua and Barry an idea of what it would cost to replace everything. The price for the building is definitely good. Joshua could lease the other space in the rest of the building and get a good return on his investment."

"I think the building will impress Joshua, plus it has potential. We'll meet you here before lunch at eleven, then we can all go eat and discuss the possibilities," I said before we left and went home.

"I can't wait to surprise Mary Jane. I'll ask her out for dinner tomorrow night," Tucker said.

"I'll be glad to have the old truck for a while. I won't have to depend on you two to take me places. Can we go back to the restaurant where that cute girl, Brenda, works on Friday?" Sawyer said. "I'd like to take her out and have her show me where the younger people hang out."

The next day, Tucker woke us bright and early to get his truck at nine when the dealership opened.

Sitting at the curb was the red truck, shiny and ready for Tucker. John came out to greet us and we let Tucker go into the finance office by himself. John had told him he didn't have to bring a cashier's check since he knew us and I was already a client. That way, he really could surprise Mary Jane.

"They said my credit was excellent, so I got a good interest rate for three years. It's full of gas and ready to go."

"Okay, we'll see you at home," I said as Sawyer jumped in the driver's seat of the old Ford and I rode beside him. "That is one excited brother.

He's been wanting that truck ever since I got mine. The money from the tour sure helped him afford it."

"When are we going to record our next album?" Sawyer asked. "We're making good money from *Green Eyes*. Do we have to wait for the recording studio to be purchased and full of equipment? That could take six months. I want to get a new truck too."

"We have to decide which studio to use. We'll get a better deal with Joshua and Barry, but we could go back to The Barn. What should we call this album? We need to decide. Let's record one primary song first and see how it does on WKMZ. Then do the full album," I replied.

"Okay, shall we talk to Bob on Friday and see what he thinks is best?" said Sawyer.

Chapter 100

After leaving the house, I drove to Mother Earth's Café where Betty Campbell had the food ready at ten. I carried on to Destin as fast as I could, maybe a touch faster over the bridge. After I turned on to Hutchison Street, Green Reef was just down the street on Scenic Highway 98. Pat had the open house signs pointing to our location. All the lights were on in number one, our designated show house. Sugar Beach had staged the living room, the master bedroom and a pleasant cottage dining setting by the window looking out at the Gulf.

"I'm here," I called up the stairs as I carried in the tray of chicken salad sandwiches. Pat had brought a pretty arrangement of flowers for the table and she put our business cards and the floor plans for the town home next to it.

At noon, the realtors started to arrive. Pat greeted them because she knew them and she introduced them to me if they didn't know me. They viewed the town home before they ate. They were complimentary about Bob's work and as soon as he arrived, Bob was happy to discover eighteen realtors devouring chicken salad sandwiches in the living room.

"Wow!" said Bob. "You two did a great job of this lunch. I'm pleased with the turnout." He shook hands and introduced himself to everyone.

"Would you like a sandwich? We have about three left," I asked him.

"No, I've already had lunch. I came to see your open house event. Well done, ladies. Bring me a contract." He left and we went back to chatting to the other realtors. Several had clients from out of town, who they said would be interested. Pat and I stayed the rest of the afternoon, and just as we were getting ready to turn off the lights at four-thirty, Bruce Witkind and his brother, David, drove up.

"I remembered you were having this open house and thought we'd come see you," Bruce said after the introductions had been made.

"Hi Bruce. I'd love to show you around," I said.

"Looks like a wonderful location on the Gulf. Who built these?" asked David.

"Bob Bonezzi," replied Pat. "I just bought number three and moved in last week. I love it. Wait until you see the master bathroom." She took David's arm and led him upstairs. Bruce and I followed.

"I've been busy with lots of surgeries lately, sorry I haven't called. Would you like to go to dinner tomorrow night? We can go to Destin, maybe eat at Marina Café and go dancing at the Sky Bar afterwards."

"That sounds like fun. I'd love to."

"I'll make reservations for seven and pick you up at six-thirty. Does that suit you?"

"Absolutely."

I showed Bruce through the rest of the house and once we returned to the living area David was there and had picked up a copy of the house plans and the information packet.

"I like it," David said. "Let's list my waterfront town home on Garnier's Bayou and I'll buy one of these." Pat looked astonished and David was looking at me to suggest I list his house. I hoped she knew he wanted to work with me, especially since I had sold them the rental property down the street in Water's Edge.

"When would you like me to come over and preview it?" I asked.

"How about Saturday around one o'clock? You come too and see what Harper thinks about the price," he said to Bruce.

Just before they said goodbye Bruce reminded me he would pick me up at six-thirty.

"Well, that was a surprise," said Pat. "I remember they were the brothers who bought that cottage in Water's Edge. I never met them, but when he introduced me to his brother, it came to me. Are you going out with Dr. Witkind?"

"Yes, he took me to the Saenger Theater and to dinner at Jamie's in Pensacola last week. You were busy moving, so I never had time to tell you."

"Good for you. He's certainly different from the country musician you were dating. I didn't realize you weren't seeing Cade any longer. You haven't said what happened. I thought you really liked him."

"I did, but he's got a drinking problem and one man like that was enough, so I stopped seeing him a while ago." I couldn't say any more. The less said the better. "Bruce is different, but I'm not ready for a big romance though, my heart still hurts when I think about Cade. But life must go on."

"Right. That's sad for you. I'm sorry it ended up that way. I'm not sure I'm ready to date after my painful divorce. But hopefully I'll meet someone when the time is right."

"I know your builder friend, Jim likes you. Does he know that you are divorced?

"No, I haven't told many people. Perhaps I'll give him a call and invite him over to see my new town house."

Chapter 101

On Friday, Joshua, Barry, Tucker, Sawyer, and I met Bob at the building for sale on Ninth Avenue. "Don't expect much, guys. It's been vacant for several years since the crash in 1987," Bob said as he unlocked the door and led everyone into the abandoned recording studio.

"I can see this working for us," said Barry. "It needs new or quality used equipment, a good clean and painting. I like the layout. Office just after the entry, then the control room. The glass is still standing between the control room and the live room. That looks like a piano room on the far left-hand side. A closet, three locker rooms and three booths. But we don't have to use all these rooms at once."

"Right," said Bob.

"What do you think, Joshua?"

"You guys are the musicians. I just want to help by being an investor."

"It's not as fancy as The Barn, but we can make it work," I said.

"It's a great location," Barry said. "It won't cost much to buy used microphones, amplifiers, and dynamics. I'll start by putting out the word we're looking for equipment if Joshua wants to purchase the building."

"Let's look at the other areas in the building. There's several square feet available for other businesses. Once the record studio is up and running, you could fix them up and rent out the remaining spaces," Bob said to Joshua.

"I like it. I like the idea. Delores said to buy it if I thought it was a good investment. Bob, should we contact the realtor who has it listed and ask to meet? I'm available tomorrow. Offer less than they're asking and see what they say. When you get the contract signed, we can meet at my bank over by my condo and I'll pay a deposit."

We shook hands and my brothers and I went back to the apartment. The purchase would be in Joshua, Barry, and Bob's hands. I knew I shouldn't get too excited. One day at a time. It was also in God's hands.

Bob called the next day. "It's a done deal. The seller accepted Joshua's offer. He signed the contract and Joshua has paid a deposit. We'll close in two weeks. Now I need to arrange for the electricity to be turned on, so we can check the AC and the lighting. Barry and Joshua are happy. They're thinking of a name for the business."

"Fantastic! Excellent job. Let's record Sawyer's latest song and release it as a single on WMZ," I said.

"Okay, I'll call Owen Bradley today and get you a time at The Barn."

When Owen rescheduled for the next day with Bob's help, we drove the few miles to The Barn and got ready to record. I could tell Bob was in a better mood and not angry with me as he had been the last time. We recorded *Just a Country Girl,* and it was a hit as a single on WMZ within a week. Our followers had not forgotten us. Then Amy called and told us to come over to The Blue Bird Café and sing our new songs. When we showed up on Wednesday, Cindy, the bartender, was delighted to see us.

"Jack and water, Cade? Beers for your brothers?"

"No thanks, Cindy. Give me a soda with lime, please. Boys, do you want a beer?" I asked.

"Give us the same," Tucker said to Cindy.

As we were setting up to play, I saw Mary Jane and her girlfriend in the audience. There was also a surprise visitor smiling at Sawyer—Brenda. We were given lots of applause and when I told the crowd Sawyer had written and recorded, *Just a Country Girl,* they gave him a standing ovation. Life was good in my new world, except for the absence of Harper. I never stopped thinking about her.

Sawyer and Brenda went out to eat. Mary Jane gave Tucker a hug and said she had to go home and study because she was going to get that finance degree. So Tucker and I ate hamburgers and French fries at the bar. We gave Cindy a big tip, thanked Amy for having us, and went home.

Chapter 102

On Saturday, Pat invited Anna, Lee, and me over to her house. We arrived around four and Anna and Lee went in first.

"Oh my, this is exquisite," said Anna. "Look at this gorgeous furniture."

"The furniture is gorgeous but look at this view!" said Lee. "You must love living here."

"I do. It's so peaceful. I love my new furniture and especially my bedroom and bathroom. I've soaked in the tub every evening with a glass of wine. What could be more perfect?"

"Nothing," I said. "I'm so glad you're happy here."

"Come, let's enjoy the hors d'oeuvres I ordered from My Private Chef, and I have some champagne," said Pat.

We sat in her beautiful living room, ate, drank, and talked about work. Anna told us Don had an interesting murder case. An older woman in her seventies had been charged with shooting her abusive husband. He had broken her arm the week before and put her in the hospital with concussion. He was a binge drinker and used to disappear for a week and come back home off his face. She'd had all she could take and one night when he came home drunk yet again, she was ready with his shotgun. He kept lunging at her until she pulled the trigger. Her daughter called Don the next morning. She was hysterical and begged Don to defend her. Don told Anna he would use the *Battered Woman Syndrome* to get her off. It was considered a subcategory of post-traumatic stress disorder.

"People living with battered woman syndrome often feel helpless and this can cause them to believe they deserve to be abused and that they can't escape it. This is often why people don't report being abused to the police or to their loved ones," Lee said.

"That was not the case with me," I said. "I didn't believe I deserved Michael's abuse. I was just afraid I wouldn't be able to support myself and the children. I thought about shooting him many times when he came home drunk and knocked me around. I just couldn't shoot him in front of the children."

"My mother-in-law used to tie Johnny's dad in a sheet when he came home drunk. When abused her, she hit him over the head with coke bottles. Once he was sober, she released him from the sheet," said Anna.

"I love that idea," I said. "Except I would've been too afraid of what Michael would have done to me when I released him. I won't tolerate any kind of abuse ever again."

"It'll be interesting to watch Don defend her and get her off," Lee said. "The man can work magic in the courtroom."

"He certainly worked magic for me," said Pat. "Thanks to him I live in this serene town home on the beach. I only wish it were warmer than we could go for a walk."

"Too cold for me," I said. "I can't wait for spring.

"You girls can come over anytime and go to the beach. Bring the kids if you want to. My son will be home for spring break. I know he's going to love his bedroom and the new place," Pat said.

I stood up. It was time to go. "Thanks for having us. We need to get home to our children," I said to Pat. "I'll see you at the office tomorrow."

Chapter 103

We were working in the studio when the door opened and a tiny blonde girl, wearing cut-off jeans, a ratty T-shirt, worn cowboy boots, and carrying a guitar almost as big as her, walked in. We all turned to look at her.

"Hey, Amy from Blue Bird Café sent me," she said.

Barry walked up to her. "She did?"

"Well, she said you might like my song and I need a guy to sing the guy's part."

"Okay, I'm Barry, the producer. This is Cade, Tucker, and Sawyer Fox, the musicians. What's your name?"

"Candy Kane. You know, like the candy with red and white stripes, only I spell it KANE."

"Come on in, Candy. If Amy sent you, we need to hear your song. Come into the live room to the mike and sing it for us," I said.

She sang *I'll Always be Crazy* and for or such a little lady, she had a booming voice. There was a scratchy tone to it, and it was definitely a country sound. I liked it. So did everyone else. "Do you have it written down? I'd like to try singing it with you," I said. She reached into the back pocket of her jeans and pulled out a sheet of paper. It wasn't typed. Just handwritten. I studied it for a few minutes. "Okay, Candy, let's try it together."

I'll Always Be Crazy
Sit down, baby. Let's have a talk, I've got something I need to say.
I go to work every day and I swear, I earn my pay
But the boss called me in, said times are tough
Babe, I got laid off today
No, I promise I didn't mean to let you down
Let me down, are you crazy?
Since we met life's amazing
You're the man I'm always dreaming of
As long as you are proud to be my baby
I'll always be crazy, oh so crazy over you
I'll always be crazy

You believed and I tried
All these songs about my life
Just one more month, Babe, I swear we'll make it
And you were right there by my side
There's no doubt you saved my life
Sometimes you're the only reason I keep breathing
You stood by me, you're so crazy
Since we met life's amazing
You're the girl I'm always dreaming of
As long as you are proud to be my baby,
I'll always be crazy over you
I'll always be crazy over you
Yes, we've both been through hell
Sometimes the good is hard to tell
With love this strong forever is where we'll take it
We're holding hands, we're so crazy
Since we met, life's amazing
I have you to love and you to hold
It's the love we're always dreaming of
As long as you are proud to be my baby
As long as you are proud to be my baby
I'll aways be crazy over you
I'll aways be crazy over you
I'll have you to love, and you to hold.

Everyone clapped. Candy grinned and hugged me.

"Can we do it, Cade? Can we record my song? I'd be ever so grateful."

"What do you think? Can we record it?" I asked Barry.

"Yep, I think it'll be a hit. You two need to practice singing and have Tucker and Sawyer back you up. We can do a couple of test runs to see how it sounds with all of you."

We spent the next few hours practicing in the live room with Barry in the control room. Then he came out.

"That's a wrap. Your last take was the best. Let me finish my work and I'll have it ready for you to listen to tomorrow."

"Come on, Candy Kane, the brothers and I are going to take you to the Blue Bird Café and thank Miss Amy. Do you have a car?"

"No, I took the bus here. Can I ride with y'all?"

"You sure can. Let's go. You can ride in the back with Sawyer." I didn't think Sawyer would mind. She was more his age. We arrived at the Blue Bird and walked up to the bar.

"Well, I see she found you," said Cindy. "What are y'all drinkin? I'll go get Amy from the back."

Tucker and Sawyer each wanted a beer. "Get me a soda with lime and whatever Candy is having," I said to Cindy.

"I'd like a shot of tequila, Miss Cindy." Cindy put the drinks down on the bar and went to get Amy.

Amy came out grinning. "I thought you'd like her," she said to me.

"Thanks, we just recorded her song. We'll get to hear it tomorrow. Barry stayed late to mix it."

"Y'all want to play it here tomorrow night?" Amy asked.

"That would be fantastic," I replied.

When we were ready to go home I asked Candy if she wanted a ride. She said no, she would hang out at Amy's for a while longer. We were tired from a full day's work at the studio and were eager to listen to Barry's magic tomorrow.

Chapter 104

It was time to get myself into gear and do something constructive such as post more cards to friends and acquaintances. I was pleased the David Witkind had listed his waterfront town home on Cinco Bayou with me. As soon as it had sold he was adamant he wanted to purchase one of the Green Reef town homes.

As I drove to the office what a shock it was to hear Cade's new song, *There's No Shame When I'm with You,* on the radio. It reminded me of the time we walked out of the hotel after the Christmas party and I was in my red dress and that older lady gave me a look of disgust. Nothing like the walk of shame. That was in the past, but the recollection still hurt.

At the office, I created a number of excellent postcards which I ordered from Vista Print and asked to be posted to Crystal Beach. There would surely be people ready to sell after owning property for five years or more.

Pat and I went to lunch at Liollio's where I ran into an old friend, Judy Elgin. She was looking for a commercial space for a second Little Caesars Pizza restaurant. She and her husband, Bob, owned one in Fort Walton Beach and wanted to open one in Destin. I told her I would start looking for the right location and call her later. Judy was one of the most positive women I knew. We belonged to the American Business Women's Association and we had worked on projects to raise money for scholarships for women in need. Since I hadn't been able to complete my college degree, I wanted to help others finish theirs.

"Here are some coupons for pizza. You can give them out at your open houses," Judy said.

"Thank you. That's a great idea."

"You see how important it is to go out to lunch and see people?" said Pat.

"Yes, I agree with you. I need to do it more often."

Chapter 105

I made myself a cup of coffee and sat down to eat breakfast with my brothers. "What a fluke to find Candy Kane. She has an amazing voice. Maybe we can incorporate her into our band. It's always good to have a female vocalist in country music. What do you think?" I asked them.

"That's a great idea," said Tucker. "She's talented. We may need to help her with better clothes though."

"I like the idea too," said Sawyer. "Let's talk to Bob about bringing her with us."

"Let's get her to the studio to do your new song *Because You Love Me*. Let her be the back-up for you on this one. Did one of you get her phone number?" I said.

"I don't think she can afford a phone or a car," said Sawyer. "But I bet she'll show up at the studio today. We need to go there soon."

"I need to go to my meeting. I'll see y'all around nine," I said.

When I arrived at the studio, Barry was already there and no surprise, so was Candy. My brothers and Candy were practicing Sawyer's song.

"She loves it," said Sawyer. "We've been practicing it together. Come join us in the live room."

Barry printed out the words for me, and we ran through the song a few times. Barry said if we played it together, he could mix it later and let us listen. Joshua and Delores came in and brought sandwiches from Subway. We all sat in the break room and I put the words in front of Joshua and Delores.

"What do you think? We can play it for you after we eat."

"I can relate to the words," said Delores after reading it. "I have my trust in Joshua that our love will last." She smiled and gave him a hug. It was wonderful to see the love in her eyes.

"I will always love you," said Joshua.

"I wrote this for Cade after he got out of rehab. I thought it would be a great song for Harper to hear," Sawyer said, but his comment fell flat and no one said anything. After we'd eaten we went into the live room again to play it for them.

Because you love me
I don't know how to take it slow
I tend to fall a little fast
I know I put my heart on the line
With just a hope that this may last
You seem to keep it locked away
Your heart's been broken in the past
Seems like all the men in your life
Never did learn how to act
But I can tell you're feeling something
I can feel it in my touch
The way you're looking into my eyes
I could swear you're in love
Just say you love me
And I won't let you down
Just put your trust in the life we build around
And it won't matter what the world outside is saying
Because you love me
Because you love me
I've never seen someone so pretty
I've never known someone so great
To put the confidence in my mind
That I can do anything
Just say you love me
And I won't let you down
Just put your trust in the life we build around
And it won't matter what the hell gets in our way
Because you love me
Because you love me

Barry recorded it as I sang and Candy sang back-up. I knew it would be a success. Bob walked in as we were finishing up.

"Listen to this," Barry said to him. "I should have it mixed by this evening."

"Wow, another good one. And who is this young lady?"

"This is Candy Kane. She found us yesterday and she has the voice of an angel. The boys want to add her to the Fox band. She'll need you to represent her," Barry said.

"Well, hello, Candy. I'm Bob, the brothers' manager. You want to come into the kitchen and chat?" Candy followed Bob, and the rest of us knew he would like her. Twenty minutes later Bob was grinning and Candy was jumping about with excitement. She hugged Bob and did a little dance.

"We need to find a place for her to live and I'll provide money for new performance clothes," Bob said.

"She can stay with us," said Delores. "Until she gets on her feet. We aren't always at the condo, and she can look after it for us. I could take her shopping, but you may have a better idea of what she needs," Dolores said to Bob.

"I'll take her down to Broadway. She needs new boots, new jeans, a white shirt like the guys and a string tie. Want to go now, Candy?" Bob said.

"Yes, sir. I can come back to the studio, but I'll need a ride to the condo."

"I can take you," said Sawyer. "We can pick up your things from where you are now."

"I'm at the Y.M.C.A."

I was pleased with the way the studio was working and Candy would be a wonderful addition to our group. I had a feeling she could replace me so I could go to Florida soon. I had decided to call John Holley, the boat captain I met in Destin. Money was really coming in from the first and second albums and I wanted to ask him about buying a used charter boat.

Tucker went out with Mary Jane after she got off work and Sawyer was with Candy, so I called John. He remembered me, we discussed boats, and he offered to look around for one for me. He had connections and said there was a rumor that one of the sport-fishing boat owners wanted to sell his boat. I intended to keep that information to myself in the meantime.

I fixed spaghetti for dinner. I needed some new recipes. But at least my brothers liked spaghetti.

Chapter 106

My kids were back in school and I was ready to restart open houses, so I went to Crystal Beach where Bob Bonezzi had another cottage ready to sell on Luke Avenue. I put up the signs, turned on the lights, and set out my flyers with the listing information. Pat had reminded me that snowbirds would arrive after the holidays.

This cottage was smaller than the last one I sold. It was only 1,400 square feet with a one-car garage. It was a charming light aqua home with a yellow door. I had brought a garden chair to sit in the living room and the electricity was on, so it was warm. At eleven o'clock, a distinguished woman walked in the front door. She had on a long black mink coat, dark brown hair in a bun, high heels, and a big smile on her face.

"Welcome, I'm Harper Hamilton. Come in."

"Happy New Year to you. I'm Regina and I'm building a home down the street on Luke Avenue. I just stopped by to see what this one looked like inside and enquire about the price."

"The price is $135,000. It has three bedrooms and two bathrooms and it's 1,400 square feet. Bob Bonezzi was the builder."

"I know Bob. He builds a nice home. My son-in-law is Phillip O'Shea. He's been building for a couple of years and is doing well. My daughter, Kelly, helps me pick out the colors and we stage our homes. I'd love for you to come see it."

"How long will you be there? I could come by at 4 p.m. This is Pat Champion's listing. I'm her administrative assistant."

"I'll be there at four. Why don't you come by and we can talk? The house is Lot 11 Crystal Beach Cottages Phase I. It's the yellow home with a one-car garage."

A few neighbors come through Pat's listing. One set of snowbirds came in, but said they were just looking and checking out Crystal Beach for the first time, to compare it to staying in a condo. At four, I closed the house and went down the street to meet Regina. When I drove up, I loved the light-yellow color of the home.

"I'm so glad you came," Regina said. "Would you like a glass of wine? Come sit in the living room."

"Yes, a glass of wine would be lovely. I didn't have any real customers today. It can get boring."

"Tell me, I know. My job is to sit at the open houses. Kelly has two small children, so she needs to be at home." Regina handed me a glass of chardonnay. We sat and got to know each other. She told me she had just become divorced and moved to Destin to be closer to Kelly and the grandchildren.

"I'm single and raising my two children. Pat convinced me real estate would be a more profitable job than working in a bank. So here I am," I told her.

"Are you from Destin?"

"No, Milton, via Tallahassee and now Fort Walton Beach. Since getting my license three months ago, I've sold several homes and a condo. Prior to that, I was a banker for ten years."

"Well, we financed the construction phase through Destin Bank. I refer the buyers to them for a mortgage. They can't do them all though because they're a hometown bank. May I have your card? I don't always list my homes with the same realtor."

The door opened and a gorgeous girl, who looked like Regina's twin, came through the door with a little boy and girl. Regina jumped up to hug the children.

"This is Kelly, Paige and Chris," Regina said.

"Kelly looks like she's your sister. How can she be old enough to have these two darlings?"

Regina laughed. "Kelly, this is Harper Hamilton. She's a new realtor. We were just getting to know each other."

"Thanks for the compliment. My mom looks so young you'd think she had me at sixteen. I know better. I just came by to say hello, Mom. Phillip will want his dinner soon. Nice to meet you, Harper."

"I need to go too, Regina. My two will want their dinner. I hope we see each other again." As I left to drive home I thought how much I would have loved a cute house like that for my family. I really liked Regina, and her daughter was lovely too. When I pulled into the driveway Sean was outside throwing a baseball with his friend.

"Play a little longer, then come in and get ready for dinner."

"Hello, sweetheart," I said to Lizzie. "Have you done all your homework?"

"I've finished it. Want me to set the table?"

"Yes, let me change my clothes and I'll warm up the lasagna. There's garlic bread left too." As I warmed up the food, Sean came inside.

"Do you want to play the guitar for me after we eat?"

He returned with his guitar.

We ate, sat in the living room and Sean played his guitar. He had remembered lots of what Sawyer had taught him. When he missed some chords, he frowned.

"It's okay, I'm going to find someone local to teach you."

"That'd be great," he said and smiled.

A few days later, I found Jimmy Stephens who lived three houses down and had a garage band.

"Yes, ma'am, I'd love to teach Sean. He can come down to my house a couple of afternoons a week around four and I'll work with him. I charge $10 an hour." He was a very polite young man with hair was long and blond, like a surfer's. He told me that the look fitted their band, which was called The Surfing Safaris. He played guitar and one of the other teenagers played the drums and they had a girl vocalist. Lizzie could take Sean down there on Tuesdays and Thursdays. The band played for high school events on Fridays. I couldn't wait to tell Sean and I hurried home.

Chapter 107

Harper never answered any of my phone calls. I still loved her so much that my heart felt like it would never heal. At some point, I was going to fly down there without telling her or anyone, for that matter. I would just turn up. But first I wanted to get together with John and a local banker in Destin and purchase my dream boat. I told Tucker and Sawyer I was leaving on the weekend. It was bad timing because we were caught up recording, but if Bob got them a gig, Candy could fill in for me. Thank heavens she could play the guitar as well as sing.

John called that night and told me he would meet me at the harbor late the next afternoon. He'd found a sport fishing boat and he said I could stay with him at his condo. His banker was Frank Burge at the Destin Bank, and he would take me to meet him.

I arrived at noon and John was waiting for me on his boat.

"Welcome back," he said. "Before we look at the boat and meet the seller, I think we need to go to the bank. Frank is expecting us."

The bank was on the corner of Main Street and looked like a large cottage, with a big front porch and rocking chairs. The receptionist, who was wearing black and white with pearls around her neck and high heel shoes, greeted us.

"Hello, John. Is this Cade? Frank is expecting you." She led us to Frank's office and introduced me.

"Hello, Cade. Glad you could come. Sit down, please. Tell me what you are looking to do. We're a community bank and like to take care of our boat captains and our locals." Frank had soft brown hair and eyes to match. He wore round glasses, had a firm handshake and a southern accent.

"Thanks for meeting me. I want to purchase a used charter boat, give you a sizeable down payment, and finance the rest. My royalties from our last two albums have been excellent and I saved a lot of money when I was on tour with Garth Brooks. The only hire purchase I have is my truck. My credit is good."

"We would love to have you as a customer. John says the boat he wants to show you has a fine financial record with many repeat sport-fishing clients. That'll help when I talk to my board of directors about finance. So, get the financials if you decide to purchase it. John also tells me you intend to hire a captain. Make sure you get a good one. John can advise you."

"Yes, sir. I'll be going back and forth to Nashville for a while to record my brother's songs and perform before I buy a place to live."

"My wife Pam and I are big country music fans. She bought both your albums, and we were glad when John said you were coming to talk to me about a loan. Let's fill out your loan application. We'll leave the amount you want to borrow blank until you get a contract."

I filled out the application. Shook Frank's hand, then John and I left and he took me back to the harbor to meet Dr. Huddleston and see his boat, the *Raptor*.

"I'm Jim Huddleston. I appreciate John telling you about my boat. I haven't advertised it yet. I just let a few of the guys know that my lovely wife wants me to retire from sport fishing and stay home more."

"It's a pleasure to meet you, sir. I'll let you do the honors and show me your boat."

"Our local boatbuilders, Steve Sauer and Budy Gentry from G&S Boats, built my boat. Their boats are renowned worldwide for fishing and setting world records. Their unique engineering and design make them the experts in maneuverability for pursuing light tackle records. This one is a 1983, 40-foot convertible, with a diesel engine." He showed me the equipment and the engine first. Then we climbed up to the second deck where the instrument panel, the depth finder, the plotter and more were located. "I'm asking $250,000."

"Thank you for the tour. Tomorrow morning I'll go to the bank and see if I can afford your boat. It's a beauty."

"I hope so. We would love you to have you here in Destin."

After we left, John told me the story behind the boat. He said the boat, captains and mates were famous for catching many billfish and giant bluefin tuna. Whether it was in Cat Cay or Cape Hatteras, she held many records. I wanted that boat. I would name her *Green Eyes* and have a set of green eyes painted above the name.

That night, I hardly slept. John and I had a few drinks at his condo. Non-alcoholic ones for me. I avoided going to Harbor Docks in case Stevie or Kitty spotted me.

The next morning I went to the bank and gave Frank all the details about the boat, including the fact that I would have the financials very soon.

"I don't think I'll need them, now that I know whose boat it is. If you can get the right captain, the money from the tournaments will more than pay your loan repayments. We checked your credit, and you can more than afford the boat with the down payment you are providing. Get a bill of sale from Doc Huddleston and bring it back to me. That could take a week and I have to get it approved by the board of directors."

As we shook hands I was shaking. I was so excited.

Chapter 108

I wanted to see my mother. I needed a hug and some counseling. Dr. Witkind was rather controlling, perhaps because he always had to be in control in the operating theater. To begin with our date at Marina Café was okay, but it reminded me too much of the time Cade and I ate there. My poor heart was still bruised. I didn't know if it would ever recover. Halfway through the meal I knew he was not for me. There was his need for control, but also we were too different. He loved expensive material things, whereas I didn't. I guess you could say the simple life was for me rather than the type of life he led where he drove flash cars and ate in expensive restaurants. Then there was his preoccupation with his mother. He went on and on about her so much that it was as if he was married to her. And last but not least, there was no chemistry between us and I didn't think there ever would be.

When he ordered for me again it was as though he thought I didn't have a brain of my own to choose for myself. He consumed the majority of the wine and attempted to hold my hand towards the end of the meal. I resisted.

Then when we arrived at the Sky Bar, he ordered two fancy, expensive, after-dinner drinks. I didn't want mine, but I sipped it anyway. By far the worst was his wild dancing. In his black suit and shiny shoes, he danced like a flamenco man. He was an embarrassment and he looked so bizarre and out of place. But little did I know there was worse to come.

When he took me home, he walked me up the steps to my door, backed me against it and without any warning began to kiss me. His tongue went so far into my mouth I almost choked and then if that wasn't bad enough, with one hand he groped my breast while the other went up my skirt. It was all too much. Without giving it a second thought, I pushed him away and slapped his face with the back of my hand. He froze on the spot for mere seconds. He was too close to me so I lashed out and shoved him—hard with both hands. As I turned quickly to put my key in the lock I heard him cry out. I glanced at him briefly as I pushed open my door. He had landed on his ass and was sprawled on the ground at the bottom of the steps with one hand on his face. I had unintentionally caught his face with the small emerald ring my parents had given me for my twenty-first birthday. It was a family heirloom.

"Bloody bitch," he spat. "You've cut my cheek."

I hurried inside, slammed, and locked the door. That was the last I would see of him, thank goodness. *Men! Who needs them? Not me! I'm far better off on my own.*

I arrived at my parents' house feeling happy. I had put the incident with the nasty doctor out of my head. In fact, if I took the time to think about it, which I didn't, I had to laugh. He got what he deserved.

I had warned Lizzie we couldn't go horseback riding because cold weather from up north had hit the Panhandle. It was forty-two degrees in the morning and the high was only going to be fifty-seven. Mom and Dad had their fireplace roaring, and Mom brought us hot chocolates. Their home was so cozy and comforting. We would stay inside and play board games.

"Thanks, Mom, the hot chocolate hit the spot. What are you knitting?"

"A sweater for your dad."

"How is everything with your real estate?"

"Good, I'm making an excellent living. It sure feels great not to have to worry about paying my bills."

"Dad and I are so proud of you. I know I was nervous when you quit the bank. I prefer security over commission sales. But you knew best."

"I must have inherited the sales genes from Dad's side of the family. I know that Grandpa sold pots and pans in Michigan before the depression with a horse and buggy and Dad said he progressed to a truck and even had a general store where he sold everything."

"Your grandfather was quite a character. Nine wives he brought to meet us. I didn't like it, but your father said I had to be respectful. I loved his mother. How could a man leave his wife and children to fend for themselves during the depression?"

"I don't know. How can Michael not pay child support?"

"Have you heard from Cade? I know you told me at Christmas that he was in rehab. It's been a few months now. I wonder how he is doing."

"No, I don't answer his phone calls. I had a couple of dates with a client, a neurosurgeon. He's rich and his family are refugees from Cuba. He likes to eat fancy food and go to the theater, but he's not for me." I saw no point in telling her in detail about the scene at my front door. It would only cause her distress.

"He sounds interesting, but I can tell by the tone in your voice that you're not taken by him. Give yourself time. It's early days yet. You'll meet someone. Probably when you least expect it."

I didn't reply, but I suspect the expression on my face as I thought about Bruce Witkind said it all.

"Let's eat dinner. Certainly nothing fancy at my house. Just a round roast, potatoes, carrots, and there's Yorkshire pudding in the oven."

"I love your Yorkshire pudding, and I can never make it like yours. I'll get the kids to and set the table for you.

"Yum, Nana made Yorkshire pudding, my favorite," said Lizzie.

"Mine too," said Sean. Once we finished a lovely family dinner, Mom and I tackled the dishes, then we settled in to watch television, a rare treat for me. We watched *60 Minutes* first and then *Murder She Wrote*.

Why was it so easy to sleep at my parents' home? Security? Whatever, I slept well. The next day was Sunday and church day. Dad treated us to breakfast at the Waffle House. On Sunday afternoon we drove home early so I could do the laundry and get ready for the coming week.

Sean checked the mail and came running in with a small package addressed to me. It was postmarked Nashville, but I didn't recognize the address. I opened it in the kitchen. It was a CD from a recording studio. The label on the song was *Because You Love Me*. A letter from Cade was enclosed.

Dear Harper,

I understand why you don't answer my calls. It hurts so much not to talk to you and share our lives like we used to. I want to explain why I went into rehab. Boone died from a heroin overdose. It was me who found him in the bathroom, unconscious. I couldn't stop thinking that it could have been me. No, I never did heroin, but Boone wanted me to try it. Thanks to God, I didn't. Cocaine, alcohol and Xanex were enough poison for me. Tucker and Mom were disgusted with me, and so was Bob. I realized if I didn't change my life,

I would lose everything, my musical career and you. Please forgive me and let me back into yours and the children's lives. I miss all of you so much and I love you like I have loved no other.

Sawyer wrote this song because he knows how much I love and miss you.
All my love now and forever.
Cade.

I went out to the garage and plugged in the CD player. The words were beautiful. Tears poured down my face. He loved me. He absolutely loved me. Of course, they were Sawyer's words, but I'm sure Cade must have expressed them. I sat in the car and cried until I had no more tears left. Dear God, help me do the right thing for me and my children. Could I let Cade back into my life and trust him again?

Chapter 109

When I arrived home in Nashville, my brothers were eager for me to explain my disappearance.

"Give us the scoop. Surely you didn't go for one day and night just to see Harper," said Tucker.

"No, I flew to meet John Holley, and the president of Destin Bank, and buy a sport-fishing boat. I didn't see Harper."

"You have to be kidding me," said Sawyer. "Just what exactly are your plans?"

"This boat has everything I want. I can't be the captain because that takes three years. But I can hire one to take the boat out for sport-fishing tournaments. The boat has made a lot of money in the past. I've given this so much thought and I know that my relationship with Harper won't work unless I live in Destin most of the time. As yet I still don't know if she'll have me back. Maybe she won't. But I really hope she will because that's what will make me happy. I want a life with Harper and her children. So, suffice to say I am working on it and doing my best to get her back."

"What about our music career?" asked Tucker.

"I won't abandon it. I can fly back for recordings and special shows and concerts. Now that you have Candy, the three of you can handle the smaller engagements. You also have Bob to manage everything and the recording studio."

"Have you spoken to Harper?" said Sawyer.

"No. One step at a time. It'll take at least a week to get the finance sorted and the boat transferred into my name. I have to form a corporation, take out insurance, and find a captain."

"Where are you going to live while you're in Destin?"

"John knows of a small three-bedroom older block home near the harbor where the boat will be kept. I can stay there. Destin has plenty of venues where our band can perform too. Y'all might want to come down for a week or two in the summer. It's a great place and the music scene is lucrative. You can stay with me."

"I feel a little better now that I know your plans," said Tucker. "You better tell Bob soon."

"I'll see him tomorrow. I also need to call Mom and tell her. In fact, I'll call her now."

Mom. She listened to everything before she replied.

"I can see your point. You learned a lot about yourself in rehab. Being a famous country music star isn't everything in life. I know you love Harper and her children. But does she still love you? She went through a bad time with her husband so maybe the similarities between you and him are too much for her. You need to be prepared for her to reject you, so don't set your heart on it. As long as you come home, help the boys with their careers and see Grannie and I, I'm in favor of your decision. I only hope Harper will forgive you. I would hate for you to move there all for nothing."

"Thanks, Mom. I knew you would understand. Before I own the boat, I have a week's worth of work to complete. I'll let you know when I'm going to Destin."

I devoted most of the next day to phone calls, securing boat insurance and establishing an LLC. I called John Holley and asked him to help me find a captain. Then I called Bob to explain my plans to him.

"I had a feeling this is what you might do. If you stay involved with your brothers and help them succeed, it'll be fine. I can handle their management."

I went to my AA meeting to talk to Joshua and Barry the next morning at eight. They weren't surprised. "I hope you'll both watch out for my brothers and Candy. They have a wonderful future ahead of them. I'll go back and forth, but my heart belongs to Harper and her children in Destin.

"Good luck, bro," said Joshua. "A great family will do wonders to help you stay sober. Delores and those twins are my rock."

"I've never been to Destin," said Barry. "Once the studio is making money, I want you to take me fishing for marlin."

"It'll be my pleasure."

The week crept by as I waited for Frank Burge to call. Finally, after a week and a half, he did. I was nervous and anxious about their decision. What if they said no? I feared my dream would be shattered. I held my breath as I answered the phone.

"It's Frank. Great news, the board of directors have approved your loan."

"I'm so relieved. Thank you, Frank, thank you. I'll be down next week to close. Any time you want to go sport fishing, just let me know."

"I'll take you up on that offer. Congratulations! See you next week."

My next call was to Dr. Huddleston to tell him the news. He said he would be in town, and we could close in seven days. Then I called John to tell him the good news and he mentioned that he had been talking to Chris Davis, a young boat captain from the Keys who was in need of a boat to captain. He thought we would get along.

Thank you, God, thank you for blessing me with a new sober future.

A week later, I drove to Destin with my clothes and money. I closed on the loan with Frank at the bank and paid Dr. Huddleston. He then took me out on the Gulf of Mexico to fish for marlin. We didn't get one that day, but I would in the future.

My heart was pounding with anxiety as I drove to Harper's house. As I knocked on the door, fear that she would refuse to see me engulfed me. With a bouquet of white roses in my hand, I stood there shaking and anxious. When she came to the door she looked hesitant and I was afraid she would reject the flowers and me.

"Come in," she said as she took the flowers. Then she hugged me. I didn't try to kiss her. I knew I had better take it slow. I was just glad she let me in and invited me to sit on the couch.

"Are the children here?" I asked her.

"No, Lizzie's at the park with friends and Sean is having a guitar lesson. Sit down and tell me what's been going on in your life for the past few months," she said.

I told her about rehab and how it had changed me and about meeting Joshua and Barry and forming a support group through AA. I explained that I went every day and had a wonderful sponsor. Then I told her that Sawyer had moved in with us, and Candy Kane had joined the band. I was nervous as I got to the last and the most important part. I felt sweat running down my back as I took a deep breath. "I've rented a house here, so I can go back and forth to Nashville. I'll find an AA group in Destin. The most important thing is, I've never stopped loving you. I want to prove

I can be both sober and the man you deserve. All I ask is that you give me a chance." Then I went silent and waited for her to say something. The seconds ticked by, then she finally spoke.

"You don't cheat on the woman you love," she said quietly.

How did she know? "I ..." I began, but my voice trailed away and my mouth went dry.

"Don't try to tell me you didn't because I know you did." She paused. "Someone called me and told me about your other woman and the drugs and drink."

"What! Who was it?"

"I don't know. It was a man, but the voice was muffled. It was no one I knew, but I knew what he said was the truth, wasn't it? Why did you do it? I thought you loved me."

"I did ... I do ... I was so depressed without you and that night ... only one night ... it was the drink and the drugs ... and I got carried away. I couldn't help myself. Afterward I was so ashamed of what I'd done and I'm still ashamed of it." I stopped then and hung my head. *Should I leave? Maybe she would ask me to.*

"How do I know you won't do it again?"

I raised my head and looked at her, right in her eyes, then I took a deep breath. "Because I've learned my lesson and I'm sober now and intend to stay that way for the rest of my life. I apologize for my behavior and I give you my word that I will never so much as look at another woman. I hope you will accept that." I continued to look at her, but she did nothing other than return my gaze. The agonizing seconds ticked by and more sweat trickled down my back. *The caller must have been Boone. He got really pissed with me when I complained about the increase in his prices. It couldn't have been anyone else.*

"Okay, I accept your apology, but we will need to take it one day at a time until you have proved you are trustworthy. Are you okay with that?" Again there was silence, but it wasn't quite so uncomfortable.

"Yes." This time I paused. "I have something to show you. Can you come with me down to the harbor?" I said at length.

"I guess so."

She looked hesitant again and I began to feel sick.

"We can only be gone for a little while," she said.

As we drove to Destin I filled Harper in on the new recording studio. At Harbor Docks Stevie and John were waiting. They wanted to be in on the surprise. I was incredibly nervous. The timing could have been all wrong in view of the conversation we'd just had in her house.

"Follow me downstairs and out back," I said. When we got to the side of the dock, the boat was tied up there. GREEN EYES was painted in large letters on the stern.

"Is this yours? Have you bought it?" Harper shrieked.

"Yes, come aboard," I said. "Let me show you the inside." I held out my hand. The expression of astonishment on her face was worth the wait. "Sit in the fighting chair, please." Then I dropped to my knees and took a little black velvet box out of my jacket pocket.

"Will you marry me?" I said as I handed her the box.

Epilogue

In the summer of 1993, under the Florida sun, Harper and Cade began a new chapter of their lives. The gleam of a two-carat diamond on Harper's finger marked the beginning of their journey as they exchanged vows in a meaningful ceremony aboard their boat, Green Eyes, surrounded by family and friends. The reception held at Harbor Docks resonated with laughter and music, courtesy of Cade's musically talented brothers.

Cade had found a charming three-bedroom home near Destin harbor where they began their married life. Harper continued to excel in her real estate career and became a top realtor.

Family and friendship ties strengthened as Joshua, Delores, and their children, along with Bob and Blackie, joined the celebration. Cade's mother, Dorothy, had found companionship with Barry, and Grannie reveled in the joy of seeing her grandson tie the knot.

The thriving recording business kept Cade and his band busy as they planned a third album with Sawyer at the songwriting helm. The Fox Brothers reunited with The Trashy White Band for a special night at the Boat House, which brought the wedding party together one more time.

As the week of festivities ended, Cade and Harper set sail for Key West on their sport-fishing boat to enjoy a serene honeymoon. The echoes of their enduring love indicated a future filled with promise.

The End

Don't miss out!

Visit the website below and you can sign up to receive emails whenever Blair Burns publishes a new book. There's no charge and no obligation.

https://books2read.com/r/B-A-RALX-UMIYC

BOOKS 2 READ

Connecting independent readers to independent writers.

Did you love *Green Eyes*? Then you should read *Murder on the Emerald Coast*[1] by Blair Burns!

[2]

A murder mystery takes place in Destin and Perdido Key, Florida. Three real estate friends live and work through the horror of losing two other friends to murder. There is greed involved, lust, love and danger. Beautiful Honey Jennings is murdered while the three friends are out of town celebrating the purchase of a beach house in Mexico Beach. The real estate office swarms with detectives. Honey was having an affair with a rich attorney, Vick Napoli from New Orleans.He is a suspect and one of the major investors in Gulf Wind Real Estate properties.

When the team goes out of town to sell a condo project in Perdido Key, Charlie Davis is missing on the day of the sale. Two days later they find him under a ledge. Drowned in the condo pool. More uniforms decend on the real estate company. In between the chaos the three friends find time for romance and some fun at their new beach house.

---

1. https://books2read.com/u/4EN1BE

2. https://books2read.com/u/4EN1BE

Vick Napoli is accused of murdering Honey Jennings and the trial is held in DeFuniak Springs, the north end of the county. Ann sneaks up to view the proceedings.

The twists and turns of thriving real estate with two murders prove to be more than the three friends expected.

Read more at https://www.blairburnsauthor.com.

Also by Blair Burns

Murder on the Emerald Coast
Green Eyes

Watch for more at https://www.blairburnsauthor.com.

About the Author

. Blair Burns has lived along the Emerald Coast of Florida since 1955. She has seen the changes from a sleepy fishing villages to a booming tourist area along 30A. She writes about the people and places from Pensacola to Apalachicola. She writes love stories and murder mysteries. She enjoys painting, writing, gardening and taking her read therapy dog to see the children at the library and elementary schools.

Read more at https://www.blairburnsauthor.com.

9 798224 040995